Careening Humanity Into Oblivion:

Prelude to Debauchery

Disclaimer

Please Note: this is the first of (at least) two books!

This is a work of fiction. The characters and situations presented herein are not real and are not based on any living person or event. This book is solely for entertainment and the overall enrichment of the soul.

Printed in the United States of America

First Printing, 2022

ISBN 978-1-7326174-2-1

Orsa LLC

3009 Wells Fleet Circle

Willoughby, Ohio 44094

For Cal.

Table of Contents

Hello and Precious Few Other Pleasantries

Hi. I'm Paul Glassburé. I need to get a couple things out of the way for context, so please bear with me. Yeah? Good.

I don't *currently* wish to impose my will on humanity, as it were, but I was accused of such a thing when I was a younger man. Aw hell, I've been accused of this for most of my years. I've only considered doing so maybe twice. Well, maybe more, but that's a bit irrelevant if you are reading these words. See, I have an odd existence, one with some interesting ramifications. I have lived the majority of my life across twenty distinctly different worlds and twenty different bodies. Why twenty? Well, I suppose it was a choice I made, because I could cite several hundred other planets I've been to. In truth, I just did toe dips in other places, primarily as I've gotten older, and gotten better control over where I am at any given time. I felt many of these other places served part of my purpose but, in truth, I was nothing but an observer in all but those twenty primary planets.

The other interesting tidbit you should know is this: I can destroy damn near anything you can think of, big or little. When I say "little" here, think anything from a tiny pebble to a planet. "Big" is more on the order of what you perceive to be the Universe. With a little gumption and a whole lot of evil, I could hit the reset button for everything on planet Earth and rain grisly, horrific, awful death on the third rock from the sun. I've thought about that, too, more than I should say, but only got close to doing so a couple times. The visual would be simply *profound*—and there has been more reason to do so that no one reading this will understand. The whole thing would be a million degrees of wrong. I certainly realize that. It would result in the deaths of my family members and friends and, as much as this would have dark comedic elements to me, I couldn't begin to do such a thing to the people I love.

"How is any of this possible, you incorrigible buffoon?" you ask. "You are clearly a deranged idiot."

You see, it's been long theorized that humans exist simultaneously in parallel universes. In other words, you have a twin self, or doppelganger, that is living a life in a planet identical to the one where you're reading this. As the theorems posit, this doppelganger is in some way a copy of you, living a (potentially) opposite life in some ways, where critical decisions have been made differently. Like, over there, you had the guts to ask XYZ person out for joe and you have two beautiful kids and the most radical sex life ever to show for it. You know who I'm talking about.

Well, no. You're in luck. This is not true at all. Get your mind cleanly off of that sex comment and come back to me.

Good, thank you.

The truth is that a version of you is having an experience in what I believe to be an *infinite* number of other worlds. These are not parallel universes, though. These are "dimensional pluralities" as I call them, organizations of solar systems occurring in copies of the third dimension separated by slight differences in the frequency each copy resonates within.

Let's roll that back, just for fun.

There are multiple versions of the third dimension, places where energy is slowed down enough for there to be stuff (rocky things, fleshy things, leafy things, watery things, etc.). They are in no way copies of one another, except for the laws of physics. There are frequency differences between them, but they are barely discernible. Why is this important? Well, if energy vibrates too quickly, atoms can't stick together to form matter. Further, without the physics you know, life in the third dimension isn't the experience it is meant to be.

Bear in mind that you only exist once per dimensional plurality. I don't, but this is due to my purpose, which we'll talk about as we go. In other words, you don't have a twin self on that super Earth floating about in Andromeda. All the people in the third-dimension play by the same rules here—ALL OF YOU. No, Earthlings, you are not an anomaly of creation. There are hundreds of trillions of intelligent hominids across tens of billions of planets in the Universe in which you reside. Yes, the "you" I'm referencing exists in the extremities of the Milky Way. All of those brilliant fleshy things—yes, all of them—have copies of themselves elsewhere, too. One of my dearest friends lives on a gorgeous planet directly catty-corner to Earth's orbit. We are also roommates on a planet called Pliqun. We'll get into my fun with your copy of the third dimension around the second third of the book. You'll get it then. I know you are sorta confused right now. Stay patient, knave, and all will be okay.

Invariably, some smart person is calling me out *right now* for not mentioning the existence of higher dimensions. Here's the thing, smarty pants: yes, they exist. Math tells us they do, and I can speak from experience that they are plenty, plenty special. But, they ain't relevant for this conversation. So, unwind the underbritches that have found their way six inches up that sphincter of yours and let's keep going. First though, please throw that pair of underbritches away. Besides the smell, you've kept them for five years too long. Have you no shame?

That Einstein fellow wrote universal truths about physics that apply everywhere in "our" copy of the third dimension. In fact, every other Albert Einstein-like person did the same thing. There have been precious few of these individuals I have learned about or known, who lived a singular purpose across every possible machination of themselves. Every planet I have visited has had at least one person who discovered and stated the laws of physics, if, of course, the planet happened to be mature enough. I promise I'll clarify this in the not too distant future.

I'll introduce you to a couple of other people who did things other than present the Theory of Relativity consistently between every version of them. In other words, they served a purpose that was consistent with all of the other versions of themselves, regardless of when each life took place or the gender of each individual. *(Yes, there are some rock star geniuses, ladies, now sit back down and take a breath.)* The time is not right for such introductions now, mostly because I'm feeling a tad irascible, if you couldn't tell.

The other physicists who did what Mr. Einstein did, didn't live in the same "times", either. They each played the same role as Mr. Einstein at the same relative point of maturity of each planet. This differed by hundreds of millennia in certain cases. Regardless, there was a primary physicist on each of these planets who authored the same fundamental laws of physics that Albert Einstein did for Earth. The language differed slightly, but the message was exactly the same. In fact, every group of scientists I know about, across every dimensional plurality, derived the same concepts as those on Earth. We still have a way to go—about two-hundred fifty-six years or so—before we really play in the big kids' pool in the Milky Way. We'll get there... in two-hundred fifty-six years. It'll take about three-hundred twenty-four more years to really understand space. That will be super exciting to witness, so let's hope you're reading a reissue of this bad boy well after I wrote the thing!

Given that I just made a time reference, let me get this little wrinkle out of the way: time is a relative human construct, and only impacts the observer. Why do I mention this? Simply put, if I were to introduce time as a construct for the experience we are all having, the meaning changes. Something beautiful and eternal becomes something with an expiration date, and that's simply not okay.

You'll note that I've just inserted a partial, mostly incorrect reference to Quantum Physics/Quantum Mechanics. Please be warned or become aware of a sense of shame—your choice.

So, to explain time and this observer thing (in a very human, non-Quantum Physics kind of way), consider two *very* human things: eating and sleeping. You know it's time to eat if your belly rumbles and you get a bit grumpy, right? Or, you know it's time to sleep if those peepers can't stay open, and those around you are asking you to go elsewhere to snore. In both cases, you are the observer because you are noticing that you are either hungry or tired. Your loved ones are making similar discoveries, parallel to yours. It's *time* to eat. It's *time* to sleep. It's *time* to chastise dad for snoring in the recliner. In the grand scheme, there is no *time* that limits what you are or how long you exist—not even death. There is no limit for the experience you are having. So, please, soak this up into that sponge in your head and squeegee it out so it's nice and even. A consistency of cake batter is preferred here, but I'll take maple syrup or that marshmallow sauce folks use for candied yams. I hate them things.

Yes, I *am* an idiot and take what I say about as serious as a damn eyelash. I think I'm funny, and at least one or two others do, too. Take that for whatever you choose to, but please keep it away from small children. Oh—and for God's sake, quit running with scissors. Your place as a moron has been well-established with such behavior.

So, it's TIME to wrap up this topic. See what I did there? 'Told you I was funny! If for some reason you disagree with this proclamation, please remove and discard the underbritches that I've already indicated are an issue. Have you no shame whatsoever?

Anyhoo, the version of you reading this may or may not be in a body in a different dimensional plurality at the moment, though it's a virtual guarantee at least a few of your dimensional selves are out there as you read this. You have already lived, or died for that matter, and you may not yet be born in other worlds. You—the thing inside that bag of bones—is special. It's eternal, and it loves to *feel*. It just has no concept of time unless it's in that bag of bones because the bag of bones is perishable. Let me give you one more example about how this all relates that seems to resonate most with children and those who knit:

> Imagine you are standing between the hash marks in the middle of the fifty-yard line of a football stadium, and every version of you across every possible dimensional plurality is connected by yarn, standing on bleachers "above" you. Where you stand at that fifty-yard line, reflects your birthday down to the second of your birth. Every seat you move in any direction, right or left, is one second to fifty years different from your birth time. Yeah, it's a big time swing but it works out. Trust me.
>
> To your left moves time progressively behind you (the past) and the right side is time that's in front of you (the future).
>
> None of the individuals would be standing in the same horizontal or vertical planes you are, and no two individuals start or end at the same time all across those bleachers. Yarn may cross where you or another individual are, but it does not begin or end there.
>
> You would see that yarn pattern travel to the extremes of the side stairwells, and would weave in a random, yet beautiful, cacophony of lines using the whole of those bleachers—something akin to layered S's or Z's—all snaking around itself. From the bottom, you see chaos, with bodies haphazardly strewn everywhere. When you look at this from above, though, it perfectly traces the lines found in the middle section of the Flower of Life Mandala, were it to be altered so that it has slightly asymmetrical (though complimentary) starting points
>
> I cried super hard when I mapped this out for the first time based on my own experience. I was a blubbery mess every time I looked at my drawing for about a year, to be honest. The profound nature of this discovery still gives me a tear or two from time to time. It's so special—*so* meaningful.

Now that we've talked about this as it relates to existence, I want to go a bit deeper into another layer of granularity. Some of you may already be dismissing me due to your faith as it relates to resurrection. Let's go there, and see if maybe I can win over those with this belief.

The truth is that you—your eternal self—absolutely can return to the same planet if you want. It is a choice to begin the life you live every time. And, in some cases doing a do-over may be warranted. Let's say your planet was in its infancy holding life, and you lived a square four days before being crushed to death by a massive, wandering land creature. The creature, and reason for it being errantly wandering, is in no way relevant for this example, so let's get both out of our minds, yeah? The fact is, you could choose to return to that planet once it evolves a bit.

Or, maybe you were male and wanted to have a female experience on the same planet for some reason or another. No, this in no way implies you to be errant or damaged, or that you are somehow confused sexually. Please remember that your body merely feels. Gender, in no way, is stamped into *what* you are. In the truest way possible, your choice to be either male or female goes to a much deeper place and is rooted in a purpose we'll talk about more toward the end of this little book. For now, celebrate whatever you happen to be, even if you're a man with lady bits. It's important to celebrate you, whatever and *however* you define yourself to be.

Borrowing our example with the stadium, therefore, gets a tad more interesting if you look at the gender of the people in the stadium. You may see just as many men as you do women, or it could be swayed more to one side or another. This ultimately is decided by the real you, the thing in that bag of bones reading these words. Indeed, I will be continuously referring to you as a thing in a bag of bones whenever I need, for the rest of the book. I am not nearly as creative as my Grandpa Waniglia in terms of naming; he gave me this phrase as a boy. Regardless, I chase that verbiage which makes me smile—bags of bones are just too damn funny, always. Thanks, Pop!

I have been married to my wife, Helena, for fifty-two years here on Earth. We have two children and five grandchildren. They, too, will be introduced, but not right now because the time is just not right to do so. I say this mainly to anger my children and make the grandkids laugh. They get me and, therefore, this is their only gift in this little collection of words.

Helena and I have something of a complex relationship, one that spans several dimensions and quite a few worlds. No, you disturbingly awful person, that was not some new age metaphor. Your tiny brain will have to stretch a bit to understand. I am confident this is so.

Our relationship has been anything but easy and has been fraught with tragedy. Bear this unsubtle premonition tenderly as she will bite you with ferocity when you are least expecting it. I will say this, though, about my wife: I am so in love with her that it supersedes how badly broken she has made me from time to time. Ours is a story that I have problems telling, simply due to its complexity. I look forward to the challenge, but am confident it won't be easy.

There is one person who is my absolute best friend, across every plane of existence I've found and no, it's *not* my wife. Her name is Eva. She's the only person I know whose lives are similar to mine in *every* dimensional plurality. She is three days younger than me on Earth, and our ages vary by no more than that in any other world. It's an oddity I've never been able to make sense of, but it's a blessing. She is my best friend, my next-door neighbor in one world and lives in India here on Earth. I've been Uncle Paul to her kids, the son her father never had, and I loved her mother as my own. Eva is the kindest person I've met that isn't in some way related to me, and that's saying something. She and one other person you will meet in the next chapter share a quality of my existence. She has a life on every planet out there, across every dimensional plurality.

So, you may be wondering how I identify people between worlds. It's never mattered the age of the person, nor the sex—it is their eyes and their smile that gives their identities away. Interestingly though, it was Eva who pointed this out to me in one of our first encounters on Earth. I'll never forget it, and no, I won't tell you about it right now. You're welcome! I'm happy to be informative as we get to know one another!

You may know my grandfather. His name was Olaf Waniglia. He wrote a book about his life many years ago, and encouraged me to do so when I got to be "old enough." He was one of my mentors, and his guidance allowed me to become the person I am, in part because I share some of his abilities. He coined the term *"vox corporis"* to describe a voice everyone has that solely speaks truth. I heard this voice for the first time when I was six, and it accompanied a rather panic-stricken month or so. Pop was instrumental in helping me understand my ability even though he couldn't understand it. As I've aged, I learned to control when I hear the *vox corporis* and when I don't. I also now control what life I am living whereas before I really couldn't. I learned how to do so from a presence in my life that I can't describe otherwise. In time, I'll talk about him, too.

Get the God reference out of your mind, my precious and currently captive bag of bones. That "heathen" reference was anything but nice. My parents, Addison and Jonah Glassburé, taught me things about life no other parent or mentor ever did. My father played professional football and then ran a school for special needs people, and my mother ran my great-grandfather's farm in South Carolina. Hard work, dedication and humility were beaten into me repeatedly and effectively. I also got a wicked sense of humor from my other grandfather, Nol Glassburé, whose story you may also know. My favorite memories of him are coupled with experiences I've had. I look forward to showing you the man I knew the way I did.

So, you may be wondering why I'm writing this book. Truth be told, there are a couple reasons. First, I've learned things I feel I need to document. Second, in the process of learning these things, I've been through some of the most impossibly ridiculous situations and feel the story of each needs to be told. Along the way, I've had something of a journey. This string of lives has served a singular primary purpose and about a dozen or so secondary purposes. When I die on Earth, I believe this purpose will consciously carry on in one of my other lives. There's also the chance that one of my kids, who again I will not mention by name solely to instigate anger and hatred, may also pick up the torch I have carried. I hope so, anyway. Earth, and maybe one or two (hundred trillion) other planets and hundreds of hundreds of quadrillions of individuals may be at risk if not. Yep, you are one of 'em, so fingers crossed, right?

This story is going to be told chronologically. I'll explain things and will introduce folks as we go.

Prepare yourself; this ain't gonna be fun. Let me just get this out of the way now: I'm sorry.

The Oddity of Childhood When You're Me

I was born on a Thursday in late August. No, this isn't cosmically significant but it does play in astrological realms. Feel free to analyze this if you wish.

Life up through age six was normal. My brother, Larry, is nine years my elder and my sister, Dylan, is three years older than me. I had a typical sibling relationship with my brother where he enjoyed beating the snot out of me, and my sister alternately loved me and thought I was gross.

Things got weird two days after I turned six. I was playing with my beloved army men when I heard my mother's voice. Thing was, it wasn't my mom talking. She was sitting on the couch doing a crossword puzzle at the time.

"Hello, Paul. You are a special boy. Never forget this," the voice said.

"Hi, Mommy. Thanks," I replied cheerfully, smashing a bevy of army men with a tank.

She looked up from her crossword and asked, "What, sweetheart?"

"You just told me I was special," I replied, moving another tank into position for an assault on an incoming assailant.

"Um, no, sweetheart, I haven't said anything. You are super special, though! That is absolutely true, baby boy!" she smiled.

"Paul, tell her you need to talk to Papa," the voice said. I was looking at mom when I heard this, and her mouth didn't move. "Papa" was what I called Grandpa Waniglia.

I instantly broke into hysterics, panicked out of my mind. I ran out of the room, up to my bedroom.

I dove under my pillow and let my six-year-old emotions explode onto my mattress.

My mom ran into my room seconds later, also crying.

"Paul, baby, tell me what's wrong. What happened? Are you hurt?" she frantically asked.

I cried harder, not knowing whether I could look at her. I thought my mom was possessed. I could thank my buddy, Adam, for that. He introduced me to horror films the week prior. I was convinced what I had just witnessed reflected the reality that mom had a ghost inside her.

"Paul, I am not a ghost. I am part of your mom. Please, talk to her," the voice

said.

"No! That's what a ghost would want me to do. You're trying to steal my life. You're not allowed to steal it! Go away! Go away!" I screamed.

"Baby boy, tell me what you're talking about," Mom implored. I could tell she was still crying.

"No! You have a ghost, Mommy. You need to go find a minister to get it out. It's trying to kill me, Mommy. Go to church!" I yelled from the extraordinary protection of my pillow cover.

Mom left my room and ran down the stairs. I heard her talking with someone as her voice trailed away.

I don't know how much time passed, but I woke up to my grandfather's hand gently patting me on the back. It was Papa.

"Little fella, could we talk?" he asked calmly. He was so good at being a soothing person.

I, tiredly yet slowly, retreated from the fortified pillow above my head. I looked cautiously at him, looking for signs of ghost activity.

"Papa, Mommy has a ghost," I said, wiping my eyes as soon as I felt safe. "I think she needs to go to church to have it removed. It wants to steal my life, Papa."

"Paul, what did this ghost say to you?" he asked, handing me a handkerchief.

"It told me I was special. It also said I needed to talk to you. It was *evil*, Papa," I replied, knowing in my heart I was right.

"I understand this was scary, Paul. Tell me this, though: did this voice you heard first say 'Hello'?" he asked, leaning in and putting his hand on my shoulder.

"Yeah, but I think that ghost was just trying to fool me," I said, my resolve strong.

"I think I solved it, little guy!" he said, squeezing my shoulder. Your mommy doesn't have a ghost. I promise. I think you heard something I call the *vox corporis*. It's really strange to hear it at first, but I promise it isn't a ghost. Do this for me: listen really close and see if you hear mine," he suggested.

I cautiously looked up at his eyes, and then I heard it.

"Hello, Paul. I promise you I'm not a ghost. You're safe. Like you heard from your mommy, you're special. Never forget this. You're going to have a couple very bad days ahead. Make sure you tell Papa. He will help you as much as he can," his vox corporis said.

"I heard it, Papa. You promise me you don't have a ghost?" I asked, completely unaware how to address this.

"I promise, my dear grandson. Tell me now, what did you hear?" he asked, smiling brightly.

"He told me I'm going to have bad days and you're going to help me. What does this mean, Papa?" I asked, my naiveté shining through like a rainbow in a storm.

"Paul, grab my hand and then close your eyes for me, okay?" he requested, extending his hand.

"Okay, Papa," I said, and grabbed his thumb. His hands were massive and powerful. He was a fighter; his hands were immense compared to mine.

As soon as I closed my eyes, I found that we were no longer in my bedroom.

The area all around me changed to a place I had seen before in Hawaii. A man in traditional Hawaiian clothing approached us. He was smiling so big I thought his mouth would break.

"Paul Glassburé, it is wonderful to meet you. My name is Akamu. I've known your grandpa for many years," he said kindly.

"Where are we? We were just in my bedroom," I said, looking around. We were on a beach with palm trees swaying to my right.

"Little fella, we are in a safe place. That's all you need to know. Akamu is my teacher. We also worked together for many years," Papa said.

"I get that we're safe, but where is this, Papa? I don't understand," I said, my panic turning to frustration.

"Paul, don't fret. Your grandfather brought you here so, together, we could help prepare you for what is to come," Akamu said and then knelt down in front of me. "Please understand, Paul—you have an interesting road ahead, one that will be challenging. I can promise you that you will be safe; you will need to be very calm when your instinct is to be anything but. Both of us will be here to help you."

"Papa's voice or whatever said the same thing. What the heck is going on? I don't understand," I replied angrily. This was getting absurd in my six-year-old brain.

"Little fella, don't be upset. We just want to try to prepare you for what is starting. In a lot of ways, this is all we can do. Just promise me that when you see something you don't understand, let's talk about it. If we aren't there, try to be calm until we are together again. Can you do this for me, Paul?" Papa softly implored.

"I'll try, Papa. I'm scared though. What is happening to me?" I asked, tears forming in my eyes.

"Paul, you're special. Sometimes special people have extraordinary lives. I think your life is about to become nothing short of *unbelievable*. Try to stay calm, and when things become unbearable, close your eyes and listen. You will always have help. Okay?" Akamu said, putting his hands on my shoulders.

"Okay," I sheepishly replied. I had no idea what was happening. None at all.

"I'll see you again soon. Olaf, it is always a treat, my friend. Be well, and please give Annie a hug for me," Akamu said, and stood up to shake Papa's hand.

"Of course, my friend! See you soon," Papa said warmly.

As soon as their handshake ended, we were back in my bedroom.

"How in the heck?" I shouted, unable to comprehend what just happened.

My grandfather said not a word in response. He hugged me tightly, in a way I'd never felt. That embrace took every last bit of confusion and angst and shredded it. I'd never felt so protected in my short life.

When the hug ended, he winked at me and said, "Just remember, Little fella. you're never alone. Try to stay calm when you see or hear strange things. It will help. Let me know if there is anything we can help you with, okay?"

I nodded. We then went back downstairs to find my mother on the couch, looking as though she'd been crying.

"Addie, what might these tears be for?" Papa asked kindly.

"Daddy, I'm… I'm just really worried about Paul. Just think about all the things we went through as a family, all the times we almost lost you. I can't stand the thought of my son going through anything like that," she replied as new tears fell.

"Addison Grace, are we talking in your living room right now?" Papa asked playfully.

"Yes, Daddy, but…"

"Well then, what did all of those awful things do to this moment? Best I can tell, you have three wonderful children and a profoundly special husband to boot. If anything, this moment is the sum total of all the others that led to it. This being the case, my dear child, I dare say we wouldn't be in this moment *without* all the others. Your son is here and he is special. If nothing else, *celebrate* this. Condemning it to something other than special is absurd," Papa pontificated. He was so good at this.

My mother angrily wiped her eyes and swept me up into her arms.

"I love you so much, Paul. I'm sorry I scared you today," she said, her eyes puffy.

"It's okay, Mommy. I promise," I said and wrapped my arms around her neck.

"Addie, if he needs to talk to me, can you help him do that? I think it will be important as we go from this point forward," Papa said, his tone much more serious.

"Of course, Daddy. If we can't help him here, I will call you. I promise you," she said and set me down.

I hugged my grandfather. He smiled warmly, put his hat on and disappeared down the hallway with my mother.

I had trouble understanding what all the fuss was about. In the end, I learned I could hear these weird voices. I really wasn't sure what the big deal was.

Well, little did I know, that was the tippity top of a ridiculously large iceberg; Davy Jones' locker was open and waiting for me.

Nothing out of the ordinary happened before dinner, with the exception of me hearing the rest of my family's *vox corpora*. I heard this voice from my dad, my brother, Larry, and my sister, Dylan, before dinner. The conversations weren't anything more than introductions, with a sprinkling of the same "you're special" content here or there. I didn't react to any of this, though my dad lightly pressed me on the happenings of the day, seemingly taking cues from my mother.

The conversation was extremely short, I think because Dad really had no idea what to say. I was okay with this, because, at six, I wasn't exactly prepared for discussion.

I also wasn't prepared for what amounted to the next three days, starting at dinner.

The fare that night was cook-out. Dad had learned how to cook from both of my grandfathers, and had made gourmet burgers and hot dogs that night. We had settled into our spots at the table, and my brother and sister had traded verbal jabs as was the norm.

I took a bite of my hamburger. I tasted the pickles as they danced with the burger in my mouth.

I was looking at my plate when I caught something out of the corner of my eye. Curious, I looked up to see something which then made that bite of my burger project across the room with incredible force and speed.

Over a period of sixty seconds, I saw my family age sixty years.

I watched as both my brother and sister grew to be adults old enough to retire. My brother had grown at least as tall as my dad, and eventually lost his hair as the minute grew toward its completion. My sister became extravagantly beautiful and remained so all through this process.

My parents' transformations were the most troubling. Both shrank and seemed to become frail, their hair thinned and became grey, and their skin became wrought with wrinkles.

I was vocally barraged by each of these people as my hamburger remnant was eaten by the dog. Their mouths were animated, but I heard nothing.

My mother cried, my sister yelled, and my brother raised his hand to hit me.

I took a deep breath, remembering what Papa and Akamu said to me.

I then yelled, "STOP!"

The animation in my family stopped. They all looked at me in varying states of anger, awe and concern.

I got up, and walked first to Larry.

"Say something to me about turtles, Larry. Something we always say. Tell me," I begged my brother.

His much too old face looked at me, a mix of extraordinary confusion and anger reflecting back at me.

"They're cowards. 'The hell is wrong wit' you, boy?" he angrily replied.

I moved to my sister and asked, "What was the last thing you and I did together?"

Dylan seemed to have been swayed more toward concern than anger based on the look on her face.

"We… we fished, Bug. Why are you asking?" she replied.

I nodded and then moved to my mother, who was sobbing. What I saw was a ninety-six-year-old body, skin that had grown thin and wrinkled. She had bad bruises on her hands.

"Mommy, what was I playing with earlier today when your ghost talked to me?" I asked.

"It was your army men, Paul," she said, tears falling into her mouth when she replied.

I again nodded and moved to my father. He was also appearing in a ninety-six-year-old body: his muscles reduced to nothing, the powerful man I knew now weak. His hair was thin and white.

"Daddy, the last thing we talked about was what?" I asked, looking into his cataract-ridden eyes.

He thought for a moment and said, "We talked about the sun being on fire, Paulie. What's this about?"

I nodded.

"First, sorry for spitting my food out. I saw all of you change super-fast, and it scared me. I think this is part of what Papa told me about today. Larry, you're bald. Dylan, you're beautiful. Mommy and Daddy, you're super old. I don't understand this, but I need to talk to Papa. Mommy, you promised, so can you please call him?" I asked, walking all around the room as I gave my synopsis.

"What's going on? I'm not bald, am I, Mom?" Larry implored.

"No, moron. It's just what our kid brother sees. Settle down. There's obviously something wrong with him if he called me anything but stupid," Dylan dismissed.

My frail mother then produced her phone with my grandfather on the other end.

"Okay Paul. Talk me through what you see," he requested.

"Well Papa, I watched everyone get a whole lot older in just a few seconds. My brother and sister are adults, and my parents are older than you. What happened?" I asked, as the rest of my family watched and reacted to this.

"Did you actually watch them change, Paul?"

"Yes, Papa. I watched Larry lose his hair, I watched Dylan get super pretty and I watched Mommy and Daddy shrink and get so old they shouldn't be able to move. I *watched* them change."

"I'm going to guess they aren't seeing the same thing, right? I mean, if they really had gotten that much older all at once, we wouldn't be talking on the phone," he said carefully.

"I don't think so, Papa. Do you want to talk to Mommy again?" I asked, realizing he didn't have any answers.

"Sure, little fella. Try something for me, though: go outside, close your eyes and listen. You might get the answers I can't give you. I love you, Paul. Just be ready for some tough questions tonight, okay? You have a worried family, and they probably won't know what to say. Just be patient, and it will be alright. I promise," he said reassuringly.

I handed the phone back to my still-old mother, grabbed my plate and went outside.

Our house had a long boardwalk off the deck leading to a dock in the Copahee Sound. No matter where I looked out back, I saw nature. Closing my eyes, I heard birds in the sky chatting, and in the distance, water lapped against anything it could.

I sat there for a moment, enjoying that what I was looking at seemed not to have changed. I found comfort in this and ate the rest of my burger with the coward turtles watching from the water.

After a short time, I heard a voice. It was a man's voice, and it wasn't anyone I knew. It was deep, and sounded like an older gentleman.

"Hello, Paul. Both Akamu and your grandfather mentioned me, though they do not know me. For now, please know that I am your guide, and this is how we communicate. No one is hearing me but you. I can hear you whether you speak or think; this is your choice. You can call me Sam," the voice announced.

"How are you talking to me, Sam?" I thought.

"In due time, I will show you. For now, let's talk about what you just saw at dinner, okay? Paul, sometimes you will see things as though you were on another planet. You just saw your family age sixty years in sixty seconds because that is a reflection of your life there. I know this sounds very strange, but that's why you saw what you did. I promise it will make more sense soon. This world I speak of is very different from Earth," Sam said.

"Sixty years in sixty seconds? Did my family really get that old, Sam?" I asked, confused at the whole of this.

"No, Paul. They are still the ages they were before you saw them age. You will see them in their older bodies for the rest of the day, though. For now, I want you just to relax. Your family will want to talk later. Be honest, and be kind. After all, they all are concerned about you. I will talk to you in the morning. When you wake up tomorrow, ask to speak with me before you open your eyes, okay? Blessings, Paul," Sam said, and then he was gone.

I sat there, my six-year-old brain doing its best to comprehend what it had just heard. It didn't take too long before I had company.

"Paul, can we talk?" Mom asked timidly. She was still appearing in her elderly body, so her voice was weak. It upset me, even though I knew my mother wasn't really in her nineties.

"Sure, Mommy," I replied, matching her shyness.

"Sweetheart, can you please tell me what you saw? I want to understand, baby. I want to help you," she said passionately. I could tell she was struggling badly with this.

"Mommy, I saw you get sixty years older in sixty seconds. I saw you and Daddy get super old. You still look older than Papa right now. I saw Larry and Dylan get older. Larry lost his hair and Dylan got super pretty. She is even prettier than Lizzie," I said, referring to my cousin who was a supermodel. "I don't think this is something you can help me with. I just think it's something I have to see. Can you promise me something?"

"Of course, Paul, anything," she said as tears fell from her eyes.

"Promise me that you won't get upset if I say weird things. I think I might," I said, thinking that there was a strong possibility of odd behavior, given that I was seeing bizarre things.

"I promise, sweetheart, but you need to promise me something too, okay?" she asked, and peered deeply into my eyes.

"What, Mommy?"

"Promise me that no matter what you see, you *tell* me. I want to know everything you see, everything you hear, and everything you do from this day forward. Do you hear me, son? I want to be part of *everything*. Do you promise?" she said, placing both of her hands on my shoulders.

"I promise, Mommy. Some of this is going to be so strange, though."

"I'll take strange, Paul. I don't care how strange or upsetting these things get."

"Well, there's this person that talks to me in my head. His name is Sam. He seems nice, I guess," I said, testing my mother's resolve.

"As long as he's nice, that's all I care about," she said kindly. "Have I ever told you about the angel that sang to me at night when I was little? She was really nice to me, too, when I needed someone to be."

"You had an angel, Mommy?" I asked.

She then told me all about her "singing lady," and I was astounded at how open she was about Sam.

When she was done talking, I smiled. From that point forward, I knew she would be the calm in my storm. For the rest of her life, she was. My mother was the only person I knew I could trust implicitly. I needed her and, for most of my life, she gave me every ounce of strength she possessed. I needed it.

Not too long after this conversation, my father, brother and sister joined us. They were still in their older bodies, and seeing my bald brother made me laugh.

"What's wrong with you, rodent?" Dylan asked coarsely. Her behavior oddly matched how she looked. I can't begin to explain why, but it fit.

"I can't get enough of Larry, stupid. Ain't I allowed to laugh?" I deflected.

"And what in the world about me is making you laugh, turd?" Larry demanded.

"Enough, you two," my father boomed. "Paul, are you okay?"

"Yes, Daddy. I'm okay. Larry's bald, though," I said. I couldn't help myself.

My brother then chased me, and I jumped off the end of the dock.

"I may be crazy, son, but that dome of yours reflects the sunset *just* right," I said, chiding my brother from the water.

"I'm not bald, idiot! Y'all's insane," he dismissed and walked back down the dock.

That night ended as most before had, with the exception of the fact that my entire family thought I was nuts. My mother meant every word she said, but in my heart, I knew they thought me insane.

Well, the next morning, I would swear to you myself that I had lost my marbles.

I woke up and felt different. My body felt light, my head felt as though it no longer had hair.

"Sam? Where am I? What's going on?" I thought, as he had instructed.

"Paul, you are in a different body, on a world vastly different from Earth. Give yourself a couple minutes to just breathe. Your memory will catch up quickly," Sam said kindly. His voice was louder, almost as though he was closer to me.

"Sam, you seem closer to me physically. Are you?"

"I'm not far, my dear boy. Now, as soon as you have your bearings, please open your eyes and observe. Your sole responsibility for the next couple days is just to listen and watch. There aren't many people here. What I want you to see will become obvious quickly," Sam instructed.

"Wait! A couple days?! Won't my family wonder where I am?" I asked, my mind racing.

"Ah, ah, Paul. Take a few deep breaths for me. I can feel your heart racing. At your age, this is not advisable. Your family has no idea you are gone because to them, you aren't. They will have the same Paul they've always had.. He will continue to address what happened last night. When you return to Earth, you will know everything that has transpired. Believe it or not, you are still living that same life, even though you feel you are gone. Now, can you tell me where you are, and how old you are?" Sam asked kindly.

As Sam talked, my mind indeed settled and I became aware of the life I was now in.

"I'm on the planet, Pai. I am three-hundred-twenty-four years of age. My name here is Nyd."

"Very good, Paul! Now, open your eyes and please make note of all you see. Please know that every experience and every memory you gain here will come with you. You will always know Pai. Enjoy this world, my dear friend. I am here if you need me for any reason," Sam said reassuringly.

I smiled. I was no longer bound by an immature mind. Indeed, people in this place lived slowly and aged at a snail's pace due to the purity of the environment and the way of life. I found myself eager to go outside, almost as though I needed to.

My hands showed signs of aging, but were nowhere near decrepit. They looked similar to my Dad's hands, but slightly smaller. His hands were massive; I have never seen another person's hands even come close—even Papa's.

I walked effortlessly on healthy looking legs. I saw a mirror across the room, but felt that I needed to be outside, so I skipped a study of my face. I knew I was bald due to the air that hit my head as I walked. I instantly felt a kinship with Larry as a result and chuckled when I made this recognition.

I stepped outside and was bathed in scrumptious light from Pai's dual stars in the sky. My house was high in the mountains, and the air was crisp but abundant. Everywhere I looked, I saw mountains. The peaks rose and fell in a concert of sight—I did not see a single house anywhere around me. I'd never seen anything nearly as awe-inspiring as this, in pictures or otherwise. The expanse was predominantly a bluish grey in color, with trees providing interruptions in the color palate here and there. The sky was a rich blue with puffy clouds scattered loosely above. The air was warm on my skin, which was odd in retrospect simply due to the altitude. There was not one part of what I saw that first morning that failed to take my breath away in some way. You see, I loved everything about where we lived in Charleston: our house, the boardwalk and the Copahee. However, none of it held a candle to the profound awesomeness of the scene before me.

The light from the stars in the sky seemed to feed me. The rumbles I felt in my belly disappeared the longer I felt the warmth on my skin. I closed my eyes and took several deep breaths. Any trepidation I had about this place, or being away from Earth, were gone. It was magical here, and I allowed myself to be enveloped in all of it.

I heard what was similar to an eagle's cry in the distance. It was the first sound I heard, aside from the gentle but constant breeze caressing me. I opened my eyes to find the source of this sound. The bird was large, bigger than the biggest eagle I had seen. It glided across the sky in front of me a short distance away. It seemed to know me. I nodded and it acknowledged me with another strong cry.

I saw that same bird each morning I was there, across three days. On the third day, he landed next to me and joined me in my sun worship. I got a much better look at the creature as he sat there, basking, and was taken at how striking he was. His chest was impressive for his body; it was notably muscular. His wings matched closest to the pictures of bald eagles I'd seen in books in their shape and how they wrapped around his body as he sat. He had a distinctive pattern running along the length of his torso with a solid rich brown line in the middle. Smaller lines started with that main line and trailed off along his wings. He was stunning, pure and simple.

As I sat with my winged friend, I heard Sam's voice for the first time since the day I arrived here.

"Paul, tonight will be the final night you spend here. I want you to pay close attention to the night sky as a planet close to Pai will become visible to your naked eye. You will be able to make out enough detail to begin to understand this neighboring world. It is important you observe carefully, my friend. Soon enough, you will see this place for yourself," Sam said, an emotional intensity present in his voice I'd not heard previously.

"Thank you, Sam, I will watch tonight. It makes me sad to know I'll be leaving Pai. This is such a special place," I replied.

"Yes, Paul, Pai is indeed a wondrous place. It is important that you saw it and know it as your first step beyond Earth. There are many special worlds, but I tend to believe Pai to be in a class of its own."

I found Sam's words to be laced with sadness. This left me without knowing what to say. Instead of saying anything further, I again turned my attention to my winged friend, who was still bathing in sunlight. I couldn't help but join him in my own continuation of my sun worship.

That night, per Sam's suggestion, I turned my attention to the sky. What I saw was disturbing, despite the fact that I had to be hundreds of thousands of miles from the object of my gaze.

There were distinctly visible metal girder-like constructs holding objects that seemed to have large flames at the end. These constructions seemed to cover most of the planet. Other objects were in orbit around the planet, and were, again, big enough for me to see. I couldn't discern whether they were weapons or not, but they, at minimum, seemed to be on some sort of patrol.

On the planet itself, I saw the antithesis of Pai. I saw unnatural light everywhere. There couldn't have been a hint of trees or, honestly, nature there. I got a horrible sense in my belly about the beings occupying this place and, on cue, Sam addressed my feeling.

"Your feeling is just, Paul. Everything you just observed is exactly as you assessed. That planet is called Cythis. It is a complete opposite of Pai in every way. It is also an important part of your journey. I will tell you more when it is necessary. For now, I want Cythis to leave your mind. Envelop yourself in Pai until it is time to sleep. You will wake elsewhere tomorrow," Sam said sentimentally.

"Sam, please promise me I will return to this place again. I'm not sure how this works; I just want to be sure I can see Pai again. I don't want to leave, if I'm being honest. This is the most special place I have ever seen. I love this life. I will be completely heartbroken if I can never return," I emotionally responded.

"Pai will always be part of your journey, Paul. You will be back. I just can't say when."

"Thanks, Sam. Will you tell me where I will be tomorrow?"

"No, Paul. I cannot tell you those things. It is beyond what is right, given your journey. I will always be with you. No matter where you wake, I am but a thought away," Sam reassured.

The next morning, I woke up back in my bed in Charleston. I immediately felt the difference in my body. One may think that my body as a child would be vastly lighter than my Pai body. In fact, the opposite was true. I felt a heaviness in my chest weighing on me.

"Sam, why do I feel like this? I mean, I have this weird feeling in my chest that I've never felt before," I asked.

"Well, Paul, you will notice these things as you move from place to place. Your body on Earth is not even close to as healthy as your Pai body, simply because of the planet itself and what humanity has done to it through pollution and war. Take a few moments to adjust. This feeling will fade. Please, though, don't forget this difference. It is key to your development, and key to the impact you will make in your life," Sam instructed.

"Thank you, Sam. Does my mom know I was gone? I mean, I know what you told me, but I'm just not sure what to say to her this morning."

"Again, Paul, just take some time and everything will come back to you. I have to believe your mother would be fascinated by what you just observed."

Sure enough, after a couple minutes, my memory absorbed the happenings of the time I was away. It was standard fare for the most part. I had been a pest to my siblings, who still considered me damaged from the night I saw them age. Dylan, apparently, was very sad, thinking that something was really wrong with me. Larry thought me to be nothing but a damaged imbecile, which was about right given our relationship.

With my brain set to go, I got up and brushed my teeth. I then went off to find my mom.

I found her in the kitchen, making some kind of egg concoction in a skillet.

"Good morning, Mommy! I have some things to talk about when you're ready," I said, hopping up on a stool by our island.

Mom was apparently taken by this, as she stopped everything she was doing and quickly came over to me.

"What is it, Paul? What's wrong, sweetie?" she asked, concern running rampant in her eyes.

"Nothing, Mommy. Why?" I deflected.

"What things do you need to talk about, Paul? What's wrong?" she persisted, her gaze intensifying.

"Mommy, this is going to be confusing, but for the past two days, I was somewhere else. It was the most beautiful place I've ever seen. It's called Pai. This is part of what I'm going through. I would love to tell you about it if you would like to hear," I said, trying to comfort her.

"But Paul, you were here. How were you on Pai? We had chicken last night that you said was yummy. You and your dad played catch. I don't understand," she said, her confusion intensifying.

Without missing a beat, Sam came to my rescue.

"Paul, tell her you were here, but were on Pai, too. I will help you through this," he said kindly.

"Mommy, I *was* here, and I was on Pai, too. This is why I saw you guys change the way you did. The next morning, I woke up on Pai. The thing is, you never would have seen a difference because part of me was still here," I said confidently. I hadn't perfected a means of describing this in my young age, and my explanation confounded my mother badly.

"Paul, you're really confusing your mom. Sam, can you help here please?" mom's *vox corporis* said desperately.

"Wait… You guys can talk? How?" I thought.

"Paul, let's fix things with your mom first. Try saying this: 'When you sleep, part of you wanders. You're still in your bed, but part of you likes to move around. I'm no different, except the part that wanders goes to other lives'," Sam instructed.

"Mommy, I'm sorry," I began and grabbed her hand. "When you sleep, part of you wanders. You're still sleeping in your bed, but part of you moves around. That same part in me moves, but when he does, he goes to other bodies in other places. I'm sorry I confused you."

"Perfect, Paul. Keep going—she's interested now," Mom's *vox corporis* said reassuringly.

"I'm proud of you, Paul. I'm here if you need me," Sam said kindly.

"So, let me get this straight, Paul: you were here, but part of you was living in a different place?" Mom asked, returning to her skillet.

"Yeah. I woke up in a body that was three-hundred-twenty-four years old, named Nyd. I was bald, and lived high in the mountains. I chuckled when I realized I was bald, but still planned on teasing Larry because it's super fun.

"There, my body didn't need anything but sunlight. I didn't eat for two days—I just sat outside and *breathed*. There was this massive eagle that sat by me the last day I was there. I have never seen a bird so big, with a pattern like he had. Pai was the most beautiful place I've ever seen, even more beautiful than the prettiest sunsets on the dock. I want more than anything for you to see it someday, but I couldn't tell you where in the heck it was. There were a bunch of planets close to Pai, and two suns in the sky. Sam told me I'd be back someday. I hope he's right," I said, and took a big gulp of juice that Mom had deposited in front of me as I talked.

"How did you feel waking up this morning, Paul? I'm not concerned anymore, but I'm still trying to make sense of how you can move from body to body and not miss a beat," she said, maintaining her focus on her skillet.

"I felt heavy, Mommy. It was weird, but I felt super heavy. Once I got past that, I gave myself a couple minutes to let my memories to catch up. I know this is weird, but I am getting used to this. Sam helps me a ton, but I'm getting used to it," I said and took another big gulp of juice. "I'm sorry I was a pest to Dylan and Larry, Mommy. I'll try to be better."

"Heavy? What do you mean, Paul?" she asked, putting a steaming plate of eggs-something in front of me.

I took a moment to smell the food. I allowed the spice-filled steam to permeate my sinuses. I closed my eyes, feeling grateful for the plate in front of me.

I found it incredibly interesting that my first instinct, like on Pai, was to envelop my senses. This had never been the case in my young life until now. *Gratitude?* Nice to meet you! Yeah, I was changing.

Mom noticed me doing this and asked, "Is everything okay, sweetie?"

"Yeah, Mommy. I'm just looking at things a little bit differently. The steam is filled with spice and smells from the vegetables and it smells really good. Thank you for breakfast."

"You closed your eyes. Were you praying, Paul?" Mom asked, leaning in.

"No, Mommy. I was just being thankful for the food. That's all," I responded without flinching.

Unbeknownst to me, Dylan was standing behind me for this entire exchange. I felt my sister's arms wrap around me and squeeze. She was crying.

"What's wrong, Dylan?" I asked.

"Shut up, bug," a muffled voice responded.

I nodded.

Larry came into the room with Dad to see this scene. There was no mistaking his disdain for me, and he blamed me completely for our sister's tears.

Dad, for his part, fluidly moved past us and kissed Mommy. Their eyes sparkled at one another; they loved one another so deeply. I'd never paid attention but, seeing this, I teared up, too.

"'The hell? Did someone die? What am I missing?" Dad implored, his senses accurately picking up on the emotion in the room.

"It's obvious Paul did something. What was it this time?" Larry asked accusingly.

"Larry, knock it off! Bug just was sweet, and it made me cry. Shut up," Dylan explained, her arms still tightly wrapped around me.

"Paul, what are your tears for?" Dad callously asked.

"I've never seen how much you love Mommy before. That's all," I said sniffing. I had no use of my arms due to Dylan's squeeze, so I was a snotty, teary mess.

My response seemed to stun my family. Everyone but Larry teared up, and that's simply due to Larry's lack of a soul. Okay, that's not nice on my part, but whatever. Deal with it.

"Paul, your brother doesn't hate you. He just can't relate. You have completely stunned him; take his words not for what they are, but instead as a representation of a person who loves and respects you—and simply doesn't know how to do so," Larry's *vox corporis* interjected.

I smiled when I heard this.

Dylan's arms gently let go and she kissed me on the cheek. She then punched Larry's shoulder and hugged our father. Yeah, to this day, this is a perfect synopsis for the person my sister is. I love her dearly for all that she is.

After breakfast had been consumed and the crowd dispersed, my mother redoubled her efforts to understand Pai and what was happening to me.

"Okay, sweetie, we never finished talking about the heaviness you felt this morning. Could you tell me more?" she asked and took a sip of coffee.

"Sure, Mommy. It's almost like I'm trying harder to breathe and to move. It's not bad; it's just noticeable. That's all," I responded.

"So, on Pai, your three-hundred-something year old body felt lighter? You didn't have to eat? This is really something, Paul. I'm coming around on all of it, but it's still hard for me to understand how what you're telling me is possible. No matter what, thank you for trusting me enough to tell me about your experience. I meant it when I said I want to hear everything, sweetheart, even when it's hard for me to grasp," she said, looking me deeply in my eyes.

"She is being truthful, Paul. Tell her about your winged friend. She'd like that," Mom's *vox corporis* suggested.

"Mommy, there was one thing—one really special thing—that happened on Pai. There was this really big bird, like an eagle but bigger, that flew through the valley by my house. The last day I was there, he landed on my porch and sat with me for almost the whole day. I've never had anything like that happen before," I said, smiling.

"Really? What did this bird look like?" she asked and leaned in to me.

"He had this pattern all over his body that was like zebra stripes, but thinner and crazier. The lines traced his body, off of this one thicker line in the middle. The lines were brown, and he was sorta white," I explained.

Mom smiled as I talked. She loved birds as much as politicians love fleecing their constituents.

"He sounds stunning, sweetheart. I'm so glad you got to see this bird up close."

Our conversation trailed off from there. It's almost as though my mention of the bird made this whole batch of insanity somehow tangible to my mother.

In one fell swoop, I learned that I could talk to people without uttering a word, move from body to body *and* remember the experience. This was certainly not the last experience I had as a child. But, because it was the first, it is a batch of time I will never forget.

So, you've gotten a taste—a tiny morsel—of what I've done in my little life. Should you be curious, read on. Should you care to venture forward, I have to be honest and tell you this: it ain't easy sleddin'.

Don't say I didn't warn you! Get a receptacle ready. Your precious belly may decide to precipitously produce projectiles from within. I hope at least one person witnesses this and laughs. You need that. I can tell.

A Model of Insanity

Remember that iceberg I mentioned last chapter? This chapter goes down about six inches on that thing. Progress!

After Pai, I did stints on two other planets in something of a regular rotation for three years. The first was a place called Crata, which was basically Pai with some cursory development—America during the gold rush. I was thirty-two there. The second place was Pliqun—the place I mentioned before—which was essentially a Crata copy with nicer people. I was sixteen there. I'll talk more about these places and my lives in each place later on. The more pertinent topic right now is something I continue to affectionately call "The Jury."

After each trip, Papa, Akamu and I would convene in that odd spiritual realm I was first taken to after I initially heard the *vox corporis*. Akamu has a particularly interesting skill in that he can see cursory details about one's life before they happen. Thing is, it's not particularly accurate down to the tiniest of details. As an example, he would be able to see that you were going to have a bad day on the 5th, but he wouldn't be able to see why. It's almost as though he could tap into one's future emotions and draw conclusions from there. Then, when the stuff of life fills in the gaps, the initial forecast isn't reconciled against what happened. This is the rub.

This is akin to something fairly common, like a weather forecast. Say you see a forecast for snow and temperatures in the singles digits two days out. You live a frivolous couple days and awake on the forecasted cold day. You extend a hand outside when the dog goes out in the AM, and indeed it's cold. Your clothing choice for the day includes shorty shorts, flips and a tank top. This is a perfect metaphor for this pattern, but in Akamu's case, his forecast prevailed as truth even though key details were missing. His subsequent judgment was, ahem, interesting.

Do you see where this could go a tad squirrely, especially if the emotion in question is fiery, murderous hatred?

Let me be very clear: Akamu is a vastly powerful, knowing, caring entity. I cannot begin to marginalize him given all that he has done for me. Thing is, this little bit of precognition caused more problems than anything in the first decade or so of these conversations. It's why The Jury got the name it did, and why I've asked for a juryless trial for the past several decades.

My first trips to Crata and Pliqun were nothing but observation-based. There wasn't anything to litigate, per se, so the jury conversations were light.

"So, Paul, you have been to three planets so far. How are you feeling?" Akamu asked after my first trip to Pliqun.

"I'm doing okay, Akamu. So far, it's just interesting to see these planets and learn what I can from the lives I'm living there," I responded. I was nine years old at this point; my experiences had matured my speaking self but the rest of me was still very much a child.

"Good, good. So, no feelings of uneasiness or concern then?"

"I mean… No, um… I mean…," I stammered. I had matured quickly in a lot of ways but certainly not all. I really didn't know how to answer this very anemic question.

"Paul, have you ever felt scared when you are living these other lives?" Grandpa interjected.

"Sure, Papa, I'm always a little nervous when I wake up someplace new. Once my memories come back a couple minutes later, I'm fine. Sam is a huge help, too. I always feel as though I have someone with me. He's a huge reason why this isn't completely crazy to me," I rationalized.

"I'm so glad to hear that! Have you seen anything interesting in either Crata or Pliqun? I know Pai really struck you with its beauty," he continued.

"I, too, am glad to hear this, Paul. I apologize for confusing you; that was not my intention at all," Akamu conceded.

To the best of my knowledge, this was the only time Akamu apologized to me. You see, a couple things happened that fundamentally changed me and caused this to be true. You will see shortly why Akamu didn't apologize again.

Within a day of this conversation, I again, saw my family age at dinner. I laughed at Larry's bald head, I reviled in Dylan's profound beauty, and I did my best not to be alarmed by my parents' appearances. My hope was that I was returning to Pai.

I did.

This time, Sam welcomed me with a stark warning as I awoke in my bald self.

"Paul, as you venture outside, I need you to remain calm and objective. Your instinct will not follow this pattern. Please heed this advice, my friend," he said, his voice cold. Were he standing in front of me, I would have had to believe he was shaking when he'd said this.

I didn't respond right away as I didn't know how to process this. Pai was my favorite place to be. I wasn't sure how to make sense of Sam's words.

"What's wrong, Sam? Can you please…"

"Try to remain calm, Paul," Sam insisted, interrupting me.

I begrudgingly got up and made my way to my door. I could see something was happening outside, but I couldn't make out what.

Well, my eyes saw what my brain could not process.

"Paul, please… You have no idea what you are capable of," Sam pleaded.

I was passed a point of restraint. There was nothing in me but blind rage.

There were three of them.

Three.

They were taking turns gashing my bird with a blade. He was alive, barely. He was suffering badly. I could feel his pain in my chest. This made my anger tenfold worse.

I stormed out the door, which for the moment stopped my friend's torture.

My glare fixed on these damned souls. In my mind, I had two thoughts: the pain you caused my friend, you will feel, and the life you have taken from him will be returned.

My attention turned to the twin suns in the sky. I somehow felt I was connected to them, their combined power coursing through me. My anger fueled this sensation and it was as though I had lightning stirring lava in my veins.

One of the damned took a step toward me. That's as far as he got before he started to bleed. His eyes widened as the pain expanded. He was not mortally wounded. Well, not yet anyway.

"Paul, you have to restrain yourself," Sam demanded.

"I'm making things right, Sam," I thought calmly.

"You know not how powerful you are, Paul. Please, my friend. Remain as calm as you can. This is but one problem. You must remain objective," he urged.

The other two assailants took notice of their now-injured comrade and together stepped toward me.

I was not sure how, but it was my intention for these two individuals to replace the life they had taken from my winged friend. That was my sole thought.

My right hand raised, and this stopped the forward motion of these two individuals. I looked toward my winged friend and raised my left hand, which raised him from the ground. He was near death; blood poured from his body as I raised him.

I closed my right hand into a fist, slowly, but resolutely. As my fingers closed, I choked the air from both individuals, though this was not intended to kill them (yet). I cupped my left hand and a steady stream of something light formed from the choking assailants and moved rapidly into the levitating bird.

The bird's bleeding slowed and then stopped over a period of maybe fifteen seconds.

Within a minute, his wounds had healed and his eyes no longer held pain. I could feel his pain release completely in my chest.

I lowered my left hand, softly setting the bird on the ground. He immediately began inspecting his wings.

Out of the corner of my eye, I caught a glimpse of something.

The entire side of the valley facing my patio was on fire.

With this recognition, my thought turned to this: *You will burn.*

My gaze fixed on the damned, all three of them. Each of the three lowered their eyes, a surrender apparent to me. They were afraid.

This made me happy.

The ground around me started to shake as though a very mild earthquake had begun. I slowly raised both hands with my eyes locked on the assailants. They rose off the ground, each struggling to regain the control of themselves I now owned. They seemed to beg in whatever language they spoke. I glared at them, my intent unwavering.

I believed the more fear I could create in these individuals, the more I could influence what was happening to Pai. Mind you, Sam wasn't speaking to me. I'm not sure where these beliefs came from, but I trusted them.

I moved my hands slowly in the direction of the edge of my patio, with the damned now following the movement.

There was no railing between the patio and the valley. The patio itself was just a flat slab. I moved the damned to the edge of the patio and held them there for a minute or so.

I then moved them a foot off the patio, into the expanse of the valley. There was more incoherent chatter, more struggle. I held the damned there for another minute.

With more motion, I pushed the assailants ten or fifteen feet off of the patio. I could feel their fear; this was precisely what I was after. I held them here longer, maybe two or three minutes.

The individuals' backs were toward me, and I felt I needed to convey something to them. Slowly, I turned the men toward me.

I glared at the individuals, slowly shaking my head in sheer disgust.

When I felt I had elicited enough fear, it was time. In a quick pushing motion with my hands, I threw the damned into the flames in the valley. Though it was a very large distance, I made sure they remained alive when they landed in the burning forest below; I sent them into the fire. I needed their pain to join their fear—this was important.

I watched them writhe in the grips of the fire. I coldly watched them suffer—I felt their pain as they slowly died.

I took solace in watching them perish in the flames.

"Paul, we're going to need to talk about this," Sam scolded.

"I'm sure we are, Sam," I replied.

For the rest of that day, I sat and watched my beloved valley burn with my winged friend by my side. I cried tears of anger the whole time. My precious Pai was burning.

"What demonic nonsense caused such a thing? Pai is pure," I thought.

"Look up, Paul," Sam responded.

I did, and to my horror I saw the beginnings of the industrialized mayhem I observed around Cythis.

"What can I do, Sam? This cannot happen. I will not let it happen, not here," I said as fresh tears fell to the ground.

"Right now, you can do nothing, Paul. If anything, you just made this whole situation worse," Sam responded coldly.

"Well, Sam, forgive me, but I disagree. A line was crossed, sure, but those men needed to feel fear and suffer and they did. I was not going to stand by and do nothing today. I refuse to live that way. I am learning that I can do things, Sam. When the occasion calls for it, I will not hesitate to use these things, ever," I replied with the same chilly tone Sam had used.

"Okay, okay. Let's try this a different way," Sam said with a softer voice. *"Paul, I need you to understand that just as you are connected to your lives, you are connected to all others, too. I will agree that you handled a situation today well, in part. Throwing those men into the fire was not the best use of your ability. Neither, admittedly, was letting them go so they could tell others about you.*

"You had a benefit of being on Pai where no one witnessed your actions except the men who were involved. This will not be the case elsewhere. I will tell you that you will be going to Cythis soon. You cannot display yourself to them. They will take you, and you will be lost. So, too, will be your chance to address the first part of your path.

"So, let me be clear: yes, you are powerful and this is true of every life you lead. It is not unique to the life you live here. But this power is held within your essence, the one that moves, so there is no chance for you to unconsciously abuse your abilities. In other words, your body on Earth is a normal boy until you return there. Can you imagine what would happen to one of your lives if you showed some part of your ability and your essence was not there to defend the life or lives being attacked? Trust me, my dear friend, you do not want this.

"There will be times where the full breadth of your talents will be needed. You've seen but a part of what you can do, Paul. I will help you to understand it all—much, much sooner than I had planned. Today's events were unbeknownst to me when we spoke last, and were incredibly unfortunate to be sure. My concern, that I will again apologize for, was that you would not properly control your abilities and do quite a bit more damage.

"Our plans have changed as a result of today's events, my friend. Because of this, I am going to teach you another aspect of your talent. You will not be returning to Earth from here. Your mother is concerned, Paul. You need to let her know you are okay because she knows you are gone. She has been able to pick up subtle changes in the Paul she is seeing while you are here. So, would you be willing to let her know you're okay?

"Your winged friend would also prefer for these emotions to ease in you, Paul. You saved his life today, and he knows it. He wants to save you now. So, if for nothing but the incredible creature you saved, will you gather yourself, show him you are okay, and then do the same for your mother?"

I looked over to my winged friend, who had moved closer. There was worry in his eyes.

I smiled, the warmth coming from my winged friend was overwhelming. I wiped the remaining moisture from my eyes, composed myself, and allowed the emotion to even out as I deeply breathed in Pai's mildly smoky air. The bird seemed to recognize this, and his gaze softened.

"That's it, my dear friend. I cannot begin to express how sorry I am for openly criticizing you. I was wrong, Paul, and should have handled myself properly. I will not make this mistake again," Sam said kindly.

"You were right, Sam. I took things too far today after my winged buddy here was well, and at the time everything was as calculated as I felt it needed to be. Looking back on it now, I don't know what to think. Knowing those men really had to die to protect me is something I'm not ready to face. How am I supposed to move forward? Am I always going to thirst for fear and pain? What the heck is happening to me, Sam?" I asked and took another deep breath. As I began to process the events of the day, a weight, slowly but noticeably, found its way onto my chest.

"Well, Paul, the only thing I can tell you at the moment is that your purpose is going to take over when it needs to. Today was a very good example of this; those men were going to lay complete waste to everything in the valley and the ridges above. After torturing your avian buddy to death, they were going to destroy your house and begin burning everything on the opposite side of the valley. You know the fear and pain you wanted the men to feel? The men wanted to convey dominance and destruction in the very same way. What you did temporarily stopped the Cythians from proceeding.

You see, those soldiers' biorhythms were monitored back on Cythis throughout their time on Pai, They are members of a motivated army whose sole purpose is dominance. By causing the soldiers to feel fear, it threw a wrench into the army's plans. Simply put, the men you fought felt a deep fear before perishing which starkly contrasted the dominance that was expected by all. You properly sent the message you needed to, at least for the moment. Your next objective will be to stall this further and ultimately reverse the course of this action. There is much to be discussed before that challenge is upon us," Sam said comfortingly, but resolutely.

"Can you tell me what's going on with Mom?" I asked, turning my attention to a different concern. How in the world was I going to tell my mother that I had tortured and killed three men?

"There's nothing wrong with your mother, Paul. She, armed with the knowledge you've given her, started paying very close attention to you. She can tell you're different, but she can't put her finger on how.

"Your sister has noticed this as well, but she isn't as concerned about you at the moment. She seems to have a sense of knowing; when you were addressing the situation today, she was scared for you. After all was said and done, she felt bad for you. Maybe as part of this exercise, you talk to her, too," Sam encouraged.

"How in the world would I talk to my family from here, Sam? I have no idea how such a thing would be possible," I attempted to rationalize.

"Paul, every living thing, everywhere, is connected. How is it that you and I communicate with me being several dimensions away from you? How do you interact with Akamu and your grandfather, though Akamu passed a good fifteen years ago? It all comes down to energy. Your abilities are founded in energy as you soon will see. Both of your family members know what they do because of energy, especially Dylan.

"Are we clear on this energy topic?" Sam sheepishly asked.

"Yep, we are clear. Akamu died fifteen years ago? He's not a being like you, Sam?" I asked, confusion seeping through my mind.

"Indeed, he did, my dear boy. We are different in a couple ways, but identical in others. He still communicates daily with your mother. Ask her about it."

"I had no idea, Sam. I thought… Well, I guess I… I have no idea. This is all so strange," I stammered.

"In time, Paul, all of this will seem as normal as brushing your teeth. Now then, can we please get in touch with your mother? We are going to use her dreams for this exercise, and she is in the perfect deep sleep right now," Sam said reassuringly.

"Yes, just tell me what to do. I'm not sure what to say, though, once we are talking. How do I tell her about today, Sam? I killed three men. How do I tell Mom that?" I asked, my heart pounding.

"She already knows, Paul. Akamu told her," Sam said flatly. *"I'm not at all happy with him at the moment."*

"WHAT? How did he know?"

"Remember what I just told you? Akamu knows what he does because of his ability to leverage energy. Regardless, that's not as important as getting in touch with your mother. Time is of the essence, Paul. Please take some deep breaths for me," Sam said, the timber of his voice lower and his speech slower.

I did as I was asked; I focused on my breath and felt my heart stop racing. I was calm after a few slow, deep breaths.

"Good, Paul. Now, I want you to think of your mother's eyes."

Mom had beautiful eyes. They were a deep, almost navy blue, with lighter blues all through her irises. They were stunning—and incredibly easy to remember. I had no problem visualizing her eyes.

"Good, Paul. Now, very gently, I want you to ask her to join you. Keep the image of her eyes vividly in front of you when you do. Once she accepts your invitation, you will see her," Sam said softly.

I took another deep breath, focused on Mom's eyes and asked, "Mommy, would you join me, please?"

Well, I'm not too sure how to explain this.

Mom's eyes remained fixed in my brain, and all of a sudden, she was standing in front of me on our deck back in Charleston. I was still in my Nyd body—the life I live on Pai. This confounded me.

"Hi, sweetheart. Are you doing okay?" she asked, reaching out and touching my face.

"I'm okay now, Mommy. Can you really see it's me?" I asked, my curiosity getting the best of me.

"Of course I can, Paul. You're my beautiful baby boy. I could never mistake you for another," she said kindly.

"Mommy, I… I'm…,"

"It's okay, Paul. Akamu told me. I understand. I'm surprised and must admit that I'm scared, but I understand," she reassured.

"I don't know what to say, Mommy. I don't want to be a monster. I don't want to be a murderer. I don't want you to be scared of me," I emotionally responded.

"Look at me, Paul," she said and got uncomfortably close to my face. "I know what you did today was hard. I just need to know you are okay. You will never be a monster to me; you are my baby boy. I was not scared *of* you, my son, I was scared *for* you. Do you understand?"

"I do. I'm sorry, Mommy. I asked you to join me so that I could tell you that I am okay. Sam…,"

"That's all I need to hear, sweetheart. Thank you," she said, interrupting me. Her arms then wrapped around my bald self and squeezed tightly.

I took a breath to say another word, and then found myself on Pai.

"What the heck just happened, Sam? I was just with my mother and…,"

"She heard what she needed to, Paul. When you have those conversations, they are not driven by you at all. She needed to know you were okay. You told her you were, she believed you, she left. It was that simple," Sam explained.

"So, I can't have conversations that I need or want to have? I mean, what if

I needed to talk to someone about something important? Can they just decide to stop talking to me if they don't have an agenda for the chat?" I asked.

"That's the tricky part, Paul. Your mother just needed to know that you were okay; it was founded in emotion. Once you understand this, you can determine how to manipulate the other person in the conversation to stay as long as you need them to. Why don't we try again with Dylan? See if you can read her emotion and keep her in your conversation until you are ready to let her go. Remember how to do this?" Sam asked, his voice full of joy. He loves to teach me any chance he gets. Yes, even today, he still teaches my old self new things all the time.

I took another deep breath and thought of my sister's eyes; they are a complete smoosh between my mother's and father's eyes. Dad had these deep hazel eyes, with greens and dark browns intertwined in radiating patterns. Dylan's eyes are deep blue with greens and browns accenting the blue from her pupils outward. In her modeling career, she became known solely for her eyes and how she could burn holes through you with a simple glance. Her children have virtual copies of those peepers, which has led to some confusion in my older years when I attempt to talk to them as they sleep. Those are stories for a different day, though.

With her eyes implanted in my brain, I asked her to join me. Almost instantly, I was standing in her bedroom and she was standing in front of me.

"Hi, Bug. You doing okay?" she asked and gave me a hug. I was still in my Nyd body as I was with Mother. Dylan was a good six inches taller than me and put her head on top of my bald dome.

"I'd complain but you'd destroy me, Fink," I said. "Fink" was my nickname for Dylan. My aunt used to call Dylan a "Rat Fink" whenever she'd use makeup she wasn't supposed to use. I liked the "Fink" part, especially since it made Dylan mad if I caught her in a mood.

"Aw Bug, given what you've been through today, there will be no destruction. You scared me, Paul. You scared me in a way I don't allow myself to be scared. Can you tell me, honestly, that you aren't hurt?" she asked, her intense gaze burning fresh holes clear through my skull.

Given what Sam told me, I purposefully didn't answer her question. Instead, I pivoted the conversation toward my own curiosity.

"Dylan, what did you see or feel when I was having my fun today?" I asked, leaning in.

Her gaze softened slightly as she thought. I could tell she really didn't know what to say.

"Well, I can't really explain this but I knew when you were fighting. It was almost like I was there with you, but I couldn't see what was happening. I could feel how upset you got; I felt your anger, I felt your guilt and I *really* clearly felt your sadness. I wanted to wipe your tears, Bug. I knew you were involved in something and that you ultimately did something, but all I wanted to do was to hug my brother."

My relationship with my sister changed that night. She grabbed the core of my beating heart with her words and to this day has never let go. Her eyes—those otherworldly spheres of pure angelic beauty—became a beacon of love and support I still look to almost every day. She and I still make an unusual pair, but there is no one as devoted to both who I am and my well-being as my supermodel sister.

I hugged her tightly and said, "I know when I say this that this moment will end, but you need your rest. Thank you for being with me today, Fink. I'm not hurt."

I felt her smile. I then found myself back on Pai.

"Much better, Paul! You controlled the conversation with Dylan perfectly. Remember it; you will need to use this skill frequently," Sam instructed.

"Thanks, Sam. Should I be concerned that my family can feel when I am behaving badly?"

"No, my dear friend. You should find comfort that they are always with you."

The day ended with my winged friend and I watching the fire die in the valley as the suns set and the moons rose. In total, there were three moons in the sky that night, all seemingly more vibrant than the last time I had observed them. He sat close to me as long as I lingered on my patio—his wing pressed into my shoulder so much that I could feel his bones.

****

I woke in the middle of the night to Akamu's voice—and the first jury I can remember wanting to cause extraordinary harm to my mentor and his surroundings formally began.

"Paul? Paul? Are you awake, Paul?" Akamu asked abrasively.

I was still on Pai, waking up in my bald, thrice-centenarian-plus body. As such, I said, "My name is Nyd. I had a rough night last night and am not yet ready to greet the day. Can this wait, please?"

"Enough, Paul. Join me now," Akamu scolded.

"Again, Akamu, here you address me as Nyd. Until I leave Pai, that is my name. I will not have this conversation until I am awake. Please leave me alone," I asked kindly but pointedly.

"Paul!" Akamu shouted.

"No more, Akamu. I will talk to you when I am up," I said, my tone becoming less pleasant.

"Paul, would you please join us? It's time we talked this through," Papa asked kindly.

The sun was not yet up. I think I had only been asleep but a couple hours.

"Papa, please let me sleep. I promise I will talk to you in the morning," I responded, my voice less aggressive.

"Okay…," he began.

"NO! You will talk to us now, Paul!" Akamu demanded, censoring Papa.

"Okay. You want to talk? We'll talk," I shouted.

"Easy, Paul. You just have to appease him. I tried…," Sam conceded.

"What do you want, Akamu?" I asked. My heart was pounding in my chest in a way that made me feel like Nyd really shouldn't have this stress. So, I continued, "I will not do this here. My body should not have this stress. Tell me how to get to where you are."

"Close your eyes, boy," Akamu boomed.

"Fine," I said coldly. I had honest thoughts about what I might be able to do to Akamu. I was furious and still very tired.

I closed my eyes and immediately found myself standing in front of Akamu, who, himself, was standing. The look on his face matched the anger in my veins.

"How dare you, Paul? You tortured those men for no reason," Akamu scolded.

"So, you saw the whole thing happen? You knew the reason for my actions?" I jabbed.

"I didn't need to. I know what you did, and…"

"…And you have no idea why. Until you understand that, I'm nothing but a cold, calculating murderer who has learned new ways of torture," I interrupted. I was furious and hell bent on teaching my mentor a lesson.

"I don't need to know why, Paul. I know you callously took the life from three people today," Akamu blubbered.

"Akamu, Paul has a point. I took lives in my lifetime and didn't get this treatment. What is this about?" Papa asked, anger notable in his reply.

Akamu stopped for a moment and considered what my grandfather had just said. It didn't seem to help.

"That's irrelevant, Olaf. Your situations were life and death. You had no choice," Akamu scolded.

"How do you know Paul had a choice, my friend? I mean, Sam did try to explain this. Why don't we get Paul's side of today's happenings and cast our judgment when we have all the facts?" Papa suggested. I loved that he was fighting for me. I wish like anything this had been the only time it was necessary.

"I… I don't see how that's relevant, Olaf. I know what happened," Akamu repositioned. "I have enough information to cast judgment on what I know now."

"Okay. Then there are a few things I need to say to you," I began. "First, when I am done saying this, I'm going to bed. You woke me up after hardly any sleep, on a very hard day for me. If you wake me again, I will lay complete waste to whatever reality this is without a shred of guilt about it. Second, the next time you tell my mother I killed somebody, this too, will be a time that brings me here to destroy *everything* I see. That's my responsibility, Akamu. She is my mother; she knew what I did and why I did it without you telling her anything. Third, I will not accept your apology today, tomorrow, or next week. Don't find me. Don't ask to talk. I will not respond. Until you care why I did what I did, I don't care to talk about this. I am fine moving forward with Sam as my only guide. Now, as I have said, I am going to bed. Don't, for a second, consider waking me again. I will come back swinging and will not ask questions. Good night," I said and closed my eyes. Upon doing so, I was back on Pai and had no trouble getting back to the land of the sleeping.

I woke the next morning on Pai, finding the beautiful serenity of the planet having an all-encompassing comfort. It was almost as though Pai itself was hugging me.

"Good Morning, my friend. You got a well-deserved rest last night," Sam said kindly.

"Had it not been interrupted, it would have been perfect, Sam. Even so, this morning is different. I can't explain this feeling I have, just that it's different this morning," I responded.

"Well, yesterday you restored natural balance to Pai. You protected the sanctity of this planet, Paul. Whether you realize it or not, you did something profound yesterday. What you are feeling is the result of your actions. You should be proud of this accomplishment, my friend. In a nutshell, this is your goal on Cythis. That planet and its people have settled into a pattern of self-destruction. They know nothing different, Paul. This is not an easy, nor quick, task. You will not have a tiny number of assailants; you will have a global population hell bent on killing you or, at minimum, making you feel degraded. Because of this, I will teach you more about your ability today. Specifically, I want to teach you how to control it," Sam began.

"What happened with Akamu... I cannot tell you how sorry I am, my friend. I tried to explain the situation. Your grandfather is incensed at what took place. You deserved a much different conversation, and I believe Akamu now understands this. Regardless, I cannot help but feel bad for how you were treated last night," he continued.

"Well, until Akamu properly addresses the situation, I do not care to have his help. You have been so helpful to me, Sam. I don't believe I need him guiding me, especially if he is choosing to be so harshly judgmental."

"I understand how you feel, my dear friend. Give it some time. I think Akamu will listen when you are ready to talk. Between me and your grandfather, he is clear that the next conversation is yours to begin."

Sam continued, "When you are ready, go outside. Please don't rush this, though. Pai is in no way done with you."

The feeling I had—the interesting hug-like sensation—intensified. It was as though Pai had sprouted tentacles and was wrapping me ever tighter, all over and inside my body. This in no way hurt, but I learned that morning just how sentient planets are.

I got up when I felt the tentacles fully recede, a feeling of extraordinary love coursing through my soul.

"I could get used to this. My goodness," I thought as I walked toward my deck. From that point forward, I would never again suggest that planets are just rocky things with stuff on them.

"Well again, Paul, you have to understand that what you did yesterday was profound. It wasn't just that you dispatched three assailants. You protected Pai; you restored her to balance. The love you feel is grounded not just in gratitude, but in truth as well. This is a very big part of your purpose, Paul, but on a grander scale," Sam said kindly.

"A grander scale, Sam? How is that possible?"

"Should you succeed, Paul, you will learn what this feels like from a dimensional source. Before we get there, I need to teach you things. You ready?"

No pressure! I just need to restore balance to a dimension. Got it.

Like hell.

"Let's rewind that just a second, Sam. You're saying that I need to fix a dimension? How is that even possible?" I asked, perplexed beyond measure.

"Well, sort of. You actually need to fix a couple dimensions, but that's not important at the moment. If I promise to tell you more about this after some work, can we please get going?" Sam dodged and implored.

We'll get to this training goodness in just one second. First, intrepid consumer of my words, it's time to come full circle on this Jury topic. Aside from the initial conversations I had in this context as I began my journeys to Crata, Pliqun and Pai, the last documented item was, quite literally, the last time I allowed a conversation like this to happen.

I didn't talk to Akamu for many years after that day on Pai.

Indeed, I manage my life and those in it carefully for reasons that are my own, in part due to what I experienced as a boy. Some of this foments in the madness of a grudge. I tend to celebrate this madness more than most. Perhaps this, again, is due to what I experienced as a boy. I know beyond a shadow of a doubt this madness protects me, so I'm happy to be its co-pilot.

You can take that judgment oozing from every major orifice in your damned self, light it on fire and shove it where the sun don't shine so you burn from the inside out. Use a wood match; butane is *so* yesterday.

Learning

I shrugged, my mind in knots trying to comprehend what I had been told. Somehow, someway, I was being tasked to heal a version of existence.

"Sam, how is it possible to heal a dimension or worse yet, a series of dimensions? This doesn't seem like something a single person would be capable of doing. I'm still not entirely sure how I did anything that would even make a planet get a mild tickle, let alone recognize a restoration of balance. Can you help me here?" I asked, curiosity dominating my mind.

"Paul, what is the one thing we have discussed a bunch today?" Sam pointedly asked.

"Um…," I postured.

"Energy, Paul. We have talked about energy. This is the answer to your questions and your madness as well." Sam said flatly.

"I will take this madness reference as a compliment. Thank you, Sam. I maintain: I am one…. Thing," I responded, realizing that I no longer could identify myself as simply human.

There was silence after my response for a good couple of seconds too long. So, I decided to keep talking, given Sam's refusal to speak.

"That's right, isn't it Sam—the part about me being a thing? I mean, honestly, I can't say I'm just 'Paul' or 'Nyd' or any of the other bodies I have occupied on other planets. So, though I understand that all of this is possible because of energy, I, literally, have no idea what I am anymore. Can you please, Sam, seriously, tell me how to make sense of this?"

There was another slightly uncomfortable pause after I said this, but it didn't last nearly as long as the previous void.

"Paul, there is no way to say this another way, unfortunately, so please don't be upset. If I were completely honest with you, the answer to that question is not something I can respond to verbally. Please close your eyes, and feel the warmth of Pai's suns on your face. Focus just on that warmth for me," Sam said softly.

I did as I was told, which wasn't hard. This was what I did every time I had the privilege of being on Pai. There is still nothing in the natural universe nearly as special as the warmth of Pai's suns.

A couple moments passed and I gradually felt the warmth on my face change. It was akin to what an ice cube would feel, were it sentient, as it melted.

The next time I heard Sam's voice, it was obvious he was right in front of me; I felt his words as they left him.

"Open your eyes, Paul."

Okay, intrepid consumer of my words, I'm gonna try super hard to help your human mind comprehend that which it has no business comprehending. Stay with me here.

Indeed, I opened my eyes, which in no way were eyes. Instead, it was merely a change in recognition from passive to active.

I no longer was in a humanoid body as on all of the other planets.

I also had never felt quite so… *Alive*. I was in an amplified state of being, though I can't quite call it enlightenment because the very notion of it was not at all something out of human thought.

The whole of what I observed had no end as I looked down. I also felt it absolutely possible for me to expand in any direction I thought about. In a quick, albeit passive, action I embodied… *Me*.

Opposing me was Sam. I knew it was him by feel.

Sam's words had a feeling, an energy about them. I'd hazard a guess you know what I mean; just think of the last time someone special spoke to you and just feel. Let your mind do nothing but remember and embrace the moment that passed. It matters not if this person is alive. If you need to cry, cry. If you need to smile, smile. Hell, if you need to get angry as a hornet and yell, do that. The key here is to just *feel*. This person's voice is there, in that memory, along with the energy to allow you to feel their voice. In truth, you are feeling them—their energy.

If you get super good at this, you will be able to persistently feel this when you need or want to.

I digress, and you're welcome.

Because Sam's words had the energy they did, being in his presence was unmistakable.

"Hi, Sam. It is wonderful to finally meet you," I said, though not from a mouth. I had communicated something in this place that was audible as far as I could ascertain, but I'm still not sure how.

"Hello, Paul. I agree, it is wonderful to be together. Please now, I know you still have questions. I will answer anything I can, and show you anything I can't."

Undoubtedly, dauntless reader of my words, this brings up a question: "Why are you being identified as 'Paul' in this place?" Simply put, Paul is the essence that is aware of the others. In other words, Nyd was not capable of moving to Paul. Paul is the only identity with this awareness and ability. I hope that helps.

"Well, for starters, this is not a planet. Where are we?" I asked.

"Take a moment and observe. The answer will be yours as you observe," he said, every bit the professor.

I did and what I began to realize was that I was in an open plane of reality. Let me be very clear; this was not the *foundational* plane of reality. It was *a* plane of reality. This was part of the thing that liked to feel. What I realized, though, was that it too could experience. I looked up and saw a vast aurora pulsing above me. I found myself both curious and amazed as I watched the colors dance. I felt joy, comfort. I was not on a planet—this is very important to note.

What I came to understand in this observation is not something I should discuss more. I sincerely apologize, but it's for good reason.

I can tell this is upsetting you. So, let me try to make you feel better. Let me simply say this: there was so much more life beyond this place, more than the whole of the universe in which you currently reside. Though this indeed was an important place, it was, itself, connected to something much greater. This was not the "top" or "Heaven" or whatever other topmost place you have faith or belief in.

So, though you may feel I led you down a path and left you five feet from a sacred river, I want you to realize that place on the path, where you are currently, is immensely special. The life you live, and every recognition or thought you possess, is intentional. The thing you are a part of is beyond rational human description, and the *things* it rolls up to are profound but are not themselves an ending. You—that wonderful bag of bones and energy—are part of it *all*.

Indeed, if you allow yourself to wander either by spirit, meditation or curiosity, the things you will feel will bring you to this river in the way you seek, within the reason of human recognition. I know this, after all that Sam has taught me, to be the most appropriate path forward for you—namely to find your own conclusion and thus your own understanding.

Hopefully, we're friends again, yeah? Even if you're still a bit upset, let's keep going.

"Now then, my dear friend, are we clear?" Sam asked kindly.

"We are. Thank you, Sam. I know now what I must do. Let's return to Pai to continue this, okay?" I suggested.

"Agreed. When you are ready, please close your eyes and open them when you again feel Pai's suns."

I closed my eyes. No more than a second later, I felt the familiarity of Nyd's body and the scrumptious Pai sunlight on my face.

"Thank you, Sam. I needed that perspective," I thought.

"It's my pleasure, Paul. Now then, it's essential you understand the way in which you work in this dimension. Again, I need you to focus on Pai's suns and try to feel the combined energy of them beyond simple heat," Sam instructed.

I'm not sure if my experience in the "aurora place" changed me, but I found

I had a new, keener awareness. Indeed, I could feel the energy both in the suns and between them. They were individually powerful. Together, the energy between them was amplified by several million factors. I felt my ability to, in a sense, "borrow" from each sun independently or together.

Sam seemingly was over my shoulder as I made this recognition.

"Good, Paul. Now, shift your focus to Pai. See what you can feel," he encouraged.

I closed my eyes and tilted my head forward to "look" down the ravine. I saw what looked like waves coursing all over the planet. It was as though Pai was nothing but a water world, with water dancing a never-ending Argentine Tango. I sensed I could borrow this energy, too.

"Excellent, Paul! You have the basic knowledge you need to move forward. Some planets will offer you more energy than others, but every star is yours to use. Be wary of stars that are unstable; you can feasibly destroy more than you can imagine by borrowing from them what they don't have to give. You'll know right away—it'll feel wrong. If you don't feel a star being one with you, complimenting you, let go immediately. If you borrow from a sun that is near the end of its life, about to collapse, you'll amplify the collapse and release a multiple of the stored energy the star possesses.

"Worse still are stars whose life has already ended. Any star that has collapsed and is in varying states of supernova or dwarfism has no place in your purpose. Using any flavor of the dead would be exactly like setting up a corner of the Universe next to a volcano and making the damn thing erupt. You could vaporize innocent life, Paul. That would effectively end our work together and send the Universe in this and two adjacent dimensions into abject chaos. The meaning of existence in the whole of the third, and most of the fourth, dimension would change," Sam said.

"Thanks, Sam. What about moons? For that matter, what about other living things? I seemed to very easily connect to the individuals harming the bird," I rationalized.

"Slow down, Paul. Let's take this one step at a time, okay? Moons are unique tools to you that we'll explore on a remote planet. You can do irreparable damage to a planet—or entire solar system—if used improperly.

"People... I really don't... Geez, Paul...," he stammered.

"I can do bad things, right?"

"Yes, Paul... Essentially you can start with nominal discomfort, moving to torture and finally forcing an extremely painful death. In very specific, targeted situations, this is justified, but those situations are few. In most other situations, it is disastrous because innocent people get hurt or killed. You can, with a bunch of practice and careful manipulation, use people's energy and it can result in a non-lethal yet unpleasant experience for the person or people involved. One of the reasons I have so much trouble with this—and why I reacted as I did when you killed those men—is due to something I did a long time ago, something I cannot soon forget.

"You see, I was in the same role you are before you were born on Earth for many years. I held that role for all of my adult life, all two-hundred fifty-two years of it. I lived on Pliqun; my grandson is actually one of your neighbors there. I inadvertently caused the death of several thousand people by accident. I... I...," Sam said, his voice laced with sadness.

"What is it, Sam? What's wrong?" I asked

"I'm the reason Cythis became what it's become," he said sadly. *"Honestly... You are tasked with not only finishing my work, but also fixing my mess."*

"I don't know what to say. Are you willing to talk about it, Sam?" I asked, completely unaware if I was overstepping an unspoken boundary.

"Many years ago, Cythis was an evolved Pai. Nature abounded and technology allowed the population to have many conveniences without harming the planet. Most of the people lived in harmony. The key thing there is that there was a segment of the population that wanted to control the rest of it. The reason for this was greed, pure and simple. My job was to restore harmony without killing these people or causing harm to the planet.

"I studied all sides of the conflict for years. I needed to understand the reason for this greed; it made no sense to me. The rest of the population posed no obstacle to this group, which named itself 'The Faction.' In fact, I learned that what they wanted could never be had, and they knew it. That's the insanity of this; they wanted something the rest of the population didn't have, so they decided to throw a fit about it," Sam said, his voice laced with indignation.

"This was a need for chaos. That's all," he continued. *"In the end, this group got what it wanted after all. They used my gaffe to rise to power. They have conditioned the rest of the population to crave chaos. The weaponry all over the planet—literally everywhere—will not be easy to overcome. So, there are a few more things you need to learn. Have I answered enough of your question, Paul?"*

I won't candy-coat this here. I was shocked. I didn't know what to say.

Reluctantly, I took a big breath and said, *"Yes. Let's get going."*

"I know I just said things that upset you, Paul. I'm sorry for the way this has happened—honestly, I am. I need you to have a clear picture of both the problems to solve as well as awaken the parts of you that remain asleep. It's time for you to fully grasp a few things," Sam said, his tone returning to the teacher I knew.

"You're right, Sam. I needed to know. I'm ready," I replied, forcing myself to focus on something not related to Cythis.

"Excellent. Let's talk first about the things you've already experienced. First, you can take life from one and give it to another, as you did with one of the Cythian men and your aviary friend. You must be extremely careful when doing so, as you will be limited in your ability to stop other action happening against you. In your altercation, there were but three individuals, but especially on Cythis, you will have dozens to contend with.

"You can also take from many but only give to one. There is no limit here except for the fact that the one needs to be able to handle it. You can easily kill everyone involved if you aren't careful and this, too, will bring about the end of our time together. This isn't anything you can do remotely, either. You need to focus on both the damned and the saved at the same time," Sam explained.

"Is there a chance that I could make a mistake, Sam? I mean, what if I don't witness a situation and I have two people, one dying and one not, each blaming the other?" I asked, my concern growing. I really didn't know how any of this could be governed.

"Well, to be honest, you won't always consciously know. Thing is, you have a part of the skill your Papa gave you that he figured out much later in life that you need to know now. Essentially, you can hear the vox corporis non-verbally—you can engage that truth using your mind. You'll just need to be able to discern who is who when you are using this tool. You will always get truth. Does that help?" Sam suggested.

"I'll need to play with this a little bit, but yeah, that helps. Is there ever a chance on a small scale that I could make a mistake that would compromise everything?" I asked, my concern ever growing.

"Paul, I need you to relax. I've painted you a heck of a picture, and I'm afraid it's compromising your perspective. Are there things you can do today, right now, that would end our relationship and cause mass chaos everywhere? Yes, there are. I will help you to understand these possible pitfalls. I know this to be difficult to accept given our history in battle together but I promise you, I will always help you through this," Sam explained, his voice soft and reassuring.

"It's not that I don't trust you, Sam. That's not it. I just don't know the extent of my ability to make a mistake."

"Well, let's make that concern worse then, okay? Torture. This is the dark side of what you can do. Believe it or not, though, there is a light side to this nefarious topic in addition to the dark one. If you remember, everything you do is possible because of energy. Pain releases a monumental amount of energy. This is where I went wrong, so please pay attention.

"I was in the middle of my confrontation with the heart of The Faction and a multitude of innocent people witnessed the exchange. It was clear to them that I was fighting for them, and they offered me anything they had to help. I explained that the type of help they could offer would be painful, but they still agreed. There were maybe two-hundred people there that day," Sam said, and then paused. I could tell this was going to be hard for him.

After a couple moments, he continued, "I thought I had been gentle enough, but I ultimately took so much from those people that they suffered terribly before they died. I was so distraught I never used the energy I gained from their sacrifice. If I had, The Faction would have been vanquished. Instead, they used propaganda from that event to push forward their agenda. The rest is history. So, if you use this option, you must be careful and know what you are doing before you use such a skill. With careful manipulation, this can be as mute a feeling as a pinch or as insane as a hoard of angry *hornets killing you from the inside out with fire on their stingers while your bones are pummeled with hammers. I'm not kidding here, Paul. This is a horrible, horrible death. To this day, I can hear their screams if I listen closely enough. I have been forgiven by all involved; I just have never forgiven myself."*

I was going to have to learn this, but there was a tiny little problem: how does one practice torture to know how much is too much?

"Sam, how…?"

"We'll figure that out together, Paul. I think part of this will need to be done in very small batches to extremely unwilling participants. Like it or not, this is part of your task. Look at it this way: harmony has been destroyed in certain places using energy. You will need to restore harmony using whatever means you must, with energy as your guide. Invariably, this will call into question your ability to be cruel and dark when necessary," Sam explained, seemingly hearing my concern.

"There are two more talents we need to discuss, Paul. The first: you can manipulate a planet and anything immediately outside a planet as long as it is consistent with the overall goal. You know, based on your experience on Pai, that planets are sentient. They will support you; your goal is their goal. So, you can introduce radical weather or manipulations of the crust, core or atmosphere of a planet if you need to. Or, if the opportunity exists, you can pull fiery meteors, including big, big rocks that happen to be close to a planet, down to the surface. I want you, right now, to scan the entirety of Pai's sky from horizon to horizon and see what you can observe," Sam instructed, his voice energized. He sounded excited.

I slowly looked from horizon to horizon and found three small asteroids and one large one. They looked to me like energy blobs gently floating by, almost like clouds.

"Good, Paul. Very gently, see if you can move that little one an inch to the left."

I focused on the smallest rock, watching how it spun. After seeing two rotations, I waited for the thickest part to face me, instinctively raised my left hand to gain control of it and then very slightly moved my hand as close to an inch to the left as I could. I then let the asteroid go, watching its new orbit. The change was barely discernible, but it definitely moved.

"Excellent, Paul! That's exactly how you do that. Whatever direction you move your hand, that's where the object will go.

"This is a good time to talk about moons. See, you can do the exact same thing you did with that asteroid with bigger bodies, moons being one of them. Moons interact with planets in different ways. Earth's moon affects the tides and people's moods. Pliqun's moons govern the way the upper atmosphere functions, but has no effect on any of the water on the planet or its inhabitants. Cythis' moons together affect the rotation of the planet. Change those and change the definition of a day for all of the planet's inhabitants. Any change here would destroy Cythis' wildlife; their patterns of existence would be changed so drastically they wouldn't be able to adjust. So, you see, any manipulation of moons needs to be done carefully, if at all.

"You can also do this with stars and other planets, too, Paul. I don't think I need to tell you how bad an idea this is, always. The ramifications of interrupting a solar system are many. I can only think of one time such a thing would be warranted."

I fully expected Sam to explain this, but he left me in suspense.

"What is that one time, Sam?" I asked as it became apparent he wasn't going to clarify it for me.

"Well, to induce chaos, Paul. You'd only do that if you are convinced that the abject destruction of life is the right way to go. Such a decision is almost automatically an introduction of an extinction-level event for any life in a given solar system. I've never seen a reason to do this. In fact, had I done such a thing to rid the Universe of Cythis, Pai would have been badly, badly damaged and all life removed from her. This would have had enormous ramifications on the planets themselves, which could have died and become very large bowling balls, destroying anything in their path. This would have continued until they became so damaged, they exploded," Sam explained.

"Got it. Is there any chance I could do that by accident?" I asked, my curiosity again grabbing me by the throat and forcing concern.

"No, Paul. You'd have to have an intention to cause such a thing. It wouldn't be easy at all to do, but it's certainly possible," Sam dismissed.

"Thanks, Sam, I appreciate that."

"No worries, Paul. Let's talk about the last angle of your ability that remains inactive. You can move very large distances, very quickly. To anyone watching this, it will look like you disappeared. This is how I survived on Cythis after I murdered all of those people. I jumped quickly backward and was on the other side of Cythis by the time anyone noticed I was gone. "Try this for me: use the energy you saw in Pai's valley along with the energy in the wind to go to the other side of the valley. Then, come back," Sam said calmly, just as he'd order a cup of coffee.

"What? How…?"

"Set your intention, Paul. Let Pai help you," Sam reassured.

Well, though Sam was trying to help, this one had me stumped. I saw the energy in both places, but no matter how much I thought about it, I just couldn't move.

"Relax, Paul. Your panic here has paralyzed you. Allow yourself to relax. This is really quite simple if you allow it to happen," Sam said reassuringly.

I closed my eyes, focusing on the energy in the valley and also in the sky. With a calmer mind, I saw the two interacting, almost like what happens if you flick two rubber bands close to one another. If you do it right, the vibration of the rubber causes them to be close together from time to time.

I really don't know if this recognition fixed me or not, because when I next opened my eyes, I was looking at my house from the opposite side of the valley.

"Excellent, Paul!" Sam said happily. *"That was perfect!"*

"How… I have no idea how I just did that, Sam. I just looked at the energy and then I was here," I explained, confounded.

"This is the power of intention, Paul. Whether you realize it consciously or not, this was your intention. Now, try to get back to your deck, but try to do so deliberately," Sam encouraged.

Well, again, I looked at the dancing energy and somehow ended up back on my deck.

"I think this will need work, Sam. I still have no idea how I got here," I lamented.

"With a little luck, you won't need this for quite some time, Paul. We'll work on it—I promise. Now then, I want you to rest. Tomorrow, you will wake on Cythis," Sam said, concern evident in his voice.

"Thanks, Sam. I really appreciate your help today," I said as genuinely as I could, with Cythis squarely in my brain.

Knowing what I did about Cythis, I had no idea if I could be objective. I really didn't know what I was walking into. I would soon find out.

Chaos & Normalcy

Tension.

All I felt was tension. It was like waking on Earth after being on Pai and adding this insane tension to my entire body. It felt like every muscle within me had been flexing as hard as possible for years.

"Sam?" I said, hoping to unlock what I was feeling.

"Just relax, Paul. Remember what I said about Cythis and couple this with what you know about planets. Try to come to your own conclusion after considering this," he responded.

I laid in bed for a few more moments, allowing myself to adjust. Sam was right in that I needed to try to orient myself to what was going on more independently.

After a few moments, I felt the impact of the tension ease. I also made a startling realization about the planet itself: it was choking. So little space remained untouched for it to breathe. I could almost hear its strain as I laid there.

I also felt something new, something I was unprepared for.

An arm sleepily reached across my chest, gently cradling my side.

"Don't you dare panic Paul. Take a moment and allow yourself to catch up," Sam scolded.

My name was Vik, short for Vilok. I was still what was considered to be a "young adult" at age fifty-six. I was married to Ania. We had been together for eight years but had no children.

"Good morning, you," she said kindly.

I looked to my side to find the most strikingly beautiful woman I had ever seen lying next to me. The love in my heart overflowed for this woman.

"Good morning yourself, beautiful," I responded. "Sleep okay?"

"Every night I am next to you, I sleep like a baby. You have taken my breath from me from the beginning," she responded, moving closer to me.

On Earth, I had recently celebrated my seventh birthday. Here on Cythis, my wife had removed both her and my clothing in the most tender way possible. She then made love to me in such a way that when all was said and done and I held her to my chest, I felt a deep passion unlike anything I had ever experienced before.

"Hello, Paul. I'm glad you and I can finally talk," Ania's *vox corporis* said kindly.

"You know who I am on Earth, my other identity?" I thought, hoping that this worked as well as speaking to communicate with this inner voice.

"Of course, I know this, Paul. I've been literally counting the days until we could talk. You see, you will save this world, but it won't come without profound pain. I don't say this to ruin your current moment, which was magical for both of us. Please know this love you feel is coming through Ania, but is shared by a desperate people. Everything you give to us through Ania will begin to heal some incredibly deep wounds," she said, hope hugging her words.

So, um… Yeah, to sum up, that incredible feeling in my heart was being channeled through my wife, passed to me as a sort of penance, from the people of Cythis. This hit me strangely, as I believe it would just about anyone.

I was done talking, at least for that moment. I rolled my hugging bride to her back and made love to *her*. I wanted to give her as much love as I could physically, and catch her completely unaware by doing so. If what I heard her *vox corporis* say was true, this action would start the process of healing I was to undertake.

I succeeded.

"What in the world just got into you, babe?" she asked, her breath heavy and her eyes bright.

Those eyes, those beautiful eyes…

I hadn't really gotten a good look until she laid there and looked up at me. They were almost equal parts aqua blue and hazel. I had never seen anything like it, even in my family of models.

"Aren't I allowed to?" I asked playfully.

"I will never say no to that—ever!"

So, to recap our experience on Cythis so far: I woke up next to a beautiful woman who ended up being my wife, and the sex we had moments later was fueled in part with a shared energy from other individuals hoping I would save their planet. We square?

We laid there holding one another for what seemed like a long time. I studied her face over and over again. There was something so purely innocent—and at the same time so elegantly beautiful—about her face. Every time I blinked and saw her in front of me, I fell deeper under her spell.

Our bellies began to growl a bit, so we slowly separated and got dressed.

Our house was an average size. There were two more bedrooms and then the rest were nicely decorated living rooms. There was no kitchen, as just like on Pai, Cythian people got all their nutrition from the sun. So, we ventured outside and I got my first look at Cythis.

I gasped when I saw what nature on Cythis had become. There were no trees in sight. There were no flowers, no shrubs. There were weapons everywhere I looked, some with people seated in them, some apparently automated. It was clear that what Sam had said was true about this place. I was at a loss on first look how this would ever change, even over time.

The air we breathed was stifled, likely due to the reduced amount of breathable matter in it. I saw a large body of water maybe a mile or so in the distance. Most of the air had to be coming from underwater plants there. It was no wonder at all why Cythis was in the state it was. I felt awful for the planet as I could feel its struggle.

As I looked at my neighbors, I got an interesting impression of life on Cythis. There were couples in just about a third of the houses in my view. None of those folks seemed to want to be together as they didn't sit close to one another. Of the single people I saw, not one of them smiled or even showed gratitude for the sunlight, which was prevalent from the solar system's dual suns. I was taken by the amount of energy I felt between these suns as Cythis was a bit closer to the stars than Pai was.

"Sam? Are you there?" I asked.

"Of course, Paul. How are you?" he politely replied.

"I'm good, but I have questions. Why are the people so upset? I don't see a single person, outside of Ania and I that look anything like content." I explained.

"You are about to get your answer to that question. Make absolutely sure you remain calm."

No sooner did Sam stop talking than a horn sounded and everyone I saw made their way to the street.

"Come on, you. Verification is starting," Ania said.

Ah, Verification. All of the residents lined up in front of their houses, near the street. Faction representatives then began moving from person to person, fiercely looking at each individual, looking at their house and then back to the individual. Questions and admonishments would follow, anything from a house being dirty to money owed to The Faction to a look being taken as aggression. I saw one man, face as plain as one can imagine, get beaten in the stomach with a baton for supposed "aggression toward a Faction member."

I remembered what Sam said, and just took it all in. I borrowed my cues from my neighbors when it came to my turn.

A Faction member approached me, his brow furrowed.

"Name and occupation?" he scolded.

"Vilok Ghabey. I am a builder," I replied, focusing on keeping my face as neutral as possible.

"Your finances are in order, but your house is dirty. I am fining you and expect your house item to be resolved immediately," he growled. In this case, "fining" happened immediately. The Faction controlled every bank account in the area. They took money from just about everyone. Ania got the same talk. We were fined twice.

I nodded, accepting my punishment.

The Faction continued auditing the entire neighborhood. We all stood outside until it was complete.

A second horn sounded, and the residents returned to their houses. Those who had been beaten did their best to move. The one gentleman who I saw get hit with a baton had a badly bruised rib. I could see the injury clearly as I looked at him.

"Sam? Why can I see inside that man? I've never experienced anything like this before," I asked.

"Well, this is sort of an enhancement to the vox corporis *I failed to discuss with you. You will see this with injuries moving forward. Your abilities are getting much, much stronger, Paul. That's why the poor man's ribs were so readily shown to you. If you focus, you can see inside and ultimately interact with anything in a humanoid body you choose. I'd recommend you do some practicing before you attempt anything of the sort, though. Please, during this first trip, get as much information as you can. You will be returning to Earth in two days as there are things you need to address there. So, get as much exposure to the culture as you possibly can in the days ahead. You have a very important person to meet. Please be ready for this as it's going to be a surprise that will require some secrecy. Are we agreed?"* Sam commandingly instructed.

"Sure, Sam… You're not telling me anything else, are you?"

"Nope. I'm here if you need me, but you should not need me unless you do something foolish."

Ah, my dear Sam. I love that man. I love him so much, in fact, that I am allowed to hate him sometimes. He is always right, and this bit of coarse encouragement was later proven. My hatred of him was entirely misplaced, which is also always the case. *Always.*

The rest of that day, I fell in love with Ania over and over again, discovering that such a thing was never enough, no matter how many times I looked at, touched, or kissed her. I listened to Cythis' cries and watched everything I could without arousing suspicion about what I was doing.

Ania was an artist. The Faction allowed a certain number of artists to remain in their profession, though their charge was creating good looking propaganda. She painted murals wherever she was instructed to, with a creative flair distinctly her own. Her current project was aimed at promoting the local hospital, though the image was to clearly depict more weapon imagery than healing imagery.

The Faction was smart in some ways and really, really dumb in others. It'll be super fun to show you those negative examples a-plenty. This was one of the more tepid examples, but it spoke to a bigger theme. This organization led with fear and intimidation. This was their sole charge, hell-bent to keep the global population under control. Yes, this was a global phenomenon. The cost to the planet, as a result, was horrific. Natural balance was destroyed and hundreds of species of indigenous creatures were rendered extinct in the wild.

Read that last item again. There was a part of The Faction that was designed to appeal to the softer side of the people and "nature preserves" were created to house as many of these ill-fated critters as possible. The same was true of quite a few plant species as well, but there was a catch: all of these nature preserves were contained in massively fortified concrete structures. In other words, to see all that The Faction had destroyed in nature, one had to see The Faction's influence while you did so. This had gotten into the hearts and minds of a tremendous number of people all over the world.

But there was one other thing that The Faction did regularly, precipitated by Sam's actions: every week, the world was reminded of "The Senseless Murderer" via an actor-depicted and much-sensationalized video. The majority of the people alive on Cythis at this time had been born after Sam's situation and thus were none the wiser.

Regardless, the Cythian people were torn. Their "normal" involved a constant theft of their government-supplied incomes that always hurt families' and individuals' lives and normal beatings for no reason. The fear involved with "The Senseless Murders" had started to be replaced with bigger questions that threatened The Faction in ways that would ultimately compromise their message. There were definitely people who knew from relatives the horror involved with Sam's mistake. There were also a growing majority of people who rightfully saw the whole thing as propagandized horseshit. These people subconsciously felt Cythis dying and it fueled their disgust. Regardless, weapons of any kind were prohibited for individuals. The Faction were roughly forty percent of the global population. If you do the math there, the deficit was small enough that arming the minority and taking away any shot of armament from the public brought about normalized chaos.

Children were designated for The Faction when they reached the age of ten and passed a series of mindset tests. It should come as no surprise that those kids with any sort of mental or personality challenge passed this test. The kids were taken from their families immediately and entered into The Faction Academy. Almost every child taken would not recognize their parents just six short months into the program. This broke the hearts of far too many parents over time, many of whom no longer live due to "degenerate" designated beatings. One such man's crime was approaching his son and simply asking if he was okay. He was beaten by six individuals, including his son, as his wife watched in horror. Had she so much as flinched during this horrific event, she, too, would have been killed.

A rather intense regimen of brainwashing and training in all things military were coupled with drugs not unlike steroids on Earth for these Faction trainees. So, at the most formative point in a child's life, their DNA was fundamentally changed and they were taught crowd control for a population that posed absolutely no armed threat. Some of these kids were so completely radicalized that there were instances of their beatings so severe that they resulted in death. One such instance happened with a woman in her "middle-late age" of one-hundred sixty-two. That poor old woman lived alone and literally was beaten to death for coughing and startling one such juiced-up youngster.

She was also labeled a degenerate who was rightfully terminated in the government-run media, with some story about her finances justifying such an action. Thing is, hers, and every other story involving a death-by-Faction incident, made its way around the world to a growingly impatient majority—an unarmed, poor, pissed off majority.

"Paul, you understand Cythis at a high level. There will be a knock at your door in a moment, a very slight knock. Be ready, turn off the light by the door and let your guest in," Sam said, his voice laced with stress.

I did as he instructed, after keying Ania into the event. Oddly, she asked no questions whatsoever. This was curious, but I didn't have time to dwell on it.

I turned off the interior lights near the front door. I heard what sounded like a piece of paper rubbing against the door, opened it quickly, let my guest in and quickly but softly closed the door again.

"To the back. I'll go, then you go. An' is already there," my guest instructed.

I went to the back of the house, which had no windows and was out of the view of the rest of the house.

When I got to that room, I found Ania and this phantom person hugging. Almost as if on cue, our guest then attached herself to me in a deep embrace. Tears fell down my shirt; the person in my arms was about at my shoulder height-wise.

"Hi. I'm Eva," she said through big, big tears.

"Hello, Paul. This is a really long time coming, which is why the tears are falling as they are. Eva knows you as Paul but knows to refer to you as Vik here. All of the prep has been done already and the story has been established with the entire neighborhood. We have a lot to talk about," Eva's *vox corporis* said emotionally.

"I am really, really confused. When can we talk?" I asked. I had nearly perfected speaking with the vox corporis after all of my conversation with Sam. It was identical in practice; I just still had no idea where to look as I was communicating with this voice.

"Soon. For now, understand this: Eva is wanted by The Faction. It was her grandmother who was killed and labeled a 'degenerate' for coughing. She hasn't been terribly silent about her disgust for The Faction; she's basically the unofficial leader of The Resistance, but they have no idea who she is or even her gender. She lives thousands of miles away; she travels at night, using word of mouth to remain hidden and strategically move from place to place. It's taken her over a year of travel to be in your arms right now," she clarified emotionally.

My heart broke when I heard this. I hugged Eva tighter and let my shirt get a bit more tear-soaked.

"I have news," she said as she separated from me and wiped her eyes. "We found him. We found Klain. He is being tracked now."

Wogin Klain was the leader of The Faction. He has been the longest running leader The Faction has ever had. He is two-hundred eighty-four years old and is constantly hidden. The one thing these idiots got right was keeping their almighty hidden so no one could hurt him. Klain dictates every action The Faction takes. It is rightfully believed, as a result, that if Klain is dead or held hostage, The Faction would fall apart. This has been the people's belief for the better part of a generation.

"They made a mistake, and let one of us in as part of his security detail. It's taken a few years, but we finally are on the inside. We need to be ready, though, because he's coming here in two weeks. This, Vik, is where we need your help. You are going to be part of the build team for his mobile stage. We need to know where the weaknesses are. Can you do that?" she asked, leaning in.

I knew I had been building something big, but I had no idea what it was. This was not uncommon for builders.

"I will keep my eyes out for sure. If I see something, I will make mental note of it. We are still so early in the project that I had no idea what the thing was. At this point, it's just a cement foundation and some really initial vertical supports. I can say that foundation is solid; if there is going to be weakness anywhere and it follows the patterns I've seen on other projects, it'll be directly in front, six inches below the center of the stage," I said.

The reason for this, ironically, was for the placement of a gun with a sensor. I had been on other builds of these things for other dignitaries and there was always a part of the design that was just this framed out hole. We weren't permitted to install the gun, but I had been asked to assist in doing this a few times. I served as the guide for The Faction member to install the gun because it had to go in from the front because of the design of the stage. Essentially, it was a square unit that just sat on the inside of the frame. I had never seen them be secured; it was my belief that The Faction felt no one would assault the gun assembly.

In truth, they were right; if that sensor caught movement it programmatically determined to be aggressive, it would spray a massive number of bullets into the crowd. This happened a few times and as news of this spread, crowds would literally stand in abject fear at these things. It was mandatory attendance when dignitaries came to town. It continued The Faction tradition of keeping the people under its thumb.

Thing is, a well-placed shot or shots directly below the gun unit would almost assuredly cause the whole gun assembly to fall down. This eliminated one aspect of the threat; there was also the dozens of Faction members with guns that posed a big issue. There would be casualties without a doubt. However, if the townspeople worked together, there was a great possibility of success.

"Those awful guns. I cannot believe they are still using them after what happened last year," Ania interjected.

"That was all by design, my dear. All of it," Eva said, referring to what most refer to as either "The Accident" or "The Mass Murder."

The last time Klain appeared, it was a year prior in a densely populated area, a good bit south of where we lived. The crowd, several thousand in size, all stood perfectly still as Klain arrived on stage. The stories of the event are tricky as no one from that entire province survived. No one, that is, except a little boy who was protected by the bullet-riddled bodies of his brother and aunt. His account, per the grapevine, was that the gun started firing when Klain got particularly spirited in his speech. It seemed to indicate that Klain himself had caused the gun to fire, which absolutely incensed a good many people all over the planet. Cracks had begun to form in The Faction's rule. The people demanded answers.

The government-run media claimed it to be an accident. Oddly, they didn't discount the boy's description of that awful event. Instead, they apologized and said they would fix the problem.

I think if that kid had been taken or outright killed, there would have been a mass uprising. He was taken in by a family not far from town. Many looked at him as a beacon of hope, a lone survivor of a horrid attack.

"It's getting late. Eva, you are staying here tonight, right?" Ania asked, concern apparent in her voice.

"No, sweetheart. I am going to be on my way to protect you. I just need to have a word with your husband before I go, if you don't mind," she replied, embracing Ania as she spoke.

"Of course. Thank you for coming. I know this has been a long time in the making. Please be safe, okay?" Ania asked sleepily.

She gave Eva a kiss on the cheek, me a kiss on the lips and disappeared upstairs.

"She's amazing, isn't she? She's such a sweetheart, Paul. This is special," Eva said, wrapping her arm around me. "You're heading home tomorrow night. There are things you need to practice, *to perfect*, Paul, before that day with Klain. The full breadth of your talent will be needed, and there are things that are still rusty. In particular, you need to learn to use your talents discreetly. Vik will need to be able to live on here; he is still young. Do you understand? Sam is aware."

"Wait… What? You know Sam? You know me? How…," I asked, my brain in abject disarray.

"Of course I do, Paul. Let's not get hung up on silly details, yeah? You clearly heard what I said, right? You know what you are working on back on Earth, right?" Eva pressed.

"I'll sort this out with Sam. Where are you going tonight?" I asked, trying to dismiss my confusion.

"I'll be okay. For now, you need to go lay next to that beautiful woman that somehow agreed to be your forever. She probably has questions. Be careful," she said and took a deep breath. "It is profound magic to meet you for the first time, my dear. Next time, we will have more time to talk. My window to move safely is disappearing, unfortunately. So, I will see you again soon."

Before I could say a word in response, she disappeared.

"Sam, what in the…," I began.

"Go to bed. Ania has questions. Answer them honestly. I mean it. Honestly, but creatively. Eva—we will talk about her when you are back on Earth. Tomorrow is another day of observation and staying quiet. Right?" Sam interrupted.

"Fine, but you have a ton of questions to answer. Tons of them," I angrily responded.

I took several deep breaths before heading up to our bedroom. I felt like this might be challenging and, boy, was I spot on about that.

I found Ania sitting up in bed, her eyes fixed on me intently as I entered the room.

"There is something about you that's different, a different Vik. What is going on?" she asked agitatedly.

"What in particular about me do you feel is different, love?" I asked, hoping I'd hear what I needed to hear.

"The way you looked at me today—with so much love—where is this coming from? The secretive conversation with Eva—again, what in the world is this about? Do I need to be worried that my husband is becoming a liability to my safety?" she asked, her eyes laser focused on my everything.

"Well, let's break this down one thing at a time, okay? The first thing, the way I looked at you—did I make you feel uncomfortable?" I asked, slowly walking toward my side of the bed while making constant eye contact with her.

"Well, no, but I never had this, Vik. Not since we were matched, never," she lamented.

Part of The Faction's fun was paring people randomly for marriage. In truth, they did so with the hope that the two people paired together would make one another miserable. In our case, I was a builder, and she an artist. I'm not sure where The Faction's logic decried this pairing as bad, but whatever.

"Did I overstep a boundary or something? Did I do or say something I shouldn't?" I asked, sitting down slowly on the bed. I maintained eye contact with her at all times of the conversation.

"No, but… I… I've never felt so cared about, so loved by *anyone*. I mean we've been *good* for the past couple years but today we went to *incredible*! I don't want to have my heart broken if this Vik decides to go away and not come back," she said sadly.

"Love, look at me," I softly demanded. I as much needed to make a point as I needed to memorize her eyes. I was going to see this woman every day I was away from Vik's life. Darn tootin' I was raiding her dreams!

I studied her eyes and her entire petite face. I memorized every detail. I then kissed her gently.

She, in turn, pounced on top of me, holding me down at my shoulders while she straddled my hips.

"I don't know who you are, fake Vik, but you are not permitted to leave. You are not permitted to put us in danger. Do you hear me? You are my Vik, *my* beautiful Vik. Promise me you will be this Vik forever," she demanded, her eyes locked into mine.

"Don't you realize that you are *my* beautiful Ania?" I asked, matching her intensity.

She collapsed down onto my chest into an immediate snuggle. I'm not sure how else to describe such a thing but, in one succinct motion, she had me in a body lock with her head on my chest.

"She feels the love you gave her as Paul. That's what the difference is," Ania's *vox corporis* explained.

"How do I ensure Vik continues to love her the way I have?" I asked intently. I wanted desperately for Ania to continue to feel loved.

"You already taught him, Paul. You showed him how to be a loving husband. You needn't worry. She is going to remain happy," she encouraged.

I wrapped my arms around my still-attached wife and felt her heartbeat. It began to slow, and eventually she fell asleep. I smiled when I felt this and allowed myself to drift off into the unconscious.

****

The next morning, I awoke to find her still attached to me, drooling up a storm. I also found something else.

Just as I had seen that poor man's bruised ribs, I could feel that something was different in Ania's body. I found that I was able to extend my eyes in a sense and consciously go wandering inside her body. This is how I found the change: our baby.

Yeah, it seemed that ol' Vik's stuff had it after all! Ania was pregnant. Cythian gestation took place over six months due to the twin suns. The baby already had a functioning heart—a heart that I sat and watched flutter for an absurdly long time.

"Sam, I don't wanna go. The baby…" I lamented.

"You heard what Eva said, right? There is work to do before you come back. Understand?" he scolded.

Ania slowly got up, looking deep into my eyes with her sleepy peepers.

"We stayed like this all night?" she asked, yawning.

"Yep, we did. How are you feeling?" I responded.

"Slept like a baby, even better than the night before," she said, studying my face. "Same Vik?" she asked hopefully.

"Of course I am, love."

We spent a vast amount of time in bed that day. There was no Verification that day for some reason, so after getting some sunshine nourishment, we hopped back in bed.

"You know, don't you?" she asked pointedly after we had settled.

"I know what, love?" I asked, attempting to play dumb as much as possible.

"There is a big change happening. I think you know," she pressed.

"What is she asking me about?" I silently asked her *vox corporis*.

"The baby, Paul. She picked up on the sentimental tone in your voice. She also somehow subconsciously knows that you were with the baby this morning," she responded.

Uh-oh. It seems my wandering wasn't as covert as I had thought.

"So, about this change…," I began.

"Ready to admit you know now, sneaky pants?" she jested, her eyes again connected to mine like laser beams.

"I will do no such thing! I believe it is you who are aware of something and you're hiding it," I said, rolling her to her back and connecting *my* eyes to *hers* like laser beams.

"This right here… Don't you move, unless it is to kiss me," she commanded, her words changing course notably.

Kiss her I did.

"So, this change, this really special change… Are you happy?" I asked, showing my cards.

"I've quite literally never been happier in my life," she gushed. "We're going to have a child, Vik! A baby that is all ours!"

"I literally cannot wait! This is incredible!" I also gushed.

The Faction had made it mandatory that any woman who was pregnant register as such with the nearest hospital. There was a media nightmare a few years back where a pregnant woman was beaten during Verification and the baby died. There was a horrible cover-up to the whole thing. The next day, Klain announced the requirement.

"We're going to the hospital before the day is over, right? I want to be sure you and the baby stay protected as much as possible," I said, a notable amount of fear entering my brain.

"Of course, babe. There's something though... Something...," she replied, slowly undressing us both and starting an extended session of love making. I will spare the details because they are still some of the happiest memories I have.

After a copious amount of heartbeat to heartbeat closeness, we went to the hospital and received the formal protection for Ania's pregnancy. Her course of treatment was also established.

I resisted that day ending, knowing that I was headed back to my childhood on Earth as I slept. I had gained a true appreciation for the problem I faced. What I didn't realize is that this was being discussed in the Glassburé home back on the Copahee.

I held Ania as she fell asleep and alternately watched her beautiful face sleep and the baby's heart grow stronger.

"I love you, my precious son. I will see you again soon," I whispered to the baby and then crashed into unconsciousness.

Complications & Pressure

"Talk to me, Bug," my sister said, sitting on my bed.

"Why are you waking me up, Fink? God, my head," I said, the familiar heaviness of Earth pressing on my forehead.

"Paul, I know. Out with it," Dylan demanded.

"What are you asking me about? What do you know?" I asked, saving my *vox corporis* tooling for the next step. I needed to know what she was talking about from her. It was important to me.

"Look, I know you—the real you—has been gone for a while. I know you killed some dudes in one place and you have a really crazy situation in another. The girl, the sex, the baby. Go," she demanded.

"Sam, help, quick! What do I do?" I asked, panicking. I feigned a yawn to get the question out.

"She and your mother know all of it, Paul. Be honest. You will need all of their help if you are to be successful when you return to Cythis. You have eight days, Paul. That's it. We have monumental amounts of work to do and you have school sprinkled in the mix," Sam lamented.

"Let me brush my teeth and then have this conversation once. Mommy needs to hear, too. Okay?" I stalled. I needed a moment to really get my thoughts together. This had the markings of insanity written all over it. I needed to somehow make the insanity palatable.

So, I made my way to the bathroom and did some energy playing, heeding Sam's words. I brushed my teeth without using my hands; I moved the brush all around with my mind. I turned the water on and off using the same method. I pulled the water to my face to rinse basically using the same method.

I took a cursory glance at my teeth from the inside as I had a couple loose ones and wanted to see the new teeth. Yeah, I proved this remote eye thing works super well, wherever I happened to be planet-wise. The energy stuff was clicking, too; Earth was a willing partner with my lunacy. This was good, because I was about to have a fairly significant test.

I made my way downstairs. It was Saturday morning and everyone was in the kitchen. When I got there, five pairs of eyes fiercely dissected me from top to bottom. My grandma and grandpa Glassburé were also in the kitchen.

"Ah… Good morning?" I said self-consciously.

Mom had been cooking. As she turned to see me, the tie from her apron just barely nicked the edge of the gas flame. I saw the fire start—I'm not sure what drew my eye to it, but I saw it as clear as day, looking through her body. That damn apron was going to light up like a candle if I didn't do something quick.

"Focus, Paul," Sam encouraged. It felt like he was standing behind me.

I quickly surveyed the room, looking for water. I found it in the dog's bowl.

In one quick motion, I pulled Mom away from the stove, coated the end of the burning apron string with dog water and waited for it to completely douse the flame.

What I didn't quite pay attention to in this transaction was that I had suspended my mother a good couple feet off the ground to do so. When I was comfortable that the fire was out and Mom was safe, I slowly put her down.

"What the…?" my dad exclaimed.

"Her apron string was on fire, Daddy. That's all," I calmly responded.

Mom grabbed the back of her apron to see the burned part.

"Oh my God… Paul…" she exasperatedly said, running over to me and swept me up into her arms.

"Well, I believe we are officially off the reservation. Squirtbud, we talkin' an' we talkin' now," my grandfather demanded. "Squirtbud" was his nickname for me. I called him Papa G.

"Can I have something to eat while we talk? My head is killing me, Papa G," I explained.

"Aw sweetheart, of course," Mom said, releasing me from her grasp.

"Paulie, why did you just, um…," my grandmother began but lost her words. I called her "Gammy" because it made Papa laugh.

"So, Papa G, Gammy, Daddy, Mommy, Fink, Larry… I need your help and, if you are willing to give me that help, I will tell you everything. First though, Daddy, when did you hurt your shoulder?" I said, seeing what looked like a partial dislocation of his throwing shoulder.

"Champ? 'The hell?" Grandpa demanded.

"I knew it, Jonah. When were you going to tell me," Mom asked, angrily.

"How… I…," Dad began.

"Hold still," I said, and began looking at the insides of everyone's shoulders. I saw the issue with Dad's shoulder—there was this rubber band looking thing that was wrapped weird over a bone.

"Paul?" he asked confusingly.

I moved his massive arm up, like a shrug, with my arm. I then energetically unwrapped that rubber band. I moved his arm down, watched it for a minute and saw the inflammation subside.

"There. Feel better?" I asked, slowly letting his arm return to normal.

"Oh my… I… How… Addie…," he fumbled.

"Did our son fix you or not, Jonah?" Mom, still angry, replied.

"Yeah, he did. I don't understand. How did our son, our scrappy seven-year-old son, just diagnose and fix an injury our trainers couldn't understand?" Dad replied, himself reflecting a bit of nervous anger.

"Daddy, haven't you noticed Bug being a little different for the past few months? He'd be what he is now, and then a more muted but similar Bug for a while, and then this Bug…," Dylan explained.

"Jonah, we talked about this. We talked about this several times, as a matter of fact," Mom added, disappointment dripping all over her words.

"Yeah, we talked about this, but Paul has never done anything like this before. I've certainly seen other changes, but this is incredible. You have to admit, being moved through the air while dog water flies across the room to douse a flame none of us saw. Come on, Addie. Give me some credit," Dad backpedaled.

"Can I try to help?" I interjected. "I just need some food to ease this headache and I think I can make all of this better. I meant it when I said that I need all of your help."

In less than a minute, orange juice and some egg concoction made its way to a place setting in front of me. The entire family patiently but intently watched me eat. I think they all felt I would combust or something.

I finished eating and felt the pressure in my head dissipate. This new pressure was concerning; I was aware it was something Earth was showing me, but not clearly enough for me to understand. Sam was proud when I later revealed this.

I digress…

"Okay. First, the basics… Everything you see is made up of energy—*everything*. You each are who you are because of your *unique* energy. To complicate this a little, understand that the thing you are, your soul, if you want to call it that, is actually part of a very large group of individuals spread out over different dimensions. In my case, I actually live the lives I am a part of. The best way for me to explain this is using dreams: at night, you dream but return to your body here. In fact, this is what ninety-nine percent of the people all over the place do. The difference for me is that sometimes I wake up in other lives I am living. This is where I have been for the past couple weeks," I explained.

"So, this is what Olaf was telling us about, right, Sadie?" Papa G asked.

"Yeah, but I had no idea it was like this, babe," she replied.

"Okay, so you bounce from life to life… What happens when you—the you I am talking to—aren't here? How does that Paul continue to live?" Dad asked intently.

"He learns what I teach him through experience, Daddy. He does the same thing for me. He can't do this energy stuff, but he knows about everything else. He also knows that he has to keep everything very secret. You all get that, right? This is *not* something you need to talk to anyone about," I said nervously.

"Baby boy, I grew up with a Daddy who talked to and healed people using their body and these orb things. This is really not that far outside of my wheelhouse," Mom kindly encouraged.

"I have loved Olaf—Papa—for lots of years, son. I don't mean to be hard on you. I'm just slower to the game, okay?" Dad explained, his eyes sentimental. "Thank you from the bottom of my heart for fixing my shoulder. It hurt really, really bad."

"Jonah, I told you. I *told* you. Slide—don't take the hit. You're not a rookie anymore. I will whoop on you, boy. Dammit, son," Papa G lamented, addressing his quarterback son.

With that, there was a knock on the door, and my grandma and grandpa Waniglia appeared. For reference, I called my Grandma Waniglia "Gam" from the time I was first able to speak through the time I was a parent myself. Judge away, Heathen.

"Tell me about the baby, Tiny One. I need details pronto," Gam demanded, hugging Gammy.

"Annie, give him some room. Paul, how are you?" Papa asked kindly.

"I'm good, Papa. Thank you. I need your help, too, okay?" I responded.

"So, this battle, Paul… Papa and I may have figured a couple angles out but not others. Can you fill in some gaps?" Larry said, changing the direction of the conversation.

"After the baby talk, okay? Tiny One, details please," Gam requested, usurping Larry.

"Yeah, I need to hear this," Gammy seconded.

"He's… He's so…," I said, tears falling from my eyes in mass quantities. "His heart… I watched his heartbeat for hours. I could literally sit and watch that for days."

Everyone, including soulless Larry, cried with me.

I caught my breath and continued, "My wife and I have been married for eight years. Her name is Ania. We live on the planet Cythis, which is the huge project I need everyone's help with."

"That is such a beautiful name, Bug," Dylan said, wiping new tears from her eyes.

"If we are good with the baby thing, can I ask my question?" Larry sheepishly interjected. To this day, the man has awful timing.

"One more question and then he's yours, Larry. You can do things and see things I'm not sure we fully understand, things I can't even do. Can you run this down one more time for my benefit, little fella?" Papa asked.

"Sure, Papa. The 'do things…,'" I said and lifted everyone a foot off the ground. I also lifted the flame from a candle along with the people.

"It's all energy, Papa. You are up off the ground because I am using Earth's energy along with your energy to lift you. Everything I do is possible with energy, no matter where it comes from. The flame is up using its own heat to fly and still stay lit," I explained and then set everyone down.

I continued, "The 'see part…' I can see that Daddy's shoulder is better, you have a sore right wrist, Gam still has scars from bullets hitting her belly on the inside, Papa G is still hungry, Gammy's low back is sore, Dylan's knees hurt because they are stretching, and Larry has some…,"

I couldn't resist.

I just barely flicked a *bunch* of gas built up in Larry's digestive tract and the loudest, longest bout of flatulence I'd witnessed in my young life was thrust into existence.

I looked down for a brief moment before abject hysterics consumed me.

"Squirtbud, y'all… Y'all… *Oh* damn…," Papa G muttered through his own laughter.

"Damn, son… That was *epic*!" Dad proclaimed as his laughter subsided.

"Paul… Squirtbud… This is serious now. Focus here, boy. *Focus*. You *have* to promise me you can do that again. Not to Larry, necessarily, but *please*. My sweet, sweet Paul. This has so very much potential. So very much potential indeed," Papa G begged.

"Nolan, behave. Ignore your grandfather, Paul," Gammy commanded.

"I can do it again, Papa G. Larry?" I said and just lightly tapped a little more gas in Larry's gut.

A mini version of the prior epicness made its way through Larry's lower cheeks.

Everyone, including Larry, laughed for a good few minutes with that display of fun.

"I think I'm clear now. Thank you, little fella! How can we help?" Papa asked.

"I can help with some of this," my stinky brother interjected.

Larry produced a cursory drawing of the entire city on Cythis where Ania and I lived, complete with gun locations and Faction stations that housed the armed corps.

"Papa G and I have been talking and have most of this figured out, but there are problems," Larry began.

Larry was a major war history buff. So, too, was Papa G. Somehow, they had gotten this map and had time to discuss it before the morning.

"How… When… Who… This is…," I stammered.

"Ask Papa," Larry instructed.

"Sam and I talked, little fella. He helped me draw all this and asked that I have Larry and Papa G talk about it. I gave it to them about a week ago," Papa clarified.

"Paul, you need to create two things for there to be a chance here and, even then, there is a complication. There are guns at every corner of the area and also above it, in the sky. You'd have to disable the big guns to enable the fight to be fairer. Also, you'd have to somehow move the residents quickly because none of this happens neatly; their houses are right in the line of fire from every angle.

"This doesn't solve the complication, which is the potential for the massive influx of both armed fighters and literal battalions filled with weaponry to enter the fight. You can see here where there are four possible places where additional troops could enter the fight," Larry explained, pointing to the map.

"Squirtbud, if there were people helping you, the playing field becomes a little bit cleaner. I'm with Larry in that the big guns have to go for there to be a shot. These guys figured a defense system that overlaps everywhere. You need to remove some of that overlap. Do you have help?

"The thing that is so tricky here, Paul, is the overlap these guys created. You have to remove that overlap and then figure a way to either neutralize incoming troops or have an armed group ready to fight with you," Papa G explained.

"There's one other possibility, Paul, but it's a long shot. There's one leader, right? This whole thing is controlled by one man calling the shots. You hunt and publicly murder this dude, and a power vacuum happens. You can trace back thousands of years and see how this, too, could be really viable," Larry added excitedly.

"Wait a minute, here," Gammy began. "Paul, how in the world are you going to do any of this? I mean, the stuff you did here is remarkable, yes. I'm not sure how this translates to a fight, though."

"Well Gammy, this is exactly what I want all of your help for. Sam has 'work' I need to do that will get me close to ready. I just need other ideas, other really crazy things I can try to work into a plan. Larry, I love the 'kill the leader' thing. I need a couple more of those kinds of plans to cover all the bases.

"I can already do some bigger things that I can't really show in the house. Like—those sky guns may be able to be damaged if I can find enough asteroids, I could throw those at them. The tough part there is that I need to hit them up and out instead of down and in. Those things falling onto the planet would hurt or kill a ton of innocent people. I cannot be the cause of innocent lives lost for this to work."

"Well, I'm no genius when it comes to this stuff, but why not take the bad guys out from the big guns and put good guys there to basically be that help that Papa G mentioned?" Gam suggested.

"That's perfect, Gam! Paul, if you could get the big guns turned on the bad dudes, it's almost problem solved," Larry said excitedly.

"That could work, Paul. I hadn't thought of that," Sam said, encouraged.

"Yeah, that really could work, Gam! Thank you! The other thing I need your help with is gonna sound mighty strange. When you each go home, could you wait for me?" I asked, hoping this would help me with my location challenges. Both sets of grandparents lived a good forty or so minutes from our house. Given that I basically went invisible when I did these big leaps, this was one big thing I could repeatedly practice without arousing suspicion.

"Little fella, could you give us a little more information?" Papa asked.

"It might be easier to show you," I said and focused on the other side of the kitchen.

In a blink, I was standing on the opposite end of the room, a good twenty feet from where I had been previously standing.

"I need to get this down on a much bigger scale. I figure going from here to Gam and Papa's house and then from there to Gammy and Papa G's house and then back would be a really good test. Plus, that would allow anyone who wanted to follow me to do that. Make sense?" I asked the curious group.

"Makes sense to me, but I want to go, too, son. I'll go to Gammy and Papa G's house and meet you there," Dad said.

"…And I will go to Gam and Papa's house and meet you there," Mom seconded.

"Larry and I will wait here and make sure you get home safe, Bug," Dylan said kindly.

"Good thinking, Paul! This is a wonderful test for you. Involving the family is perfect, too. Nicely done, Sir!" Sam said excitedly.

"Okay! Let's get a move on and see if this kid can fly," Gam said sarcastically.

One by one, they hugged me and told me to be careful. I would wait for the high sign from my Mom and go to that grandparents' house first. Then, same thing with Dad that they were at my other grandparents' house.

****

When it came time, Sam reminded me of my cues.

"Remember, Paul: use the planet's energy along with the sun's energy. This will be a little harder than on Cythis because of this being a single-star solar system. The sun is still young enough that you will have plenty of help there," he instructed.

Dylan got the message from Mom that they had arrived.

"Listen to me, Bug, I need you to be safe. I have a horrible, horrible feeling in my belly about this. You need me, you let me know and I will come get you," she said, her hands on my shoulders and her eyes cutting holes in my head that went clear through the hills a few miles away.

"I'll be okay, Fink. I promise," I said, smiling. My sister is still this protective, all these years later.

"I'm gonna film this so you have a point of reference, okay, Paul?" Larry asked.

"Thanks, Larry. That should help if we can see anything," I replied. This was not the brother I knew, the brother who literally could not stand to be in the same room with me without berating me. I liked it, but I waited for the other shoe to drop.

I focused on Earth's energy, which moved slower but more freely than on Cythis. I then turned my face upward and looked at the sun's energy. It ebbed and flowed; this was not going to be easy.

"Just balance the two, Paul. You'll be fine," Sam encouraged.

I took a deep breath, concentrated on my grandparents' house and went. About a second later, I was standing on their dock out back.

"Well, looky here," Gam said, chuckling. "It seems we have a flying child in our midst."

"Do you feel okay, Paul?" Mom asked, surveying me for damage.

"I'm okay, Mommy. I think I'm getting the hang of this," I replied, smiling.

It felt great! I did it! Now, if I could do it twice more and then maybe do a bigger move another day, I'd have solved this riddle.

"Okay. I'll let Daddy know you are on your way. Please be safe, sweetheart," she said, worry, clear as can be, in her words.

That dock led to the Intracoastal Waterway, itself teaming with life and energy. I decided to use this along with the sun to see how it might work. So, I closed my eyes and got a clear image of my grandparents' house in my mind. I watched the energy in the water, looked up to grab the energy from the sun and went.

Less than a second later, I was standing on their front porch soaking wet.

"What'd you do, boy? Why y'all soakin' up the sittin' porch?" Papa G asked.

"You okay, Paul? Aside from being wet, you feel okay?" Dad asked before I could answer.

"Yeah, I'm okay. I used the Intracoastal to come here—the energy from it. I didn't think I'd actually *use* the water, though," I explained.

"Okay. Well, get on home, boy. Y'all makin' a watery mess 'a my sittin' porch," Papa G lamented. He was kidding; this was in no way a serious complaint.

"I'll let Dylan know you're on your way home, okay?" Dad asked.

"Yep, I'll head there and then rest a bit," I said. I was getting tired. This required a decent amount of effort to do.

So, I got home clearly in my mind, synced up the energy and went home.

About a half second later, I was standing on our dock right by the Copahee.

"I knew you'd come back here, Bug," Dylan said, smiling. "This is easily your favorite spot at home. You feel okay?"

I smiled and hugged my sister. "I'm good but super sleepy, Fink. The energy here is way different than other places."

****

I then fell asleep and slept for a good four hours. I woke up next to a very worried Dylan.

"What was that, Bug? You basically said you were tired and collapsed into my arms. Are you okay for real or are you putting on a brave face for me?" she asked, as motherly as she had ever been.

"I swear to you, I'm okay. I didn't hurt you, did I?" I asked and yawned my sleep away.

"Of course not, Bug! You're still lighter than my purse. I'm just glad your sweet self was hugging me so I could catch you," she said, smiling.

"So, you know now that I can see things, right? When are you gonna fess up?" I asked, invoking my parental right.

"What are you talking about, Bug? I feel fine," she deflected, confusion rolling through her brow.

"Your heart, Dylan. You don't feel anything at all? Nothing? I would fix this if you want me to," I pressed.

"What's happening with my heart, Bug?" she asked, fear making its way into our conversation.

"There's a little hole in the side of it. You leak blood every time your heart beats. You really don't feel anything? I looked at everyone's hearts twice today to make sure I was seeing what I just said. I just want you to be healthy, Dylan. If you want to go to the doctor, I completely understand. Just promise me you will get this looked at, okay?" I asked, hoping she would agree.

"Tell you what: I will tell Mom and go get checked out. If this is something that needs to be fixed, I'll get it fixed. Forever more, you will be my health care. We good?" she negotiated.

"Yes, for sure," I reassured.

She went to the doctor the next day and the issue was confirmed. A little procedure followed a couple days later and fixed the hole.

While she was recovering in the hospital, Dylan pulled me close and asked, "Did they do okay, Bug?"

"They did, sis. No more leaky heart," I said reassuringly. From that point forward, Dylan trusted me with her health. Well, all of it with the exception of a couple things we will talk about later.

****

Sam and I worked on the fundamentals of my ability on a really small scale every day in some way. This, ironically, was where I was tested on my ability to be discreet—to not be caught using parts of my talent.

The best example of this is something I am still proud of today: the remote wedgie. Yes, my lovely friend, I yanked not one, not two, but *fifteen* distinct sets of underbritches up into the caverns of the human rumprump—where the sun don't shine. Best part: Joe Chava was blamed for it *all*. To this day, it is a shining accomplishment of mine, along with the discovery of my ability to invoke some of the most majestic fart magic this planet has *ever* witnessed. Papa G and I had a field day with this you will read about in another chapter and a half or so. Simmer down there, Skipper. We have more sleddin' to do on this hill first. Don't go skipping ahead or nothin' because you will get lost and have lots of disappointment and shame. We do not want such a thing, right?

****

Every night I was on Earth, I talked to Ania in her dreams. As it lined up, Earth's night on the East coast matched up with Cythis' night in our city almost exactly. The topic was always the same, and because those were such incredible conversations, I'll give you but a snippet of the last conversation we had before I returned.

"Hi Vik. I missed you today even though you're here. How are you?" she asked, running her fingers through my hair.

"How are you feeling, love? Is the baby okay?" I asked, my hands gently wrapping around her waist.

"He is your son, Vik. Sweet as the sunset is beautiful. You are my real Vik, right? The one that showed me love for the first time?" she asked, wrapping her arms around my neck and then kissing me.

"I will always be your real Vik, Ania. I will always love you, forever more."

With that, she smiled and drifted away.

Plans & Accountability

I woke up feeling the familiar pain of Cythis filling me.

I immediately looked to my right to see my wife, who I had missed more than I can possibly explain. She was still asleep, but the baby was up. I spent a good while saying hello to him.

As my memories from Vik settled in, I learned a few things. Firstly, construction on Klain's platform had completed but there was no announcement about when he would be in town. Secondly, The Resistance had grown immeasurably, and The Faction had taken notice of a change in society. This change: people smiled more. This caused a panic amongst The Faction, who had been stepping up assaults against the public as a result.

"Sam? You there?"

"Of course, Paul. I can tell you are confused. The only thing I need to make clear is that you must remain calm. Times are tense here."

"I understand, trust me. Is The Resistance still planning their attack?"

"I don't think they can. They lost the trail—Klain is missing and has not been heard from or seen in several days."

"Thanks, Sam. This should be interesting."

No, it really wasn't going to be interesting. It was going to be insanity— stress and abject insanity.

The sun later rose, and my beautiful wife gracefully woke up.

"Good morning, babe," she said sleepily and snuggled into my chest facing me.

"Good morning, love. How did you sleep?" I asked, wrapping my arms around her.

"Perfect, as always," she whispered.

We laid there for a short while before she uttered, "We need to get up. Verification is earlier today."

"Really? How come?" I asked, a ridiculous feeling brewing in my entire body. Something was happening today. I could feel it.

"No one knows, really. We should get ready, though. Don't want to kick the hornet's nest, right?"

"Paul, I…," Sam began.

"Sam?" I was confused.

"I'm right here, okay?"

"I need to know what's going on, Sam," I demanded.

"I am right here."

"Come on, Vik. We need to get ready," Ania urged.

Reluctantly, I got up and got dressed just in time to hear the horn sound. So, we gave each other a kiss and headed to the front of the house.

There was a massive presence of Faction might that morning. There seemed to be equal parts guns to batons. The game had officially been upgraded.

The typical process of verification took place, and I repeated my expected speech: "Vilok Ghabey. I am a builder."

The Faction member then moved to my wife, who said, "Ania Ghabey. I am an artist and am pregnant."

A look of confusion, and then anger crossed the face of our verifier.

"Please repeat, ma'am," he growled.

"My name is Ania Ghabey. I am an artist and I am pregnant," she respectfully replied.

I'm not sure if she smiled too much, or if her eyes somehow captivated this man and he couldn't handle it, but within a blink he had removed his baton and began violently beating Ania. He hit her in the head so hard she fell with the first blow.

"What are you doing?! She is pregnant!" I yelled as soon as my brain connected what had just happened. The shock of this made time stand still when I could not afford such a thing.

My neighbors looked at the scene in front of my house with immense sadness.

"I love you, Paul. I'll see you again… Goodbye, my true Vik," Ania's *vox corporis* said. She had died sometime in the flurry of blows from the baton.

This asshat had just killed my wife and unborn son! A rage unlike anything I have ever experienced in my life, one laced with intense sadness, filled me.

I looked to the suns in the sky and filled myself with the murderous nectar of hell itself.

Cythian bodies were constructed exactly like human bodies, physically. There is a heart, lungs, bones, blood and brain that makes the whole thing go. The only difference is the digestive system, but for all that comes next, this is not important.

"GO BACK INSIDE, ALL OF YOU! NOW!" I yelled as a group of gun-wielding assailants got closer.

I tackled and then stepped on the throat of Ania's assailant and watched his brain for the location that invoked shock. I blocked it, because this man was about to feel the kind of torture—*all* of the torture—that I was about to thrust upon his dying body. The only thing that was going to stop the torture was the death of either his brain or his heart. Keep this in mind.

I first ripped each finger off of his hands and propelled them at the speed of sound toward The Faction that approached me. This slowed them but still a few moved forward, guns firing.

So, one by one, I ripped the ribs from his chest, through his skin, and propelled them into the advancing Faction, again as fast as the energy would allow. Enough of those went through the assailants' necks that the majority of them died with this exchange.

My wife's murderer screamed in pain throughout all of this. I kept him alive and feeling everything, because I was not yet close to being done with him.

More Faction approached from my left. I felt bullets whizzing all around me. Some hit me, but not significantly enough to cause damage. I found I could easily remove them as they began to pierce my skin, so I returned them to the approaching gunners. I was a better shot, hitting all of them in the eyes. They stopped advancing.

Still more Faction approached from the left. And—the turret closest to me had begun firing, too, and the shells were exploding close enough to make me uncomfortable. So, I ripped the toes, one by one from the asshole murderer, accelerating them as fast as possible toward the turret. Think of a shotgun shell made out of toes, if that would help. The turret stopped firing, though I was confident this was temporary. I still had The Faction approaching from the left, and they had gotten uncomfortably close.

So, I ripped the bones from each leg, one at a time, turned them horizontally and threw them at the advancing Faction, which had gotten within five feet of me. I cut them all in half at the waist with the bones from the still screaming asshole. The top half of those Faction fell backward as their bottom halves had momentum forward. They screamed in pain for a minute as the contents of their chest cavities emptied onto the street.

The turret began to fire again, and the big guns above me also had started sending shells to my location. I knew my time was limited, so I raised my still conscious, mostly boneless, asshole murderer, ripped the heart from his chest, showed it to him, and then threw both as hard and as fast as I could at the turret. It stopped firing, but again, I felt this was likely temporary.

I heard more massive booms above me. The big guns had increased the frequency of their shots and the shells were exploding close enough to me to throw copious amounts of shrapnel into my legs and belly. I removed everything I could as fast as I could, but I was hurt and was running out of time.

I threw a ball of energy around me, kind of like a protective egg shell, to keep as much new shrapnel from hitting me as possible. This allowed me to quickly get the rest of the shrapnel out of my legs so I could run.

Running toward the turret, I fumbled around my belly and got as much of the shrapnel out of my chest and belly as I could. I was still hurt, but I could function enough to still do what I needed to do.

More doomed Faction ran toward me. Remember that thing about raging torture Sam mentioned? Yeah, they all died super painfully, their blood running in the streets as they screamed.

I got to the turret and threw the gunner occupying it as hard as I could into the side of a building. He was liquid goo going slippity slip down the side, last I saw.

I grabbed the controls of the turret and turned it to the sky. I was able to destroy one of six big guns with it before that turret was gunned to bits by the remaining big guns in the sky. I escaped as the thing exploded, but I took more shrapnel in the side in the process. I ripped it and a load of meat from my body out with my hands and did a cursory repair job on the wound as I moved. I knew that standing still was not an option. I had to keep moving.

Even more doomed Faction ran toward me, guns firing. I grabbed a handful of the shrapnel from the gun and threw it toward the group as hard as I could, again accelerating it to near the speed of sound. I don't know if they all died at that point, but the gunfire stopped.

The big guns found me, apparently when I threw that stuff.

"Paul get out of there now! NOW!" Sam screamed.

I launched myself quickly to another turret across town. The Faction member who had occupied it was running away. I tortured him for his cowardice and threw him into the street, face down. Goddamn coward.

I put my hand on the ladder to climb up and take control, but I was stopped. I turned to find Eva, tears covering her face, holding my hand tightly, preventing me from moving.

"There's no time, Paul. I'll take this one. Others are willing to help. Go… Go clear the other guns and let us help you," she sobbed.

"You shouldn't do this, Eva. This is my fight. They took her… They… I…," I couldn't handle even saying another word before the sadness completely overwhelmed me.

"Paul, you have to keep moving. There will be time to grieve, but this is not that time. Get the other turrets cleared and use the help. GO!" Sam yelled.

"They took her, they took my son, Sam. I…"

"You have to keep moving, Paul. Please, my friend. Please," he was crying, wherever he was.

"Go, Paul. Let us help you. I'm shooting anything I can. Others will do the same. GO!" Eva yelled.

I angrily wiped the tears from my eyes and leapt to the next turret I could find on an opposite side of town.

I ripped the arms off of The Faction member in that gun and threw him headfirst into the street.

"I am so, so sorry. I will help," a man I'd never met before said. He quickly got into the seat and started firing into the sky. "I'll cover you as best I can. Run, Vik! We got this!"

"Thank you," I said, and moved as quickly as I could to the last turret in town, diagonal from where I was standing. This stopped the big guns, at least temporarily.

There was already a resistance member in this last turret, shooting the big guns in the sky.

"I got this covered. Keep moving!" the lady encouraged.

There were two large groups of Faction moving in from either side, just as Papa G and Larry had showed. I had to take one and get creative with the other.

Well, it so happened that the one group coming in would pass by Klain's stage. So, I leapt over there, switched the sensor gun on, and hoped for at least a little time. Ironic, no?

I went onto a small hill so I could see all that was coming toward me. Only one big gun in the sky remained, but it had found me. It was damaged, but those shells were still hurting me, and the damage was definitely getting worse; I couldn't keep up. So, I arrived at a plan.

I began throwing oncoming Faction members at the big gun, which at a minimum obstructed the big gunner's view. I had to have thrown thirty or so bodies at it before I saw the resistance-controlled turrets finally finished off that big gun.

I still had a big group of Faction coming my way, and bullets were flying all around and into me. I saw that there was nothing flammable on their path, no houses, no civilian buildings. So, I borrowed a little fire from the littler of the two suns, made it into a really big, forceful fire and threw it at those Faction members. When the smoke cleared, nothing moved.

Behind me, near Klain's stage, I heard gunfire. I couldn't tell what was happening, so I leapt close enough that I could see it.

Resistance members had taken Faction guns and were involved in a firefight with Faction gunners near Klain's stage. No turrets were close enough to assist, so I found the next best thing: Klain's stage. The worst thing for those Faction gunners:

Klain's stage.

The Faction were using the stage as a shield, ducking behind it for cover—they had to have turned off the guns. It was built with hundreds of thousands of bolts—bolts that turned into *vicious* close range projectiles when thrust at high speed into the unsuspecting Faction gunners. In the end, the only thing left of The Faction, at least as far as this side of Cythis was concerned, was a big mess of blood and body giblets.

The gunfire stopped, and an eerie silence covered the area.

"Klain. We need Klain, Paul," Eva instructed as she approached me. Her hands and face were notably bloody.

"Get a camera ready. I'll be right back."

There was only one government broadcasting channel that served the entire planet. When something was broadcasted, the whole world got the transmission.

Thankfully, I knew where the coward was, but not using any of my talent. There was only one hotel in the city, a cement monstrosity whose upper floors were reinforced. The increase in hostility that had taken place at Verification was a clear sign Klain was in town and was bearing witness to this whole thing.

I was exhausted at this point, badly hurt and emotionally destroyed. Regardless, I got close enough to the hotel to see what security I may be dealing with. There was nothing outside. So, I was left to believe that hotel was filled with security details and the coward himself.

"He's in there, right, Sam?"

"Yep. Penthouse. There are thousands of Faction inside with guns drawn."

The suns were starting to hang lower on the horizon. My timing for this was starting to be compromised. So, I looked to Cythis, which was teeming with energy I hadn't seen before. I gladly made use of it and the energy I had left from the suns to rip the top third of that hotel off and dropped it to the ground, blocking the only entrance of the building. No, there were no emergency exits.

I then dropped fire into the now topless hotel. I heard screaming and yelling and then nothing.

I ripped the side off of the penthouse portion and pulled all of the living out. This included Klain.

Each of the armed were disarmed; I literally ripped the arms off of anyone I saw in that group holding a weapon and dropped them on the ground. Anyone not holding a gun was thrown backward, against the building like pancakes.

"Happy?" I asked as I pulled the very dazed Klain toward me.

"You will pay for this, all of it," he scolded.

"I'm sure I will, and thanks for that. For now, you and I are going to have a chat on TV. Yeah?" I asked, every bit the shitty son of a bitch about to murder the man on live TV.

I got Klain over to the collection of residents and resistance members who had gathered by the camera. It was rolling.

I stopped Klain directly in front of the camera, holding him tightly to the ground. I broke both of his ankles with the pressure. His knees were starting to pop. I felt the pain coursing through him—I blocked his brain's natural protections, just as I had done to Ania's murderer.

"What do you have to say to the rest of Cythis, Klain?" I asked calmly.

"I am being held hostage. All Faction…"

I stopped Klain from speaking. Use your imagination here, and you're probably right in how I was doing this.

"I want you to try this again, because every Faction member that remains alive in the world will either be dead by morning or headed to prison for crimes committed against this global population. Now then, Klain, what do you have to say?" I asked, allowing him to speak.

Coughing, the realization of this truth seemed to have come to bear.

"I don't know what you want me to say," he scowled.

"Start with 'I'm sorry' and we will go from there," I volleyed.

"What am I sorry for? What do you think I could possibly be sorry for? Your dead wife?"

I again choked Klain, but this time it was a tad closer to the fatal variety.

"What Klain is referring to is the impetus for today's liberation. A Faction member killed my pregnant wife, Ania for not one single good reason," I said, and one by one, disconnected all the valves from Klain's heart.

Klain's eyes got big, his breathing got heavy, and then he died and gurgled. I dropped the broken asshole to the ground.

"Wherever you are tonight, celebrate the love in your life. I lost mine. Do it for her. Do it for my unborn son. If you are Faction and you remain true to Klain's vision, you will die by morning. Goodnight," I said, tears streaming down my face.

The camera turned off and I threw Klain's body into the sun. I then took all the dead Faction bits from all over the city, opened a hole in Cythis' crust, and dumped the lot of grisly death into it. I then closed the hole, leaving fresh dirt for planting.

I made my way down to the crowd, which was still assembled, and we collectively wept.

"You did it, Paul," Eva whispered.

"No, Eva. *We* did it," I said as fresh tears fell down my face.

I walked slowly back to my house, and found my beautiful bride still laying where she had fallen.

I collected her into my arms and slowly carried her to the ocean. We had loved watching the waves together.

"I am so, so sorry, Ania. I… I…," I sobbed. "I failed you, my love. I failed… I'm so…"

The moon had risen, bright and full. I used the last bit of my energy to leap to the middle of the ocean with her. I sat suspended in the air, blood from my body pouring into the sea. I tried to speak another word and just couldn't. My heart, my body and my soul were broken. I traced the side of her face and gently let her go.

I watched in complete brokenness as she faded away into the darkness of the water. My beautiful Ania was gone.

Community

I woke up after some time had passed, still suspended above the water where I had let Ania go.

Someone approached, gently put their arms around me and carried me through the air to the opposite side of Cythis. The suns were just barely kissing the horizon in the distance.

I was carefully placed on the edge of a small island. I could feel all the remaining bullets and shrapnel being pulled from my body. The damage from all of it was repaired.

I then fell fast asleep.

****

I woke to the sound of a fire crackling not far from me. It was night.

I sat up and looked off into the vast ocean. I wondered where Ania's body had come to rest, bowed my head and sobbed.

"I failed. I lost the *only* person I was here to protect. I lost my son, my beautiful son. I *failed*," I mumbled through extraordinary hysterics.

"You didn't though," Eva said. She was behind me.

"How can you say that, Eva? I can do all that I did, but I couldn't protect her. How is this not complete failure?" I scolded.

"Listen," Sam said. He was with her.

"Listen for what, Sam? What the hell should I do that for?"

"Just shut your mouth for a minute and listen," he encouraged.

"You should have let me die, Sam."

"Paul, *listen*," he said comfortingly.

Begrudgingly, I closed my eyes and listened. For what, I had no idea.

"I'm not far, my love. You mustn't cry another tear. When it is time, I will find you," Ania's voice whispered.

"ANIA!" I yelled and leapt to my feet. "Where is she? WHERE ARE YOU?" I leapt in every direction I could, feverishly searching. My wife was *somewhere*. I *heard* her. I was going to *find* her.

I had crossed that massive ocean three times before I got back to the island and collapsed. I was completely spent; not even Cythis' plentiful energy was able to help me stand.

"Paul, what did we talk about back on Pai?" Sam asked calmly.

"We talked about a lot of things, Sam," I said weakly, trying to catch my breath.

"Well, let's go back over this, okay? Eva, would you care to assist here?" Sam said flippantly.

"Gladly!" Eva excitedly began. "Paul, your work involves restoring balance and establishing harmony where it has been lost. Remember this?"

"Yeah, so?" I replied like a snotty toddler.

"What do you think you just did?" she asked.

"Half. I did *half* of the fix. Innocent people died in the process. This is *not* success," I reasoned.

"Let's get you caught up, okay? Klain had brought eighty-five percent of The Faction's army with him. That left fifteen percent, right?" she asked, her voice bouncy and yet logical.

"So? There are still the big guns in the sky on the other side of the planet. There is still an entire side of this planet that is fortified," I said angrily.

"Paul, where do you think we are right now?" she asked, remaining very patient throughout.

"I have no idea, Eva. Why don't you tell me?" I coarsely replied.

"We're on the other side of Cythis. Look up," she said.

I did. I just saw clear, dark early morning sky.

"I saw an entire structure surrounding the planet. I *saw* it. I'm not sure how it's possible that an entire structure around a planet could just disappear," I angrily reasoned.

"Cythis, he's all yours," Sam said joyfully.

"What the...," I began, but was launched into the air. I got to a point so high that I could see the curvature of Cythis' side. There was no structure where I had expected to see one.

I was then put into an energy bubble not unlike the one I had used to deflect bullets and shrapnel when fighting The Faction. I began to rise into Cythis' uppermost atmosphere.

I was stopped and turned to face an open part of the sky just to the left of one of Cythis' three moons. The light from the moon illuminated something shiny in the distance, tumbling through space away from the planet.

"The structure?" I asked.

I was then taken to the side of Cythis I had not been and lowered slowly back into the sky.

It was morning, and lights were on in some homes.

I was set down in the middle of what I could see was the biggest, most populated city. Gun turrets were still there, in bigger numbers compared to our town, but were unoccupied. Guard stations were where I expected to see them, but all were empty.

I walked through the middle of the quiet city when all of a sudden, a small boy approached me.

I was still wearing the ripped, blood-covered clothes I wore during the fight. I should have looked terrifying to the child, but he reached for me to pick him up.

"Good morning, Vik. Thank you for all you have done for us," he said. This kid couldn't have been more than four or five years old.

"You're certainly welcome. What's your name? Where are your parents?" I asked, my curiosity abounding.

"I'm Max. My parents will be here in a moment. They need to talk to you. Before they get here, I need to tell you a couple things," he said, seriousness lacing his words.

"Okay, Max… What is it?" I asked.

"Your son wanted me to tell you that he felt no pain when his mother died. The love you gave him in his short life has been shared with all of his other lives. You gave hope, love and support to many who desperately needed it. He also said he looks forward to the day when he can show you how much this meant to him.

"Your wife felt no pain at the time of her passing. The love you gave her has connected you to her throughout every other life she lives. You will see her again but you must be patient. She will remind you of this; it is important to understand that she will find you when it is time. You must not look for her, no matter how hard this may be," he said emotionally.

"But Max…," I whispered, my voice hoarse. Tears streamed down my face. I wiped a couple that fell onto the boy's face.

"There is more, Vik. You have more to do to complete this part of the work. You must address the community here, understand them, and then move to three separate locations to complete the work. You then must return to Earth and heal. Eva will help you through all of it. Okay?" he explained, his voice returning to an age-appropriate timbre by the end.

I had no time to respond. Several sets of arms surrounded me, still holding the child. Some of them wept, some of them breathed deeply; this was a heavy time for these folks.

"You freed us, Vik."

"You've given us hope again."

"You healed us."

"We will never, ever forget your sacrifices."

"Thank you, Vik."

The arms around me started to release. As soon as they did, new arms appeared, presenting new gratefulness and heavy emotion. I felt it all. This pattern continued for three more rounds.

The last batch of hands included the boy's mother and father.

Max looked deeply into my eyes, hugged me tightly and whispered, "See?"

"Hi, Mommy," he then said, every bit the little kid, and reached for his mother.

"He said he needed to talk to you. I hope that's okay, Vik," she said.

"Of course! Max is a special, special child. Thank you for trusting me with him," I responded, the reality of the situation, namely a stranger holding someone else's child, weighing on me.

"We have so much to thank you for, Vik. You would not have done any of this on our behalf unless somewhere inside of you, there is love. I will never forget the day my child spoke to the man who gave me my freedom," Max's mother said.

"Out of curiosity, where did the rest of The Faction go? There should have been several thousand of them on this side of the planet," I asked, returning to a nagging thought in my head.

"Three massive ships left here maybe an hour ago. I think they all ran, hearing your threat on TV yesterday," she said.

"It's morning here for another four or so hours, right?" I asked, the task at hand Max mentioned becoming very clear.

She smiled, saying, "Yeah, I think you could even stretch that to four and a half if you needed."

"Thank you. Please take care of your amazing child. Max is a special boy. I have to go, I have to make good on a promise I made," I said, my blood beginning to boil with all things demonic.

"Please be safe, Vik. We are all with you," she said kindly.

"Okay Paul," Eva began. I could hear her exactly as I heard Sam, nonverbally. *"Hopefully, you now understand how special yesterday's actions have been*

for this entire planet. Also, I hope Max helped you understand the truths about your fallen family. He mentioned needing to go to three locations. While this isn't incorrect, it's a little misleading. The ships are not far from Cythis. One went toward Pai, another left going to the opposite side and the third went right in the middle.

"Part of your ability you've not experienced yet, is done using the energy that runs unseen throughout a dimension. Dark energy is found everywhere in this realm. You can use it just as you do normal planet energy. But there is a catch. If you disrupt it and its natural flow, it can be disastrous—entire planets can be swallowed whole by the force exerted in such an instance. However, if you contribute to this flow, the dimension itself benefits.

"I want you to walk away from this crowd, around the next block. When you are clear, Cythis is going to take you again. As soon as you are high enough, I will show you what to look for," Eva instructed.

I walked around the corner after saying my final goodbyes to the crowd, which had dissipated. As soon as I was far enough away, I was launched into the sky. An energy bubble surrounded me as soon as I was too high for oxygen, and within a couple seconds I was sitting in the vastness of space. It was completely awe-inspiring.

"Good, Paul. It is gorgeous up there, isn't it? I want you to close your eyes and pay attention to the energy, just as you have on all of the planets," Eva said, reminiscent of my teacher on Earth. This made me chuckle.

"Thanks, Teach," I said, still laughing. *"You said that just like Mrs. Little, my teacher for this year back on Earth."*

"Interesting… Look at the energy, Paul," she responded, notably not amused.

I closed my eyes and saw a ridiculous web of energy before me. On all the planets, energy tended to run in one direction, not unlike a river. That direction could change, of course, but the energy always stayed together.

What I saw here were layers of intertwined energy, not unlike an absurdly busy plaid shirt, if that shirt had diagonals in the pattern. I could see that some energy moved quicker than others, and the whole thing pulsed and flowed with this very hypnotic trance-like rhythm not unlike a heartbeat.

"Good, Paul. What you need to make absolutely sure of is that you move with the energy you are closest to. If you do this, all will remain in harmony. Understand?" she asked.

"No, I'm still fuzzy on this. What could I do to disrupt the energy? I mean, can stuff that is thrown around mess things up? Can I use the energy incorrectly and somehow cause a problem?" I asked, thoroughly confused.

"Let's use the first ship as an example, okay? The ship heading to Pai is the closest to you and the one that can do the most damage the soonest. Cythis will navigate you since the planets are so close. It will be a very strange sensation, but you must trust it. Okay?" Eva encouraged.

The distance between Pai and Cythis is akin to five-ish times the distance between Earth and the Moon. Both are smaller than Earth so, although both planets were visible to the other, their orbits were complimentary to one another.

I was turned horizontally and was propelled quickly toward Pai. Eva wasn't kidding—this was sorta like the feeling of being squeezed by a giant gorilla while being blown out of a cannon.

Within about a minute, the first ship was visible to me.

"Okay Eva—I see the first ship. What should I be looking for?" I asked.

"Look just above you and just below you. What do you see the energy doing?" she asked.

I looked and saw two big bands; one was above me, one was below me. The bands themselves were about the size of a four-lane highway, moving in beautiful wave-like undulations.

"Two big bands of energy are here, one above and one below. The one above is moving diagonally away from me, and the lower one is moving in the direction I am moving," I responded, still watching the energy.

"Okay. Now, where you are, you're being affected by both bands. Look really closely and try to see this," she said encouragingly.

I did; I could see the blending of the two bands, almost like that fun bleeding/spreading thing that happens in a cup of coffee when creamer is poured in.

"So, I can move and work between the bands, but the closer I am to the bands themselves, the more I have to stay in sync with their movement?" I asked, still trying to understand how this all worked.

"Yes. Here's the thing, to be completely clear—the only way you can hurt the energy is to use a vast amount of it against the current of a band. In other words, if you grabbed this big chunk of energy and threw it the opposite way a band runs, you'll cause a ripple in the band and affect all of its interactions. This can throw orbits off, causing the potential for bowling at the cosmic level. It has to be big, Paul, to do this. Bear that in mind, okay?

"Please be careful. The Faction is heavily armed and expecting you. They just don't know how," she said, concern notable in her voice.

"I got it, I think. Let's see what fun we can have, right?" I responded, deflecting the intensity of the moment.

Okay. Knowing I could cause cosmic smash 'em up with a misstep weighed on me. I didn't know what "big" meant in energetic terms, and that made this first ship's demise sorta blah.

I got close enough to the ship to make out what I needed to make out. I gathered enough energy to grab the ship. So then, spoiler alert, I grabbed the ship and effectively stopped its forward motion. A volley of big bullets proceeded to fly my way quickly. They were fun and exploding and whatnot. So, I had to work quickly, something that Sam reminded me.

"GET TO WORK, PAUL! NOW!" he boomed.

My thought was to rip the ass end off and send the rest of the ship along the band that ran toward the bigger of the two stars.

I focused on the propulsion of the ship, knowing that if I disabled it, the ship would be mine to control. This would remain true as long as I could avoid the aggressive defenses. So, I moved above the ship for perspective and to establish my approach. The bullets paused briefly and then started again, harder than before. The energy bubble was good but was not nearly strong enough to withstand too many hits. I was getting hit by the shrapnel as those damn bullets exploded. It didn't feel great, let me tell ya.

I gathered a little bit more energy and threw it at the ship, being careful not to disturb the energy bands. I essentially moved in the direction of the top band, so I was okay.

Once the energy hit the ship, I quickly pulled it backward as a cowboy does a lassoed pig. This acted like a can opener and in no time, I ripped the propulsion area off of the ship and sent the now dormant ship toward the star.

Though I had no idea whether any of the ship's inhabitants survived the propulsion unit's removal, I wanted as many surviving Faction members as possible to enjoy this experience to the very end. So, I sealed the end of the ship with an energy bubble and pushed it down toward the star's band. As soon as it was lined up correctly, I gave it a little push and watched it accelerate toward the star. The ship had no way to change course with the propulsion unit gone. In about twenty miserable minutes, the lovely Cythians inside would be cooked alive and then swallowed in the star's atmosphere.

As much as I wanted to see this, I knew the other ships had to know I was coming and would be moving away from the area as quickly as they could.

"Outstanding job, Paul! That was a perfect use of everything. Like I said: you can use the energy and not cause a problem as long as you work in a common direction. Don't be afraid to use the energy—just don't overuse it," Eva said encouragingly. *"You need to hurry. Your job has gotten a little easier on one hand and much harder on another. The other two ships are now very close together. This is good for proximity's sake, but bad when it comes to avoiding the combined aggression they will no doubt throw your way. Get a good plan in place before you engage."*

"Thanks Eva. I'm all ears if you have ideas. Those shells hurt—I have shrapnel in my legs and a little in my belly," I replied, surveying yet more tattered clothing and blood loss.

"Go up from where you are—you will find healing there. You have to hurry, Paul. Get that damage corrected and get to the remaining ships. They look to be headed to Loht, which would be awful for those people," Eva said, worry in her voice.

"Understood. I'll hurry," I said reassuringly.

Loht is a planet in the solar system with Pai and Cythis. It is well developed with a fairly sizable population of individuals, though they were contained to a small amount of the planet. The majority of Loht was water.

The Faction had started harassing these poor folks, but had been unsuccessful in really doing anything due to Loht's exceptional planetary defenses. My guess was The Faction's mentality was likely a "shoot first, ask questions never" kind of thing so their overall approach was likely to be very aggressive given The Faction's losses on Cythis.

So, I quickly went "up" from where I was and curiously found an area that was mildly luminous.

"That's it, Paul. Keep going," Eva said encouragingly.

With the confirmation I wasn't heading into something harmful, I proceeded into the luminous area.

Well, let me begin this little segment by reminding you that Earth will not truly possess a proper understanding of the Universe for hundreds of years. Should you be reading this two-hundred, fifty-six years from the copyright date, please forgive the elementary review.

The Universe is not a vast expanse, a container if you will, of solar systems, galaxies, etc. Beyond the rocky things and the bright things, there are dark things. These are not evil things but, because they do not reflect light, they are appropriately deemed "dark." These dark things influence *almost* everything in the visible Universe. They *do* affect everything in the non-visible Universe.

Key among these dark things are areas of consciousness. If you were to map all of it out, it sorta resembles a map of the brain if you were to draw out all the major centers of thought and reflection and flatten it. With me so far?

You are aware that your body receives its healing instructions from the brain, right? You cut your finger, platelets rush to stop the bleeding and the brain gets to work assessing and fixing the damage not unlike a drill sergeant. This luminous area is akin to this function of the brain; anything passing through it, or it passed through for that matter, is fixed. That is—any damage is quickly analyzed and repaired.

When I entered this area, the energy bubble disappeared. In a sense, I was in a new energy bubble that was the size of Texas. I could feel the energy all around me scanning the entirety of my body, outside and in. When it reached something that wasn't supposed to be there, it removed it and quickly healed the damage. Mind you, I felt every damn thing it did, so there was no replication of comfy pain meds in an emergency room. In a sense, when all was said and done, I was given a little dash of cushy brain candy to make all the pain go away. That's what it felt like, anyway.

With the damage repaired, I exited the luminous, healing, gnarly place and tried to get my thoughts together on a strategy. If I remembered correctly, Loht had all kinds of rocky material around it due to a collision that happened thousands of years in the past between a couple tiny moons. It wasn't a ring, per se; the pieces were big, like a series of itty-bitty moons scattered around the planet. This presented me with both a thought and some concern. The energy topic was still far too unclear to me.

"Eva, if I throw space rocks around, can I do anything to the energy? I'm thinking all the material around Loht may be really helpful when addressing these two ships," I said.

"Well, the short answer is sometimes. Some of the rocks around Loht govern aspects of the planet's weather. The bigger ones for sure should be avoided," Eva said, confusing me further.

"So, the right answer is that I really shouldn't use those rocks, right? I mean, I don't want to hurt Loht," I replied, rife with concern.

"Paul, just get over there and take a look. You'll know if a rock is too big by the resistance it gives you if you try to move it. Now go—the ships are almost in Loht's orbit. Your travel this time is being governed by something a little bigger. You may want to prepare yourself," Eva instructed.

"What…," I thought and was interrupted by the fact that I had been grabbed by something massive and pulled at an incredible velocity.

I couldn't breathe and I couldn't struggle. It felt like I was in a crushed car that was dropped in the ocean from twenty stories up. The pressure was *unbelievable.*

After maybe ten seconds, things slowed down, a new energy bubble was thrown around me, and I found myself looking down at the two ships. They were in Loht's upper atmosphere; I had to work fast.

"Sweetheart, PUSH!" I thought, hoping my hunch on planetary consciousness was right.

The ships forward momentum stopped. This was an opportunity for me to pull them backward, so I surveyed the energy and found that it all was flowing in the direction of the smaller sun.

I took a deep breath and focused on one of the bigger bands. I attached to it and let the energy move down to the ships, across and through my arms. I watched the energy surround both ships, detached from the band and yanked the ships back. I made absolutely sure the energy stayed in place while I did this. I thought, the energy being what it was, I could just pull the ships into the smaller sun using the energy bands. Easy-peasy, lemon squeezey.

Well.

Yeah, I'm an idiot.

A massive amount of armament flew my way—I was hit by no fewer than twenty shells at once. I was thrown backwards and completely disconnected from the energy.

I hurtled through space, hurt, bleeding, disoriented. I was in bad shape—really bad shape.

"Paul! Speak to me! Oh my God! PAUL!" Eva yelled.

"PAUL! Say something! Please, my friend, say something," Sam begged.

I tumbled, bled some more and found myself completely unable to think.

Again, that crazy apparatus that had delivered me to the fight collected me and moved me into another healing section.

I yelled in pain as the damage was repaired. Not to be too gross but, my belly was completely rebuilt, parts of my gut had been thrashed, and chunks of my innards were all that remained before I arrived in space triage. My right arm was gone, too, from the shoulder down. My pelvis had been shattered into bits; my legs were all but falling off of my torso. That felt super, *super* great when it was being fixed.

This whole transaction on my body took a couple minutes. At the end of the physical rebuild, my mind was sorted out. I was in shock, and the mechanics to resolve it were not unlike the licking of a big cat momma on a freshly born tiger. It felt that way, anyway—the pressure, the comfort, the sloppy love, more pressure, more sloppiness…

Eventually, that baby tiger complains, mom licks some more, slaps a big old paw on the helpless kitten and makes damn sure it's okay before licking some more. This is what happened in my brain, almost to a T.

"Wow," I thought. *"I'm okay, I think."*

I didn't hear a response, because that gnarly hand grabbed me and put me right in the middle of the two suns.

"It's time," a voice not Eva or Sam said.

"Um…,"

"Feel and proceed," it bellowed.

I heard nothing from Sam or Eva. So, heeding the instruction from the phantom teacher, I closed my eyes and focused on the energy in the suns. Slowly, but resolutely, I was filled with ridiculous amounts of both energy and anger.

I had no idea how I was breathing. I'm not even sure I was still Cythian after my time in the space clinic.

I focused on these intense feelings. I have never felt so powerful, but in the same way, so unbelievably angry. This feeling was what I felt after Ania was slain, times a factor of several hundred-thousand.

I yelled out the most horrific sound I had heard in my short life on Earth, demonic and hell-born. Well, the latter for context; I was factually in the heavens at the time.

I digress, with apology.

Loht was in the distance. I could not see the ships.

As I approached, I saw an island surrounded by a vast sea. I felt this was a good place to touch Loht for the first time and get to know the planet's energy.

I was not in an energy bubble. I wasn't thinking about this, per se, but it is worth noting. I entered Loht's atmosphere with no issues—I should have burned up but good. I glided down to the surface, over the water.

I dipped my hand in the cool sea, appreciating Loht's beauty, as I drifted toward the island.

A notably-sized sea creature joined me in my short journey. I didn't feel threatened or scared; I felt very much as one with the beautiful individual.

As I got closer to the island, my traveling partner went her own way. I could see a small clearing near the beach. I figured this a good place to begin familiarizing myself with Loht's energy.

I gently landed on the sand and walked onto the clearing. I found a nice place that was lit by the suns and sat down.

Loht was a pleasant planet but, because most of the surface was water, the potential for massive loss of life was quite real. All the people were in one relatively tiny spot on the planet. I knew that I had a small window of time to get my thoughts together and address The Faction.

I felt abundant energy everywhere, especially in the water. This shouldn't be too surprising given the things researchers on Earth have discovered about water. If you aren't familiar, I recommend you take a gander at the research. You may look differently at that stuff coming out the tap forever more.

In any case, I figured that I could pair this water energy with the suns' energy and have some success. I knew I had two ships to dispose of. I knew they were heavily armed and certainly capable of ending me and lots of Loht's people and creatures. So, this was to be a stealthy and all kinds of messy endeavor.

I closed my eyes and heard the faint vibrations of assault coming from just west of the island.

"I will protect you, sweetheart. I promise," I thought. Talking to planets may be a little odd, but your judgment is not appreciated.

I leapt toward the conflict and saw what I had suspected: both ships were in place destroying whatever they could.

My first goal was to protect the people. Then, raise ridiculous hell.

So, I started at the back of the area and quickly formed a big energy bubble. In seconds, I had formed that bubble over twenty or so square miles. I saw some very scared eyes as I did this. It only took a single shell bouncing off of that bubble for the people to see I meant them no harm.

I also knew that bubble was only going to hold The Faction off for a couple seconds. In that time, I needed to get rid of those guns shooting the big shells.

Loht had defenses, but a good amount of them had already been destroyed. Bearing this in mind, I quickly moved out over the water and focused both on it and the suns above me. I was filled with rage and a fun new tool: water energy.

See, water reacts to emotion. There are a few truly profound folks who have experimented with this and documented the outcome if you're curious. In my case, I inspired an aggression in the water that gave weight to everything else I did. Think of the energy in a twenty-foot wave as it crashes into the shore. Now, add that same intensity to me and it was time for some fun.

The guns had found me, but I was able to move out of the way quickly enough to avoid taking any more damage. I positioned myself directly on top of the ships and gathered as much of the suns' energy as I could safely, forming the energy into a column of fire.

When I couldn't grab anymore, I moved directly over the guns, waited for the shooting to stop, and then forced that insane flame through the first ship's guns with the strength of the ocean. It took less than a second for the ship to begin to break when the fire came out the other side.

As soon as I was sure the ship couldn't fly or shoot anymore, I connected the fragmented ship to the closest energy bands I could find running toward the suns. In a slingshot-like movement, that first ship was thrust out of Loht's atmosphere so quickly that there is little chance anyone inside would have survived the pressure alone.

Thing is, this happened so fast that it meant I was now wholly exposed to the other ship's guns, which had started lobbing those lovely massive shells my way.

As quickly as the first shells approached me, I moved and got out of the gun's range. I barely avoided getting hit again, but I was able to position myself directly above the ship.

This incited The Faction to shoot a huge amount of those shells at Loht's surface. I had to act quickly—hundreds, if not tens of thousands of Lohtians would perish unless I did something fast.

So, I focused on every one of the shells that were hurtling toward the surface and caught them just as they were making contact with the energy bubble I had created.

I then pulled all those shells directly back toward me as hard as I could.

As soon as the shells got close, I leapt back down to my place on top of the ocean and watched the fireworks. The shells badly damaged the ship and it started to fall from the sky.

So, I decided to play The Faction one final visit and then deal with the errant vessel before Loht or its people were in any more danger.

I leapt toward the ship and entered it through a hole one of the shells had formed in the front. I knew I'd be facing aggression. So would they.

Maybe they saw me through the hole. In any case, their aggression came first.

Gunfire met me before I fully entered the ship. I wrapped myself in an energy bubble as soon as the first bullets found their way into my legs.

As soon as I got into the ship, I knew I needed to work quickly. The ship was falling and I had very little time to "work" as Sam put it. I missed having him in my head—badly.

My feet touched down and I focused on the gunners. I summoned all kinds of evil and ripped all of their still-beating hearts from their chests. Shock, then death, followed in kind.

The next round of victims, knowing they would die no matter what, attempted to pick up the guns that had fallen on the ground. There were maybe fifty or so The Faction left, give or take a dozen.

Those who went for the guns received the same kind of death many of their colleagues on Cythis had experienced. Let's just say they felt all kinds of lovely things as their blood rained from their bodies when all of their bones fell to the floor. What a mess!

I'm awful…

The rest of The Faction seemingly realized it was over and went to the opposite side of the ship, toward the back. I figured this was my opportunity to end the conflict. I was hurt and needed to ensure that Loht was protected.

I leapt out of the ship, found the closest energy band, attached the ship to it and let it go. The ship flew into the sky—and I fell toward Loht.

I was completely spent. My injuries were a touch worse than I thought and this ultimately stole a bunch more of my energy.

As in the other oddities experienced, I was grabbed before I hit the ground. I was flung into that healing blob in space and fell unconscious as the pain of bullet removal made its acquaintance again.

Strangers Who Are Family

I woke up on Earth. I knew the feeling of that body without opening my eyes.

I was not alone. I heard four other sets of breathing with a smattering of whispering among the other occupants of the bed.

Having mastered a bit of my own body-space control, I levitated above the bed, flipped over and opened my eyes to greet my bedmates.

Thing was, one such bedmate was someone I had never seen before.

"Paul! You're back! My baby boy is okay! My God, little one—we were so scared for you. Eva was a godsend through all of the things you just went through. Are your legs okay? Your head? Can you talk to me, Paul?" Mom interrogated.

"Geez, Mom! Let him breathe! He just got back! Bug, you good? Your head okay? Your legs?" Dylan asked, adding her own concern to the mix.

"Paul? Recognize me? Look close," the stranger said.

I still had not said anything. I had woken up in my parents' bed with Mom, Dylan, the stranger and Dad, who was apparently horrified I was airborne.

I enjoyed this immensely. My demented self was growing nicely in my almost nine-year old Earthling self.

I lowered myself over the stranger, who was smiling at the whole thing.

"Look at my eyes and pair it up with the smile," she said kindly.

"Hi, Eva. Why are you in my mommy's bed? Why are we all sleeping together?" I said, realizing the stranger was one-half of my instruction team from Cythis. Little did I know that she was a uniquely persuasive little girl.

"Without her, I think we would have lost our collective minds, Paul. Can you come down? This is super hard for me to look at given the past two days," Dad asked, his voice notably strained.

I moved slowly over him, kissed his cheek, and stepped onto the ground. I could not help myself.

"Is he okay? My God that was awful last night!" Larry said, running into the room. "Paul? Are you okay?"

"Hi, Larry. I'm okay. I owe you a thank you—your strategy with Papa G worked *perfectly*," I said.

"I'm glad, but I think there are bigger things we need to talk about. What happened last night?" he demanded.

"I dunno. Eva, what happened last night?" I asked, not sure what this group knew or didn't know.

"Well, Paul, let's talk over breakfast. This is not a story that will go quickly or without a lot of questions and I'm starving. Mrs. Glassburé, can I be so crass as to ask you if we can start making breakfast?" Eva asked sophisticatedly.

"Sweetheart, as I told you, no 'Mrs. Glassburé', okay? Besides, I think your mom may have already started cooking," Mom responded.

"Wait—Eva, your parents are here?" I asked, my confusion returning.

"Yep. They have wanted to meet you for the past couple years. It sorta became very necessary now. This will be a whole other round of conversation you'll endure," Eva explained.

I scratched my head, shrugged, and made my way into the bathroom. I must say this was one aspect of my Earth life that became one of the most annoying. See, on Pai, Cythis, Pliqun or Loht, bodies eat like plants do on Earth. Waste is basically recycled and burned inside. Sexual organs are, by design, just used for sexual pleasure and reproduction. Shocking, right? Earth bodies are probably not going to ever mutate to the level of the other bodies because Earth may never be healthy enough for that to happen. I don't want to be a downer, but it's just a fact and that fact is annoying.

I brushed my teeth and headed downstairs.

I was followed closely by everyone from the bedroom. Something had clearly happened I was not aware of. This was not going to be pleasant.

A petite Indian woman saw me, shrieked, and enveloped me in an uncomfortably tight hug.

"It is a true pleasure to meet you, Paul. I am so glad you're here," she said.

"Indeed, Paul. Welcome home," an Indian man said, patting my back gently.

"Hi. Are you Eva's parents?" I asked, putting two and two together.

"Yes. I am Hansh, and she is Anika. It is truly special to meet you, Paul. Eva has told us so much. My heart breaks for you as much as I am wowed by you," he said.

Ania.

At once, the profound heaviness of her loss hit me square in the chest.

"It is so nice to meet you… Would you please excuse me for a minute?" I asked as tears introduced themselves to my cheeks.

I ran out to the dock. I needed nature and a place to cry. Little did I know unresolved feelings had a nasty way of finding you, even when you are a monster who rips bones and organs from people.

I sobbed, alone, for a good ten minutes. The weight of Ania's death had found me again. Yes, Eva and Sam had educated me on the truth of our relationship and I was able to function to protect Loht. I almost died twice, but I was able to function.

Look, I knew my tears were selfish. I gave into the emotion because I wanted to.

Then, that insane thing in the sky grabbed me and yanked my almost nine-year-old self into the depths of space.

I have no idea if anyone saw this, but it had to be strange—a boy flying helplessly through the sky at a ridiculous speed couldn't be normal to see.

I was flung into a different kind of bubble. Yeah, I really had no idea these things were in our Universe, too. Thing is, this was not a healing bubble. Not even close.

"Your tears, Paul, are silly. Stop now and understand that when it's time, we will be together. Do you understand?" Ania's voice demanded. This was the first time she called me "Paul."

"But..."

"No, my love. When you need me, close your eyes and say 'Hello, Love.' I will be here—I will always be here, Real Vik. I will know you as my true love for as long as there is life to express it," she said. *"Now, someone else needs to talk to you. Hold still."*

Well...

That energy-tentacled hug customary from planets wrapped me in a mummy-like way—a tight mummy hug, to be completely clear.

"You freed me, Paul. I cannot thank you enough," I heard. I wasn't sure if this was Loht or Cythis, but it felt different. It was definitely a planet hug, though—this much was confirmed.

In my mummy-like position, I was thrust into a deeper place in space. I have no idea how I didn't die, intrepid Reader. Indeed, the Universe is a freezing vacuum that fleshy things don't survive in—at all.

I arrived in a place that seemed like an edge to reality. It was bright and warm and simply breathtaking—but there was a vast expanse of nothingness in front of where I was "standing."

"This is a special place, Paul. This place carries a dependency on all of its siblings. Your work on Cythis and Loht has healed one of my siblings. We are healthy for the first time in thousands of years due to your actions. We owe you a bevy of thanks. Your work is nowhere near complete, but in this corner of existence, we are balanced, finally.

As a token of our thanks, enjoy," a voice said.

Yeah, remember what Sam said a while ago? Heal a planet, get a nice hug. Heal a dimension, it's a little different. This was a level of existence akin to what you probably feel Heaven is, if you believe in it. It was bliss on steroids. It was comfort reinforced with profound love. The visuals were akin to Godlike creation—gorgeous patches of light pulsed together, a richness present throughout. There are literally no words I can choose to properly express this experience. How does one properly convey a state of being not implicit in reality?

The mummifying arms released and a new set of arms collected me from behind.

I turned, a knowing feeling in me that I had missed, returned. I recognized her eyes and her smile.

I hugged my wife tightly. She matched me.

"I'm so sorry. I should have saved you," I said, squeezing tighter.

"You did, Paul. You have to understand this," Ania replied, though this was not Ania's body.

"But…"

"No, Paul. The thing you must realize is that the love you showed me—the truest, purest love—connected us. Whether you realize it or not, you did the same thing for our child. This love was not something you had to give. Just as you didn't have to save a single blade of grass on Cythis or Pai or Loht, you didn't have to show me the truth of love as you did. Whether or not you realize this, everything you have done to this point comes from a place of love. Those who you have taken know this—they all know this.

"What you must do is show your family this love. They felt every time you got hurt, Paul. *I* felt every time you got hurt. It means the world to me to feel you in my arms again. This place is special—and this chance was afforded us because of the entirety of your sacrifice. As I said, you simply speak to me as you do Sam or Eva. When it's time, we will have a life together—a full life. Have faith in this, my love," she said and hugged me again.

"You are not in Ania's body. What should I call you? You are calling me Paul—I think it only right I call you by a proper name," I said, overcome by all that I had heard.

"Just 'Love' will do, Real Vik. When it is time, you will know my name," she said, smiling.

Then, she was gone.

"But…"

"Remember what I said, Paul. Your family…"

I had a second to embrace the beauty of that place before I was grabbed by the space hand and pulled at a ridiculous speed back to Earth. I ended up falling comfortably into the Copahee right by our dock.

Eva was there, with a towel.

"I let everyone know where you were. You okay, Paul?" she asked, handing me the towel.

"Eva, before we go inside, can you help me? Ania, or whoever my wife was when I just talked to her, said the whole family knew what happened on Loht. How is this possible?" I asked, wiping off my face.

"Sit, Paul. Dry off, okay? They knew because the whole thing—*all of it*—played out in their minds. When you got hurt, especially when you got really badly hurt, your body (here) reacted. At one point, you simply said, 'I need to lie down,' and collapsed where you stood. Your dad carried you to bed, crying the *entire* way. Your sister, mother, brother and my parents were hysterical. I got upset because you couldn't hear me anymore.

"I, too, saw the whole thing and knew you needed me and Sam. For the record, he is beside himself with pride. You did it, Paul. You *did* it. I mean, you healed an entire corner of existence, Paul. You restored balance to a section of reality. You need to keep that balance, but my goodness, Paul—you did more than half of this alone.

"This doesn't change the fact that your parents and siblings experienced you being torn to pieces and almost dying, Paul. I could help them as long as you could hear me. When you couldn't, I became a helpless participant watching the whole thing, too. You're thrust into the Loht thing, almost die, and go in for round two and still get hurt. Paul, we saw the whole thing. It was like an awful dream that played out—your body convulsed with every injury. Your dad—your powerful father—could hardly breathe through it all. You have no idea how much it means for you to be here, with all of us. Your grandparents will all be here in a little while. In particular, your Papa needs to see you are okay. Your Grandpa Glassburé needs you to have silly fun. Your Grandmothers don't care about anything but your child and your love life. Shocking, right?

"So, be patient and show them you are okay. My parents want to see your talents, so be patient there, too. Just please show them the love that your Love spoke of. She wasn't wrong, Paul—about any of it," Eva said kindly.

"So, let me get this straight… My body failed and twitched and moved as I was getting hurt? Is this normal? I thought I was separate when I was there," I replied, confused.

"Well, your body on Cythis—yes, Vik is still alive—has slept for a week. Nyd has been sitting on his deck, unmoving for the same time with a very nervous avian buddy nudging him, constantly. Your body on Pliqun is basically a stateless being. Sam's grandson has been caring for you, based on Sam's guidance. Thing is, all of the individuals you are connected to felt this, those you've already touched more so than others. You need to know that, in the future, this is something you'll need to properly manage with the people in your life the next time you get into a fight like this. Think how terrifying it may be for your children, Paul," she explained.

"I'm not even nine yet, Eva," I dismissed.

"It doesn't matter! Remember what I told you about your dad. Your brother was so distraught he needed to seclude himself. Your sister would not leave your side. I think she cried herself to sleep last night. Well, we all did, come to think of it. So, look, my dear friend, there are people who hurt that need to know you are okay. I'm one of them. Sam, too. Can you please do this for me?" she asked, tears falling from her eyes.

Instinctively, I wrapped my still wet and towel-covered arms around Eva. I hugged her until I felt her sadness go. I knew I'd have to do this with an entire household in one way or another.

"Thank you, Paul. I needed to feel you alive. You were so dead, twice. So, so dead," Eva said despondently.

"Well, I owe you a huge amount of 'thank you.' Eva, you and Sam taught me how to do this—you are responsible for as much of the success as I am. I cannot do this without you. I know we are connected in at least two bodies, so I'm going to guess there is a pattern, right? I mean, you and I were almost exactly the same age on Cythis and we have to be really close here, too," I suggested, releasing the now wet Eva.

"Yep. We are almost exactly the same age everywhere we exist," she said matter-of-factly.

"So… What in the world… How… I don't understand," I stammered.

"Well, Sam told me there are many people whose lives intersect for energetic reasons. I'm going to guess this is why we are aligned. It's convenient if nothing else, right?" she explained.

"I mean, sure…,"

"Paul, if you're thinking this means we need to fall deeply in love and live all of our lives together, stop. Think about what I just said for a second. There are likely tens of thousands of us that intersect in order for the energetic differences to be meaningful. Besides, I have my own 'Love' I am looking forward to finding here. That is a story for another time, my friend. Our relationship is, beyond a doubt, akin to family. This will be true everywhere we go. So, hopefully, this helps your boy brain to relax," Eva quipped.

I smiled. "I'm sorry, Eva. There is so much of this that I just don't begin to understand."

"That's what Sam and I are here for, Paul. I mean, we can help you a little in the physical sense, but we can't do what you can do—not even close.

"Here's the thing: I am starving. Can we please take this inside so I can eat?

Besides, your grandparents are here and you do not want to keep Gam waiting. God, between her and Gammy, they are the busiest, chattiest people I have ever seen," Eva said, pulling me by my wrapped towel toward the house.

I prepared myself for some big questioning and got my strategy down. This was going to require things Sam and Eva had taught me. I was ready.

****

I entered the house and took a deep breath. I heard the entirety of the collective in the kitchen first interrogate Eva, who very calmly addressed every question. When I felt I was able to enter the room and only get semi-mobbed, I proceeded.

Papa was the first person to see me. His smile could have ended poverty.

His massive hands collected me into his chest. He said nothing—this was equal parts relief and joy. I realized in an instant that that whole group likely had experienced the events of the previous forty-eight hours in some way or another.

"Well, there's my tiny one. What say you, child?" Gam pressed.

"Give him a minute, Annie. I think he just scanned every one of us in the room. What were you looking for, Paul?" Papa asked, releasing me but keeping a single hand the size of half of my body width on my shoulder.

"I just did my normal check, Papa. I want to be sure I understand," I explained in a not terribly specific way.

"What do you mean, Bug? Understand?" Dylan asked, walking toward me.

"Would I be able to explain a few things before anyone asks any questions? I don't mean to be rude, but I think I can clear up quite a few things all at once," I said, hugging my grandfather and releasing from his grip.

"I think that's reasonable, but can I eat while you do this? I'm not kidding that my stomach will begin to digest everyone in this room slowly and painfully if I get no food in my mouth real soon," Eva said, her eyes wide.

As if on cue, my mom handed Eva a plate, smiling. Eva found a place at the table and began consuming her food as though she'd not eaten in days.

"So, based on what Eva told me, you all felt or saw quite a bit of what happened the past two days. I'm sorry you had to go through it with me.. I… I had no idea anyone would experience that stuff except me.

"Here's what I can tell you: Ania and the baby died. This is what started the whole thing and why I was so dumb when I fought. But something kept me alive somehow and I was able to help rid that part of reality of horribly bad people. So, Papa G and Larry—you helped me so, so much. That whole 'overlap' thing helped a lot! In fact, all of your advice helped me. Thank you!

"Now, about Ania and the baby… Here's what I know: both are going to see me again, somehow. I'm in the dark as to how this happens, or when for that matter, but she just said that when the time was right, I'd see her again. Yes, I was flung into the sky a few minutes ago and talked to her, and no, I have no idea how any of that is possible at all. Grandmas, does that answer your questions?" I asked and looked at my grandmothers, who were holding onto one another.

"I think that does it for me. Sadie?" Gam said.

Gammy nodded.

"Okay. Daddy, I need you to know a couple things, okay?" I asked, walking toward my father, who was holding himself up on the counter. He didn't look so good, if I'm being honest.

"First thing, you should have never had to feel what you did last night. I am so sorry, Daddy. Second, your neck was really messy. I moved a couple vertebrae back into place and checked your heart. Please be careful, okay?"

He stepped toward me, knelt down and hugged me. He was crying.

I could feel his sadness. I could also feel a sense of helplessness. So, I squeezed him tightly and thought, *"No more sadness, Daddy. I'm right here."*

His *vox corporis* responded, *"This is helping, Paul. He just doesn't know how to fix you. He wants to, but can't figure this out. Time on the dock today will help. Okay?"*

"I promise," I thought.

"I'll be careful, Paul. I had no idea my neck was bad, but I feel a difference. Thank you, son," he replied.

I smiled and walked over to my mother, who was at the stove.

"Mommy, you shouldn't have had to know I was doing what I was doing. I don't want you to ever feel like I am a monster even though I kinda am," I said, wrapping my arms around my mother's waist.

"Having you here is helping more than anything, Paul. She wants to know about the planets but not here. Make time for her today, okay?" Mom's *vox corporis* requested.

"Absolutely—I will do that today," I thought.

"I will never feel like you are anything more than my son, Paul. I'm just glad you are safe. I made you yummy bacon. Will you eat?" she asked.

"In one minute, I will. I am starving! I need to talk to Dylan, Eva's parents and Larry first. Okay?"

She smiled and nodded.

I turned my attention to Dylan, who was feverishly studying me as I walked toward her.

"What is it, Fink?" I asked, needing her to ask the question I heard in her mind.

"Bug, I just can't imagine you doing this crazy stuff even though I saw you do it. I can't get this question out of my mind, but I don't want to upset anyone—especially you," she said, obviously searching for the right words to say.

"You know I already heard the question, right?" I asked, every bit the shit-starting little brother I was.

"Yeah, I figured that. So here goes… If you can protect a planet, how come you couldn't save your wife?"

The room all around us lit up in a bright, but warm, light. "He saved me in the most important way, Dylan. Paul, you should answer the door," Ania's voice said and then the light dimmed.

The whole room, including me and Eva, were stunned.

As the dutiful spouse should, I headed for the front door.

When I reached for the handle, a faint chuckle was audible outside.

I opened the door and was immediately swept into the arms of a twenty-something man.

"Sam?" I asked, trying to steady myself to see his eyes.

"You did it, my boy. YOU DID IT!" he yelled without confirming or denying his identity.

"Oh my God… It is you. Sam… How?" Eva asked, still clutching her plate.

"Before this gets weird, I need to meet your family. Your dad and grandpas both could put me in the hospital. Yes, Paul—it's me," he said and put me down.

"Come in. I'm just telling everybody about…"

"I know, Paul. I need to tell everyone something before you continue," he said, interrupting me.

By the time he finished his sentence, the stunned collective began taking in this stranger.

"My goodness… Sam? Is that you?" Papa asked.

"It is, Olaf. It's wonderful to see you in the flesh, finally. Listen, everyone: my name is Sam. I am part of this puzzle with these two astounding children. I come bearing news, so if I may, let me tell you some things all of you must be aware of.

"Paul's actions yesterday had an effect on this Universe, though it's subtle. The implication I am here to talk about is in regard to what you just experienced.

Indeed, that was Paul's wife on Cythis, Ania. Well, to be perfectly clear, that was her essence but not Ania, the person. Hopefully, you understand what I'm saying.

"The implication this group—Eva, you and your folks included—has to be aware of is that wherever the kids are, parts of this wider, more expansive reality will surface. This is why you just experienced what you did. All of you should know that the girl in your dream last night was Ania. Now, the good thing is that the bad stuff—like the folks on Cythis that terrorized an entire solar system—cannot come here. But you are likely to have parts of your world get a little weird, but good weird.

"Now, I cannot understate the importance of what Paul accomplished. I know the lot of this group, me included, watched helplessly as this brave soul fought, got hurt, fought more, got more hurt and came back home. In no way was this the last time Paul will face danger, but he will have a reprieve for a while. The job Eva and I have is to ensure he remains as supported as possible in every situation. The thing we will not do is interfere in your life here. Eva's presence over the past couple days was to help, and I believe from the bottom of my heart she has. Thank you, my dear!

"But I have a big, big request and subsequent demand that is coming from a truly special place. Despite the good weirdness—please, please, please, please, please—do not allow life to be constrained. It's going to be too easy to crawl inside a shell and stay inside your own little world. The thing is, this planet has become a bit more aware. As she pays more attention, she will have both questions and responses to things she's ignored. Kids, you need to spend a bunch of time listening, okay? Between the three of us—and Olaf, if you're willing—we can and should help.

"Now, does anyone here have any questions?" Sam said, surveying the room of stunned souls.

"You're telling me that my tiny Paul did all this stuff and now our planet is waking up? Seriously?" Gam said sarcastically.

"Gam, would you close your eyes for me?" I asked, taking her hands in mine.

"If I must, child," she protested and closed her eyes.

I thought I might be able to help her understand this if she could feel Earth the way I could. So, I focused on all of the energy around us and pushed it slowly toward my grandma's heart.

"Gam, do you feel that?" I thought.

"She does, Paul. She is starting to understand; keep it up!" Gam's *vox corporis* said.

I pushed a bit more of Earth's energy into her heart and her head and she started to cry.

"It's so beautiful, Paulie. I had no idea! Thank you, tiny one," she said and hugged me tightly.

"See? She's more awake. The more we help her, the more our world and everything around us will improve. It's no different than a body with a bad ticker. Fix the heart and every other organ improves. This is no different, but the improvements will eventually affect human life for the better," Sam explained.

"So, I'm going to guess that Paul's son is in some way going to stay in his life, right? I think I had a conversation with the boy last night. It was simply unreal," Papa G said happily.

"I think so, Papa G. That's what Ania just said, but I'm not sure if he is tied to me just on Cythis or if he's tied to me here, too," I said, attempting to explain my understanding.

"Well, that is one thing I know about, but will not spoil what promises to be one of the most special events of any of your lives," Sam misdirected.

"Fair enough, but I need to make sure I understand something, if that's okay. First, Paulie, tell me *how* the strategy worked—the strategy Larry and I came up with," Papa G said, his eyes really bright.

"Well, you were both right about everything you said. I needed help, and I certainly got it. The rest of it worked because you taught me to look for places the troops could merge. I used that to my advantage, and I also murdered the dictator guy on TV.

"But I was super, super dumb when I attacked the ships—like, toddler stupid. Those awful guns… Look, I know you all felt what they did to me, and I am so, so sorry. Sam, maybe you can answer a question I have: what kept pulling me into the space hospital thing? I certainly didn't go there under my own power," I said, taking a bite of my yummy bacon.

"Paul, tell me what you just experienced with your wife," Sam said, holding a cup of coffee like it was liquid gold.

"Well, the same space arm grabbed me, took me to Cythis and then tossed me to that… place," I attempted to explain.

"Okay, and this space arm—it took you to the healing place when you needed it, involuntarily, right?" Sam said in his teaching cadence.

"Still the professor, even here, huh?" Eva said, though she was still eating as though life itself was leaving her.

"I love you even more for doing this, Sam. I know Akamu feels the same. Thank you," Papa glowed.

"Yes, Sam. So, are you saying that somehow I'm controlling this thing?" I reasoned.

"Paul, what have we talked about more than anything else? What was the first thing we talked about and the thing that enables you to do everything you do?" Sam asked, taking a sip of coffee.

"I get that it's energy, Sam. But, energy in the way I understand needs to be manipulated by something," I said, confused.

"Mom, would you care to interject here?" Sam said suggestively.

"Well, when I knew you needed help, I asked for help, Paul. I didn't think…," Mom said, furrowing her brow.

"Dylan, what was your experience last night?" Sam asked, walking toward my sister.

"I cried a lot. When Paul got hurt, I hugged his body here and told him I would never let him go. Ever," she explained, tears falling down her cheeks.

"Quarterback Dad? How about you?"

"I kept wanting to protect you, Paul. I didn't think I was doing anything, though," Dad replied.

"Larry?" Sam said, continuing the inquisition.

"I have to be honest, Paul. I about lost my mind when those guns hit you. You were destroyed, boy. I hated it, and seriously just wanted it to end," Larry said angrily.

"Okay. So, Paul, take everything you just heard and take a stab at what manipulated that energy," Sam said, smiling.

"It was the combined intention of my family? Is that right?" I guessed.

"Eva?" Sam pressed.

"Well, sort of, Paul. Yes, your family had a hand in this—especially in you coming home. That was all due to Dylan last night. The hand thing was controlled by your family and every engaged soul on Cythis, Pai and Loht who knew you were somehow protecting them. The chorus of gorgeous thoughts from Cythis was unlike anything I have ever heard. The sum total of all of this energy, all of this intention, was instruction to forces in the Universe that summarily agreed. So, while fighting, the hand was controlled by hope.

"But the hand that just grabbed you was controlled by gratitude and love. The former was sourced from Cythis, Pai and Loht. The latter was encouraged by your wife, but sourced from the place you visited with her. That place was broken, Paul. It was unbelievable when it came to life again.

"You have to understand—well, not just you, Paul, but all of you, too—the love in your heart will do more than you ever could possibly expect it to. Your love as a family goes so much deeper than you realize. This is as important to understand now as it is to understand as you all age. Paul will have parts of a life that are really normal. He will also have parts of his life that are really not. Know in your heart, and know in your mind, that you will never *not* be connected to all of it, and in a sense, will be able to influence it," Eva explained.

"I couldn't have said it better myself. Beautiful words, my dear," Sam beamed.

"Your mind is vast, my child. I am grateful," Hansh said, and hugged Eva tightly.

"I think I understand," I said.

I then made my way through everyone in the room, hugging them until I knew they were okay. Well, I hugged Larry and then made him produce what one may construe as the flatulence of the Gods. The epicness of it all reduced me and everyone else to tears.

I had to; it was beautiful.

By the end of that meal, I had fixed all of the mental angst that had collected during my fight with The Faction. I also fixed my dad's neck and ticker, and little things on everyone else, too. By the end of the day, I had honored every request the *vox corpora* had made. My conversations ran the gamut from fighting to Ania to Earth to the Copahee and everything in between.

I learned that day the horrifying detail that my family and connected lives would know and react to times of stress. This is honestly something that I have tried to mitigate for the entirety of my life, unsuccessfully.

Maintenance

For the next five years, I settled into a pattern with the Pai/Cythis/Loht solar system of checks and balances. If you're keeping score, that put me at fourteen by the end of this chapter, give or take a year.

On Pai, as an example, I spent time with my avian friend and made absolutely sure the sanctity of Pai remained as the planet needed. The population there was tiny; life throughout Pai balanced itself with the planet taking the lead and rewarding its inhabitants with extraordinarily long, healthy lives. Bear in mind, I wasn't murdering people or doing anything resembling evil. Everything I did there simply supported Pai by being Nyd. There was nothing at all hard about this; Pai is still the most beautiful rocky place I have ever seen.

On Cythis, my life as Vik took something of a radical turn. After all the murderous craziness, I accepted a fairly big role in helping the whole population of Cythians to move on beyond The Faction. See, even though there was agreement The Faction's way of governing life was wrong, there was anything but when it came to what should be in place as the ultimate type of governance.

With Eva and a myriad of others from all over the planet, we formed a means of unifying the population. Think of it as a central government (albeit tiny; there were eighteen of us) that established the rule of the (whole) land. There was representation from every pocket of population on Cythis, even though our government is as minimally staffed as it is. By the end of two years of debate, the rule of the land for Cythis was aligned and fully in place. I worked tirelessly to fix the planet's energy; this was as important as getting the population aligned.

As you can imagine, The Faction had taken a huge toll on the natural environment on Cythis. All of the weaponry and cement structures had robbed the natural order in ways that surprised even me. It was almost as though the planet was in shock at first—the energy around the planet was weak. This caused a rather notable die-off of plant life and some radically awful storms until I was able to get things stable. I was seen repairing a patch of the sky one night when I heard several *vox corpora* of people on the ground.

"Be careful, Vik! We know the work is important, but please be careful," I heard one woman say.

Recognizing this, I returned to the surface to find a group of maybe twenty people.

"What are all of you doing out here so late?" I asked, concern apparent in my voice.

"You've been fixing Cythis, haven't you? Like for a couple years now, right?"

the woman whose voice I heard asked timidly.

"Yes… How long have you been watching me work?" I asked, shocked at the knowledge that my work had been observed for so long.

"Well, I saw you one night when I couldn't sleep. I hope you don't mind, I mentioned this to the others," she said nervously.

"I don't mind at all! How would you like to help me?" I asked, addressing the whole group.

"How in the world can we help? You're doing unbelievable work for us. We've seen the difference, Vik," one man said.

"Well, I have had a thought that emotion might speed things along," I said, echoing a conversation I'd had with Sam the week prior. Essentially, he thought that using people's emotions would give a boost to the energy available. I figured this to be a good place to try the theory.

"So, if all of you are willing, I would like you to close your eyes and think about whatever makes you really happy as long as you can. The goal is how you feel; I want you to genuinely feel happy. Your challenge is to get as much consistent, good energy as possible for the next twenty-five minutes. Sound like a plan?" I asked.

A random, but complete round of agreement followed. One by one, they closed their eyes and I could see the energy grow to a consistent level after a minute or so. Encouraged, I grabbed it and headed for the spot I had been working on.

Long story short, I was able to fix an entire segment of the environment by combining the people's energy with all the other available nearby energy in the Universe.

After twenty-five minutes, I returned to the group.

"That was amazing, Vik! I could feel you, um, taking how I felt into the sky. That was surreal!" a man said excitedly.

"Yeah, I felt that, too. Did we help?" another man asked.

Like a proud father at his kid's baseball game, I beamed, "You absolutely helped! Believe it or not, you just helped me to fix *three times* what I had hoped to do tonight. Thank you all so much for this! I have to ask you to go to bed now, though. It's late and we all need rest. Deal?" I suggested.

"Are you sure you're done for tonight? I'd be willing to stay a little longer if everyone else is," the original woman replied.

"Yes, I think it best we let Cythis rest now, too. We did a bunch of good tonight, but we need to let Cythis adjust. It's no different than exercise—after you work on a certain part of your body for a while, you need to rest so that area of the body can heal. This is exactly the same thing, especially with how much work we did tonight," I explained.

"Well, okay. Can we do more tomorrow?" she asked hopefully.

"How about we rest and let Cythis decide that, okay?" I dismissed.

The group took turns thanking me and eventually disbursed.

The next morning, the changes were notable to anyone who chose to pay attention to their surroundings. The air felt different. The sky was clearer. There was animal chatter at a level I'd never heard before. I'd say the experiment was a rousing success! For fun, I went out to the water, near where Ania had been laid to rest, and played with aquatic critters for a while. They seemed happier.

"I cannot believe how different things feel today, Vik," the woman said later that morning. It turned out that she lived one street over from me.

"I know! Look how much good you all did last night! Thank you!" I happily replied.

This pattern evolved to have a bunch more people, consistently around one-hundred-twenty, for the remaining work I had to do on Cythis. After all the damage was fixed, Cythis functioned exactly like Pai. It was enlightening to see a planet behave like this with Cythis' population. In total, I used "the group" for three solid years. The first six months reflected the biggest perceptible changes, but the rest of the time fed the soul of the planet. Plants grew better, the air was cleaner, the planet's energy increased by thousands-fold—the differences were *profound*.

On Loht, unlike Pai, I was a ghost. The population there only knew me as Vik from when I fought the ships. So, from there, I did all of my other energetic repair in the dead of night over the vast expanse of Loht's water. More than anything, using those vast oceans allowed me to do more alone, quicker, than on the other planets. From Loht, I actually kept the suns in balance and the energy of the solar system aligned to support the entirety of it all.

It took me five years to do it, but in those five years, I cemented peace and balance in that solar system. By extension, I did the same thing in that dimension as well—in every possible aspect. Those patterns have remained intact to this day with just little nudges here or there over time. It was during this time that Sam, Eva and I truly shaped our relationship.

It was also during this time that I became comfortable that I could talk to— but very impatient that I could not see—Ania. We talked every day for at least an hour at a time. There were many conversations, however, that exceeded the five-hour mark.

The conversations were as much about the work I was doing as they were about getting to know one another. Think of it like the most ridiculous long-distance relationship ever, if you need context.

Though the conversations helped, I was definitely *still* affected by Ania's death. As much as I was instructed not to be, and understood the dynamics at play, I felt the weight of her death when things were quiet.

My family knew this and made it their charge to fix it.

One such person was my Papa G, who contributed to the effort by arousing the most ridiculous behaviors in me. It was during this five year stretch that my dad's football career enjoyed the highest highs and lowest lows.

Papa G and I went to every game, no matter where it was. In every stadium, we would focus on certain people in the crowd and I would introduce them to profound bouts of flatulence. My Lord, my grandfather would turn shades of red no human should turn. Tears streamed down his face as he tried to contain his emotions.

For his part, my dad made me promise not to ever influence his games. I kept that promise, with the exception of one game.

That year, Dad was on pace to break all kinds of records. Unfortunately, this gave him confidence to do things he shouldn't do.

It was the third quarter of that one lovely game, and we were winning by three.

"Paulie, that last one was insane. I could do this every day for the rest of my life and nevah, evah get bored," Papa G said happily, rubbing his eyes.

"It's fun, Papa G… What is Dad doing?" I asked, watching my father take a nasty hit. I knew he was getting hurt—I could see his vertebra moving.

"He's being a damn fool, Paulie. He cannot afford to get hurt," Papa G said angrily.

The next play was third and two. All Dad had to do was hand the ball off.

He didn't.

Dad took a vicious hit and fell backward over a fallen player onto the back of his head.

I saw it; I saw my father become paralyzed.

I then yelled, "NO!" and both fixed him and knocked him unconscious. He wouldn't be paralyzed, but he was done for the day.

"What did you just do, Paulie?" Papa G whispered, horrified.

"I just made sure that Dad could walk again, Papa G," I whispered, shaking mightily.

I was then smothered by my grandfather, who was crying big tears and angrily blubbering nonsensical words.

We won that game, but my father was furious at me.

"How dare you take me out of the game, Paul? What in the world were you thinking?" he yelled at me that night.

"You want to know, Dad? Let me show you," I replied and severed the connection in his spine at his neck. He fell limp, and I laid him down gently so that there was no irreparable damage.

"You're going to listen to me, and you're going to listen damn close. How do you expect me to allow this to happen to you, Dad? How do you expect me to allow this for Mom or Dylan or Larry or Papa or Gams? This is the *exact* injury you suffered. Does this feel good? Can you speak?" I pressed.

Tears fell from his eyes; he couldn't move or produce anything but a mild gurgle.

"The only thing I influenced was your health. I didn't influence the game at all. I'm going to fix you, but don't think for a second I won't reintroduce this injury permanently if you don't get your head out your ass," I said angrily. I was freshly fifteen at this point.

I fixed the damage and helped him stand.

The tears flowed from both of our idiot faces and no more words were said that night. Neither of us mentioned this to anyone. Well, my grandfather pressed and was informed as to the events of the night. He then was sworn to silence with a threat of an outright flatulence ban. He never spoke of it.

Dad was able to play the rest of that season, but changed his approach. He protected himself; his statistics stopped their meteoric rise, but that was okay. I made good on my promise and never did a single thing to influence any of his remaining games.

****

The last game of the season, Papa G took to addressing my love life.

"Paulie, we need to talk about yer lady. I know this bugs you, and you don' wanna talk about it, but we talkin'," he insisted.

"Papa G, I don't know what to say. I've been told so many times that this is a 'wait until the time is right' thing. I get it, but I'm really impatient," I said, allowing the silly emotion of the moment to reflect in my voice. Puberty was alive and well in my human self.

"Well, you talk to her every day, right?" he said suggestively.

"Yeah, we talk every day," I confirmed. "Papa G! Did you see the throw Dad just made? That thing went forty yards in a blink. God, Dad's arm is a canon!"

"Focus, boy. My son is doing 'is thang. Now, then, yer lady. Y'all talk every day and y'all still miss her. Explain this, you fool of a human being," he demanded, looking me in the eyes.

"But Papa G, Dad just...,"

"Explain, Paulie. It breaks me up you can do what you do, but you do it with that sad puppy face. Kills me, Paulie. Not good, Paulie. So, we talkin' this out," he said, emoting his best Southern Baptist preacher impression. Sounded like it, anyway.

"Look—I watched her die. It was a horrible, awful, ridiculous, life-changing thing to see. I watched her *die*. I'm literally not going to be able to let that go maybe ever. But, if I was able to just look into her eyes again, it'd help. Does that fix how y'all feel?" I asked, wiping tears from my face throughout my response.

"This is what I mean, Paulie. I know y'all saw awful thangs. I know y'all got really damn hurt, too, on account of yer angry fool ass head a' steam. Look, I'm yer Papa G. I will never stop worrying about you, kid, because I *also* saw y'all die. I felt it, I saw it, and it *broke* me. Selfishly, I got y'all back and we have had our fun ever since. But it's because I got you back that I worry 'bout y'all. It's weird, but ever since that day I've been able to feel how *y'all* feel. I cain't hear nothin' else, but I can feel when y'all's sad.

"Paulie, I want you to be able to have fun. 'Cause here's the thang: she *is* alive. Y'all's lady walks on this same Earth y'all do. Well, when y'all here, anyway. Thang is, boy, she *here*. Well, she *somewhere*, but she breathin' the same air, lookin' at the same stars, knowin' in her heart y'all doing them thangs, too. So, look—I know y'all seen her die. Y'all cain't keep this sadness, Paulie. It ain't *right*, boy," Papa said, emotionally shaking me as he spoke.

I hugged him as tightly as I could. I didn't listen to the game; I didn't say anything. I poured myself into that moment, loving my grandfather for the lesson. He made a major influence on my life—all of them.

We watched the rest of that game in complete silence. Dad broke all kinds of records that day and cemented their place in the playoffs. When they won, we exchanged an accepting nod and hugged.

Two things happened that night: Dad had a record night and a grandfather taught a grandson a prophetic lesson. It would not be the last time Papa G taught me something universal, but it was definitely the first. Perspective has never been an issue for me—not since that day. In retrospect, I struggled with it across every life I lived for *years* prior to that conversation. It was the first time I can remember something important echoing through hundreds of thousands of individuals all at once—and hitting home in the most resolute way possible.

I Done Got My Ass *Kicked*

The next five years encompassed some key things in my human life. I learned to drive, I gained the right to vote, I graduated high school and I started college. I also started talking to Akamu again.

Let's talk about the happenings, shall we?

My fifteenth year progressed through fairly normal checks and balances until Sam approached me one day on Cythis.

"Well, the past few years have been incredible, Paul. We have something of a new assignment that I need you to be ready for," he said with obvious trepidation in his voice.

"What do you mean, Sam? Is something wrong on Crata or Pliqun, or is this something different?" I asked, turning my attention away from the suns in my face. Though Cythis was part of a binary star system, the two suns were rarely in the sky at the same time. This day happened to have one such occurrence and I was soaking up every second of it.

"Paul, you're going somewhere new—and I'm truly unsure what to expect," Sam said, his voice shaking

"Okay, Sam—what is it? What is making you feel this way?" I asked, turning my full attention to my mentor.

"Paul, your next assignment is not something we're prepared for. Truthfully, I'm not sure I'm ready for it. I say what I do because you're going home tomorrow and you need to prepare your family for this.

Family, by this point, was partly defined by my twenty-four-year old brother living in Charleston with his college sweetheart to whom he had just proposed. I knew this period of relative calm had made all involved insensitive to the chaos that played out with The Faction. Given Sam's sentiment, I had some work to do to prepare everyone for what could possibly happen.

Dylan was eighteen and about thirty seconds away from graduating high school. She wasn't going to college right away as some modeling agency had scouted her social media feed and signed her to an entry level contract. She was leaving for New York in less than two weeks.

Dad was getting ready for another season of football and seemed ready. Mom had started her modest pressure on him to retire, given the injury from the end of last season. Dad's team had done well in the playoffs but lost after the second round. He ended that year sore and starting to show his age.

"Sam, can you tell me anything about this new assignment? I mean, what has you feeling this way?" I asked, allowing Sam's emotion to seep into my psyche.

"I... I wish I could. I've been asked to solely inform you and make sure you have your affairs in order. Just... Just be sure you prepare yourself for the potential of being away. As in all new places, you need to adjust when you wake up. Look, I'm sorry Paul—I cannot say... I can't say anything else," he puked at me verbally. Something was definitely bothering him and he could not say what.

I went to bed that night feeling the weight of the preparation for this new assignment. In truth, I had to just wake up in a new place and remain conspicuous. My family represented the bigger task.

So, advantageously, the next day was Saturday and I could handle all of the necessary details around communicating this new wrinkle in my assignment. I figured I'd start with my parents and then figure out the plan from there.

In truth, this did not go well at all.

At breakfast, I had my first opportunity to address this. Dad was leaving for a training session and Mom had work to do at the farm. I had right around twenty minutes to get this done.

"So, I need to tell you both something," I began.

"You failed that math exam, didn't you? God, I knew it," Dad angrily replied.

"I got an A on that, Dad. I've literally never struggled in math. You know this," I flatly retorted.

"What is it, sweetie?" Mom asked, shrugging off my father's idiocy.

"I am going away again, Mom. Sam...,"

"He told us, Paul. You're going to some hush-hush thing and will be gone for a while. Promise me you'll talk to me in my dreams, okay?" Mom said casually as she put a plate of egg scrambled goodness in front of me.

"Wait..."

"He told Papa G and Papa Waniglia, too. I have to assume the grandmothers know and your siblings know, too. Any idea what this is all about?" Mom interrupted.

"Sorry Paul. I... I couldn't let you do this alone," Sam interjected. I think he was on Cythis at the time.

"Uncool, Sir. Very, very uncool," I thought.

"I don't know what this is about, but I know that creepy Sam is all skeeved out by the whole thing. I just want you all to realize that this might not be pleasant. I don't know what you will experience. I mean, remember all the awful fights on Cythis?" I asked, hoping to stoke a tiny bit of emotion in my parents.

"You'll be fine, Paul. I mean, correct me if I'm wrong, but did you not get disemboweled and essentially have your limbs removed in that fight? We got through it okay, right?" Dad suggested.

"Don't you remember what you experienced? I mean, yes, those things happened—but you witnessed it all. I truly have no idea what is in store for this trip. I wish I did, so I could prepare you. No matter what, it seems I'm going to be gone for a while and more than anything I just want you to be okay," I said sentimentally.

"Sweetie, yes—we did go through all of those things and it wasn't too fun. It's hard for us to understand what to expect this time. Sam made it pretty clear that the experience would be a new one. I'm as curious as you are to find out what this means," Mom explained, clutching her coffee as though her life was dependent on it.

"Well, I just… I just want you to know… I love you both so much and don't like that I might not be around for a while. I mean, Dad—we needn't recall the events of last season for you to understand why I might be concerned. You weren't too bright at times. Right?" I asked, openly mocking my father's attitude.

"Paul… That's not fair," he complained.

"Isn't it?" Mom retorted.

"Babe…," Dad deferred.

"Paul has a point. You didn't protect your health, and your son, well, the healing one, won't be there to protect you. You're not a spring chicken anymore. Cortisone shots in your joints, all the physical therapy. My love, you have to see that this is a concern for all of us. Paul is right to bring it up," Mom reasoned.

"Addie, I get it. I *know* I'm older. Paul, I haven't forgotten *anything*. I promise you that I will protect myself. This might be my last year—I don't know if my arm will hold up for another two seasons. Plus, I told Dad that I'd plan on being full-time at Rick's school *real* soon. So, look, I promise you both that I will be careful this year.

"Paul, I don't mean to dismiss you. I seriously don't *ever* want you to get hurt. That horrible day was not anything I want to live through again. I… I didn't mean to be flippant before. It's hard to imagine what might hurt you, though, given that you survived what you did. Make sense?" Dad said, backpedaling.

"I'll be careful, too, Dad. I promise. I… I just have no idea what I'm walking into," I said sentimentally. I really had no idea what I was going to experience, and it was eating me alive.

Dylan walked into the room as this discussion was wrapping up. I attempted to talk to her but she said, "I know, Bug," as she casually dismissed the whole thing.

"No need to call your brother, Paul," Mom said kindly. "I talked to him this morning. Apparently, he and Blue were going to some farm market and hoped to get the 'good' eggs before the 'heathens' took them," Mom said, her voice rich with sarcasm. Blue is Larry's love, um, thing. She grew up on some chicken farm and somehow her dad played football with Papa G. She's a *very* interesting person you will meet in a few chapters.

I spent the rest of the day trying to extract information from Sam and Eva, who apparently was keen on the new plan. Neither would say a thing.

That night at dinner, I again saw the change in my parents that reflected the likely changes I was to experience the next morning in this new place. I don't know how to properly say this… They grew to be approximately four times their size. They were entirely ablaze. Yep—head to toe fire.

I sat there, unmoving, the absence of any proper headspace finding me. I didn't know if I should take this as a threat or as something else. Regardless, I saw what my parents would look like if they happened to grow to be massive and be on fire

Sam and Eva both refused to answer questions. To be fair, I didn't answer my parents' questions, either.

I went to bed that night scared. I'm not ashamed to admit it, either. Well, maybe a little.

****

As I started to gain consciousness, I felt a profound heaviness in my body. Within a couple seconds, my memories caught up with me and I started to make sense of things.

My name was Wryp, and I was thirty-eight years old. I was married; my wife Jly laid by my side. I was on the planet Xsip, which was ruled by massive, roving, menacing creatures who never slept and were eternally on fire. The population on this planet lived in abject fear every day of their lives. The average lifespan for people on this planet was around forty-four. My wife and I did not have a good relationship at all.

Before I had a single thought more, the roof was ripped off of my house and one of these massive on-fire bastions reached toward us.

Instinctively, I wrapped Jly in an energy bubble and sent her away from the conflict.

There was one massive problem, though: there was almost *no* energy for me to use. It took everything I had to just move her away from the fire thing.

"I KNOW WHO YOU ARE, HUMAN. YOU WILL NOT DEFEAT US!" The creature yelled and again tried to grab me. I went into full assault mode, first moving my incredibly distraught bride to a place less likely to be destroyed and then doing everything I could to get outside. I *had* to find energy.

Well…

I found just enough oomph to get away from the imminent danger and hide. I saw no fire things around me and figured I had at least a couple seconds to try and figure a plan.

"Sam? Eva? Can you guys hear me?" I asked, out loud, in full panic.

There was no reply. I was in a dense, yet incredibly desolate forest—nothing appeared to be alive. The trees themselves were barren—branches were devoid of leaves. The forest floor was so dry that wherever I walked, the ground crunched. I honestly could not reconcile what I was seeing, given that amid the dead trees were copious amounts ash. It was as though nature was too worn out to die.

I figured I had very little time to get my game plan together, putting everything I had learned into practice.

I kept moving. I did not have my bearings in any way; I didn't know which direction was home, nor where I had leapt in my getaway dash.

I heard the pounding feet of giants behind me. I didn't have much time.

I found a small lake and searched for signs of energy. It was tiny, but it was there. It likely was enough to create a diversion, but little else.

The giant became visible in the not-too-far distance. He had two others with him. They were yelling something undecipherable, in unison, as they charged toward me. It was impressive, if not just a tad adorable that they coordinated their death chant.

As they got within range, I moved out to the center of the small lake and slowly grabbed the energy in the water. It was so, so weak—I had not felt energy like this in any naturally occurring substance on any planet. Even sleepy Earth had more gumption in its waters. I started to put together part of what I knew had to happen: the planet had to be free. I just had no idea what was keeping this rocky thing so dormant.

The giants got to the edge of the lake and, predictably, leapt toward me. I formed the water into the pointiest spear I could and threw it at the semi-aligned fire things. It was strong enough to hurt them, and this meant I had a chance to run.

I grabbed the rest of the energy in the water and got out of there as quickly as I could.

I leapt up into the sky, hoping to find a big body of water, maybe with an island or two. While up in the air, two things happened: I found the place I wanted to go, and a fire spear not unlike my water creation drove right through my chest.

Touché..

I was grabbed by an unfamiliar interstellar hand and my burning, writhing body, was put into a healing patch. I lost consciousness.

****

When I woke up again, I was on one of the islands I had seen from the sky prior to being skewered. There was a small forest but I didn't feel that anything was alive there except the trees and other foliage around me.

I immediately became afraid that those fire giants would somehow find me and hit me with an attack before I could react. See, I knew there was something I was missing. There was a way to disable those things—a way to fight them—without imminent death seconds later.

"Sam? Eva?" I thought, hoping for a friendly voice.

No such luck. I heard only the miniscule lapping of water against the shore. Geez, even an ocean seemingly bigger than the Atlantic was weak. Weirder still, I heard no birds or birdlike things in the sky, and the familiar breath of big sea creatures was also absent. It seemed that this was a planet ruled by these fire giants, who choked life itself into absence on Xsip.

That's how it felt, anyway.

I also found that I couldn't communicate with anyone—no dream speak, no Ania speak, nothing. I was here with only the strange interstellar hand and fire giants wanting to kill me.

For you sentimental purists, yes—I was there with a wife, too. I didn't think it was one of Ania's bodies, but it was absolutely my bride. This likely brings up some questions for you, questions I will address when I am good and ready to do so. Be patient; this horrific insistence of yours is unattractive.

I digress, but will not apologize. I am confident you know why.

Somehow, these fire giants knew who I was and that I served a purpose. What the purpose was wasn't yet known to me, but it clearly was an affront to them in some way. I had to learn more, and the only way I could figure this out would be to observe them.

How in the world would I do this…? I was at a loss. I figured I'd start by getting a lay of the land I was on from the sky. It seemed I was far enough from the beasts that it represented some kind of safety.

Slowly, I moved up into the night sky. The massive ocean had but two small islands in it. I had woken up on one to the east. There was another due south from it. The closest land to the island I was on looked to be very developed. I needed to get to that other island to get its' perspective.

Carefully, I moved south from the shore to a small forest. I could feel something else lived there, but I couldn't tell what.

Unexpectedly, the sun started to rise. I wasn't going to be able to hide as easily, so I quickly moved into the small, dense forest.

What I found was—well—insane.

Everything I expected to find on the surface—or that other island—was contained in this southernmost island. There were birds, sea creatures off to the south, and small woodland critters that climbed trees. There was no sign of other people but, given that all the wildlife thought nothing of my presence, I knew they couldn't be far.

Well, indeed not. A rope wrapped itself around my ankle and thrust me off the ground. I hung there maybe five minutes or so before I heard a woman's voice behind me.

"How did you get here? How did you find this place? Did they see you?" she asked, nervous aggression in her voice.

"I don't think so. I got here without a ship of any kind. I'm not a threat to you; I will leave if I make you uncomfortable," I said as kindly as I could.

"I will let you down, but anything funny and I will turn you over to the Xsint. I won't think a second thought. Do you understand?" she demanded.

"Yes, I understand."

I was lowered to the ground and was promptly knocked unconscious.

****

I awoke sometime later with an aching head and ropes tying my arms and legs to a wooden structure. I was in the middle of a small village. There were small huts arranged in a square; I was in the middle of that square. Best I could tell, there was dense forest all around the village.

The sun rose and fell four times before I saw anyone again. The days here were short, maybe eight or ten hours at most. I wasn't hungry; it seemed this body had evolved to feed from the star as well. Aw, humanity… Why?

A woman approached me. I wasn't sure if it was my savior assailant, but I was sure to soon find out.

"How did you get here? Did you swim or something? How did you survive?" she asked. This was not the same person.

"You likely would not believe me if I were to tell you. No, I did not swim here," I replied as kindly stoic as I could.

"Why are you here?" she asked, nervously walking around me.

"I was just looking at the islands. I needed a place to hide. I'm trying…,"

"Are you Paul?!" she asked excitedly.

"Um…"

"Paul, the one the Xsint are trying to find? The Paul that is here to ruin our way of life?"

"I'm not trying to ruin anything. I just…,"

"I'm not sure how you got here, but you aren't staying here. Goodbye, Paul," she said, walking away.

With that, still tied, I was dropped down a chute and thrust into the water. I quickly shot to the surface. During my ascent, a giant sea creature took a fancy to me and tried to take a pretty big nibble out of my nimble self. I dodged just enough to have one end of the rope severed and moved quickly north to the uninhabited island.

I had just landed on the shore when one of those fire giants—the Xsint—joined me.

"THERE YOU ARE!" it yelled and threw a fireball at me.

I dodged it, and was able to rid myself of the rope. I wanted to see if I could extinguish this thing. It was my thought of the moment, anyway, knowing that its' friends weren't far behind.

So, I grabbed as much water as I could and threw it in several smaller blobs at the creature.

It had a moderate effect, wounding the individual enough for me to take a look inside its body. I had to quickly figure out how these things worked. If they had a semi-predictable human-like anatomy, they'd be easy to fight.

Thing is, it wasn't like anything I had ever seen. It was *just* fire. The whole body was nothing but flame, even the head. There was some type of consciousness organizing the whole mess, but as far as I could tell, they were just energetic beings.

So, I grabbed more water and threw it in the biggest barrage I could at the still-wobbling Xsint. His friends still hadn't shown up, but I knew they couldn't be far.

All of the blobs hit, and the creature fell down.

I grabbed still more water and got closer to it. I threw the water as hard as I could at the remaining flame. I thought maybe I could kill the thing if I put out the blaze.

The Xsint growled as it writhed in pain. I felt I had almost solved the riddle; I grabbed more water and got closer.

It threw a small fireball at me, wildly missing. I threw half of my water at it, leaving only a small portion of the face.

"I'm not sure what you've done, but I will undo it all. Goodbye," I said and dropped the rest of the water on the beast's face.

Indeed, I was left with a large patch of wet on the ground. The Xsint didn't flame up again.

Regardless, this raised a big concern. I couldn't trust that I was safe here. I wasn't trusted or wanted on the southern island. So, I figured I'd pay a visit and help them understand a couple things.

Yep, I am full idiot and, though I am not ashamed of this, it has caused a fair amount of discomfort in my lifetime.

As I neared the shore, emerging from the woods were none other than three of my dispatched friend's family. I had no sooner made this realization that I found myself skewered by three massive pillars of fire. I immediately went into shock and lost consciousness.

****

I'm not sure how long after my fire spear fun it was before I woke up, but I did so on a cement pyre in the middle of the town I'd initially woke up in. A quick survey of my surroundings told me this was not the best place to be.

There were a good hundred or so Xsint and what looked like a couple thousand people facing me. The pyre around me was black with soot and my wounds had been patched *just* enough for me not to die. I was not tied to anything, but was maybe twenty feet in the air.

"THIS HUMAN HAS COME HERE TO DESTROY OUR PLANET," one of the Xsint in the middle began. "IN NO UNCERTAIN TERMS, THIS IS A FLAGRANT AFFRONT TO EACH OF YOU."

I tried to listen to the *vox corpora* of the people in the crowd, but I found no one willing to allow me to communicate.

"AS PER OUR TRADITIONS, THIS HUMAN WILL BE TORTURED UNTIL DEATH. NO THREAT TO OUR WAY OF LIFE WILL BE TOLERATED," the Xsint professed.

Given that I hadn't been grabbed by the new space hand thing and in a sense, rescued, I had to think fast. Sam and Eva had taught me well, and the experience on Cythis was a true education. I knew energy well, especially that of assailants, intention and weaponry.

There were twenty beings of fire in front of me, full of vim and vigor. I took a deep breath and used every last bit of my energy to pull the fire from the Xsint toward me. My thinking was that I could diffuse them by disassociating the focus of their bodies. I still have no idea what they were.

I pulled the fire close enough that I could really feel it and the angry panic of the Xsint. I then sent it as high into the atmosphere as I could. As soon as they vanished from sight, I collapsed and again fell unconscious.

****

I woke up some time later, still on the pyre. The woman from the southern island stood in front of me. She had some kind of a staff in her right hand. I hurt really badly and was bleeding everywhere.

"You shouldn't have done that, Paul. They were our guardians," she said and hit me across the face hard enough to knock out a couple teeth.

Again, I was faced with a choice. Let this continue or use her negativity against her. So, with what little strength I had left, I stood, forcing my way up against the pyre.

"You clearly believe that, but unfortunately, I'm going to have to show you how wrong you are. I wanted to help you to improve your lives. Now, I just want the planet to breathe again. So, whether you like it or not, we're doing this a different way now," I said and attached to her energy. I used her life to heal my fire wounds and those in my head. Yes, this was something of a no-no but, in a similar circumstance, I pulled all of the blood from assailants' bodies to stop them. In contrast, this was pretty minor; I basically stole some of her health to fix me—she was in no way going to perish.

I pulled her in close and whispered, "See, you did a very, very bad thing attacking a helpless person who is simply here to help. Now, you will be mine until I don't need you anymore. Maybe, just maybe, you'll get to see what a healthy planet is. Or, maybe not."

I choked her with my mind hard enough to scare her badly. I was going to spitefully exact the kind of revenge the raving savage in me knew best. See, I *couldn't* kill her quite yet, though I was semi-obsessed with the thought of doing so.

"I am here to help you. This is all you really need to know," I broadcast to every one of the people still around the pyre. I couldn't emote quite like the Xsint, but I could do the mind-talk thing even if the people didn't want to listen.

I took my now *extremely* weak captive back to that southern island. I didn't know where she belonged, so I put her down in the middle of the village where I'd last been.

"It's a shame we arrived in this place of malice and chaos. If you cross me as you have in the past, I will show you no mercy, nor patience. I will torture you in ways you cannot fathom before your eyes shut for the last time," I said coldly and walked back to the shore.

I had to find a place I could go and really be alone. I had no idea if the Xsint were all gone or if, somehow, they'd re-form in the upper atmosphere. I didn't really have time to think about it, though.

Using the energy from that much-more-alive southern sea, I headed south toward what I hoped was a pole with a land mass. It was doubtful civilization would be there.

During my journey, it hit me hard that I had been cut off from my family, Sam, Eva and Ania. I wasn't sure if time behaved as it did on Earth or even in Pai's solar system. There were *seconds* separating Pai from Earth time. I couldn't be sure the same was true here; given the short days, time *could* be moving faster. I had a legitimate fear that I would get home and be an old man, having missed the chance to experience early adulthood, marriage, children and the like.

I arrived at what I thought was the bottom of the planet in just over two hours. Indeed, there was a land mass where I expected, and it seemed to be uninhabited. I decided to take a cautious look and see if this is where I could do some thinking and exploring without interference.

The land was full of rolling hills, trees and foliage. It reminded me a bit of the floor of the valley on Pai. Nature had survived here—this had to be a clue for what happened in the North. I scoured the area as best I could from the sky, and when I was sure no fire spears were headed my way, I headed down to the ground.

To my surprise, I found a small house not far from the shore, hidden by trees. I think this is why I didn't see it in my initial survey. I readied myself for anything, and carefully approached the front door.

"I won't hurt you if you agree the same for me," a woman's voice said.

"I have no intention of hurting you, I promise. Can we please just have a conversation?" I replied.

"I don't see why not. Please, come around back."

I did as I was told with extreme trepidation. The voice of the woman seemed to indicate she was older but by no means elderly.

I found her sitting in a rocking chair on a wooden deck that reminded me of home.

"Don't be afraid, Paul. I have been waiting for you to arrive for over one-hundred years. Please, join me. You have questions; I have answers and several big requests," she said with a kind but firm conviction.

"How do you know my name? How did you know I would be here?" I instinctively asked, taking a seat next to my host.

"I am similar to Sam. In fact, I have been communicating with him throughout your stay here. He was proud of you, but wanted me to remind you that harming innocent people with your mind is not acceptable," she began. "Look, I know you were put into a terrible place and you did what you had to do. You need to be careful, okay? You have one shot at this."

"Is Sam… Eva…?" I said as tears flowed down my face.

The woman put her hand on my back. "You have been through a heck of a lot in the past couple days. How about we just get acquainted and go from there, okay? My name is Xase; I am two-hundred twenty-four years of age. I have outlived most people on this planet by almost six times. I have tried, unsuccessfully, to heal this place, though these southern passages and islands have been able to be cultivated. The rest of the planet is in a sense, dormant. Those Xsint came here, initially, as hired hands and then unleashed terror on generations of people.

"I think they somehow damaged the atmosphere in the north—I could never get close enough to see. It never rains and there is rarely any deviation in seasons. There is muted sunshine and dry air that moves from very cold to very hot through most days. People here are unhealthy, with much lower than normal life expectancies. Nature has been completely stifled for a long time. They have pilfered all the freshwater lakes for drinking water. They used the same sources to water trees and foliage that subsequently die every couple of years. Because of this, they have desalinating equipment on the western shore that supplies all the water for the planet. You can imagine the quality of life the folks here have.

"I came here on assignment, as you have, but have not been strong enough to succeed. It is your show now; I am here to help guide you, but I'm afraid I will be of no use to you otherwise," she explained.

"Do you know if there are more Xsint anywhere? I have to have really poked the bear this time," I said, apprehension apparent in my question.

"No, dear boy. You had the entire squad gathered to kill you. They came damn close, too, you fool. What were you thinking?" she asked, her tone much more aggressive. "I mean, seriously, you opened yourself up to all of it."

"I know. I have only had one other big fight and I died a couple times in the midst of it. This was not my most shining moment. I have to ask: what were the Xsint? I scanned the one I killed for signs of anything inside and it was just energy. Did I miss something?" I asked, getting more comfortable with my host.

"The Xsint were energetic beings—I'm not sure where they came from, but I think context might help you understand. That lady who tried to kill you twice—that's Xash. She is something of a politician; she convinced most of the population that the Xsint were protectors, and their practices were justified as a result. That pyre you were on was used to burn people to death weekly for meager things like 'disturbing the peace' by coughing or sneezing. Or, my personal favorite was 'disruption of daily life' by sleeping in too long or not working long or hard enough. Xash is a monster, plain and simple. She protected the Xsint in exchange for her and her family being left alone. In fact, though I can't confirm this, there is a good chance Xash somehow recruited them. With no Xsint, she is in some major trouble. You don't have to worry about her anymore—she has millions of people on this planet who would love to see *her* burn.

"Honestly, this is going to be one of your biggest problems. You have a population waking up from several generations of incredible oppression. The result may be worse than what the Xsint represented. So, the first thing you need to do is repair what you can and get nature fixed. If those folks in the north—almost the entire population is there—feel rain again, you may witness the most tears shed in the Universe at any one moment.

"From there, as you felt when you got here, you help Xsip feel again and the problems will be easier to solve. You have to be deliberate in how you work; the people *have* to see you work and then see positive change. You will not get them on your side if you don't," she said kindly.

"Can you…,"

"Your bride is a lovely person, Paul. She loves you and understands, even though there are things you don't know that she does. For that matter, the same is true of your family. Eva and I talk daily and she reports to all. I think she's still living with your folks. Sam is in the same city and has been working with your grandfather. Look, I would love to keep chatting, but I want you to get some work in today. Start where I left off—you'll see it as soon as you get there. Spread north from that boundary. Come back here when you're done. I have a place for you to stay where no one will disturb you. Jly is here; I think you need to talk to her, but—not before you get some work done," she said, her eyes fixed into mine. I knew Xase was scanning me just as I do everyone else. I just wasn't sure what she was looking for.

I wasn't sure how to reply. I sat there dumfounded for a good minute or so, nodded, and launched my way into the atmosphere. The energy here really had been fixed; though Xase gave me several reasons to believe her, I still didn't fully *trust* her. The one truth she said for certain was that there was a clear line between the healthy and the completely dead (energetically speaking).

Because the days were so short, I only had a narrow window to use the energy from the tiny little star that Xsip orbited. It wasn't a white dwarf per se, but it was several hundred times less luminous than the Earth's star—and hundreds of thousands of times less than either of Pai's stars. I wondered if this was part of my responsibility, but felt it could wait for the moment. It was strong and pure enough to use, which was most important.

I got a good bit of fixing done that night, enough to give life a better chance in the sea up to the boundary of the North. At minimum, the people closest to the water would start to see an immediate difference by morning.

I also got a good introduction to the energy in that solar system. Best I could tell, there were at least three other planets orbiting that star and the usual wandering stuff that drifted from galaxy to galaxy throughout their lifetimes, too. There was some kind of interference happening beyond my vision, strong enough to truly pique my interest. I realized I had a ton of work to do, and was absolutely certain I hadn't fought for the last time.

As the sun started to set, I made mental notes for my work the next day. I found a natural path of energy that had been somehow redirected that Xsip needed for balance in the atmosphere. I'd seen the same thing on Cythis; I was going to start with it in the morning. There were still so many things I needed to know, and I decided to go talk to Xase and *try* to make sense of all the madness to Jly.

When I got back to that southernmost island, I found both women standing on the shore.

"I cannot believe how much work you got done tonight, Paul. This is unbelievable! You fixed the entire sea—the difference is already astounding," Xase said excitedly.

"Yeah, I don't understand anything that happened over the past couple days, but I have never seen anything like this. I can't call you 'Paul', though—I hope that's okay," Jly said shyly. I hadn't had a moment to look at her at all when I first woke up. I wasn't too sure what I was in for.

"I saw all the progress you made, Xase. I also saw quite a bit I have questions about. Do you mind filling in some gaps after Jly and I talk?" I asked, walking toward the pair.

"Of course, Paul. Why don't you two walk along the beach? It's a pretty night. I will be awake for another couple hours. I'll probably be on the deck when you get back," Xase said kindly.

I nodded and Jly walked toward me. Using the same trick Eva had taught me, I looked at her eyes and her shy smile.

It was the first time I saw Ania's eyes in a living body since they closed for the last time on Cythis. Our time in that energetic boundary didn't count; neither of us were physically there.

I know where your brain just went, and you should be careful Smarty Pants. You think you know something, but you don't. *Man,* you disappoint me. Just as I thought we had something going… Boom! You go thinking silly things and drawing incorrect conclusions.

I digress, again *without* apology.

I'm still super disappointed, and you should know that.

Okay?

"Let me… Can I just look at you a minute?" I asked shyly. I was doing cartwheels in my head. Fireworks were sprouting rainbows in every possible dimension throughout creation.

"Don't be weird, Wryp. Am I ever going to just get my husband back?" Jly retorted, arms folded.

"I am your husband. Ask me anything," I said confidently, knowing this was a battle I was going to win.

"Okay. Where did we meet?" she asked, eyes squinted, arms still folded.

Due to the Xsint's harsh rules, marriage was a form of punishment. Marriages were arranged between people who intentionally would not connect on any level. Jly and Wryp were no different.

"We met on our wedding day, at the hall," I replied, recounting the incredibly uncomfortable meeting.

"Okay, that was an easy one," she continued, still not unfolding her arms. "What did I study in school?"

"You studied mathematics, as you had been directed to do," I said, feeling perhaps this would *not* be a battle I would win.

"Look, I know things are changing and somehow you are the one making the changes. I'm still not sure how you are alive or how you got rid of the Xsint. Thing is, I don't want you pretending we have some kind of magical relationship or something. You've never looked at me the way you just did and, to be completely honest, I want nothing to do with any of this," Jly said flatly.

"That's fair; I don't want you to be uncomfortable. If you want to know more about why things happened as they have, or why people are calling me 'Paul,' I'd be happy to address them," I said kindly.

"Leave me alone, okay? I am going back home tomorrow. I'd prefer it if you'd just stay here. The house was almost destroyed because of you, but should be repaired enough for me to go back. Don't speak to me again, okay? I don't care who you are or what you're doing," she said, and left me standing there on the beach.

This hit me pretty hard—the cartwheels and rainbows turned into flamethrowers and gasoline. My emotions were already pretty raw given both the struggle of the past few days and the disconnection from all that I knew. I sat down and let the feelings drain out of my eyeballs.

Leaking Life

I'm not sure how long it was after Jly left that I remained there alone. The sun set and darkness had enveloped me. There were no moons lighting up the night—it was pitch black all around me. The only thing helping me to know simple direction was the gentle lapping of the tide against the beach.

As the sun started to rise, I waited to see Jly's ship arrive and then leave to return to Xase's house. She was on the deck, as she had promised.

"Rough night, huh?" she asked and chuckled. "Not one soul on this planet will give you the time of day from here on out, Paul. Welcome to my world; this is the place I came to almost two-hundred years ago. It took literally one day of work for me to be banished from the population and left to find a place to hide. On the one hand, the location allowed me to leverage the absence of the Xsint due to the deal with Xash. On the other, it meant a life of solitude, stuck here with a job unfinished. My only hope of going back to my home is if you finish my work.

"As it is, I have missed most of my kids' childhoods. I know I'll get the memories back, but it doesn't change the fact that I—the 'real' me—have been stuck here, leaking life right down the drain," she said coldly.

"Hold on a second, Xase. How is it that I will find acceptance from the people if they feel rain? Best I can tell, it will take generations to change perceptions of life here. Jly straight up broke me with her words. She is my wife's essence—I haven't seen her alive since she was murdered on a planet called Cythis. I will finish the work—trust me, I will. I won't begin to remain here, completely cut off from my family, working to resolve something that will take three-plus lifetimes in *my* home to accomplish. I will work night and day to finish the job and get the hell out of here," I said, frustration filling my mind.

"I… I didn't want to discourage you, Paul. I thought maybe Jly would be different, but the conditioning is too strong. You're probably right that it will take a long time for things to change. Maybe we're both wrong—but, at the risk of being right, you should get back to work," she said sadly.

"I've given you the courtesy of not trying to read you. I know you scanned me yesterday; will you please tell me what you were looking for?" I asked, a sense of betrayal setting in.

"I think you already know the answer to that, Paul," she said coldly.

I shook my head once and shot into the sky. I figured I would figure out what I needed to figure out and get on with what the planet needed. I knew from the work yesterday where I would start—that's exactly what I did.

As on Cythis, there was this band of energy originating from the star that had somehow been redirected away from the planet. It was a unique band, one that I could tell was more planetary energy than Universe energy, if that makes sense. I saw it on Pai, Pliqun and Crata in terms of the way it was supposed to be. Ironically, all three planets were incredibly healthy with happy people.

I'd thought that this was a natural anomaly on Cythis but, because I saw it for the second time with a similar overall situation between planets, I felt I'd stumbled on a trick of someone or *something*. Simply put, the absence of this energy made a planet weaker and life on it became unstable. This was two out of two planets with this situation.

Somehow, you're wondering about Earth. Be patient; it is an enigma all its own.

It took about half of my day to repair the connection, but even when I checked it at the end of the day, all was good. I expected more positive change by the morning—I had worked the entire day.

When I got back to Xase's island, I went directly to my room in her house. She had proven herself to be another aspect of this planet I could not rely on or trust given her candor about Jly, Cythis—and the fact that she scanned me without being up front about it. So, I kept to myself. Despite how tired I was from the work that day, I slept strangely. The only way I can explain this is to tie it to what people say about extremely haunted places. Randomly, throughout the night, I was awakened by something but was paralyzed in bed. I knew something was there, but I saw nothing—no energy, nothing physical. By morning, I was not at all rested and the experience truly unsettled me.

I left at daybreak, before the sunrise and got back to work. I checked that connection I'd fixed and it was stronger than the one on Cythis. Mind you, Cythis had that band sourced from two stars—Xsip had but a small, semi-dim star. I found this to be odd, but moved on and continued working. By the end of that day, the majority of the energy in the atmosphere above the main land mass was repaired, mostly due to that main energy band. Everything else I did was in support of it. As the sun started to set, it began to rain there for the first time in almost four-hundred years.

The emotion I felt from the people below was as Xase had predicted. Normally, this would have warmed my heart. Instead, I noticed it, dismissed it, and went back to my room.

By the end of that week, I had repaired enough damage for the planet to begin to really function again. By no means was the work done—but for the first time, I felt the warmth of a grateful planet as I closed my eyes to sleep.

****

"Paul, could we please talk?" Xase asked as I made my way toward the door.

"I don't believe there is anything to talk about, Xase. If you'll excuse me..."

"I was unfair to you. I did not tell you the truth. I feel terrible about this, considering that I was to support you. You've done so much I could not accomplish. You should feel…"

"I need no one's support but my family. They aren't here. Again, if you will excuse me, I have work to do," I replied, ending the dueling cut-off challenge.

As I made my way into the atmosphere above the northern land mass, I started to hear the voices of the people. They were grateful; they knew I was truly there to help. I didn't care—I did not reply.

Instead, I focused on the next phase of my work, which was to solidify the energetic structures around Xsip and truly help the planet to fully engage. Mind you, Xsip was awake and its natural processes had started. What I knew was left to do was to bolster the natural energetic order to strengthen it. This was the same thing I had done on Cythis, albeit over several years of a day here, a couple days there and with over a hundred Cythian helpers. I neither wanted nor felt the people on Xsip would or be willing to help me.

After another three solid weeks of all-day work, I had Xsip as far as I could take it. The weather patterns normalized, air quality notably improved and the planet's natural energy defenses were again alive and fully active. I had done what I felt had to be done in the first minutes of my time there: I helped Xsip breathe again.

When I returned toward Xase's house after my last day of really intense work, I again noticed both her and Jly standing on the shore. I was so disinterested in seeing either woman that I went to the opposite end of that polar land mass, a good two-hundred miles from Xase's house. I knew I could sleep on the beach if need be and hopefully go back to Earth or Pai as I slept. I was so homesick and bitter that no matter how much good I'd done, all I wanted to do was leave.

I found a place on the beach that seemed like a good place to rest, laid back and watched the sunlight leave the sky. I could feel Xsip's spirit as I laid there—a grateful, free, healthy spirit. I drifted to sleep with those lovely planet tentacles embracing me on my sandy bed.

I woke up the next morning with both women sitting next to me. The sun wasn't up yet, but the light from the sunrise had dimly lit the horizon.

"Why are you here?" I asked, wiping the sleep from my eyes and the sand from my hair.

"I think we both have things to say, if you'll let us," Xase sadly explained.

"Is there really anything to say? Jly, you were clear in what you said. It hurt, but I respected you. Xase, I believe our last conversation should resonate in your mind as that which severed the reason for us to continue speaking. So, respectfully, I'm not sure why either of you are here," I said, standing and brushing the sand from my legs.

"Am I not allowed to try?" Jly asked, her words heavy.

"Try what, Jly? You yourself explained you did not want this. What has possibly changed in a few weeks? Do you honestly believe your life to be something that would be 'normal' with me in it?" I asked, not looking at her eyes. It hurt too much to see her. It literally broke my heart to have her standing there. I missed Ania so much.

"Paul, you have no idea what has taken place on the mainland. I think you should maybe go there today and see for yourself. I can't speak for Jly, but I think maybe you owe it to her to listen a little bit more," Xase explained.

"It *kills* me that she is standing here, knowing how she feels. It hurts me so deeply that I simply don't care what is happening up there. My charge was Xsip. I have done right by her. I don't believe I really have anything left here. Maybe once I leave and Wryp continues on in a more terrestrial existence, he'll feel differently. I…,"

"Why does it hurt so bad that I'm here?" Jly interrupted, tears running down her cheeks. It was the first nonaggressive emotion I'd seen from anyone on this planet.

"You and I have a history, a history filled with love. Maybe you haven't ever felt that with Wryp, but I have felt it with you. I'm speaking as 'Paul' here, and…,"

My soliloquy was interrupted by an awkward hug from a crying woman. I had no idea what to do with this.

"Give her a chance to explain, Paul. You need to go to the mainland. Maybe take her home by air and have a conversation there? The boat ride can be choppy in this very alive sea," Xase said smiling. "From the bottom of my heart, thank you. I am going home tomorrow and am not likely to ever come back. I have you to thank, and a mountain of apology that I doubt you will sit to hear. Please know, my friend, that I am truly sorry. Please take care of yourself and say 'Hi' to the folks back on Earth," Xase said kindly and leapt away, toward her house.

"That is so strange, how you both do that jump-fly thing," Jly said.

"It's just energy. Xsip is stronger now, and her energy makes it easier. Close your eyes," I requested, my heart beating out of my chest.

I gathered a little bit of Xsip's energy and pushed it gently into her heart. I then lifted her up with me, high enough to see the sunrise.

"Open your eyes," I said, holding us still above the vast expanse of water.

"It's… I can't believe… So, so beautiful," she said, fresh tears running down her cheeks. "I felt whatever you did in my chest—I've never felt anything like that."

"That was Xsip's energy. This really is a special planet, a beautiful home. I cannot believe how badly damaged it was. I'll take you back; just tell me where I should leave you so you aren't embarrassed," I said, still not in any way trusting this experience.

"Just take me home, Wryp. I have nothing to be embarrassed about," she said, smiling.

So, carefully but swiftly, we flew back to the mainland. I had to rely on Wryp's memories of the house to find it. The last time I was there, the roof was ripped off and I ran. As we got close to the shore, I could feel something was definitely different. Our house was maybe three miles from the southern shore, two hundred miles inland to the east.

I stayed about two-hundred feet off the ground. It was still very early in the morning, so I expected there to not be many people out and about.

As we pushed north, just past the first buildings, I saw crowds of people looking up and cheering. I found this to be strange, so I asked Jly, "Do you mind if I talk to them?"

"I think you should, Wryp," she said and smiled.

I had barely touched one foot on the ground when a whole bunch of arms wrapped themselves around us. The hug wasn't aggressive or pushy; it was grateful.

Not one word was spoken for the first minute or so. I saw a little boy just off to my right, and he broke the quiet.

"Thank you," he said politely.

The hug got a bit tighter, but no other words were spoken.

After a couple minutes, the embrace ended and I was left looking at people who really didn't know what to say. I smiled and thought, *"It's okay. Please don't be shy."*

"You should go toward your house. There are people there who want to see you," a voice behind me said.

Now look: as much as this was nice, I completely readied myself to fight.

The crowd dispersed and Jly grabbed my hand.

I was startled by this, as I was mighty ready to fight.

"Why are you so tense?" she asked as we started to walk.

"I… I don't know what people might want to see me. I'm… I'm just ready," I explained.

Jly chuckled. "Do you honestly think you are in danger, Wryp? I don't know…"

"The last time I was here, I fought. I have spent weeks in the sky. I don't know what people think or what they might want to do to me," I said, sweat pouring down my back.

"Wryp, stop. You need to understand and understand *now* that people just want to thank you. You ended life as we knew it and gave us our planet back that we didn't even realize was lost. Relax a little bit, okay?" she encouraged, tightening her grip on my hand as she spoke.

I nervously nodded, but remained in full battle preparedness mode.

As we walked north, I could see a massive crowd gathered at the pyre I'd bled all over. We weren't far from our house.

I cautiously walked toward the massive crowd, Jly holding my hand like a vice.

As we got close enough to see, most people were crying or visibly emotional.

"Why…?"

"Just listen."

"But…"

"Just *listen.*"

When we got close enough, I could see there were people standing on the pyre. There was some sort of sound system there—I heard, "Paul, please find the platform facing the pyre and get on it."

When we first entered the massive crowd, people just moved out of the way. I still could not reconcile this, even a little bit. I passed in between a couple thousand people who moved as though I had some mutant virus, obtained by touch.

We found the platform, and I got up on it. I had hundreds of thousands of sad eyes on me.

"Paul, thank you for joining us here today. We'd hoped you would come back. My name is Xoob; I was appointed to help this community rebuild with the others standing here with me. Just as you've been diligently rebuilding our world, we have been doing the same, albeit down here on solid ground. We've made notable progress.

"You see a whole bunch of sad eyes here. Obviously where I stand today is where you were gravely hurt. I believe we, as a community, pushed you away despite your promise of help from this very pyre. We have watched you tirelessly work, day in and day out, and then return to a place as far away from here as one can get.

"Please know that there is a home here for you, a community waiting for you to be a part of our rebirth. Will you please allow us to repay you for all you have done for us?" he asked, genuineness in his words.

I picked up a microphone-looking thing and said, "I will gladly be a part of this community if you will have me, but you don't *need* me to evolve this community. We all need each other.

"I just have one request of all of you. See, you know me as 'Paul' from all the threats the Xsint presented to you. Please, call me 'Wryp' from here on out, okay?" I asked and a massive roar of happiness replaced the sadness.

"I would be happy to oblige that request, Wryp. Bless you, and all you have done. After you have some time at home, could we please talk? I would like you to help us, if you are willing to do so," Xoob asked kindly.

"I'd be honored, Xoob," I said and put the microphone down.

It took almost three hours for Jly and me to get home. It was not far from that pyre—which, in retrospect—is creepy as all get out. The reason for the time delay was a multitude of group hugs. I would guess there were somewhere in the neighborhood of two to three *hundred* no-speak hugs along the way.

When we finally got home, I went straight for the shower. I was pretty ripe from the previous day and just needed to get clean.

I wasn't even a tenth through my initial rinse when a pair of arms wrapped around me from behind. I slowly turned, looked into those beautiful eyes and kissed that woman like I'd felt her die.

That shower didn't offer me much cleaning, though it did work to make our bed extremely wet.

"So, um… I need your help understanding… I've never, ever felt like this—and I have emotions I can't… I can't describe. I don't care how weird the conversation gets, or how upset you think I might be when you tell me things. The fact remains that we were intimate for the first time in our marriage and I don't feel like I can let go of you… maybe ever," Jly said, laying on top of me.

"Some of this is hypothetical, some of this is history. Let me tell you the parts I know to be true first. The reason I was called 'Paul' is because the part of me that can do the energy things, the fixing things, is named 'Paul.' This part of me is from a planet called Earth, in a different dimension than this.

"Every person lives in a multitude of bodies, but few travel between them. I am able to move between my connected lives and do work to keep harmony in the Universe. See, 'Paul' is connected to 'Wryp' as an example. You are connected to 'Ania,' who was my wife on a planet called 'Cythis,' again in another dimension.

"Ania was murdered; I haven't seen 'you' in a body since I carried Ania to her grave," I explained.

"Oh my God, Wryp. That's why it hurt you so bad to see me," Jly said, fresh tears falling onto my chest.

I wiped away what eye droplets I could and said, "I can identify people by their eyes and their smile. As soon as I saw you, I was so overjoyed I almost couldn't breathe."

She put her hand on my cheek and kissed me. "So how is it that we went from not talking in this house to me laying on your chest unwilling to move?" she asked and kissed me again.

"Well, I'm going to guess that by me fixing the energy of the planet, you were able to feel the energy of your connections. This is my hypothesis, anyway," I said.

"Hello, Paul. You are right; by what you were able to do to fix Xsip, Jly finally felt the incredible bond between you, but only began to accept it in the last day or so. For me, real Vik, this is but the start of something that will change our lives. Now, kiss this woman and make absolutely sure you will remember every inch of her body. You still have over a decade to make up and you only have about four hours to accomplish this task. Proceed, Sir," Jly's *vox corporis* said.

I'm not sure if the shock showed on my face when I heard this, but I used the next two hours to do as I was asked before I fell asleep holding my wife. I held onto her as tightly as I could, because sometime in the next few hours I would be no longer be in her arms. I wasn't sure where I was going, but it was clear I was going somewhere.

The Edge of Infinity

There are good things and there are bad things.

Right?

Do you recall something that Sam told me a while back about healing a dimension or series of dimensions? Ring a bell?

When you think about something on a dimensional scale, what enters your mind first? Do you look at something in your immediate surroundings or perhaps your hand to ascertain dimension?

I ask simply to help you have perspective. Everything in the third dimension includes everything in the observable Universe. One might posit that said observable Universe contains more than three dimensions, and again, Smarty Pants, you would be right. In fact, it furthers what I am trying to communicate in this rather jagged opening to a fresh, new chapter. Especially, a chapter with a title as deftly suave as "The Edge of Infinity." I got a unique twinkle in my eye when I came up with it— and no, Smart Ass, it was not a stroke.

For shame, for shame.

See, when I fell asleep the night prior, holding Jly tight, I was on Xsip, a planet.

When I woke up the next "morning," I was not, *ahem*, in a body—and I was most definitely not on anything rocky.

For my religious friends out there, please understand that this, too, falls under the guise of whatever deity you presently worship, talk to, or in general fear and avoid. For you atheists, it was a place of energy—and you mustn't assign meaning to it. Yes, you may weep if necessary.

The primary reason I was in this place was to learn. See, implicit in my movement from place to place are moments of action, moments of learning and moments of reflection. Yeah, I'm getting ahead a bit here, conveying a lesson learned much later in life. But—I think it will help you understand this section, so I am telling you this a smidge early.

The night sky you look up to has these regions everywhere, especially along the boundary of the Universe. If you wish to use a metaphor, it is the thickness of the glass on your fishbowl in addition to being the space unoccupied by water.

Good so far?

What you probably don't realize is that these areas have intermediary entities that are all part of the order of life. Yes, you too have a couple/few of these around. When you have nights of profoundly deep sleep, you probably helped that part of you to do *something*.

No, I will not say with what.

In this place, there were sections of both expansion and stasis. I was in a place of stasis to learn. This was all part of the bigger picture that included action.

"You did a wonderful thing on Xsip, Paul. I'm sorry we weren't able to communicate. I am so, so proud of you. I think you may have learned a little something with Jly, right?" Sam's voice said excitedly. I wasn't sure where he was or how he was communicating with me.

"Thank you, Sam. How are you talking to me right now?" I asked.

"Did you really mean to ask that question? At the present moment, you are what, Paul?" Sam pressed.

"I'm energy; good one, Sam. Thing is, I'm not sure what kind *of energy. I have no form to speak of and am operating solely on feel."*

"Well, you are on a boundary, my dear boy. You will know what to do should you need to do something. For your short time there, just do what you're doing. Feel and observe—it's wholly unlikely you will need to do anything at all," he said kindly.

"Thanks, Sam. How is everything?" I asked, curious about all the work done to that point.

"Paul, what did I just ask you to do? Did it include worrying about anything other than where you are right now?" Sam retorted.

"I'd like to address this if I may, Sam. Paul, the last time we communicated, I was cruel to you. I wish to help you and, in a sense, apologize," Akamu began. I hadn't communicated with him since after my first encounter with The Faction on Pai when I was barely out of elementary school. *"This is a place where you exist everywhere and nowhere at the same time. It is a place of flow; it is a place of careful reflection. It is most important that you focus on this reflection."*

"I didn't die, did I, Akamu? How've you been?" I asked naively. I was genuinely glad to hear his voice.

"I'm very dead, Paul. Very, very dead. You are not. You are here because you have mastered the relationship of planets to stars. It's time you understood the relationship of space to everything else. Part of your purpose involves being sensitive to this relationship and knowing when action is necessary.

"If you like, you are currently a form of dark energy. You can remain still, you can remain active, but you will be both everywhere and nowhere at all while doing whatever you're doing. The feeling you have is the energetic relationships in the dimension containing Xsip. You perceived a curious disturbance on the opposite side of Xsip's star. This disturbance was strong enough to pique your interest, but it was not something you could see. I'd like you to find this disturbance and tell me what you've found," Akamu

said, every single bit the teacher.

"Thank you, Akamu. I'll look," I respectfully replied.

I switched my focus from communication to observation. In very little time, I found a problem area and moved to it.

"I found it, Akamu. It's as though something is pinched, squeezing the energy in such a way to cause a disturbance. My hunch is to address it. Yeah?" I asked.

"I must warn you, Paul: this carries greater weight than the risk Eva mentioned when you were learning about energy bands. If you do too much too fast, you could collapse a corner of the Universe and cause galactic structures to be blown apart in the biggest bumper car session you've ever seen. Please take a moment and start from the smallest place and move incrementally backward. You work from the inside-out always. Do you understand?" he said, instituting the greatest fear I've experienced, ever.

"Paul," Sam began, *"Akamu isn't wrong, but you being nervous isn't anything we can have. Not in this plane. Here, there is to be no such human emotion as it vibrates too slowly for you to exist. So, before you begin your fix, go to the boundary and rest a minute to allow this energy to escape."*

"Thanks, Sam. I will."

I moved to the boundary and allowed my energy to normalize. It didn't hurt that I was right next to the edge of the Universe, a place of both profound calm and blurred definitions. It was the end of the physical Universe, a place which naturally makes one question what is beyond. That, like so many other things in this book, is not something I will address. In all seriousness, the relevance of your experience need not consider such a thing because you subconsciously already know what lies beyond that boundary.

I returned to the problem area and asked, *"Gentlemen, am I right that I am to address this based on feel?"*

"That is precisely correct, my dear boy. I am next to you should you need me. Gently, yet resolutely, do what you feel is right," Akamu encouraged.

The disturbance was approximately three-hundred light years across, give or take a parsec or two. "Slow" in the dark energy sense was anything but. If you consider the speed of light as measured on Earth, I was moving at about twice that speed.

"Excellent, Paul. You are doing this exactly right. Don't change a thing," Akamu said happily.

"I second, my friend. You are not going to believe the difference," Sam agreed.

When I finished the fix, I allowed myself to expand into the space. Think of it like a toe-dip in the pool to see how the water feels.

"Feels perfect to me, Sam. Agree?" Akamu asked.

"I'm not sure we could have done any better, Akamu. Can we all please return to the boundary for a moment?" Sam asked. I had no idea he was near.

"I'd be happy to. Thank you both for your help and encouragement," I gushed.

Once back at the boundary, a profound calm rushed through me. It was akin to the greatest massage ever.

"That, my dear boy, was acceptance. Please remember that we are operating as part of something much greater than ourselves here. That wonderful feeling is the best 'Thank you' you will ever experience.

"Now, please know that you can enter this plane as you deem necessary. As you journey forward, this will be a tool to use. Now, it's time you go. Pleasant journey, Paul— it was a joy to witness your work," Akamu said sentimentally.

Before I could reply, I was back in bed with Jly, who was still fast asleep in my arms. She mumbled, "Welcome back, you," from whatever state of consciousness she was in. I didn't think about this too much—I just sank into the cadence of her heartbeat against my chest.

It wasn't too much longer until the sleepy girl in my arms stirred herself awake, looked at me, and pulled herself in closer.

"What happens when you go? I mean, when the part of you that's portable goes wherever you go, what happens to Wryp?" she asked from her freshly snuggled place.

"Well, in theory, nothing. The only difference is that Wryp won't be able to use energy the way I do. I'm not sure how that works with the people's expectation—or yours for that matter—but everything else is the same. The memories, the emotion, the feelings are all just Wryp's." I explained.

"Do you promise me that the life we are starting now can… can never stop? I…," she whispered and pulled in even tighter.

"Jly, look at me, please," I needed to see what her eyes were doing.

She looked up, smiled, and kissed me. She moved from her snuggled position to laying on top of me.

"Our problems before stemmed from things beyond our control. Those things are gone. It's up to us and what we decide," I said, and gave in to the intimacy of the moment.

As in my first encounter with Ania on Cythis, she demurely started making love to me, sitting up from her place on top of me. Both of us had fallen asleep without a stitch of clothing on, so this was as much an operation based on convenience and opportunity as anything else.

Again, as in that first encounter on Cythis, I took control of the situation and made absolutely sure I heeded what Jly's *vox corporis* said the day prior. I wasn't sure what changes were in store, but making sure my wife knew that I loved her was a topic I was happy to physically reinforce.

We stayed in that bed for a good couple of hours, talking about the parts of our lives that we'd never learned. I learned about her childhood and we mutually discovered we had intersected all over the place despite growing up a good distance apart. Her grandparents lived two blocks from my parents' house, and she spent large swaths of time there. We happily tried to remember possible intersection points from a time that was far less happy.

Jly was interested in the entirety of my existence and what I had experienced. I told her everything that I could, respecting her own experiences. Just as I won't tell you some things, I withheld a couple key things simply because it was the right thing to do.

What I did share with her was the event of the night before. Well, I attempted to anyway.

"So, last night, I…," I began.

"Um, Wryp, I think you changed me last night. I mean… I have never felt such… I have never felt love in a way that I could absolutely say was love. I honestly didn't believe it was possible to feel like this—and I'm so, so scared that it is in some way temporary. Please…," she said, and tears began to fall from her eyes.

"Please tell me that it's okay for me to… fall. I never thought you would care about me, Wryp. I… I hid for so long just because I didn't feel I had a place in your life. Now, I don't know that I can let you go, whether you're Paul or Wryp or any of the other people you are. The way you look at me, the way you talk to me, the way you touch me is different."

"Jly, our life before was dominated by hatred and oppression. We *both* hid— I'm not hiding anymore. I'm also not ever going to let *you* go. This is how we should have felt from the beginning, but life itself didn't let us. Fall with me and don't, for a second, believe you'll ever stop," I replied and pulled her close to me. I needed to feel that heartbeat on my chest; in so many ways, I second guessed this whole conversation simply because of Ania's death.

"But…"

"There is no 'but' in that reply, my wife."

"But there is, my husband. You see, despite all of the amazing things developing between us, I can feel how nervous you still are. Wryp, you're practically shaking holding me. Tell me how I can fix this," she said quietly, pulling me in tighter. She wasn't wrong.

"Just… I…," I stammered and let the tears I had held captive inside find freedom.

"Look—you may be able to do crazy things I still cannot truly understand, but hear me when I say this, okay? I am very much alive, Paul; I am in your arms. I promised you, right? Not only am I here—I *may* just be elsewhere, too. Therefore, these tears need to stop, husband. I need a kiss, and I need it now."

That kiss is one that I will never forget. Not just because of the message proceeding it, but because of the years of hurt that Jly mitigated in a couple sentences. Just as in the way Ania had firmly commanded my understanding of romantic love, Jly provided a kind of support I'd never experienced. She took the notion of what I was, accepted it and made it hers to keep.

I did not question Jly's statement about being "elsewhere." I knew enough to know the significance of her words. They came out of her mouth, but their source was something far bigger than either of us. In this single conversation, I learned more about existence than at any other point in my life.

As the day wore on, I could feel the heaviness of Earth begin to press on my chest. Out of sheer protectionism, I committed every millimeter of Jly's face to memory. I wasn't sure how much more work there was to do on Xsip, nor how often I'd be back.

I fell asleep holding Jly tight, but by morning I would be gone.

Surprises & New Challenges

I woke up in a place with unfamiliar smells, in a bed that was not mine at home.

"Give yourself plenty of time to adjust, Paul. You are back home on Earth, but as you suspected, much time has passed. Allow your memory to catch up a bit before you open your eyes—you will feel quite disoriented if you don't," Sam said kindly. It was so nice to hear his voice again.

"Sam, did I do what I was supposed to do on Xsip?" I thought, the memory of Jly fresh in my mind.

"You did, Paul. You needn't have your heart strings in a bundle, my friend. Jly is just fine. Heed what she said, quickly."

"Morning, you. I'm going to make coffee—I have an early day today. Clinicals—so, so fun. You have a busy day, too, so don't lounge too long. Remember, Paul: we have dinner at my parents' tonight. You need to get your clothes from the laundromat on Townsend.

"You dead in there? If so, I got dibs on cutting you straight the hell open. Ain't nobody claiming this body but me," this person proclaimed, moving me from side to side.

Um.

That was a voice of a woman. My brain was in the process of downloading nearly *seven years* of life in a hurry. I had no idea who this person was. I went from a fifteen-year-old high school student to an almost twenty-two-year-old college student finishing up doctoral and masters work in college. I got that far as a high-level synopsis but didn't yet have my bedmate's name or even a pet name I could respond with.

All of a sudden, it came to me: my pet name for her was "babe."

"I ain't dead, babe. Crazy headache… I just need a minute," I finally responded, feigning sleepiness.

I still didn't have her name.

"Well, damn, because I have a scalpel handy. This headache… We talkin' migraine or just hissy fit?" she asked.

"I think more hissy fit than anything," I deflected.

"Hmph. Okay. I'm off to make the motor oil. Y'all best be up before I leave. Hear me, Paul? I know it was a rough night. We have much to discuss and you have much to show me," she said and went to another part of the domicile.

"Sam! I lost seven years? What? Who the hell is this woman in bed with me? Where the hell am I? How are my parents? My grandparents? My brother and sister? How am I going to catch up on seven years of life? How can this be part of my experience? I wasn't on Xsip for more than a couple months," I thought, losing my mind in the most uncontrolled way possible.

"Paul, the only thing I will address in this diatribe is the time aspect. You lost an average of three years per month you spent on Xsip, or thirty-six and a half Earth days for every Xsip day. You were there for two months and ten days, which matches to almost exactly seven years, give or take a week or two. You have a busy day today and much to adjust to. First things first: do the human things, kiss the girl goodbye and get ready for your day. To speed the recovery of memories and overall life recognition, get to nature and let Earth help you. You did some incredible things for her, and she's more than willing to help. You have just enough time. So, get your old ass out of bed, brush your teeth and get on with it," Sam pontificated.

"Sure will, Teach. Where the hell is the bathroom? I've not the first clue where I am."

"Walk straight and it'll be on your right. Only door you come to."

"Much obliged."

I slowly opened my eyes and took in the bedroom. It wasn't small or large, but consistent with an apartment. My memory wasn't helping at all; I didn't recognize anything I looked at.

I did the abhorrent human things of going to the bathroom and brushing my teeth and nervously went to find the scalpel-wielding woman I slept next to.

I turned a corner and headed down a curiously long hallway. There were pictures on the wall I paid no attention to.

I seemed to walk down that corridor for much too long. I was exceedingly nervous about the entirety of my being. I had no idea what this woman knew or didn't—and it played on my human mind like a clown with blood-covered teeth asking me if I wanted ice cream.

I finally got to an opening. One direction was a living room with a TV. There was a fish tank in the corner and a black cat asleep on a chair.

The other direction was the kitchen, where I saw the back of my bedmate for the first time. She was tall and thin, with long, straight blonde hair.

"I have both coffee and your notes. I have little time, but know you need some help. Paul, close your eyes for me, okay?" she said kindly. "When I say so, open the peepers. We good?"

"Yep… I don't…"

"Do as I say. No questions."

I closed my eyes and kept my mouth shut.

"Hello, Paul. There is nothing to be nervous about, but you have loads to remember. Just take your time and do what Sam suggested. There is a pond out back. Go there with your coffee. You have time," my mystery woman's *vox corporis* said comfortingly.

I felt hands gently applying pressure around my waist.

"Okay. Peepers open, please."

I did as I was instructed and looked into the smiling face of the mystery woman.

"I understand this is an eyes/smile thing, right?" she asked, still smiling.

"It's…" I said and tears fell down my cheeks in unison.

"My name is Helena, Paul… Um, why are you crying?" she asked.

"You look *just* like someone I used to know," I whispered. Helena looked *exactly* like Ania, though taller with different hair. Ania's hair was shoulder-length and brown.

"Kiss me, please—I have to go. We have much to talk about. Remember: notes with coffee, laundromat. The rest will be later," she said.

I kissed her, seemingly for the first time. I then angrily wiped my eyes.

"Eva told me it'd be this way, and I didn't, in any way, believe her. I cannot believe this," she said.

"Wait… You know Eva?" I asked, my friend now dominating my thoughts.

"I have to go, Paul. Best of luck on your finals. Please wish me luck—last day. We are done after today, boy. You, me, booze of your choice later. I'll fill in whatever gaps remain. Is it seriously seven years?" she asked, gathering random things.

"Yep. I've never had a gap like this," I said despondingly.

"Well, saddle up, bucko. Y'all have two finals today, big ones. I am with you in spirit," she said and whisked out the door.

I went to find my coffee and this note that Helena mentioned, and found a ten-page compendium. High-level, this is what I learned:

- I was in the final year of a double-major in astrophysics and psychology at the University of South Carolina;

- I had a final in astrophysics that would result in a Master's degree and a verbal/written final in psychology that would result in both a Doctoral degree and a certification to be a practicing psychologist in South Carolina;

- There was a ton of family news;

- Eva and Sam had informed everyone about every single happening on Xsip;

- My mother missed me, and my father wanted to make sure I was clear on his career;

- Dylan was abroad. Larry and Blue had twins—the first girl liked me, the second did not;

- There were things I needed to be told about grandparents;

- I needed to go to the pond with coffee to try to remember things.

I tried to contain myself due to the enormity of the information I had to acquire. First things first: I needed to get myself whole for these finals. The family stuff promised to be a ride. Hell, the Helena stuff promised to be mind-blowing.

I grabbed the notes and cup of joe and wandered to this pond I had heard and read about.

I found a bench on one side of the pond not far from our building. I was still reeling quite a bit and paid little attention to anything but the task ahead of me: sit at the pond and remember.

It was a beautiful morning. I found myself completely enamored with this, and herein began a very strange few minutes.

In a rapid-fire series of images, I saw the entirety of my scholastic life play out as a reflection in the pond. I had finished high school with more than half of my psychology bachelor's degree complete. I accelerated my way through it and finished up my bachelor's degree and most of the astrophysics degree at the University of Charleston. It was close to home for me as a high school student.

I moved to South Carolina University on the urging of one of my professors, Dr. Upton, who wanted to remain in my educational life and was moving there from the University of Charleston. He had become my mentor.

The astrophysics aspect was a bit nuttier as I'd been pursued by several schools nationally to pursue my studies, but I chose to keep things simple and unify to a single place to finish out my schooling.

As soon as I had the synopsis of the happenings, I was given a mind-numbing amount of information about both topics over no more than two minutes. It was so intense that I dropped my coffee mug in the act of passing out.

I was awakened by someone patting me on the back.

I coughed my way back to consciousness and saw the broken mug on the ground.

"Dammit," I uttered and reached down to pick up the mug.

"Ah, ah, Paul. Not so fast. I was told you needed help and it's clear you do. Are you okay?" my human alarm clock asked.

I turned to look at said human, but the sun was in my eyes.

"Who are you? I'm sorry; I can't see," I said, wiping my eyes.

"Hold on—I'll come around and sit. We should talk," he said. I did not recognize his voice. As he moved to the bench and picked up my mug shards, his identity was revealed.

My mom had one brother, my Uncle Lou. I hadn't seen him in a few years as he had spent time out of the country. He was a farming genius—he helped farmers around the world as a part of an outreach program.

"I haven't seen you in a while, Paul. You have accomplished so much in so little time. I hope I didn't startle you," he said. "Your mom told me that you'd need some help today. How can I be of assistance?"

"I'm not sure where to start, Uncle Lou. I...,"

"Son, I know today was to be intense for you. Seven years is a *hell* of a long time to recoup. If I could be so bold, might I recommend you focus on the scholastic stuff first and the rest afterward? I was given quiz notes to issue. If you're ready... Yeah, you're ready," he said confidently.

I'll spare you the details of the quiz as the only people that would be enthralled by such a thing are brain squeezers and people who study things in the dark. You are all officially on notice and have been labeled. You're welcome.

"Well Kid, I know none of this and you hit every point on this quiz. I'd say you're ready. If I feed the cat, could you shower and then we go grab breakfast? I'll get you to school; Helena is bringing you home. Is this a plan, my dear nephew?" he asked politely. Lou was such a smoosh of my grandparents. He had my grandpa's sensitive candor and my grandma's looks.

"I'd appreciate that, Uncle Lou. Out of curiosity, do you know which building is mine? I stumbled out here and paid not one lick of attention to my surroundings," I admitted.

He laughed mighty hard, slapped my shoulder and said, "Up, boy. I'm hungry."

I found my clothes and took a shower. When I emerged from the long hallway, Uncle Lou was studying the fish tank with the cat sound asleep on his lap.

"You look scholarly, kid. Let's get some eats," he said, transferring the cat to his perch.

He drove me to a diner that looked to be close to school. I had zero context where I was.

We ordered and he talked at length about the farm and all the work he'd done abroad. His wife's family had come to South Carolina from Mexico with the help of my great-grandfather. My grandpa had continued the relationship and that led to my uncle marrying one of the most entertaining individuals I had ever met. My Aunt Julia was one of the most vivacious people, always smiling and kidding with anyone in her purview. She and my Uncle Lou have three children, my cousins Vick, Gabriella and Nicolas. Each are more than ten years younger than me—you will hear more about them later on.

"Uncle Lou, I know I'm not supposed to ask any questions, but could you entertain just one?" I asked hopefully. My memories had halted. The school stuff was it.

"I have strict guidance, boy. I'll entertain the question but may not choose to answer. I hope you understand this," he replied.

"How was this seven-year thing communicated? I mean, it's pure insanity if taken at the surface and I'm not sure how any of you are okay with this," I explained.

"This is one thing I am not allowed to address, Paul. I have two more things to give you, though: a picture of both of your professors and a map so you know where you are going. I must say, this is one heck of a job to get you where you need to go," he said, pulling out an envelope.

The envelope had pictures of Dr. Upton and landmarks to look for between the two buildings I was visiting. It had a detailed map of both the interior and exterior of the buildings, replete with a photo of the surroundings for the rooms I needed to be in. Finally, there was a map with a photo labeled "PPS: Paul Pickup Spot" with a smiling, apparently waving, Helena in the photo.

"You can't tell me anything?" I asked.

"I have solely been authorized to give you both the details and content I have, Paul. There are people who love you dearly that understand this situation in all of its glory, who have prepared both you and the rest of us incredibly well. You will hear all about it, but you must focus on these tests. Get your mind right because I don't believe this will be easy," he replied.

"Come on now, boy. It's time for you to get a Master's degree for the stars."

We left the diner and drove a short distance to the first building in the photos. The Anderson Observatory was the location for my first evaluation.

The test lasted three hours and was a commingling of both essay work and telescope evaluation. My professor, Doctor Szymanski, smiled and shook my hand at the end of the test.

"PLEASE tell me you are continuing on, Paul. I want to discover more with you! My *God*, man… We found *so* much together, Paul. Please! You could have your doctorate in no time at all with the work you've already done. I will petition the university to make this happen. Please, Paul. Don't let this end," he pleaded.

I smiled. "I need to take a look at what the future holds, Dr. S. I promise you this: I will let you know, regardless of the decision I make. I have truly loved working with you; please know this implicitly." I had literally no idea why I hadn't planned on a doctorate here. More fun sorting out awaited me.

"I'll take it. Regardless, brilliant work today, Paul. Nicely done."

I had a little over an hour before my psychology test, and there was a small café on the map where I was instructed to go. It was right next to my second test building.

"They know you in here. Be kind and order 'your regular'. Jimmy will want to chat. Just be you."

There was a photo of a smiling Jimmy on the map.

So, I went in, ordered my regular and had a conversation with the smiling Jimmy while I sipped my coffee/espresso goodness.

I said my goodbyes to the café staff as the time drew closer for my time with Dr. Upton. I walked into the door in my photo and wandered, using the map, to my third location. None of the surroundings were familiar—at all.

I went into the classroom and was greeted by Dr. Upton, who was the first person on Earth not related to my love life I recognized from another planet. Do you remember Xase, the old lady on Xsip that I took over for? Dr. Upton was part of her "chain" and yes, he was male. This was the first of many examples that proved my model to be correct. He also had a few other surprises waiting for me.

The exam began with a set of written evaluations, which I finished with no problem. The second part was a verbal exam with Dr. Upton, which, though intentionally challenging, was enjoyable. The final portion of the exam was a mock diagnosis and treatment discussion.

A girl in her late teens approached the front of the room and sat opposing me. I looked at her to try and glean some clue what I was evaluating. I didn't recognize her.

After an interview lasting approximately twenty minutes, I issued both my diagnosis of Borderline Personality Disorder and my recommended treatment that included cognitive behavioral therapy, primarily.

Dr. Upton erupted in celebration. "OUTSTANDING, Paul! It is my honor to announce that you have successfully passed all phases of the exam. Your contributions in the written portion of the examination in addition to the content previously supplied as part of your thesis work are likely to become noted briefs in my next paper. Thank you, from the bottom of my heart.

"It gives me profound pleasure to say the following: Welcome, Dr. Glassburé, to the start of what promises to be a brilliant career! I look forward to celebrating with you tonight.

"Cassie, wonderful job as always. You *nailed* this one, sweetheart!"

"Thanks, Daddy! See you tonight, Paul!" Cassie said, hugged me and bounded out of the' room.

Um.

"I can see the consternation in your eyes, son. I didn't mean to confuse you," he said, putting his hand on my shoulder.

"I'm not sure what I can say or ask or...,"

"Paul, listen to me: all of us are here to help you. I am intently interested in hearing more of your story. For now, you are to pick up your laundered clothing and move to the PPS. I have strict instruction and will respect both you and all involved in sticking to it. You were positively *brilliant* today, son. I cannot say this enough. Now then: map out and proceed to the PPS," he said commandingly.

"Thank you, Dr. Upton," I said and retrieved my map.

"Soon enough, the formalities go away. Now, off you!"

That last lobbed bomb hit. This guy was likely Helena's dad. Cassie was likely Helena's sister. I knew neither of them, even a little bit.

I smiled and left the room to go find the PPS.

The map led me first to the laundromat on Townsend, where I picked up my clothes. It then had landmarks and a path right to the meeting spot, which was at an intersection of sidewalks, underneath a collection of massive trees. I stood there for no more than a couple seconds before hands wrapped around me from behind.

"You found the PPS *and* have laundered clothing. Nicely done, Dr. Glassburé. May I claim you and take you to our next spot, please?" Helena asked kindly.

"You may. How went the clinicals?" I asked and kissed her.

"Nailed 'em. Our house has two doctors! We did it, babe! We so, so did it!" she responded excitedly.

"That's incredible! I'm so proud of you!" I said excitedly.

"Any other memories come back yet? Anything familiar?" she asked, her tone moving to one laden with concern.

"No, but through the process of observation and some leaky talkie-talk, Dr. Upton is somehow related to you and Cassie is your sister, right?" I asked.

"Oh Paul... I know this is super hard for you, but I have to let your brain get itself righted as it's ready. That question literally kills me inside, but I know it's all part of it. Now then, there are people waiting. We must be off," she said. It was obvious to me that my blank mind was hard for her.

I wasn't' sure who might have been waiting for us, but I accepted what I was told among the mountain of life that I was digesting. It was early afternoon.

We drove back toward our home, or so I believed, and stopped at a restaurant. I didn't bother looking at the name; none of it was familiar to me.

"Come on, you. Maybe this will help," she said, her eyes sad.

We went in the restaurant and a huge roar enveloped us.

"Oh no...," I said under my breath.

"It'll be okay. I promise," Helena sadly encouraged.

The restaurant was full of people for us. I quickly scanned the crowd, which was several layers deep, and didn't recognize anyone. I also did not hear a single *vox corporis* at all.

"Stop the scanning process, Paul. We need to do this slowly," Sam said from somewhere. "We are here to celebrate our new doctors! Now then! People! We have two new doctors! Let's hear it!"

The crowd erupted.

A woman walked toward us and grabbed my hand. "Come on; we have a table over here," she said. I had zero idea who she was.

I helped Helena into her seat and sat down. We were at a big table, with our "people" filling up all the other tables in the restaurant.

The seat on my opposite side was quickly occupied as I got settled. Before I could turn to look, I had a sobbing woman hugging me.

"No more dead Paul, okay?" Eva asked.

"I didn't die, Eva...," I said, returning the hug.

"You were so, so, so, so dead, Paul. You couldn't hear me or Sam or anyone. I saw it all, Paul. I saw everything you did. You need to be super proud—not only for the doctor thing, but what you did for that whole corner of existence was unbelievable. Your memories are likely to come in spurts and you probably will pass out a bunch. We have help for when you do.

"It's just so good to see you again, Paul. I need you to meet someone... again. Paul, this is..."

"Dante. It's good to see you again, man," I interrupted, and extended my hand to shake his. I met Dante after his and Eva's first official date. He was likely the easiest person to recognize simply because of my and Eva's connection.

"Wait! You know Dante? What else do you know?" Eva demanded.

"Ah ah ah... No. Remember what we discussed? Slowly, people. He's going to have moments and then overwhelm. Patience," Sam said from a place behind me.

I turned to see him. He looked at me, I looked at the people at his table and fainted.

"Give him room. Paul, you in there? You fell hard, Sir," Sam said, carefully examining me. For that matter, my doctor living partner was also evaluating, with tears in the corners of her eyes.

"Wow that sucked. I'm sorry," I said, trying to gather myself.

"Drink some water, babe. Okay?" Helena asked, handing me a glass of water. Her hands were shaking.

I accepted the glass and took a drink. I then instinctively excused myself, went outside, got away from the windows or places where people might see me and launched myself into the sky. I was intercepted maybe two-thirds the way up by a Universe hand, put into an energy bubble and taken to a healing place.

I'm not at all sure how long I was there, but my mind was sorted out, at least in part, with me in a very unconscious state. When the process was done, I was returned to the back of the restaurant where Sam, Eva and Helena were waiting. At minimum, I felt I had staved off the fainting spells for the minute.

"You went where, exactly?" Helena asked, studying every inch of me.

"This pattern was good for no one, babe. I was hurting my brain badly with the information dumps. I went to a healing place in the Universe, I think just out past Venus. I hadn't been to the one in our solar system yet," I said as casually as I could.

"So, wait… The father of my baby, the husband to be mine in, like twenty-eight hours, really is this, this…,"

"He saved so many lives, Helena. Your fiancé is the same incredible man you have always known, but he has a wider purpose. He's told you about this for *years*. Now, you just saw an aspect of this for yourself. You okay?" Sam asked guardedly.

"It wasn't real until I just saw him disappear into the Heavens and then return from the sky like he was on a high-speed elevator," she said.

"It's usually not that coordinated. If there's water, I typically fall in it," I explained.

"So *that's* why we just bought the lake house. *Got* it," she said. It was apparent that the reality of this was not as easy as she'd hoped.

The "lake house" is a four-bedroom house on the northeast side of Lake Murray. It is almost exactly due North from Helena's folks' house, which Dr. Upton had mused was the *perfect* boat ride. He reasoned it had to do with the angle of the sun, relative to the movement of the water. His soliloquy on the topic was a smidge long, so that's what I remember.

Anyway, we had mutually agreed that moving out of the condo after graduation was an appropriate step in transition from the student life to the adult life. Or, perhaps more appropriately, the right thing to do as newlyweds. So, with the help of Savannah's mom, we sold the condo and bought the house. We were due to get the keys and move in the week after the wedding.

"Dr. Upton, I promise you that the person I am has not changed. What I believe you've been informed about is the truth of what I am and what my ultimate purpose is. If it sounded unbelievable, it is. The unfortunate truth is that it is real," I explained, hugging her. I'd gotten the memories back about our impending marriage and our freshly-in-belly baby while in the sky.

"Babe, I will start my career as Dr. Glassburé. Let's keep this straight, yeah? I'll be fine, you guys. On some level, I've known it but it was always theoretical. Let's get some food; I have time to ask questions before we go to dinner tonight," she said, grabbing my hand.

We spent a little over two hours in the restaurant. Most of the people there were those from our friend and colleague groups. The thing that had set me off was when I looked at the collection of Sam, John (my research partner from my astrophysics studies), his fiancé Judy and her older sister, Stephanie—who had married Sam five years prior. I had immense history with every person at that table.

The enormity of the gap between my last conscious moment on Earth before going to and returning from Xsip was profound and troubling. It wasn't entirely resolved as I had zero family memories whatsoever. I had recovered enough to make it through that meal without fainting again. This introduced a question for Eva and Sam that I didn't want to ask as I was afraid of the answer.

Before we left the restaurant, I pulled Eva and Sam aside to address this.

"Look… I think I know the answer, but this is more so I can rip the band-aid off quicker. How likely is it that I will have huge gaps like this as we move forward? I can't…"

"Paul, it's all like a puzzle. You sorted out one of the bigger pieces—one of the most distributed pieces on Xsip. If I'm being super honest, the bulk of the work you need to do over the next several years is here, in this dimension. You will certainly have touches to the Pai/Cythis/Pliqun/Crata realms, but there are angles of this reality that are in need of more than slight touches," Eva explained.

"Yep, I agree. There is by no means a way of predicting outcomes, Paul— but I think you can be comfortable here. This does not mean there will not be time gaps, but it does keep you local to help you stay in touch with Helena, the baby and everyone in your life," Sam said, smiling. "I cannot wait to see you get hitched tomorrow!"

"Thank you both! This is incredibly rough, with all of the life lived in between. I still have a way to go, but I'm closer. Thank you for keeping everyone in line; I'm not sure how you did it," I said, gathering myself to leave.

"Expect loads of questions and requests, Paul—*loads* of them," Eva said, smiling.

"Lovely. Thanks Eva," I said, and went to collect my soon-to-be bride.

"Dr. Glassburé, I'd like to retire to the home place, if you'd be so kind," I requested.

"I'd be honored to fulfill that request, Dr. Glassburé. Thank you," she playfully replied.

As soon as we got into her car, she laid into me with a wickedly passionate kiss.

"A preface," she whispered.

The car ride back home was quicker than when my uncle had driven me to school. I recognized more of the landmarks, but the street names and where they went were still mysteries.

As soon as we got in the door, Helena grabbed my hand and led me to the bedroom. Our clothes lasted maybe a minute total from the time we got in the house to the moment round one of two commenced.

When the crazy sexcapade finished, Helena laid on my chest, seemingly listening to my heart.

"It's beating differently, Paul. I know your heart better than I know my own—and it's beating differently. It's like… It's like it got stronger. I mean, the rest of you still works *just* right, but this is… something," she said, catching her breath.

"Can I look at the baby?" I asked.

"I mean… How…"

"Just keep still. If he decided to have us as parents, I might cry," I said, not realizing how crazy this might have sounded.

Regardless, just as I had done with Ania, I "moved" and looked at my tiny baby boy for the umpteenth time. I'd recognize that tiny bean anywhere.

I think my body registered my emotion, and my tears were plentiful when I "moved" back.

"Okay—what did you just do?" Helena asked, her brow furrowed with the absurdity of the moment.

"I looked at the baby. He's got a heartbeat!" I said excitedly.

"Okay… How…,"

I cut her off lifting us off the bed, flipping her over and kissing her.

"I can do things, Dr. Glassburé, things you probably heard about but never experienced. Trust me—the real me—and I will give you a life worth living again," I said, and kissed her.

"So… Okay. How are we just suspended up here? I mean, it's nice, but I don't understand this at all," she said, chuckling.

"Energy; close your eyes," I asked.

She did, and I pulled a chunk of Earth's energy into her heart. As I did, tears fell from her eyes.

"What in the world was *that?*" she asked, her eyes still closed.

"That was Earth's energy. It's all around you—I just pushed a little extra into your heart. It's good fer 'ya," I explained.

"I absolutely promise you I will not freak out, but I need to know it all. All of it, Paul. I need to know what all of this represents," she said, wrapping her arms tightly around me.

"I will tell you what I can, responsibly, okay? I can't tell you all of it, or your experience will change more than it already has. I can't do that to you, or anyone. I hope you understand," I said calmly.

"I think I get it. I will accept what you're willing to give," she said and kissed me.

I set us down on the bed but was swiftly corrected.

"Nope. Back up—I'm not done kissing you up there yet, Dr. Glassburé," she explained.

I moved us back up, above the bed, and we began to catch up seven years of make-out time.

"Promise me, Paul… Promise me that the horrible dreams I had with you getting filleted and beaten won't be things I will have to experience again. I do not want to see my husband like that ever again," she said, turning the mood a bit.

"I can't. I'm sorry, but I can't. There's a reason I have a permanent ticket to the places in the sky where I can heal. I have stamped that passport something like six times now," I explained.

"So those fire things and your blood-covered, beaten self was real?" she asked, her eyes really big.

"Yep. All real. That place is called…"

"Xsip. I heard you saying, 'Come on, Xsip… Wake up, Darlin',' as you slept. I had no idea who this 'Xsip' chick was or how damn many pieces I was cutting her body into. Seriously, Paul? That happened? How did I see it all? Why did I have to see that?" she asked, her tone turning.

"You and I are connected at a much higher level, Helena. You get the show because of this. I'm sorry you had to see that," I said, running my fingers through her hair.

"At the restaurant, Sam said something about 'scanning'. What is that?"

"I can scan and manipulate pretty much anything in the human body. The latter is only true if I have permission from a person in some way, conscious or not. I was panicked and used that to try and see if I found anyone that could help me remember. I hit Sam and he told me to stop. If Eva had felt me doing it, she wouldn't have been as kind," I explained.

"Wait, wait, wait. What kind of manipulation are we talking about here?" she asked, her doctor smock on, though invisible on her naked self.

"Pretty much anything, good or bad," I said, hoping this sufficed to stop the conversation.

"Define this, Paul. What do you mean?" she asked, her tone much more serious.

"The entirety of the human body is energetic, Helena. I can use this energy to do what I need to. I spared my father from a life in a wheelchair when he was being an asshole in a game one day. I saved his spine after a vicious hit. I knocked him unconscious to take him out of the game by forcing his brain to sleep.

"I made Larry fart epic farts in front of the whole family. For that matter, I did this in stadiums with my Papa G, too. Judge this if you wish.

"I saved my mother from a cooking fire that would have badly scarred her.

"I've done bad things, too, but I'll spare…"

"Nope. Out with it. All of it."

"Okay… I blocked an assailant's brain from going into shock as I tortured him mercilessly, using the bones from his body to impale others. He died simply from blunt force trauma to his face, though the rest of him no longer existed.

"In the same vein, I ripped all the blood out of people's bodies as a means of torture and murder. I have used a building to crush almost half of an army to death. I've sent members of the same group to die by being cooked alive as their ship collided with one of that solar system's two stars. More of the same group was buried alive after being tortured.

"I've choked people to death, I've tortured people to save others, and I've dispatched fire creatures both with water and wind, and I don't know how any of that is possible."

"What in the world caused you to do such things to those people?"

"You and our son were murdered for no reason whatsoever," I said and pulled Helena in tight to me. "I will not ever let anything harm you or our family, ever. Do you hear me? Ever."

"I'll gladly allow you to be my murderous husband, hell-bent on ensuring our family's protection, Paul. I have so many more questions, but we need to get ready and go to dinner. Can I just ask one more thing?" she asked as I set us down on the bed.

"Sure, babe."

"Who is 'Real Vik'? I have been writing 'I love my Real Vik' in my notebooks since I was, like, ten."

I smiled as widely as my mouth was capable. "So, listen, my incredible almost-wife: this is a story that shouldn't be a quick one. Let me tell you about Vik when we get home tonight."

"You are home solo tonight, genius. We hitchin' up tomorrow, so I'm sleeping at my parents' tonight. Massive sleepover with the ladies of hitchdom."

"Well, then, it'll be a story for our wedding night. Maybe that's most appropriate, anyway," I said.

"Um Darlin'… If there is time for stories on our wedding night, something is drastically wrong. Please bear this in mind, Dr. Glassburé," she said, kissed me, and walked into the bathroom.

I laid there in silence, knowing there was more to know, more to remember. I had no memories of meeting Helena, her family, my family, or lots of locations. I had no idea where Helena's parents lived, as an example, and I was likely there hundreds, if not thousands, of times.

When Helena emerged from the bathroom, I had to confide this in her.

"Babe, I need you to know something. I still have big, big gaps in my memory. The healing place is one that just gives me enough for self-preservation. In other words, that group today would have likely put me in the hospital with the amount of fainting I was going to do.

"I have zero family memories, babe. None. I may need major help tonight to not ruin relationships or our day tomorrow," I said nervously.

"Way ahead of you, boy. We have planned for this ever since we knew you'd be back, which was sometime a couple weeks ago. Everyone tonight loves you and is prepared to help you remember. My mother is especially excited about this, so saddle up, son. She is so, so ready to re-educamate y'all," she said reassuringly. "Now, sex fiend—get ready so I don't have to look at y'all's nakedness anymore."

"Yes, ma'am," I said and walked my naked self *really* close to my bride-to-be en-route to the bathroom.

"Not nice, Dr. Glassburé. Not nice at all," I heard from outside the door.

Once prepared, we set off for dinner. I'd be lying badly if I said I wasn't nervous in ways I'd never been nervous.

It took us just under an hour to get to Helena's parents' house, which was on the southeastern edge of Lake Murray.

"Any recollection of this place, Paul?" Helena asked intently.

"Not one. It is super pretty, though. That sunset is supreme," I said, taking in the stark redness of the setting sun.

"God alive, this will be a trip," she said, chuckling.

There were six other cars in the driveway. I was in Hell.

We went into the house and were immediately met by Cassie, who stopped us at the front door.

"Paul, do you remember anything about this house?" she asked intently.

"No, Cassie, I do not," I replied.

"When was the last time you saw your brother?" she asked.

"I shouldn't…"

"Answer the question, Doc," she persisted. Helena was extremely entertained at this line of questioning.

"No cheating, either, Paul. Answer from memory only," my bride enforced.

"But…"

"Memory only."

"My last memory of Larry was right after he moved into the apartment on Lafayette with Blue. He was starting to work with Mr. Toth, I think," I said honestly. Truth be told, I did not hear Cassie's *vox corporis* at all. This was concerning.

"Okay. Now your sister," Cassie pressed.

"She was in the kitchen the day before I left. We did the Bug/Fink thing and that was it," I said.

"You're doing well, Doctor. Just one more question: what was your last memory of your mother?" Cassie asked.

"It was at dinner before I left. I was fifteen," I said sentimentally.

"You can prove your absence how, exactly?" Cassie pressed.

"I can't prove anything, Cassie," I deflected.

"You can prove something, Paul. What is this something you can prove?" Cassie asked.

I did the only thing I felt one could do in this instance: I wrapped her in an energy bubble and pushed her toward the ceiling of the large foyer.

"Um, what did you just do? What is this?" Cassie asked nervously.

"Why, it's proof, Cassie. Isn't that what you asked for?" I mused.

"So, the things we heard were true then—the things about you. Is this thing going to hurt me?" Cassie asked. Helena poked at the bubble with apparent curiosity.

"I'm not sure what you heard. That bubble will withstand things that could kill you, Cassie," I explained and brought her down a bit. I then removed the bubble and gently set her on the ground.

"Should I be scared of you, Paul?" she asked. Helena seemed amused by the question.

"Do you pose a threat to me or my family?" I retorted.

"Um, I am your family," she volleyed.

"Then, no, you have nothing to worry about, unless you go rogue and do foolish things. I would have to address said foolish things. 'Capisce?' I asked, doing my worst gangster impression.

"Okay. I won't do anything. I have been asked, however, to reintroduce you to people, places, things and animals. My sister is to assist us in the event that you faint. 'Capisce?' she clarified, openly mocking me.

She grabbed my hand and pulled me into the first room that had three people in it. She then led me to a chair opposing these people. I heard not one *vox corporis* offer me guidance.

"Paul, again—these people love you and understand your memory is challenged. Please take a look at each and see what you remember," Cassie instructed, placing her right hand on my shoulder. Helena stood on my opposite side, touching my arm.

"May I…"

"You may not cheat. Memory only," Helena scolded.

I took a deep breath and looked at the first person on the far left. She looked to be my age, maybe mid-twenties at best. She was athletic, with long brown hair.

"Would you say something to me? I don't need a clue; just tell me one random thing, please," I asked this person.

"The sunset was gorgeous today," she said.

"Savannah. How are you?" I asked. I'm not sure how, but hearing her voice returned a snapshot of her to me. Savannah is Helena's best friend. She remains a pain in my ass to this day.

"Did I give it away?" she asked Helena.

"I certainly didn't think so. Middle person, Babe. Who is that?" she responded.

This was a middle-aged man, well-dressed and mildly chunky. I had no recollection of this person at all.

"Sir, would you please…"

"Pancakes. Not one damn place makes pancakes the way they are supposed to be made. Not one," he proclaimed from his soap box.

"Saul, it is wonderful to see you again. I concur on the pancake item," I replied, identifying Dr. Upton's brother, Saul.

"Paulie, I'm just so sorry your head did this to you. Unkind," he said kindly.

"Okay, Paul, final person. Who is the person on the right?" Cassie asked, her hand still on my shoulder.

"Migraine. Opal. Juniper. Chainsaw," the person said, pre-empting my question and using a tactic that worked extremely well. I had no idea who this older gentleman was based on his fragmented words.

"Um… Firstly, genius approach. Secondly, an apology: I don't know who you are," I said, embarrassed beyond belief.

"I completely destroyed you, son. I will enjoy this for the rest of the evening," he said.

"Two out of three. Your next location awaits. Come with me, please," Cassie instructed.

I did as I was asked, still horrified that I didn't know the older man on the right.

Cassie stopped me in the hallway, in front of a collection of pictures.

"Paul, take a…"

I wandered to a photo in the middle-left of the bunch, ignoring Cassie's instruction. It was a picture of Helena and I with both sets of my grandparents. It had to be fairly recent as Gam was in a wheelchair.

"When was this taken?" I asked, as sadness washed over me.

"Babe, come on," Helena said, pulling me from my enamored state.

Cassie stopped us prior to the entrance of a room. I could hear quite a few (physical) voices in it.

"Paul, this is going to be a bigger challenge, and one that might be a tad overwhelming. So, I need you to sit in this," she said and produced a high-back rolling desk chair. "Sit, please."

I did as I was asked and was slowly rolled in front of the collected bunch.

I saw Sam, Eva, Dr. Upton, Mom, Dad, Papa—and fainted.

"Paul? Can you hear me?" I heard Eva ask.

"Babe? Please," I heard Helena say. She was crying.

I started to come to, feeling wetness on my face.

I opened my eyes to see a fairly large dog with sad eyes licking my face, one lick every couple seconds. I reached up and weakly pet the pup.

"Dammit, Paul, this is becoming a concern. Cassie, I think we need to try something different. He's going to hurt himself," I heard Sam say.

"Bug? You in there?" I heard Dylan ask.

"Fink? Where are you?" I asked. I hadn't seen my sister in a *very* long time.

Appearing in my face was my beautiful sister. I was lying on a couch.

"You are killing people, Bug. I get it, but it's, like, high time you cheat your way out of this," she whispered.

"Can you help me get outside without anyone seeing?" I asked, whispering.

"With help, yes. Go along with me, okay?" she said and disappeared.

I heard discussion in the background, and then a sizable human picked me up and took me outside.

"Do I know you?" I asked.

"Yes, Paul, y'all do. And dammit if y'all ain't breaking my heart right now," he said.

"I'm sorry. Are we out of sight of the house?"

"Yes."

"Thank you for your help. I'll be back," I said and lifted myself into the twilight sky.

I wrapped myself in an energy bubble and figured I'd heal in a different way.

The Milky Way has a massive black hole in the middle of it, Sagittarius A. As a result, though each solar system within the galaxy has their unique energies, the overwhelming commander of energy flow is the supermassive black hole.

I was not looking for a healing space this time, but rather a way to enhance my brain's ability to process information quicker. Sam was right—this was not a situation going well for anyone.

So, I pushed myself up into the nearest energy band I could find whose source was that black hole and merged my energy into it. I'd never done this before, but I felt it to be my best shot to reconcile all the memories in my subconscious mind with my conscious memories quickly. The process itself was akin to adding the flame of a match to an already burning candle—same idea.

Time had become irrelevant to me. I was going to have to do some interesting things with space-time to make my rehearsal dinner into something different.

"Sam, I will need assistance when I return. Can you please prepare for a water landing in the lake?" I thought.

"I'll get on it, Paul. You okay?" he replied.

"Yes. I am returning soon. If dinner has been on hold, please ask it to recommence. I'll just need a towel and some fresh clothes. There are conversations to be had; you, Eva and I need to discern the best way forward for those at the house. I'm relatively sure we can wipe both fear and this memory should we need to," I suggested.

"You likely will not believe me, so I'll reserve my response for when I see you next."

"Is Helena okay?"

"Yes."

"We have something else to discuss, Sam."

"I know. Just get back here when you can. I'll try to have the boat ready."

When it was clear that my memory had been restored and no gaps remained, I disconnected from the band, closed my eyes and thought, *"Thank you; love always."*

Gratefulness and love are perhaps the most powerful tools in all of creation. I highly recommend you heed this and make whatever changes you feel are appropriate. You see, my statement simply reconfirmed my commitment to all that is. I was given the gift of healing, and for this I was extremely grateful.

The Recognition of Responsibility

Before we go further, I believe I need to take a moment to reveal everything that I had missed while on Xsip. Indeed, this is a step back in time—a full seven years—but let's go there, despite your penchant desire and wicked talent to complain.

The day I left for Xsip, I was fifteen, Dylan was eighteen and Larry had just turned twenty-five. I'd like to start here as it fits the chronological model best. It also happens to contain the simplest stories to tell.

Let's start with Dylan, because when Larry reads this, and is not first, it'll twist his underbritches so far up that active sphincter of his they'll pop out of his nostrils. I both love and cherish this thought.

Ten days after I left, Dylan went to New York and started her modeling career. My aunt Lizzie had been her mentor—she was a model herself, though her career had slowed way down by this point. Aunt 'Zie (as I called her) taught Fink everything about modeling. Our father and mother, in turn, beat responsibility and business acumen into her until she dreamt about it.

Her career took off over the next two years and took her all over the world for both fashion shows and photo sessions in exotic locales. One would imagine with all the sweaty sex gods she worked with that she'd end up with one of them or some celebrity.

You'd be super wrong if you thought Fink to be that person. I'll tell you why in just a second.

Larry and Blue got married in a family-only ceremony six months into my time on Xsip. Mind you, their wedding had over eighty participants with that group—Blue has eleven siblings alone. One such sibling, a groomsman in the Larry/ Blue union show, caught my sister's eye.

Hatch was the definition of a farm boy. He worked about as physically hard as anyone I'd met with a really quiet disposition. He's also the most skilled carpenter I have ever met. Where Blue was likely to be an angel descended from Heaven above who obliged being cast into physical form, Hatch was a massive, kind, quiet, strong-as-the-day-is-long kind of man.

They shared a dance when the wedding party joined bride and groom as they were matched as partners. There was a look in her eye that I'd never seen before when she looked at Hatch, even from moment one.

What transpired over the next couple months included my sister rushing to Georgia, where Hatch's family farm was, at every possible gap in her schedule she found. It wasn't uncommon for her to fly from Paris to Atlanta and drive four more hours for the chance to spend a day or two with him.

Feel free to picture a stiletto-clad, decked-out-to-the-nines woman running across a dusty field to jump into her sweaty man's arms. This still happens today, though the farm location has changed.

They were married in the greatest clash-of-two-worlds wedding ever almost four years into my tour on Xsip. On her side were us, models, athletes and a couple farmhands from our farm. On theirs, there were just salt of the earth farmers.

They have one child, a boy. Charlie, who was two very grown-up years of age when I returned from Xsip, had already begun helping his dad in the fields. He brushed mom's hair, too.

Larry became an architect. Blue became a veterinarian, one of the most sought-after animal docs in the region. They were blessed with two kids, twin girls, during this time. They were born during the third year I was gone. Josephine, the first child to enter the world found me to be agreeable and liked me to hold her as a baby. The second girl, Annabelle, had a dislike for me from jump that was unexplainable but very present and remains so to this day.

Their life is steady-as-she-goes happy.

Larry is bald. That dome reflects sunlight like a mirror—it is simply glorious.

****

That little patch of words literally sums up the lives of my siblings over *seven years*. Looking at it again, they are incredibly boring people.

I'll admit that I laughed a profoundly deep belly laugh, pointing fingers at nothing at all as I wrote that last sentence. Judge if you must, infidel.

My parents are equally boring, and their history is told simply. Mom kept running the farm with Gam. Dad played one more season of football, won the championship and retired. He took over running the Richard Carolas Glassburé School from his father, following the same pattern *his* father initiated. Papa G retired from football the year his brother Rick passed away to run the school.

Papa G stayed on with the school in an advisory role for three years before he retired.

Speaking of Papa G, he and my Gammy spent copious amounts of time fishing and doing grandparent things. I won't summarize this further as it will get redundant rather quickly.

My other set of grandparents, my mom's folks, shaped my future during this time—and I believe this was carefully choreographed at levels way, way above my pay grade.

My grandfather, Papa, ran an exceptionally successful, multi-national psychotherapy business—part of which he started with Akamu in Hawaii. When he got his certification, it did not require a ton of schooling—certainly not a doctorate degree. His success with his clientele was in part the result of his abilities. Just as I can hear the *vox corporis*, he can heal the willing using a subset of the energy practice I have used for almost my entire life. However, I cannot minimize his talent for helping those who asked for it with nothing but his exceptionally caring soul and quick wit.

My grandmother, Gam, ran the family farm with my mom and grandpa as second fiddles. This was true until two years ago.

I'm getting ahead of myself; I apologize.

Two days after I left, my grandfather asked me to help him in the orchard. The orchard was his father's, outside of Papa's childhood home. He converted the house into his office, in part to tend to that orchard. He and I never spoke of this, but there was something deeply rooted in him to spend as much time in that orchard as he did.

The curious part about this is that he tended to work in the orchard alone. There was a time when Uncle Lou was the "orchard guy" but with his travel abroad, the responsibility switched back to Papa.

We would get fruit from time to time, but he never asked for help from anyone in that orchard. This is why the request introduced questions in both my and my mother's minds. She drove me to the orchard, but left at my grandpa's polite direction when they spoke about the visit by phone.

"I need to talk to Paul, Addie. I need him to focus on my words, so can you please drop him off at the orchard if I bring him home?" he asked during that conversation.

When I approached Papa in the orchard, he directed me to a specific tree to his right.

"Sure, Papa; what would you like me to do?" I asked, getting on the ladder leaning on my assigned tree.

"Paul, I need to get some things off of my chest, things that are not easy for me to talk about because they are the things that hurt and frustrated me the worst when I was your age. You see, I worry about your future in the same way my family worried about mine. I know you can do unique things, but I am hoping you will be willing to use your *humanity* to do good things first, and allow the bigger parts of your path to serve the wider good that humanity cannot see.

"My sweet grandson, I have seen you grow into a powerful being, capable of profound things. Akamu has told me about the things I cannot see. Paul, hear me when I say this: it is likely you will, in some way, save billions, if not trillions, of lives.

"Before we continue that count, I want to impress upon you what I feel will help you to accomplish this feat here on Earth, respecting your raw talent as a man.

Here is my challenge to you, Paul: I want you to prepare yourself to take over my practice, becoming a fully licensed psychologist. However, this is not enough given your wider task at hand. Because your kingdom includes the Universe, I challenge you to learn what you can about astrophysics at the highest levels of education, if for no other reason than to help you in your wider purpose.

"These two things combined will do what I feel is most important: protect you and empower you through education. Now, I've done all of this talking, what is your impression of this challenge?" he asked. His eyes never left the tree he was working on throughout the entire soliloquy.

It took me a minute to process the enormity of the request. See, the Paul I am when I am in another dimensional plurality has the knowledge of the experience of my abilities. He cannot hear anything out of the ordinary or do anything spectacular—and he knows it. This developed into a *thing* during this timeframe. I picked up weight lifting from my father's team trainers and a little bit of boxing, too, compliments of Papa, to help quell the competitive spirit burning within.

See, the other side of this is that I crave knowledge—it's like a drug for me. At fifteen, I was in my sophomore year of high school, and was bored to tears getting straight A's in accelerated classes with little to no effort. One of my teachers had gotten treatment from Papa and took a keen interest in helping me to find an educational challenge. I've always wondered if Papa nudged this man to help, but I never asked him.

That teacher paved the way for me to begin college work at the University of Charleston in the fall while still fulfilling my high school requirements. By Halloween of my junior year of high school, I had already completed my general curriculum work for my bachelor's degree and had enough credits to graduate high school. By the first day of my senior year, my declared double major of psychology and astrophysics was both accepted and well underway and I never again set foot in that high school building. I met Dr. Upton when I was seventeen; he was my first law professor at the University of Charleston.

I'm again getting ahead of myself. This time, I'm not at all sorry.

From my place on that ladder against that specific apple tree, I looked at Papa and said, "I'd be honored to do this, Papa. I'm just not sure how I'd take over your practice due to its size."

"Paul, those are details you and I will work through when it's time. One of the first things I need to make clear is that this orchard will become solely your charge from the first day you have the ability to drive yourself here. I will teach you everything I know; Uncle Lou will help as much as you need, as well.

"I want to make sure you do this challenge in the healthiest way possible, heeding your responsibilities with high school, the farm, and Rick's school. I will leave that to you to negotiate with your parents—I've said not one word of this to anyone but you," he said, still focused on his tree.

"Okay, Papa. Can I just ask you one thing?" I asked timidly. For the first time, he looked at me.

"I know, Paul. I will need your help as much as you are willing and able to help. By the way, the tree you are leaning against is the first one my father ever trusted me to care for," he said with no prompting whatsoever.

My question was simply, "I'm concerned; is everything okay?"

My "negotiation" with my parents was more of an introduction to panic about my grandparents' health, which was surprising. See, from the age of ten forward, I was expected to work at the farm a minimum of eight hours a week. During the same timeframe, I was expected to work at Rick's school with Papa G for an additional eight hours. The time requirement itself was not negotiable.

At the end of that conversation, I got the, "As long as you meet your responsibilities, go for it," speech. I went headlong into *all* of it.

When I hit fifteen, I got my learner's permit and forced my parents, grandparents, aunts, uncles, Blue, and anyone else willing to help me learn how to drive. The first day I was eligible at sixteen, I got my license and bought my first car with money I had earned, saved and invested.

That last part might seem a little weird but bear in mind that my mother co-ran ninety-ish percent of our multi-million-dollar farm, growing it by two to three percent every year, for all of my childhood. My father was a professional athlete for the majority of my childhood. The structure around our life from a monetary, legal and security perspective was vast and extremely well-defined. I earned every penny I received, and said penny was then taken and placed into a brokerage account, managed by the people entrusted within the structure. There was no exception to this rule, ever. The benefit to the theft of my financially incompetent childhood was buying my first car, a full-size pickup truck, with cash, at age sixteen. This was a lesson I passed on to my children, destroying their dreams of blowing hard-earned money on candy and the frivolous dumb shit kids obsess upon. I've never heard the end of it, though my children are now doing the same thing with our grandkids. Hypocrites, all of 'em.

With my truck goodness in play, I began learning about the orchard. I also began shadowing Papa in his appointments, forging relationships and learning how to truly give therapy to those needing it.

The orchard, I learned, was the result of a competition of sorts between my great-grandfather and my great-great grandfather, who started the farm. It seems father and son didn't see eye to eye. My great-grandfather, Papa's dad, was a heavily revered surgeon, specializing in oncology. This was an affront to the farming lifestyle my great-great-grandfather had envisioned, and static between the two grew, but his career was a reflection of losing his mother to cancer as a young man.

The orchard was my great-grandfather's thumb-to-nose to all. He tended every tree with a surgeon's hand—every tree was pristine. It was only when he became unable to care for the orchard that Papa and Uncle Lou got involved. Thing was, the trees responded to this surgical approach more so than conventional farming. This threw Uncle Lou for a loop, but what he learned from it benefitted all the work he later did in disparate farming locations around the world.

I, in turn, learned how to be surgical with fruit trees. What this did, both for my psychology work and astrophysics work, was revolutionary. Simply put, I approached my education with the same expectation—every topic was addressed with a surgeon's mind and steady hand. This line of thinking resonated well with another surgeon you have already met. Helena and I met accidentally, and lucky for you, this is what came next. Well, sort of anyway.

My graduation from high school was celebrated more by my family than me. I had cake, talked to the people who came, briefly, and then went on the deck to study for an astrophysics exam. I had filled my summer with classes at the University of Charleston, and my astro-work was rounding out the summer. My work for my bachelor's degree in psychology was done.

"Bug, why in the world are you out here when the party in your honor is going on in the house?" Dylan, home for the party—just the party, asked.

I set down my book, stood and hugged my sister.

"Sit with me a minute?" I asked, still holding her willingly captive.

"Okay," she said quietly, and we sat down.

"I have missed you so much, Fink. How is everything going?" I asked.

"Well, I've never flown so much in my life. Things with Hatch are amazing. Do you like him?" she asked, leaning into me.

"You know that if he makes you happy, that's good enough for me," I deflected.

"Bug—no. Look, as a surprise to you, he and I are taking you on a little trip next weekend. I am putting you on official notice, so handle your affairs," she said diplomatically.

"Fink… I… The orchard, brain studies, comet trajectories…" I stammered.

"This is my point, Bug. It's time for you to be eighteen for, like, a day. Uncle Lou will gladly tend the orchard. I have blessings from your main professors that you can have a break for a weekend. It is the end of the summer semester for crying out loud! Again, Paul—this is not negotiable. It's happening, so strap up and be ready," she instructed. I had turned eighteen a week prior.

"You talked to Upton and Painter? How?" I asked. Dr. Painter was my astrophysics professor at the University of Charleston.

"I have my ways. Now then: walk with me into that house, talk to some people, and then come back out here to your comet studies. Again, this is non-negotiable, so up," she said, pulling me out of my seat.

See, this is the sister that has always kept me straight. She still knows when I need a break and injects her influence into my life.

That night, I spent about ninety minutes of more than six hours total talking to people at my party. Some of dad's old teammates came—mammoth human beings. It was fun hearing their stories. Everyone I talked to, regardless of age or occupation, did not understand why I was so driven in my education. I heard more cries for frat parties than I did congratulations for my achievements. I took it all in stride and as the crowd dispersed, I went back out to the dock.

Incidentally, I found that I retained information better when I'm in nature. That dock was my gateway to the world in more ways than I can count.

When I went back into the house, both parents were waiting for me. I thought I was in major trouble.

"I'm sorry… I just…"

"Paul, sit," Dad said gently, inviting me into the living room.

"I didn't mean…"

"Sweetie, this is not an assignment of guilt or punishment. Take a breath," Mom said soothingly.

"What you have accomplished to this point in your life is nothing short of astounding, Son. Have you taken time to realize your accomplishments?" Dad asked, his tone firmer.

"I don't know what you mean, Dad. High school was sort of a blur. I don't look at it as anything but a step in a direction," I explained.

"Paul, you are taking time to breathe now and again, aren't you? I mean, you have fulfilled every expectation we have enforced, and your schoolwork, across the board. I am concerned, baby boy, that we haven't given you the opportunity to just be a kid," Mom explained.

"This is why there has been a concerted effort to get you the hell out of your zone, Paul. This trip with your sister and Hatch is something we all contributed to. I know your penchant talent for ducking out of plans to study, so hear me: you will not have the possibility to miss this. We have made absolutely sure of this. It will be futile to resist, boy," Dad said, laughing through the second half of this.

"Um…" I replied, stunned.

"It's all done with your health in mind, sweetie. We are so, so proud of you. I mean my Lord, Paul—positioning yourself to take over Papa's practice is no small task and you've hit it head on. This little distraction will be good for you," Mom explained.

I made it through three exams and loads of work by midday Friday. My sister had been right in her assessment of the summer. I was basically done with my summer session by that Friday. When my last class ended, Dr. Upton pulled me aside.

"Paul, I'm not sure how to tell you this, but I am transferring to USC in Columbia to take over the behavioral and mental sciences division. I will continue to teach both masters and doctoral studies, which you will be ready for by the start of fall classes, in a few weeks.

"I do not want to presuppose anything, but I would like you to come with me. I have already spoken with the head of astrophysics, Dr. Ted Szymanski. Dr. Painter announced his intent to retire, and I believe your studies will benefit greatly with Szymanski. Will you please do me the favor of considering the move? I know you have a tremendous amount of responsibility here," he said sincerely.

Little did I know, this, though topically relevant, was intended to distract me.

A lasso surrounded my torso and tightened my arms to my body, a bag went over my head and giggling a-plenty happened. This was the signature work of Houndon and Loundon, two of Hatch's brothers. Both boys were several years older than Hatch and both had played professional football for at least ten seasons each. To say these boys were anything other than extremely large children is stretching it. Both have since reproduced and persisted their brand of debauchery for a new generation to enjoy. You are free to relish in this… Now.

I was put in a car and eventually transferred to a small airplane. It wasn't until we were airborne that the lasso and bag were removed.

In the plane were my sister and Hatch; my kidnappers were not in sight. It was a private plane.

"Okay. Out with it. Where are you taking me?" I asked, my nerves frayed.

"You will know soon enough, Bug. It's a longish flight, but one that you are to assist on. Head to the cockpit, please," Dylan asked. Hatch sat, smiling the whole time, taking the whole scene in.

I had taken flying lessons at my father's urging when I turned sixteen. In fact, this was his gift to me and was one of the only activities I did for leisure outside of studying. I had a bunch of both classroom instruction and flying time in, but was not yet certified to fly a jet. It was the next upgrade to my license that I was working on.

"Fink, I can't…"

"Go to the cockpit, Bug."

Reluctantly, I did as I was asked and sat in the co-pilot's seat, which was vacant.

The pilot, who I did not immediately recognize, motioned for me to pick up the headset.

I did as I was instructed and buckled my seatbelt. He then handed me a set of dark sunglasses.

"Paul, it is a pleasure to meet you, finally. I'm Ted Szymanski, professor of astrophysics at the University of South Carolina. I understand that you have your pilot's license, right?" he said and extended his hand.

I shook, as my grandfathers had taught me. There was an onus on control, they taught me, and it began with the firmness of one's handshake.

"It's a pleasure to meet you, Dr. Szymanski. I do have my pilot's license, though I'm not certified for jet engines," I replied.

"Well, Paul, after today, you will be. I talked to your instructor at Wright— me and Frank have been friends for years. You have the classroom, simulator and flight time needed for the next license. Where we are going will give you the experience needed for the jet certification.

"See, I am a flight instructor and, as long as you agree with the plan, you will be flying this specific tin can as much as I do for the next few years. I am going to show you the particulars of the jet engine controls for this particular class of jet, a super light jet, on the flight out. You will land us. When we go home, you do all the pre-flight checks, pass a verbal test and fly the whole distance back to Charleston. It should be fairly familiar to you based on your instruction to date. We will need to refuel at about the halfway point, which is where we will stop both going and coming back.

"This is not the purpose of this exercise—it is but a single part of a couple objectives. You see, Paul, I talked to Painter and Upton and, frankly, am blown away by your resumé. As we fly today, I'd like to pick your brain a bit. Once we land, your sister owns you all but Saturday night. During the hours of nine to midnight, you are mine at the observatory. Do you have any questions?" he asked, nervousness in his voice.

"Thank you for the kind words, Doctor. I truly appreciate everything you just said. Dr. Upton mentioned the change to USC as I was being kidnapped today. I haven't been able to process this quite yet," I said, being completely open.

He laughed harder than I would have expected. When he settled down, he said, "My God, Paul. The whole kidnapping thing was hysterical. There is video. Look, I know you have many, many responsibilities in Charleston that will persist during and well after your studies. If I might be so bold… You could use this or any of the other university planes to go back to the Low Country. I'd be willing to get you a parking spot or a car or whatever you need at whatever airports you choose if you would be willing to study with me.

"I mean, look: top to bottom, you could take off from the campus airport and land at the regional airport by your grandpa's office and be off the aircraft, on your merry way in about forty minutes— versus over two *hours* in the car. The bonus: the route has one check-in and the rest of the time is yours to appreciate the sky and think. I dunno—could be a super intriguing opportunity for you. You wouldn't pay a thing to fly—not one dime—as long as you are a contributing member of the two programs, which are core expectations anyway. And, with one tweak to your license achievable over time, which we can figure out on this trip, you'd be able to be a paid pilot to ferry bodies from place to place in this class of airplane. That could be a nice boon for your bottom line when you're going to make the trip *anyway*. I have reconfirmed this with both university leadership and the FAA and have it all in writing.

"If it's not obvious by now, this is a *hard* sell, kid. I want to drive discovery with you in the same way that Upton wants to just be a part of your brilliance. You are a discipline-filled, determined person, Paul. I don't know where this comes from, but it's impressive. You are *impressive*. I've been verbal puking again. What say you?"

I was blown away! Not only was this a request to study with certain people, this was that request along with a way to continue the things for which I maintained responsibility.

"It sure sounds like all of my concerns have already been addressed. It's important for me to honor my responsibilities, wherever I study," I replied.

"Trust me, Paul—the things we can offer you are *well* worth your consideration. I will leave my sales pitch there; let's talk about jet engines and butts in seats and get you certified," he said.

The rest of that flight, I learned the little bit about jet engines and passengers that I hadn't learned previously, which turned out to be a tiny little gap for both topics. Dr. Szymanski had retrieved all of my pilot certification work from my teacher at Wright Flight School and had determined the extra teaching and demonstration I needed for both certifications.

Additionally, I had a glorious conversation with Dr. Szymanski about all things astrophysics and landed the plane myself. He, literally, kept his hands up, as though he was on a roller coaster, throughout the landing. We were on the Big Island of Hawaii, *twelve hours* later. Despite the flight time, it was Friday evening due to the time change.

"Okay, Paul—nice landing! I will see you tomorrow night—I will pick you up. Think about what I said, okay?" Dr. Szymanski asked as we were gathering our things together to get off the plane.

"I certainly will, Dr. Szymanski. I look forward to our next conversation," I replied and was promptly grabbed by Dylan and whisked off the plane.

We had landed at a small airport in the northern part of the Big Island. Once we had our luggage, we got into a waiting car. Incidentally, I had not packed my suitcase and had zero idea what was in it.

The car drove us to a hotel on the coast.

"Paul, this is the place I stay when I'm here. This is where the majority of my work is, so I know it pretty well. I have dinner for us planned. So, let's get checked in and get some food in our bellies after the long flight," Dylan said.

I nodded. We got checked in, and I headed to my room. There was this massive balcony overlooking the beach. I fixated on this scene for so long that when

Dylan knocked on my door for dinner, I hadn't done a single thing else.

During dinner, I got to truly know Hatch. I learned about his and Blue's uncanny childhood and the work he did in the community.

"So, look… I will admit that I know not one thing about space or head shrinkers or nothin' but Paul, I will say it's wonderful to finally get a chance to really talk to you," he said, and took a sip of beer.

"Thank you, Hatch. I'm not sure what Dylan has told you about me. I…"

"I know you live a unique life, Paul. I can truly respect this, even if I don't understand it. Look, I know you are working super hard to take over yer granddad's business. I truly respect that, Paul. I know it ain't easy to be a kid and be asked to jump right into adulthood.

"Bonus points, too, that you know how to bail hay. I don't know too damn many head shrinkers or space boys who can do that," he said proudly. "But look: this is not supposed to be a talk about work or school or anything like 'at. Yer Pop played QB and yer otha granddad played nose pro. My brothers, well, some of 'em, were in the league a long time, too. It ain't easy being a kid of a ball player," he continued.

"No, it wasn't easy—especially when I was younger. On one hand it was hard that Dad was gone, but I had my mom, my brother and Dylan. It wasn't *so* bad because we had each other," I remembered. "Still, it wasn't easy, no. The farm in Georgia—is it yours?"

"I get it, Paul. No, the farm isn't mine. In fact, I just bought a family farm not far from y'all in Charleston. I'm maybe an hour southwest of the city. It's a two-hundred-acre farm with an option for an additional parcel directly behind. I am seriously kicking around that idea," he replied and wiped his brow.

Throughout this exchange, Dylan took the both of us in like a proud parent.

"I can't tell you how much it means to be sitting here with the two of you. Bug, it's just nice to take you out of your element for a minute. Love, I could say the same thing to you. I just so appreciate the chance to be away with you both, even if it's just for a couple days," she gushed.

"Ah, sweetheart, ain't this where y'all work though? Didn't we just jump into y'all's element?" Hatch appropriately pointed out.

She smiled and kissed him. "I work here, yes. Thing is, I work all over the world, my love. This place was chosen so Paul could get his jet thingy done and because tomorrow's activity likely cannot be done anywhere else. So, you're not wrong at all. I just promise you that this is not a work trip for any of us, save the three hours that professor is taking Paul for," she explained. "Now then—it's late and it's been a long day. Let's turn in and plan to meet downstairs at 8:30, okay?"

"Works for me! I'm pooped!" Hatch said, standing up immediately.

"Yeah, I could sleep," I agreed.

I got back to the room and went right back out to that balcony. Back on Xsip, I was hugging Jly for the first time. Somehow, I knew this, smiled, and listened to the calm of the Pacific dancing on the shore for a while.

The next morning, I met my sister and Hatch downstairs at the prescribed time.

"Bug, did you… Have any dreams or anything last night? Seems like things changed," Dylan asked, hugging me.

"It wasn't so much a dream as it was just something I knew. I was hugging that girl—the one that didn't like me at first. I felt… I felt love, I think," I replied.

I should point out that my love life as an adolescent was zilch-o. I had friends a-plenty, but zero romances. It was suggested several times that I was gay, but I would just smile and say that I was picky.

In fact, a couple of my gay friends had an intervention at one point to address my sexuality, which they were convinced was conflicted in some way. I did my best to explain the situation, respecting my friends for their concern for me. My family understood my plight; no one else did.

"Yep, I got the same thing. You doing okay?" she asked, still hugging me.

"Yeah. That room is something! The ocean was downright hypnotic last night," I said as the hug ended.

"Well, lucky for you, that's a big part of the plan today. First, though, food. There is a great place, right on the water. It's a short walk, and they are expecting us. Vamos!" she commanded, pulling Hatch toward the door.

The restaurant was a relatively small place, right on the beach. A couple of my sister's model friends were there, and they giggily embraced. Hatch was introduced and reduced both females to fumbly, bumbly messes. It was fun to watch.

After breakfast, we walked maybe ten steps to a man waiting with surfboards.

"This is Brad. He's a champion surfer and a really good teacher. I figured we'd give surfing a try if you both are willing," Dylan said as Hatch shook Brad's hand.

"I'm very prepared to make an ass of myself," Hatch admitted.

"I second," I said.

"Let's just get out on the water and let her decide, yeah?" Brad suggested through a thick Australian accent.

We changed into board shorts and some kind of tightly fitting long sleeved thing, grabbed our surfboards and met Brad closer to the water. Dylan marched right into the foam and started paddling. Those two models from the restaurant came from somewhere and did the same thing.

"Okay guys—we are just going to paddle out and sit for a bit, okay? It's a glorious morning and the ocean is the perfect place to celebrate it. C'mon!" Brad encouraged and headed for the water with his surfboard.

The water was relatively calm, so paddling out to deeper water wasn't too hard. We got to the place where the models had collected and were sitting.

"Gentlemen, let's join these mermaids as I believe they have the right idea," Brad said, switching his position and sitting up.

"There is a whole pod of dolphins right over there," Dylan said, pointing.

Hatch and I clumsily sat up. Well, Hatch fell over and had an extended amount of trouble getting back on his board. He laughed the whole time.

When Hatch finally got himself righted, we sat there, watching the dolphins who all seemed to be observing us at the same time.

"Listen: the essence of surfing is this. We are one with the sea, as the boundaries blur between what we are on land and what we are in the ocean. Enjoy the oneness, the beauty of this moment," Brad said eloquently.

The five of us sat there, on those surfboards, for a good amount of time. When the waves started getting more intense, the calm of the moment stopped.

The girls all paddled with the movement of the ocean, finding waves to ride with what looked like absolute ease. I could not believe what I saw Dylan doing!

"Boys, it's that simple. I honestly have given those girls maybe two lessons each. It's as simple as finding your balance and letting the waves carry you. So, first, let's practice standing on our boards. Watch the movement," Brad said confidently.

He then, in a single quick movement, got to a standing position.

"It's that simple—just spring to your feet. Try," he encouraged.

Hatch and I looked at each other and started laughing. This laughter continued long enough for Brad to shyly ask, "Was it something I said or did?"

I gathered myself and said, "No, Brad. It's just that the thought of having that control is kinda funny."

"Paul, you are both incredibly strong—*way* stronger than me. Give it a go!" he replied.

I shrugged and made my first attempt. I fell over immediately and had a hell of a time getting my belly back on that board.

Hatch saw my attempt, laughed again and tried his first attempt. He actually flipped his board somehow and fell too. He emerged from the ocean and asked, "How was my form, Paul? I need a score!"

"Easily a nine-point-five, Hatch. That was impressive. Once you get settled, I need a score as well," I said.

"You both are closer than you think. Try again, Paul. Just this time, pretend like you are hopping like a frog instead of standing up like a person. It's one movement; try again," Brad instructed.

"Y'all so got this, Paul. I need to see how it's done," Hatch encouraged.

I thought about what Brad said and changed where my hands were. When I tried the movement again, I got to my feet really easily and then lost my balance in the still water.

"Ten!" Hatch said, clapping.

"That was it, Paul. Balance comes later. You *totally* nailed the movement. Hatch, give 'er a go," Brad said energetically.

"Leap like a frog, huh? Paul, what did you change?" Hatch asked.

"I moved my hands closer, and pulled when I moved my feet. Does that make any sense?" I replied.

"I dunno. Let's see."

In what seemed like the most incredible turnaround ever, he got immediately to his feet and was stable for about ten seconds before tipping over.

"You've done this before," Brad mused, rubbing his chin.

"I swear to y'all I haven't! That little change Paul suggested made all the difference in the world. Thanks man!" he said, wiping his eyes.

"Okay. You both have the movements down. Now, it's just letting the sea take you. Wanna give it a go?" Brad asked suggestively.

Hatch and I again looked at each other. We'd both seen the girls surfing with no issues at all.

"I'm game to try," Hatch said.

"Yeah, I'll try," I agreed.

"Perfect. Watch how I do this. It will take a couple tries, but it will be so worth it," Brad said and paddled toward the shore.

In a fluid movement, he paddled to a developing wave, got to his feet and glided with the movement of the wave. When he finally got to his stopping point, he waved in our direction.

"I predict failure, Paul. Ugly, painful failure," Hatch said, grinning.

"I am on the exact same page, Hatch. This promises to be awful," I agreed.

Well, we both paddled toward shore, though I let him go first. He got to his feet, rode a wave for maybe three seconds total and wiped out.

A new swell started, so I paddled, got into position and fell over just as the wave crested. I learned why I was wearing that awful shirt!

When I got to the surface, Brad gave me a thumbs up. "Try again, Paul! You almost had it!"

I saw the girls and Hatch on the shore. Undaunted, though a bit waterlogged, I decided to try again.

I paddled, got into position and rode a wave for maybe four or five seconds before losing my balance.

When I got to the surface, the collection was cheering.

"Y'all did it man! Nice ride!" Hatch said excitedly.

"You looked like a pro, Paul. How did that feel?" Brad asked, putting his hand on my shoulder.

"I totally get it. That was immensely fun! Thanks, Brad!" I said, shaking the water out of my ears.

"We have spent most of the morning in the sun. Let's dry off and get some lunch," Dylan said. "Brad, thank you for the help, as always. Can you join us? Sylvia, Candace—you guys, too?"

There was acceptance from all in a cacophonous response.

So, we dried off a little bit and changed back into our clothes. We then walked up the beach a little bit further to another restaurant, where the model collection was welcomed back.

We had lunch. The three girls talked a bunch while Hatch and I sat back and listened. The conversation was nothing either of us could relate to.

That is, until Dylan looked at me and asked if I'd be in the wedding party.

"Wait… what?" I asked. "You guys are engaged?"

"As of about an hour ago, yes," Dylan said, smiling.

"I was official, Paul. I talked to yer Pop and everythin'," Hatch said nervously.

"This was not the plan at all, Paul. This is still your weekend with lots more to do," Dylan confessed.

"I couldn't resist. Proposin' on the beach in awful git-ups just fit. I've carried that ring around with me everywhere for a couple months. I never found the right time until bein' on that beach," Hatch said, grabbing my sister's hand.

"I would love that! I am honored you'd ask!" I happily replied.

The rest of the meal had a celebratory feeling. It was honestly one of the first meals that I completely let go of my studies for a couple minutes.

When the meal was done, hugs and handshakes were had with all. Those models were so, so thin. I honestly wondered if the lunch they'd just eaten was going to remain in their bellies. It was like hugging a skeleton covered in a cotton sheet. No joke.

The afternoon was spent touring different parts of the island, culminating in a very unique park.

Again, if you read Papa Waniglia's book, you know the significance of the park. I'll try not to be too duplicative. Without further ado…

For simplicity, Papa's grandma's dad was a man named Louis Dolby. He built a house on a bunch of vacant land on the northwest shore of the Big Island as a vacation home for his wife and daughter (my great-great grandma). He then donated about three-quarters of the land to a group of Hawaiians who had been displaced from their homes because of a volcano eruption. He helped them build their homes, and they, in turn, asked that the rest of the land be left as a natural park.

My great-great grandpa met my great-great grandma after a war (I can't remember which one, and it's not relevant anyway). My great-great grandma then traced the walk that she said was their "path of love" with ornate colored lights she made. These lights then wove their way into Papa and Gam Wanigla's life after some chaos hit. The way it's been told to me, "Grandma Madelyn's lights defined love for one couple and begat love for several generations." It is said that every person in the village by the park walked the path of those lights with the person that would be their forever spouse.

As time has gone, I went to the house in Hawaii with Papa, once—and Mom and Dad, once. Both visits were before my ninth birthday. My parents' schedules, coupled with all of our activities, left little time for trips across the country.

We all clear now on the relationships, the park, the history and the significance?

Fast-forward to my trip with Dylan and Hatch…

We drove from the beach maybe twenty minutes north and ended up at the far end of the park.

"Paul, we haven't seen the park or the house in *years*. I thought it might be kind of nice to spend the balance of the afternoon here. It's closer to the place you're going to with Dr. Szymanski, too, so I arranged that he pick you up from here. We have dinner arranged and a whole lot of just hang time," Dylan said, smiling.

"Makes sense to me. I vaguely remember this place, but would love to see it again," I replied and got out of the car.

We made our way across the park to the house. Dylan had a key and we filed inside.

Papa and Gam had come to this place with Mom and Uncle Lou religiously through their childhoods and into their young adult lives. As schedules became what they did, my grandparents continued to travel here. A good portion of Papa's clientele from the islands came to the office on the first floor. The echoes of all of the life in and out of that house were everywhere.

Dylan and Hatch decided to go back out to the park to walk the path of lights. I decided to stay in the house and relax on the upstairs balcony that overlooked the beach with very picturesque views of the Pacific. I could see so clearly how my great, great, great grandfather designed the house.

I also saw something else, standing on that giant balcony: the single most attractive girl I'd ever seen in my life. I was drawn to her immediately, and helplessly watched her bikini-clad tan body walk out of my view.

It was not in my character, necessarily, to chase a girl. I had devoted my life to my grandfather's challenge and all of my other responsibilities. Here, I had neither, and I decided to give chase.

I ran down the grand staircase and out the front door. Dylan caught sight of me running and shouted "Bug?" but I kept running.

There was a small bridge over a creek that led to the beach. I kicked off my sandals and ran in the direction the mystery woman walked. Thing is, when I got to the beach, no one was there.

I felt a sense of dejection I could not resolve. I saw a girl, chased her, and lost her. The way I felt, I had just been dumped by my girlfriend of five years and had lost custody of both my dog and my manhood.

I walked down to the water and let the tide nibble at my feet.

A couple minutes later, I heard Hatch say, "There he is," and my sister and future brother-in-law approached me.

"Okay. Spill—why did you run, Bug?" Dylan asked sternly.

"My guess is that it has something to do wit' a female. Am I close?" Hatch asked, chuckling.

"Yeah, it was a girl. Look—I can't resolve this. I saw her from the balcony and I just went for it. I don't know why, but that's what I did," I explained.

"Y'all eighteen, Paul. It's only right that you give in when you see something you like. Add this to the list of atta-boys I have on y'all. You tore ass after somethin', boy. Seems the man in y'all is alive and doin' jus' fine," Hatch said, his hand on my shoulder.

"I could choke on the male bravado, but I agree. It's damn time I saw you chase a girl, Bug. Thing is, any girl you find has to pass my test, so just make sure that's clear in your mind. Got it?" she asked, getting in my face.

"Fink, I… I think it was *her*." I whispered.

"Well, I believe when it's time, you'll find her. For now, though, it's time for dinner. Come on," she said, and grabbed both my and Hatch's hands.

There was a small cabana facing the ocean where the town ran a restaurant on the beach. The kitchen was in the cabana with a couple tables, and tables were spread out on the beach across a pretty large area. It had been Gam's idea to open it and she basically had the whole thing built for them. If I remember correctly, Papa cooked in that restaurant every time he came to the island.

Gam's concern was that the town didn't really have a great way to make money. There was no developed infrastructure for miles around, so people came from miles away to have freshly made dinner based on village recipes and traditions.

The menu, basically, had two choices: vegetarian or not. The portions were healthy and the smiles and laughter were everywhere.

As the sun had set, Dylan indicated that it was almost time to meet Dr. Szymanski across the park. The shortest distance to the street was through part of the light path. So, I crossed the little bridge and started walking through the dimly lit path.

When I got to the part between the second-to-last and last lights, the path was much darker. I slowed my pace accordingly, looking up at the light in the distance for guidance.

Out of nowhere, someone collided with me.

"Geez! I am so sorry! I can barely see," I confessed.

"It's okay. Honestly, neither can I. I'm just trying to get out," a girl's voice replied.

"That light up ahead is the last one in the pattern. Just past it is the way out," I said, motioning to the light up ahead. "Grab onto my shirt and I'll get you out."

"Okay. Thanks for your help. What's your name?" she asked as we switched positions.

"I'm Paul Glassburé. I live in South Carolina. What about you?" I asked as we started to walk.

"Wait… You're Paul? Small world! I think you are one of my dad's students. His name is Dr. Ted Upton. He teaches psychology at the University of Charleston," she said.

"Wow! This is a small world! I didn't know he had any children," I said getting closer to the last light.

She stumbled and steadied herself grabbing around my waist.

"Good Lord, you're strong! Do you have any body fat at all?" she asked, moving her hand onto my belly. By eighteen, I'd become a fully licensed gym rat. My dad's trainers from his football days taught me how to lift weights. It was a big part of my stress relief.

"I have plenty of fat," I said, blushing in the dark.

"Yep, all one percent of 'ya. Sorry for my stumble, but I am not at all sorry for getting touchy-feely," she chuckled. She kept her hands around my waist for the balance of the short walk.

When we got to the last light, I saw that Dr. Szymanski had arrived. Well, I thought so, anyway, given the car at the end of the park.

"Well, we are out and I'm sorry but I have to run. Tell Dr. Upton I am looking forward to fall, okay?" I said as I walked toward the waiting car. I was plenty embarrassed from the commentary. My shy nerd emerged from its shell and cast me on my way.

"Thanks for your help, Paul Glassburé," I heard her say. I did not turn around. I won't lie—I was horrified.

I got into Dr. Szymanski's car and he shook my hand. "Perfect night for some observing, right?" he asked excitedly.

We drove about forty-five minutes west, and up a steep incline.

"This is one of the best telescopes in the world, Paul. I would like to spend some time in an observation sense to see how we work together. I don't mean to question you, son, but what I have been told thus far is sensational in my mind. I want to level-set and see where things are," he said, honesty laced in his words.

"I completely understand. Truthfully, we should see how we relate to one another given the work ahead in the program," I agreed.

We made our way into the massive building and entered the room with the controls for the telescope.

"Astrophysics and Astronomy go hand-in-hand. Let's take a look at a couple things and see if you can recognize them with both optical and general locational information," he said.

"Sounds perfect," I said excitedly.

The telescope was moved a couple degrees and the shutter opened. I got goosebumps.

"Okay, Paul. What are we looking at?" he asked.

"I believe that is one of the stars in Andromeda, based on the coordinates I'm looking at. Based on its' absolute magnitude, I am guessing this to be 7 And, but I'm not sure about the small comet off to the left. I haven't seen that before," I said, confounded by what I was seeing.

"Wait… What?!" he said and moved up to the lens. "Oh my God, Paul.

You just found a comet! And you nailed that star. How in the world…"

"I basically memorized what has been documented about all of the discovered galaxies and clusters. Andromeda is actually something I just wrote a paper on," I confessed.

"I mean, I get it, but how did you… It doesn't matter. You found a comet tonight, Paul! Want to try and ascertain what we can about it and then study its behavior in the coming weeks?" he asked excitedly.

"I'd love to, Dr. Szymanski."

"So, you're accepting the offer, then?"

"Yeah, I'd be foolish not to. I looked at your background and your achievements. I can absolutely learn from you. This is the most important thing," I said.

He extended his hand, and we shook.

"Let's get this comet properly documented and then see if I can stump you. Up for it?" he asked excitedly.

"Absolutely."

He didn't stump me. Over two more hours, he showed me all kinds of objects and asked about their movement. He did a little teaching, which I absolutely appreciated. It reconfirmed for me why the move to USC was the right one.

When the night at the observatory was over, Dr. Szymanski drove me back to the hotel.

"Profound night, Paul. I genuinely cannot wait to work with you," he said, again offering his hand for a handshake.

"I agree, Dr. Szymanski. I learned today, and I love that. Thank you!" I gushed.

He smiled and patted me on the shoulder.

I then left the car for the lobby of the hotel and went about searching for my key in my wallet.

"Mind if I apologize?" I heard off to my left when I was midway through the lobby.

This caught me off guard, as I was fumbling with my key and my wallet. I was tired and clumsy.

"What?" I asked, amid my mess.

The person stood up. I hadn't paid an ounce of attention to the voice or the person talking, so I had no idea what this apology was about. Truthfully, I had no idea about much.

I had just gotten myself sorted out when I recognized the person talking. It was the girl in the white bikini. She was wearing a t-shirt and shorts, but it was the same girl.

"What are you apologizing for?" I asked nervously.

"I got really handsy today and did not like how that little dance ended," she confessed. It was the first time I matched the voice to the girl. It was Dr. Upton's daughter.

"Ohhh. Um… Don't worry about it," I said, my boy nerves firing on all cylinders.

"My name is Helena. I'm your psychology professor's daughter. He told me about you, but…"

"What did he tell you?" I asked, finding the whole thing kind of strange.

"He described you as one of the most driven people he'd ever met," she said.

"Why in the world…"

"What he didn't say was how attractive you are," she said, blushing a little bit.

I won't lie; this both horrified and thrilled me. I had no experience in these waters, and there was chum and sharks everywhere.

"I do not mean to make you nervous. I'm so, so sorry," she said, observing my struggle.

"Walk with me?" I asked, finding gumption from somewhere.

"Really?" she asked, completely taken aback.

"Come on," I said calmly, extending my hand. Ironically, this was a technique her father had taught me.

She nervously grabbed my hand and we went outside. The beach was a twenty-minute walk to the west. There were lit gardens around the hotel. I had no idea where we were heading—I just knew I was walking with both my professor's daughter and the girl I had chased on the beach.

"Are you in college?" I asked. She looked to be around my age.

"I will be in the fall. I am going to medical school," she said. "Dad wanted me to do the psychologist thing, but I'm more into surgical medicine."

"Makes sense. I'd think being in the same discipline as your dad might be hard, especially in medicine," I said.

"Yeah. Is it true that you're almost done with your bachelor's degree for psychology and close to done with your degree in astrophysics, too? Didn't you just graduate high school?" she asked and interlaced her fingers in mine.

"I am, yeah. I think there's maybe two weeks left of the summer session. I'm done with the psychology degree and am less than a semester away from the astrophysics degree," I replied.

"Why in the world are you doing both, and why so fast?"

"Well, the truth is that my grandfather has asked me to take over his psychology practice that is rather large. That's why I'm pressing as hard as I can on the psychology front. The astrophysics part is a little bit harder to explain. To simplify the answer there, I'll just say that it's a part of me that I need to respect," I said, avoiding the rabbit hole of my existence.

"That's fair—I don't want to make you uncomfortable again. I'm sorry, Paul," she said and squeezed my hand.

"Helena, hold on a sec. Can we stop walking?" I asked. We were next to a bunch of palm trees that were lit from the ground.

"Sure," she said and got in front of me. I really studied her face for the first time. I was smitten from jump.

I grabbed her other hand. "You're not making me uncomfortable. If anything, it is a true gift to be spending time with you. My life is complex—there are a *ton* of moving parts. It's hard for me to speak about it intelligently."

She leaned in and kissed me. It was my first romantic kiss from a girl, save a kiss on the cheek I got in third grade when I was trick-or-treating.

"Thank you for saying that. I can't explain this, but I feel like I know you already. I… I don't want to come off as some crazy person, but I kinda feel like I am," she said, still facing me.

"Uh… I was sorta the crazy person today. Were you wearing a white bikini earlier?" I asked, hoping beyond hope it wasn't a mistake.

"I was, but I was not on the beach here. It was much further north, by the park."

"I saw you from the balcony of my grandparents' house and ran after you. If anything, *I'm* the crazy person. I can't explain my reaction in the park, but I absolutely admit that I chased you," I confessed.

"I think I saw you run right by me. I was on my blanket under a couple palm trees. Was it the bikini that you chased or something else?" she asked and hugged me. It almost felt like she was trying to find my pulse in some way.

"The absolute truth is that I think I know you, too," I said, allowing my guard to completely fall down. "I was chasing *you*."

She squeezed me harder, not saying a thing at first. Then, she said, "Paul, I don't want to be weird, but please pinch me. This, in no way, can be real."

"What part can't be real?"

"All of it," she said and kissed me again.

I hugged her tightly. "I won't pinch you, but I will squeeze you."

"I'll take it. Can we find a place to sit and talk?" she asked through strained breath.

I let her go and she promptly kissed me again. And then, again.

"Can I tell you something potentially very embarrassing?" I asked after her lips left mine.

"Of course."

"You are the first girl I've ever kissed," I admitted.

"Well, wanna know something crazy? You're the first boy I've kissed," she said.

"But… You're beautiful, Helena. I don't understand," I said amid bewilderment.

"And, you are stunningly gorgeous with one of the most perfect male physiques I've ever seen. I am equally confounded," she said, looking me square in my eyes. "Look—when I touched you, I knew it was *you*. I don't know how else to explain this. I came here with a couple friends to celebrate graduation. In no way was I looking for anything or anyone, just as I have spent my entire life. I am not one to believe in love at first sight, but I have completely believed in love at first recognition. I knew I'd find you, but *how* I found you is entirely strange."

"I'm in exactly the same boat. I was literally kidnapped and put on a plane to come here for the weekend. I have held a similar belief, though I've never been able to explain it. I think we absolutely need to find a place to sit," I replied.

We were in one of the lit gardens around the hotel.

"I think there's a swing thing over there," she said, nodding in the direction of another lit section of trees.

That's where we headed and started talking.

I won't detail the whole thing, as it lasted the rest of the night. In summary, I learned that she had a younger sister, Cassie, and a brother, Devin, who passed away tragically five years prior. Like me, she'd never gone to school dances, including prom, with anyone but friends. Despite some of those friends' advances, she remained single simply because she felt that was right. Again, same with me. Her family had several small interventions addressing her single-ness, though every one of them ended with her saying, "When I find him, you'll meet him." She was heading to USC on a full ride due to her insanely smart self. Lastly, she had heard her father speak of the kidnapping plan to her mother and thought it to be both genius and super mean.

We literally sat on that swing, swaying gently, until the sun began to rise.

"I wish to be in your arms before the sun touches our faces, Paul Glassburé. Further, I need you to know that this has been one of the best nights of my life. I need you to promise me this isn't the only one," she said from her place against my shoulder.

"Well then, Helena Upton, I need you to allow me to gather you quickly as the sun shall crest the horizon in no time flat. Further, as I have proven, I will literally chase you—I will also prove that I will not let you go," I said, wrapping my arm around her torso.

The sun rose seconds later, seemingly sealing our night together.

A couple minutes later, I heard footsteps behind me.

"Bug?" I heard Dylan ask.

"Hi, Fink. I need you to meet someone," I said, not moving. Helena didn't move either.

She and Hatch came around the front of the swing and both erupted in smiles as they took in the scene.

"Y'all look comfy. I'm Hatch, Paul's soon to be brother-in-law," he said, his smile growing.

Dylan had a tear fall from her right eye. "Comfy indeed. I'm Dylan, Paul's sister," she said, and was immediately enveloped in Hatch's giant arms.

"I'm going to be really rude and not move, if that's okay. I'm listening to Paul's heart and don't really want to stop. I'm Helena Upton. It is wonderful to meet you both," she said, her ear pasted against my chest.

"Have you been out here all night?" Dylan asked, still captive.

"Yep," I replied.

"How's 'bout the four of us get some mornin' grub? Might be nice to fill 'em bellies after what had to be an incredibly special night. My treat. How 'bout y'all go freshen up and we four go to breakfast?" Hatch suggested.

"I love the idea, Hatch. Helena?"

"Give me three more minutes, okay? I don't want this to end just yet. Is that okay?" Helena asked, still unmoving.

Dylan freed herself, kissed us both on the cheek and said, "Helena, you take the time you need. We'll be in the other garden when you're ready."

I smiled. Helena nodded.

Hatch and Dylan walked toward the other garden, where we had started.

"Your sister is so pretty, Paul. And Hatch… Man, he's nice," Helena said, still pasted against my chest.

"She's a model—a very successful model, at that. Hatch is a farmer. He is buying a farm of his own near Charleston, I think," I said and tightened my grip on her. "Is anyone going to be looking for you?"

"No, but I'll make sure they know where I am. I doubt they'll be up before nine," she replied. "Okay… Though it pains me to say this, we should get up. Before we do, you must promise me more time, Paul. Breakfast will be great and then days will happen with travel sometime in the mix. Promise me that no matter what, I will see you before we both fly home. Lastly, promise me I will see you next week."

"Well, I am flying us back to Charleston and I think our flight window opens in about eight hours. I'll need to sleep a bit in order to do that flight. So, let's get breakfast and figure out the rest of the day from there. In terms of next week, I will try to work something out. That is the most honest thing I can promise at this point, knowing what next week holds," I replied.

"I'll take it. You are a pilot, too?" she asked.

"Yeah."

"Okay, Paul Glassburé—you have now purchased a full week of my time so that I can learn more about you. This is not negotiable. Do we understand? I will not move from my spot until I hear a verbal confirmation of this agreement," she said, still against my chest.

"I accept the terms of the agreement. Thank you for your business, Ms. Upton," I formally replied.

"Okay," she breathed. "Just like a band-aid."

She slowly sat up and stretched. She then grabbed my hand and we walked back to the hotel.

About fifteen minutes later, we met Dylan and Hatch and walked to a small restaurant about three blocks away.

The entirety of the meal was spent in a get-to-know-everyone sense. The conversation was light, yet pointed. By the end of the meal, Dylan invited Helena to fly home with us and stay in her room for a few days so we could spend more time together. My sister also proclaimed Helena to be the sister she never had. All details were arranged and parental acceptance of the plans was excitedly obtained. I could hear Mom's excitement on the other end of the phone from across the table.

As the meal ended, I was concerned about time.

"Fink, I need to sleep a bit to be able to fly today. Are there any plans that I'm ruining?" I asked, concern rife in my words.

"You are good, Buggy-Bug-Bug. Go nap and meet downstairs to check out by two o'clock. Sound like a plan?" she calmly replied.

"Absolutely. Thanks, Sis."

We walked back to the hotel and I headed for my room.

"Would it be too forward of me to ask to nap *with* you?" Helena asked innocently.

"As long as the nap part is truly a nap part, I would love that. I have to get at least five hours of sleep," I said, destroying generations of patterning of implicit sexual advances.

"Open the door, Paul. We have six and a half hours," she whispered.

"I…"

"Open the door."

"But…"

She grabbed the key out of my hand, opened the door and we were undressed before the latch clicked the door shut.

"Helena, I don't have…"

"I've been on birth control since the age of thirteen," she said. "Here's the thing… This is a first for me so…"

She pushed me down and slowly got on top of me. "I just need to make sure."

I could see the concern in her eyes move to pleasure almost like raindrops on a window. It was stunning and beautiful all at the same time.

Well, that first round was brief, but when our rather vibrant sex life began that day, Jly's chilly thoughts of Wryp did a one-eighty, and a longing—a wanton desire for connection—began.

We mutually took a breath after what had been our first sexual experience. We then formalized what became our pattern and had a second round of relations. This was less clumsy, more sensual and notably longer.

"Thank you for being my first, Paul. You now have new promises to make," she said, catching her breath.

"I believe you are the one whose promises are more poignant, Helena. Now then, let's set an alarm and see if I can hold you, us both naked as the day is long, and sleep. Up for the challenge?" I asked.

"As long as you understand that when that alarm goes off, all bets are off, then wrap those arms around me and show me if you snore," she whispered.

I smiled, wrapped my arms around her, took a deep breath and fell asleep.

Five hours later, the alarm went off. Round three was had and, again, was better than the prior two.

We packed up, checked out, and headed to the airport.

The flight home, though long, seemed to be minutes in length. We were to land in the extremely early morning on Monday, to be completely clear. The first three or four hours, I could hear Dylan, Hatch and Helena talking constantly. In my headset, Dr. Szymanski talked excitedly about the comet and all the work he had planned for the fall.

When the sun had set behind us and darkness set in, quiet filled the cabin.

"It seems there's been a change, Paul. I am genuinely happy for you," Dr. Szymanski said randomly toward the end of the flight.

"It was unexpected, Dr. Szymanski. I'll take it, though."

We landed in Charleston, at the same airport Dr. Szymanski had talked about.

"See what I mean, Paul? The runways are perfect for this plane and the air traffic controllers know you now. This is a perfect airport for you to fly into," he said, sleepiness setting in.

"Oh—and I almost forgot. Here," he said and handed me an envelope.

"What's this?" I asked, opening the envelope.

"Your certification to fly super light jets anywhere your heart desires. I call this plane 'Bessie' for no good reason whatsoever. Regardless, she can be the other lady in your life, now. I'm thinking you fly me and Helena back to Columbia in a couple days? Up for it? Maybe you stay there for a day or two, see campus and meet people? I dunno; it's late, I'm rambling and we all need to sleep. Let's talk in the morning," he said.

"Let's do it. I'll figure the details and make appropriate accommodations."

Merging Worlds

We got back to our house and sleepily shuffled in.

"Congratulations, son. Jet pilot, extraordinaire. You shall take me places, son. Places at my beck and call. Places… for football," Dad said excitedly. "Who is this person I have heard about?"

"We'll need campus okay if I am flying the USC plane for football games, Dad. Um… I… Her name is Helena. I…" I stammered.

Dad hugged me, which wasn't odd, necessarily, but was strangely timed.

"I'm pulling your chain on the plane thing, son. If it comes to pass, if you're able, we'll figure details separately. I'm just happy about Helena. This is not what I expected to hear about. Look, son: you are eighteen. I expect you to be responsible—but know that I respect you as a man. You will have privacy. We good?" he said, still hugging me.

"Um, Dad…"

"Don't reply, Paul. Just know," he said then let go and walked away.

We settled in. Helena slept in our guest bedroom, which was across the hall from my room.

I woke up with her next to me.

"Sorry, you. Couldn't resist. Besides, I sleep better than I ever have next to you. It's that heart of yours. I practically can hear it beating," she said, stretching.

I smiled.

The week was a smattering of a couple random classes and orchard, farm and Rick's School work. It started, however, with Mom hugging Helena—and both women seemingly getting lost in the moment.

Mom made us breakfast, Dad joined and then Dylan and Hatch appeared. She had to fly to Paris in a couple hours, and Hatch was going out to his new farm to finalize the plan for the extra land.

The conversation was normal, if that makes sense. It was as though Helena had been a member of the family for years. In a very abstract way, she had been, but we didn't put two and two together until much later.

I offered to take Hatch to his farm, but he'd already asked Blue, who missed her little brother badly and craved the time with him.

As I reviewed the next couple days, I included the time to be spent in Columbia so that Mom and Dad knew my availability for the week. Uncle Lou was staying in town for another month, so I asked for his assistance with the orchard. Apparently, I struck a chord because he excitedly accepted and then hung up the phone.

"Can I tag along, Paul? I'd like to see your world if that's okay," Helena asked.

"You are welcome to assist at Rick's school when Paul is there if you like," Dad said happily.

"I second. If you would like to help me in the office while Paul works around the farm, I would love that," Mom said amid sips of steaming coffee.

"I'd love some company with the orchard, but need to be sure Papa…" I began.

"Papa is fine with the assistance, Paul. They're fruit trees. *Just* fruit trees. I swear, between my father, my brother and my son, we would think that this collection of trees was sacredly placed upon the land, requiring specialized hands and chants and witchcraft for their care. Us mere mortals needn't involve ourselves with these trees that give fruit to humans and animals *lucky* enough to grab what falls to the ground," Mom said from her itty-bitty soapbox.

"Yeah—no fruit falls on the ground. So, there's that," I volleyed.

"I *have* to see this orchard now. I'm going, even if I have to stay in the car," Helena proclaimed, laughing.

"You'd be able to see Paul's future office, Helena. You're staying in Papa's location, right, Paul?" Dad asked.

"I think so, yeah. I love the family history there," I replied. "Besides, that is where I've already met some of the trickier patients. Changing locations would be really hard for some of them."

Well, as the time wore on, it became time for Dylan and Hatch to part ways. Blue arrived to collect her brother. First though, she pulled me aside.

"Paul, this is a blessing," she said, her saintly nymph-like voice proclaimed. "Trust your heart and you will never be lost."

I hugged her and smiled. I seriously think that woman is actually an angel who elected to help humanity to be just a little bit better.

Helena and I took Dylan to the airport before heading to the orchard, where both my uncle and grandfather anxiously waited for our arrival.

Oddly though, again, the conversation was more bent toward a relationship that had been in place for years instead of simple, awkward introductions. This was true of everyone in my family, though both of my grandmothers took things a touch far.

That night, an impromptu family dinner was planned at Gam and Papa Waniglia's house with both sets of grandparents, Larry, Blue and the twins, Uncle Lou, Aunt Julia, Vick, Gabriella and Nicolas. This gave my grandmothers a forum to, *ahem*, do their thing. See, the two of them together were a bit much—always. They were best friends for decades and their favorite pastime was gossiping. When they met Helena, they doted so much that they pulled her into their cult with some witchcraft and lemonade. It took days of negotiation to remove her.

I digress.

That night, Mom, Dad, Helena and I sat on the dock and talked.

"Well, Helena, you've met the family. What are your impressions?" Mom asked.

"Honestly, Mrs. Glassburé, it's as though I've had conversations and meals with my own family. It's never felt like the first time I met anyone. Does that make any sense at all?" she replied.

"It does. Paul, you are meeting Sam and Eva tomorrow before you fly to Columbia, right? Geez that sounds strange to me. My psychologist/astrophysicist son is a jet pilot. Jonah, are you taking all the credit for this, or do I get to claim my standard twenty percent?" Mom mused.

"I'm taking full credit for this one, my wife. I'm not really sorry, either," Dad flatly replied.

"Figures, quarterback," Mom shrugged.

I laughed and said, "Two things, Mom: yes, Sam and Eva are joining us for lunch tomorrow and you are on the contract as having thirty-three percent of my accomplishments."

"Who has the other two-thirds, Paul?" Dad asked leadingly.

"Well, quarterback Father, as you are well aware, the contract details are sealed, and that information is confidential," I quipped, matching my father's earlier tone.

Indeed, the next day was to be the first time Sam and Eva would meet Helena. I was nervous about this, simply due to the absurdity of the relationship from a conventional human perspective. When the "wandering" part of me was indeed wandering, Eva talked to me daily. Sam talked to me every couple of days. The purpose of those conversations was to provide recognition of the events that would become part of my human memory, especially the traumatic events.

See, just as I had trouble reconciling seven years of information, the "normal" human part of me had an equally difficult challenge to pull in the weighty experiences from my wandering. The catch here was the trauma and the violence— Sam accurately worried that some of those memories would cause nightmares or behavioral problems, not unlike the experience of those people who have lived through war or assault victims. The conversations prepared me for what I'd have to reconcile.

This left me wondering what they'd talk to Helena about.

The next morning came and I again woke up next to my girl. I cannot understate the magnitude of the impact this simple thing had on me. There was a comfort—a knowing—that I had with Helena. My non-wandering self had memories of Ania, but they were from when I was eight years old. My deep dive into my education and all of my responsibilities had softened many of the memories from The Faction fights and Ania's death in my non-wandering brain. As a result, waking up next to her was something that created comfort and a connection in me that I didn't consciously relate to the experience I'd had in other locations. In other words, my human self figured out all on his own that he liked this girl and needed her in his life. There may have been Universe underpinnings or nudges to push Helena and I together, but the rest was all human juju.

When the time came, we got our belongings together and headed out to lunch.

Eva screamed when she first saw Helena, running and enveloping her in her tiny arms. Helena went with it, and Sam laughed mightily through it all.

After some initial pleasantries, things got a little strange.

"Paul, have you told her anything?" Sam asked innocently.

"About what, Sam?" I asked, not putting two and two together.

"Helena, would you mind if I showed you something?" he asked.

"Um… Sure—what would you like to show me?" she asked, notably confused by the question.

"Close your eyes for me, okay?" he said softly.

What I witnessed over the next three-ish minutes was Eva, Sam and Helena all with eyes closed, passing through expressions of happiness, discovery, shock and profound sadness.

When it was over, Helena looked at me, eyes still wet with tears, and hugged me.

"What in the world did you just do?" I asked.

"We showed her some things, Paul—things you know. It's going to be important that when we talk week-to-week that she be part of the conversation. There will be work to do when the current assignment completes and the next phase begins. It will be important over the next several years to prepare all involved because it promises to be a challenge.

"Because here's the thing: she's involved. You know the connection. She knows it, too. Maybe you haven't chosen to recognize it yet, but y'all's connection is way, way deeper than many in the whole of creation. I will allow your connected humanness to evolve as it already is—but I will make a two-thousand-dollar wager right now, with all involved, that you will not have anything constituting a 'fight' *ever* in your lifetime. You know I'm good for it somewhere, Paul. I make this wager right here, right now," Sam said, ending his pontification.

"Not fair, Sam. You know why," Eva said, wiping her eyes.

"Was all of that real? I mean, seriously, was all of that real?" Helena asked, still holding onto me.

"All of it, sweetie. The current assignment is especially hard because we can see him but he can't see or hear us. The work he is doing is unbelievable by himself. By *himself*. I am so, so impressed. He's been so dead again, and I hate that. The beating was awful, too. He choked that lady, which was *so* bad but just thoroughly amazing, too.

"Here's the thing, Helena: when he sleeps, he might pick up emotion from the current assignment. I've seen this before. If you hear weird things, they will be his thoughts. From time to time, he may have a nightmare. This happens for the same reason. Sam and I purposefully will never tell you proper names as it would convolute your understanding. We will, however, tell you situations. We do this with Paul's family, too.

"But, none of this takes away from who you are together. Tell me something: have you found any part of the family hard to relate to?" Eva asked, ending her sermon.

"Come to think of it, no. It was like I had known them forever," she admitted.

"This is my point. Paul, I dare say you will find the same thing as you travel today. Helena, it took me a couple days to warm up to Paul's family, and that was with me helping them through some of what you just saw. They have instinctively protected themselves from outsiders given all of their experiences," Eva said passionately.

"Yep—took me over a week *with help* for the family to open up to me," Sam said. "This is part of the fabric of who you are together. It will never matter whether or not an assignment is active—who you are together is special. It celebrates a part of existence that is truly sacred."

"I think I understand. It also explains a whole, whole lot," Helena replied, pulling herself away and having a drink of water.

"So, look: the four of us need to prepare the lot of all involved for what will be a tremendously tricky situation. There is a big, big time gap that will need to be reconciled. We have the gift of time to prepare because of the time discrepancy. It will be years in the future, which is good. Diligence is mandatory, though.

"For now, please know this: it is glorious to me to see you together. I am so glad we had the opportunity to meet," Sam said, smiling warmly.

"I completely agree. I speak from a unique perspective, having had experience with both of you in the past. Oh sweet Lord, I love this more than I will ever be able to say. It reconfirms things for me that I love to believe in," Eva sighed with fresh tears falling from her eyes.

With the meal and the weirdness complete, hugs were collected and we headed to the airport.

****

When we got to the airport, my gate agent asked for my credentials and then handed me an envelope. In it, there was a letter and two forms. The letter said:

> Hello, Paul —
>
> Bessie is all gassed up, but you need to still do your preflight checks as per normal. Your flight plan should be ready when you get in the plane. Call me with questions.
>
> You will find two forms inside. The first is for Helena to fill out. You are not an airline pilot, per se, but she is a passenger. She has to agree to accept the risk of flying with you on the college's airplane. Straight forward stuff.
>
> The second form is for you to fill out, but I want you to read it carefully. It details the University's commitment to you and its expectation from you. Please make sure you are comfortable before signing. It will be given to the gate agent, who will witness your signature and send it to back to us by mail.
>
> Please plan on stopping by my place while you're in Columbia. Upton knows where it is and can give you directions.
>
> Cheers,
>
> Dr. Ted

By the time I had finished reading the letter, Helena had signed her form and had handed it to the gate agent.

"I already know how you flew me here from Hawaii. I'm fairly confident the trip to Columbia, all thirty minutes of it or so, will be fine," she said, smiling.

I read over my form and understood the commitment I was making. I had thought through the move to USC and was comfortable with the expectations of me. In truth, the University was giving me a tremendous gift in being able to get to Charleston so fast.

So, I signed my form and handed it to the gate agent, who watched me both read and sign the document. With that, she gave me an ID badge that allowed me to get into the protected space of the airport. A non-pilot badge was given to Helena for the same purpose.

I got our luggage into the cargo area and did my preflight check. I had about fifteen minutes after that to get Bessie started and in position to take off.

I heard the voice of the same air traffic control agent as I awaited permission to take off. "N1510U, you are cleared for take-off. Travel safe, y'all," he said kindly.

With that, my first flight without another pilot on Bessie was underway.

As soon as we hit our cruising altitude, we stayed there for what felt like seconds before beginning our descent into Columbia. Helena sat next to me and had a headset on so we could talk.

"This seems pretty natural to you. Are you nervous flying this plane for the first time alone, you?" she asked.

"I'm not as much nervous as I am excited, babe. This is such a nice convenience for me, or us, or however it works out," I said, not wanting to presuppose anything.

"Paul Christopher Glassburé, stop. Where you go, I go. I will help you wherever you want me to help you—but every time you fly this plane back to Charleston, I will be on it with you. I just signed a paper saying so," she said defiantly.

"Well, okay then," I backpedaled.

"Are you excited to meet my family?" she asked, her tone vastly different.

"I am. I have to ask you though… How worried are you after the lunch with Eva and Sam?" I honestly had no idea where my existence played in Helena's mind, or how any of it would work with her family.

"Paul, Paul, Paul. If I was nervous or emotional or in some way skeeved out from what I heard today, I would not be on this plane with you."

"But, how…"

"Paul, listen to me. There has been something about you that I have felt since I was a little girl. This isn't some fantasy thing born out of dollhouses or girl crushes or whatever. I have felt you in my life since I was old enough to pay attention. What that conversation with Eva and Sam did was legitimize every belief I have held and every excuse I've ever given to anyone about remaining single. This does not come without *something*. I will admit that what I saw was a mixture of such unbelievable things and such *awful* things. What I have known since I was little— and what I know now—is that I am here to accept and help you through all of it. I'm not sure what to expect with this big change in a few years, but I will absolutely embrace it for what it is. And, you can be damn sure the whole of my family will, too," she explained, putting her hand on my shoulder.

"It's a lot, Helena. It is something that affects my family. It likely will affect you. Are you sure you're up for that?" I asked, doing my best to ruin the flight.

"I found you. It took me eighteen years and four and a half months to do it, but I *found* you. I'll take the entirety of you as long as I am able to keep *you*. Please understand that I intend to, indeed, keep you until I am done with you. Do you understand me?"

"I do. Now, sassy pants, we're going to land. Please make sure you're secure."

"Sure thing, Captain," she said in her most seductive voice.

We landed at a small airport just northwest of the city. The University was about forty minutes away and was where we headed first. Helena's car was driven to the airport, making things exceptionally simple.

We drove first to the mental and behavioral sciences area, where we found what became an incredibly emotional Dr. Upton unpacking boxes in his new office.

"Hi, Daddy!" Helena said gleefully and hugged her dad.

"Hello, Sunshine. How was Hawaii?" he asked, his voice shaking.

"Daddy? What's wrong?" Helena asked, looking into his eyes.

"For years, I have worried about you being alone, Helena. Knowing the man you have talked about for all these years—your 'love at first recognition'—is Paul… Well… I must say that there is literally not one other human on this planet that I would like to see you with more. I honestly wished for this for the entirety of the last year but couldn't figure a way for the two of you to ever meet without it being weird or contrived. How you randomly found one another is… is magical. Paul, I had no idea you were going to Hawaii. Your sister just asked for a respite for the weekend. No location was given.

"Szymanski said you flew the jet? Really?" he asked with wet eyes.

Helena hugged her dad again. "Thank you, Daddy. That means a lot to me."

"It certainly means a lot to me too, Dr. Upton. Thank you for the trust you've given me," I said, fighting my own emotions. I adored Dr. Upton—he had become a mentor to me that I hadn't sought, but consciously never wanted to lose. "I did fly the plane both to and from Hawaii and from Charleston, here."

"He's such a good pilot, Daddy. I literally didn't feel the wheels touch down when we landed for any of the flights. Is there anything we can help you with?" she asked, assessing all the boxes yet unopened.

"Well, if you'd want to help me for a couple minutes while Paul goes over the astronomy/astrophysics buildings, I would welcome it," he confessed.

"Am I close to that area of campus, Dr. Upton?" I asked. I did not have my bearings.

"Go straight out the door you came it, past the cafe and hang a right at the first street you come to. You'll run smack dab into the side of the observatory. The lecture halls connect to it," he replied.

I kissed Helena goodbye and headed to find Dr. Szymanski.

It was a straight shot for the most part, once I made that turn. I found Dr. Szymanski's office a few minutes later.

"Paul! Welcome to your new home, one of two. I heard that you took exemplary care of Bessie and that the airport staff loves you. I expected nothing less—everything I have observed about you thus far is on par with your reputation, which is still unbelievable to me.

"Could I take you on a tour?" he asked, standing to shake my hand.

"I'd love that, Dr. Szymanski. Thank you for your kind words!" I replied, smiling.

He first showed me the observatory, which had a small radio telescope.

"Look—she doesn't look like much, but we can do all kinds of research without having to go back to Hawaii. In my master's program, which I intend to start you on early, we will have occasion to travel to the Big Island to expand on our discoveries here. Any questions thus far?" he asked, beaming like a proud parent of a kid who just hit a home run.

"Just one. How am I allowed to do the masters work early? I probably have…"

"You have ten credit hours to finish your bachelor's degree. You will finish the work needed for those ten hours in the first three weeks of the semester. Selfishly, I will not let you go and squander the opportunity at more discovery.

"So, that little comet you found? Paul! You were the first to see it! We are going to study it more, as it may lead us to find some unique things lurking about in Andromeda. I took the liberty of naming it 'Glassburé's Comet' and registered the name with all appropriate registrars. You will have a certificate sometime next week and some kind of correspondence from my colleagues in Europe," he said excitedly.

"Really? It truly was a brand-new discovery?" I asked, dumbfounded.

"Indeed, it was, Paul, indeed, it was. Let's go see the places you are likely to frequent and then I'll walk you back to Upton. On the way: coffee. My treat," he replied, and led me out of the observatory.

We walked to three lecture halls and then headed to the café.

"Jimmy! You're back! I missed you, man! How's the family back home?" Dr. Szymanski excitedly asked.

"Dr. Szymanski! It is so good to see you again! Long time! Everyone is really good. It was nice to see Momma again. Are you having your usual?" Jimmy asked, grabbing a cup.

"Yes, and make it two, okay? This is one of my new students, Paul Glassburé. You likely will see a lot of this man over the next few years. Believe it or not, Paul found a comet last week! A brand-new, never before documented comet. Isn't that so cool?" Dr. Szymanski said, mildly bouncing up and down.

"Paul, I get coffee with espresso in it. I'm a bit of a caffeine hound—I hope you like it."

"You found a comet, man? Damn… Impressive. On the house on account of the comet man!" Jimmy said excitedly.

"Thanks, Jimmy. I appreciate that," I replied, taking in the scene where my professor and Jimmy seemed to increase one another's energy output by a factor of three.

Jimmy finished off our coffees and shook my hand. "It's so nice to meet you, Paul. I'll see you soon," he said kindly.

"Thanks, Jimmy. This is delicious; is it truly just coffee and espresso?" I asked.

"Oh, God. You did it now, Paul…" Dr. Szymanski said, dread in his voice.

Jimmy bowed his head. "Paul, I need to make something really clear for us to get off on the right foot. You're new, so I'll be gentle. Just know that I'm only gentle once, so accept the get out of jail free card because you just used it.

"There is no such thing as 'just coffee', Paul. Not here, anyway. I roast every bean myself and I know every farmer *personally* who sends me the raw beans. See, coffee is a delicate dance of balance. To properly achieve this balance, one must understand acidity, heat, ratios and water constitution.

"Espresso is properly achieved with pressure and heat. Not just any pressure—nine bars, minimum. I use a touch more. To properly pull shots, it, too, requires specificity in approach. That cup has perfectly brewed beans with perfectly pulled shots. I hope we are clear," Jimmy said, leaning forward on the counter.

I was taken aback by the tongue lashing. I honestly didn't know what to say.

"Thanks Jimmy. I have to deliver Paul back to Dr. Upton. See you again soon," Dr. Szymanski said, rescuing me.

When we got outside, away from the door, he said, "This is why we stick to asking for 'the usual' when we go in there. Jimmy is a great conversationalist away from the coffee topic. You venture into those waters and you're on your own."

"Got it. Yeah, I didn't expect that at all," I lamented.

"Don't worry about it. He does that to every person who asks for 'just coffee', multiple times a day. I have colleagues who do it just to be able to argue. It's a *thing*, Paul," he explained.

We walked back in the psychology building and found Dr. Upton and Helena sitting in his office. Almost all the boxes had been unpacked.

"Wow! You made a bunch of progress!" I said.

"Yeah. My helper here is rather superhuman when it comes to organization. Did you get assaulted by Jimmy?" Dr. Upton asked.

"Paul was brutalized. He asked about '*just* coffee'," Dr. Szymanski said, chuckling.

"Oooh… Ouch, Paul. Jimmy's a great guy, but coffee is his life. I think you will find him a lovely research subject as time goes. Perhaps you can help unlock some of his aggression?" Dr. Upton suggested.

"Jimmy?" Helena asked, notably confused.

"The guy who owns the café just outside, sweetheart. He roasts all the beans and I think does all of his own maintenance on the machines, too. He is hard core!" Dr. Upton explained.

"I see. Babe, are you ready to go meet the fam? Mom just got dinner going and people are arriving," she said.

"Yep, I'm ready when you are, love," I replied.

"Still tugs my heart… I could not be happier the two of you found one another," Dr. Upton gushed.

"I told you, Daddy. When I found him…"

"I know, Helena. I indeed met him," Dr. Upton interrupted.

"You all have a great night. Paul, it was great seeing you, as always. I will see you in a couple weeks. Keep Bessie with you—if you want to go anywhere else, just make sure the trip is recorded in the log at the airport. Okay? Otherwise, if you are just down to Charleston and back again in what, ten days or so, there is no reason for Bessie to come back here in the meantime," Dr. Szymanski explained.

"Thank you, Dr. Szymanski. I'm looking forward to it!" I replied.

"An outstanding scholar who finds comets and gets a bachelor's degree whilst still in high school, a great man who wins my daughter's heart and now a jet pilot. What's next, Paul? Do you have political aspirations? Am I speaking to the next president?" Dr. Upton jested.

I chuckled. "I literally have just two more plans: make your daughter happy and treat my grandfather's patients so he can retire."

Out of nowhere, Dr. Szymanski reappeared and said, "…And find astronomical objects no one else has!"

"Yeah, that could be fun, too," I conceded.

"I will allow you to make me happy, babe," Helena beamed. "On that note, we need to head home. Daddy, are you about ready to go?"

"Indeed, I am, child. Let us make our exit," Dr. Upton replied.

With this agreement, we gathered ourselves and headed out of the school.

The drive to the Upton's house took just over a half-hour from the

University. It was on Lake Murray, a touch northeast of both Columbia and the University. It was a very pretty house! They had just moved in a couple days prior.

"Ready to be mobbed, you?" she asked and kissed me.

"I think so but, I could use maybe one more kiss," I admitted.

Her hands surrounded my face, she looked deeply into my eyes and then kissed me so sensually I've never forgotten it after all these years.

"I will do that forever if you let me, Paul Glassburé," she said.

I knew I was in love with her well in advance of this kiss. After it, I knew I'd never let her go.

"I tell you what, if you still feel that way at the end of the year, we will progress things to more formal waters. Deal?" I asked, extending my pinky finger. This was my way of sealing a promise with Dylan, so I figured it to be applicable here, too.

"I'll take it," she said and kissed me again. "Come on."

We marched through the garage, into the house. As soon as the door opened, a screaming child raced in our direction.

"You're home, Helena!" she yelled and hugged my girl. "Who's this?"

"This is Paul. Paul, this is my sister Cassie," Helena said, still captive in her sister's arms.

"Hi, Paul," Cassie said, still hugging Helena.

"Hi, Cassie. It's nice to meet you," I replied. She promptly released her extended embrace and held out her hand for a handshake.

As we shook hands, Mrs. Upton appeared from what I think was the kitchen.

"So, this is the famous Paul, huh? It is wonderful to meet you finally—I have heard so much about you," Mrs. Upton said kindly.

"Hello, Mrs. Upton. It's very nice to meet you," I replied, recognizing that what Sam said had held true with the first two members of Helena's family. There was no nervousness in me whatsoever.

"Come in, come in! There are a few other people you will need to meet," Mrs. Upton explained, putting her arm around me.

She led me to the kitchen, where an older gentleman sat at the kitchen table.

"Hello, Paul. My name is Joe, Dorothy's dad. It's a pleasure to meet the man that finally broke into my granddaughter's life. I've wondered if this day would ever happen or if, perhaps, my granddaughter swung to a different tune," he said, standing to shake my hand. Dorothy was Mrs. Upton's first name.

"Dad! Be nice and reduce the vulgarity, please," Mrs. Upton scolded.

"Never!" he objected. "I call it like I see it, and that grandchild was more likely to like Paula than this *Paul* for the past five years. So *there*!"

"Not nice, Grandpa. I told you…"

"I *know*, Helena. I have now met this person you've informed us about for many years," he said, interrupting Helena before hugging her. "I am so happy for you, Tiny. It's been a long time coming."

"Thanks Grandpa," she smiled and hugged him tighter.

As this embrace evolved, there was a knock at the door. Cassie ran toward it.

"Hey, chunks," I heard her say.

Upon hearing this, Helena ran from her grandfather's arms toward the front door. Screaming then happened.

A couple moments later, Helena emerged with a very slender girl that looked to be around our age.

"Paul, this is Savannah. We've been best friends forever, but she couldn't go to Hawaii with me because she was away with her family. I think that was the longest we've ever been apart," Helena said.

"See what I mean, Paul? These two…"

"Dad!" Mrs. Upton interrupted.

"So, this is the magical Paul, huh? Yeah, I see what you mean, girl," Savannah said, looking me up and down. "Do you speak, boy?"

"I do. It's nice to meet you, Savannah," I replied.

"It has a voice, too. This is a plus," Savannah jested.

"Knock it off, Ess," Helena scolded.

"Nah, I like this. Beat the kid up a bit, Savannah. You have it in 'ya. Make me proud," Joe said from the table, where he again was sitting.

"Where have you been hiding, Paul? We have literally heard about you for a long, long time. Is there a reason you refrained from meeting us until now?" Savannah pressed, her arm around Helena.

"Honestly, I needed you to go away for a minute so I could have Helena to myself for once. So, yeah, you've heard about me *and* caused me to stay away for *all this time*. Maybe, *just maybe*, you should apologize to your friend," I volleyed.

"Paul one, Savannah zero," Joe proclaimed.

"*Well* then," Savannah conceded and hugged me. "It's so very nice to make your acquaintance, Paul. Just know one thing, okay? You do anything to hurt her and you die by my hand. Are we clear?"

"I think we understand one another," I agreed.

Over the next twenty minutes, Dr. Upton's brother, Saul, arrived with his wife, Mary, and Dorothy's sister, Gail, arrived with her son, Chase.

We had a cook out on the porch as a collective. All of the conversation was easy as we both enjoyed some yummy grilled stuff and took in a beautiful night. It honestly was all so comfortable despite the never-ending barrage of questions. The lot was curious as to how I had finished what I did by the time I was to graduate high school. There were lots of questions about the night sky as darkness took over. I obliged all of it—I loved the conversation.

When the crowd dissipated, Dr. Upton pulled me aside as bedtime approached.

"Paul, I need to tell you a couple things," he began. "My daughter and I are very close and she has confided in me on a couple topics. Among them, she has said that she sleeps more soundly when next to you.

"Look—you are both adults and I respect that. I'm not naïve to what led the two of you to be sleeping next to one another. Please know that if she chooses to sleep in the same room, I have no issue with this. I am genuinely overjoyed that you are here with us, in this capacity," he said without clarifying that statement about sleeping arrangements.

"Thank you, Dr. Upton. I cannot thank you enough for opening your home to me. It is especially meaningful given the respect I have for you as my professor," I replied, hoping that flattery was the way to go here.

"You are more than welcome, Paul. I will see you in the morning," he said, patted me on the back and disappeared down the hall.

I got ready for bed and walked to the guest bedroom, where I found Helena standing, covered in a robe.

"Close the door, Paul," she instructed and walked toward me.

"Your Dad…"

"Your job right now is to listen," she interrupted. "I have waited all of my teenage years, through countless fantasies, for this moment. The way I see it, a tradition will begin tonight: any new room we sleep in will carry the same theme. Are we clear so far?"

I nervously nodded.

"Okay. Under this robe is something for both of us. I want this experience to be something we both remember, but I also recognize it will take some time for us to learn," she said, wrapping her arms around me and kissing me. "Now then, I need you to remove my robe," she whispered.

I untied the belt and moved my hands up the opening of the robe. I pushed it down her arms to the floor and found that she was wearing rather elaborate lingerie. There were straps and clasps and pieces of cleverly placed lace everywhere. Her beautiful body was partially visible under the thin lace.

"Your challenge, Paul Glassburé, is to unwrap me. Every time you reveal a section of my skin, it is your responsibility to recognize it in the way you choose," she instructed. "Where would you like to begin?"

I traced every strap with my fingers. I figured this to be a wonderful first step given the abject abundance of torture she'd introduced to this point.

I found two clasps in the back and undid them. This revealed her left side, down to her belly button. I kissed every relevant inch of her left side, paying appropriate attention where attention needed to be placed.

I found the same clasps on the opposite side and undid them. I repeated the same attention on her right side.

"This last part isn't as straightforward. I wish you continued success, boy," she said through heavy breath.

The bottom half had no clasps that I could find, so I instead investigated each strap intersection and found a single end that moved differently from the rest. It was in place with a hidden snap.

I undid the snap and Helena pushed me to the floor, onto the open robe, and kissed me.

"This last part has another interesting twist, Paul. You may no longer use your hands on the straps. Proceed as you need," she breathed and kissed me.

I flipped her over and found the place where the hidden snap had been undone. This was on the right side of her lower back.

Using my teeth, I undid the strap and pulled backward. This ultimately loosened the lace around her midsection but did not remove it.

So, I turned her back over, keeping that strap in my mouth.

As I pulled the strap, she began to undress me, removing my shirt.

I flipped her again as the strap wrapped twice around her right leg. As I moved left, the lace pulled away from her right side, revealing open skin. Heeding my instruction, I kissed it all.

There was notably heavy breathing happening from both of us at this point. So, I again grabbed the loose strap in my mouth and continued left.

It went around her left leg twice and then once around her waist. When I got the whole thing on the floor, she had me magically naked and we had an incredibly passionate twelve seconds.

"That was unreal, Paul. I am nowhere near done with you, but I want to move to the bed. I'm not…," she said, grabbed my hand and led me to bed.

She held me close, and we straight up made out for a good few minutes. In what seemed like a seamless movement, she got on top of me and we made love again. The energy of the lingerie adventure was still extremely present, but the entirety of the session was appreciably longer.

When the denouement of the session arrived, she laid on my chest and whispered, "That was so very much worth the wait."

"I am not at all sure… how…," I mumbled.

"So, you enjoyed yourself, boy?" she demurely asked.

I flipped on top of her, leaned down and kissed her.

This led to a third round, still fueled by that incredible lingerie extravaganza.

With the third round complete, I collected her in my arms and we both fell fast asleep, naked as the day is long.

When we awoke the next morning, I was still holding her close to me.

"If I could wake up like this forever more, I would be extremely happy," she said, unmoving.

"I'd certainly be willing to oblige," I replied. "What was the tradition you mentioned, the thing about new locations?"

She chuckled. "Yeah, that was a hit last night. Wherever we go, on the first night of our time in the new place, I want to have a similar challenge. I have collected some rather exotic lingerie that I have saved for the right moment."

"I see. So, does this mean that the lingerie from last night has been retired?" I mused.

"Not at all! If anything, I believe it earned a spot in the rotation. Thing is, Paul, I think I may be saying that quite a lot. Are you into it, or…?" she asked.

"I think you know the answer to that question, love," I replied and squeezed her tightly.

"You're gonna make me pee! Stop it!" she laughed.

I released my grip and she ran into the bathroom. Laying there, I reflected on what
Sam said about our relationship. If it was true that we were somehow connected differently than other couples, I wondered how our sex life played in the whole of our connection.

I need to pause here and say what is likely incredibly obvious: yes, Helena blessed me documenting this. If she hadn't, I'm certain I'd be dead through some nefarious surgical method as I slept. See, throughout our life together, we've had a lively, yet incredibly loving, sex life. The spark we felt as teenagers never left—it remains to this day despite us being grandparents, and it is the single most magical thing I have ever felt.

Helena emerged from the bathroom dressed in what she likely was going to sleep in.

There was a look in her eye in that moment—perhaps recognition or simply gratitude—but it told a story. I believe my smile served as my rebuttal.

"Get your sex lord self outta bed, boy. Go get dressed—Momma likely has breakfast started and we have a full, full day today before you fly home," she said, leaning on the bed.

"You got it, sex goddess. I look forward to trying to act normally around your parents this morning," I replied.

"Well, here's the thing, Paul: you are mine. We are eighteen. I was given a green light to do as I please, and I did so three times after an incredible experiment gone right. So, know that you are my kept man, your body is actually my possession and mine is yours if you'd care to sign the title," she said, and kissed me on the cheek.

"Do you have a pen?" I asked, pulling her close.

"That was a trick question, boy. Y'all signed the title over with your tongue last evening. Now then, let me go before I take what's mine and do as my brain has suggested," she said, struggling to free herself.

I let her go and she disappeared out of the room. I then got myself settled and ventured out to find the kitchen.

The smells of the coffee and bacon swirled in the hallway. In no time flat, my belly reminded me that it needed food.

I arrived in the kitchen to find Mrs. Upton cooking and Dr. Upton and his daughters sitting and chatting about the bird that just took a fish out of the lake.

"Good morning, Paul. Did you sleep okay?" Mrs. Upton asked, stirring potatoes in a skillet.

"Good morning, Mrs. Upton. I slept soundly, thank you. Breakfast smells incredible! Is this one of your specialties?" I asked, looking at the array of pans with food in them.

"She is a master, making most any meal one might want, Paul. Breakfast, lunch, dinner—it's all good," Dr. Upton beamed.

"Thomas, that's enough. Paul, tell me more about the orchard you tend. Did I hear that it was started by your great-grandfather and is outside the office you'll be inheriting?" Mrs. Upton asked.

"Yes, it was originally planted by my great grandfather as something of an insult to my great-great grandfather. It's a ridiculous story, but the trees themselves respond to the way my great grandfather tended them. It's interesting that the trees learned how he cared for them and expected nothing less as time moved on," I replied.

"Yeah, Momma—I saw how both Paul and his Uncle tended the trees. It was much more delicate and precise than I would have expected," Helena interjected.

"Someday, I will need to see this orchard, sir. I also expect fruit. So, on one of these trips back and forth, could you maybe bring me something? I am not at all picky," Mrs. Upton said, handing me a plate. "Sit and eat while it's hot, okay?"

"Thank you, Mrs. Upton. This looks incredible," I said, surveying the breakfast deliciousness in front of me.

As we ate breakfast, we talked more about the orchard and Rick's School, which seemed to really interest Cassie.

"So, wait—you work at a school for people with special needs? Who was Rick?" she asked.

"Rick was my grandpa's brother. He had Down Syndrome and died too young. Rick's passion was that school, and my grandpa completely supported him. I mean, when Rick died, Grandpa was in the middle of his career. He retired from football to run the school. See, Rick created this revolutionary system of teaching people who have a myriad of challenges, preparing them to live independently. A large portion of our students have Down Syndrome, but not all," I explained.

"Could I go back with you and help there sometime? I would love the chance to do that," she asked.

"I certainly don't see why not, Cassie. Let's absolutely do that," I said enthusiastically.

"Wait… Your grandfather is Nol Glassburé?" Dr. Upton asked, setting his fork down.

"Yep, that's right. Did you ever watch him as a pro?" I asked innocently.

"Well, Paul, this is complicated. I played against your *father* when I was a freshman and he was a senior, though I was a backup offensive tackle. I have never seen anything in person like his arm, ever. I watched so many games of his and saw the same thing I did standing on the sidelines. I'm honestly nervous to meet the guy.

"Your grandpop, though—I watched that man lay chaos on our entire conference. No one could block that man, Paul. No wonder you are the driven kid you are. I had no idea your granddad was that one-man wrecking crew," he lamented.

"Daddy, Mr. Glassburé is such a nice man. Well, both of them—father and son—are pretty great people. They're large, funny people," Helena intervened.

"This may be true, child, but the fact remains Paul's grandfather pretty much knocked us out of the playoffs every year by himself. I'm not sure how to reconcile this," he replied.

Helena hugged her father and said, "Well Daddy, you have time to think this over before you meet. You're a smart man; do some mind juju on him or something.

"Paul, we have a bunch to get done in not very much time at all. You ready to go?"

"I am. Thank you so much for breakfast and for having me! I genuinely appreciate it," I replied and shook Dr. Upton's hand.

"It was a pleasure having you, Paul. Travel safe today, okay?" Mrs. Upton said kindly, hugging me.

Cassie stood and extended her hand to shake. "It was nice meeting you, Mr. Glassburé. I must inform you that you owe me a conversation."

"Of course, Ms. Upton. I am happy to oblige this request. I will be back in the area in ten days' time. Please consider said conversation taking place over milkshakes at that time," I replied, shaking her hand.

She smiled, nodded and sat back down.

In a flurry of activity, I grabbed my bags and Helena and I set off for a few hours of activity. Because I was entering school as a master's student for psychology, I did not have the requirement to live on campus despite the fact that I still had undergraduate work to do in astrophysics. So, I needed to secure living quarters close to campus.

It so happened that Savannah's mom was a real estate agent and was bribed to help me find something within budget that wasn't typical student housing. So, the four of us went property shopping. Savannah noted that entertainment space, specifically for her, was needed in whatever place we picked.

After maybe an hour of driving around, we found what would end up being "home" throughout our collegiate life.

Do you remember the pond I talked about a couple chapters back? That single detail got me to buy a one-bedroom condominium. Location-wise, it was close enough to both the school and airport, but yet far enough from student housing that I wasn't likely to have drunken visitors in the early morning hours.

Helena liked the closet and the size of both the bathroom and bedroom. I felt the initial pings of despair as my closet space—that I never got to actually use— was summarily taken from me before I even had the key to the place.

The living room was big enough for a pull-out couch, which Savannah made sure of by lying on the floor and pointing out the room she had in all directions while doing so. My questions asking when she would have occasion to sleep in my living room went unanswered.

This amused her mother—perhaps too much.

With the property arranged, I needed furniture. So, we said goodbye to Savannah's mom, but somehow retained Savannah. I still struggle with this, to this day. Why she needed to go with us for furniture shopping is a mystery.

We went to a total of three stores and secured an easy chair, an end table, a pull-out couch that Savannah tested (there were several in the test), a bed and mattress that Helena chose, a dresser and chest of drawers set that matched the bed and two nightstands of the same ilk. Everything was due to be delivered in nine days.

Lastly, I needed other living essentials: plates, silverware, cookware, paper products, towels, etc. I let the girls pick everything and then said no to almost all of it. The plates and every lick of bed accoutrement were floral and pink. Nope. The silverware was flimsy. Again, no. The cookware was all cheap nonstick crap. I subbed for stainless steel and cast iron.

I kept the towels they chose. They were fluffy.

Everything would live in the spare bedroom with the Upton's blessing until I returned. Helena was going to fly back to Charleston with me and stay for about three-quarters of the time. She'd then drive my truck up to Columbia and park it at the airport. The University had arranged for a car to be available to me at the airport back in Charleston once school was back in session.

As we took off from the University airport and headed south, I reflected on how much life had changed in such a short amount of time. On Earth, Helena and I had found one another after entire childhoods with abstinence in every romantic fashion. We had entwined our lives as we had our bodies and found nothing but comfort and joy throughout.

Footholds, Cadences, Plans

When we landed back in Charleston, I got an eerie feeling in my gut. I couldn't place it—I just felt like something was amiss.

I got Bessie all cleaned up and settled in for her nine-day slumber. When we got into the terminal, the gate agent stopped me and handed me a written message. It read:

Welcome home, Paul —

Take your stuff home but then head to Mercy Hospital. Mom and I will be there and will explain everything.

See you soon,

Dad

"I wonder what's going on?" I mused. The fact that it was a written message was strange enough. My father abused text messaging about as much as teenagers used the social media platform of their peers. Why this was written instead of texted was strange.

"I doubt this is great news, Paul, if everyone is at the hospital. Let's just go there—we have nothing in the car that needs to be refrigerated and it sounds like your folks may need some help or love or support. So, take me to the hospital, boy. I might work there someday," Helena replied.

This is exactly what we did. When we got to the hospital, I wasn't sure who I was asking about. When I finally gave the desk person my name, she said, "Ah—head to room twenty-two fifteen on the second floor."

I thanked her and we headed to the second floor.

"I could see myself working here, Paul. I like the vibe," Helena offered.

When we got to the room, I found both parents, Papa, and Gammy and Papa G huddled around a bed.

"Safe flight, you two?" Papa G asked with heavy eyes. He hugged Helena tightly and then grabbed me.

Gam laid unconscious on the bed. It looked like she was breathing on her own, but there was no other movement to speak of.

I went over to my mom and hugged her.

"You okay?" I asked.

"Nope, I'm not sweetie," she replied and I felt tear drippings on my neck.

I wiped Mom's tears with heavy eyes myself. It killed me to see her sad.

"We're not doing so well here, Paul," Papa offered through scratchy words. "She fell at the house and hasn't opened her eyes since. The reality of this is that when she wakes up, there will be a few challenges to address. She knows we're here, but needs to rest. Hopefully, she will be awake by morning, but that is up to her."

"What can we do? How can we help?" I asked.

"Can you stop at the house and let the dogs out and then feed them? I'm afraid at their ages you may have a mess to clean up. Would you mind doing that for me?" he asked. My grandparents had this uncanny thing with dogs all the way until they died. They never went a day or two without having two dogs, always Rhodesian Ridgebacks—but they never, ever bought a single dog. The dogs always found *them*. Their current pups were Violet and Gale, and both were nearing the end of their trips on the third rock.

"No problem at all, Papa. Mess or no, no problem. Do you want me to let them out later tonight, or do the feed and let out in the morning?" I asked.

"It all depends on whether they kick me out or not. I'll call you or message you as soon as I know. Regardless, thank you both for your help. Helena, sweetheart, how are you? Not the best circumstances to return to," he said politely.

"It's okay. I'm just so sorry about all of this. Paul and I will take care of the dogs. Mr. and Mrs. Glassburé, do we need to do anything at the house?" she asked, looking at my sad parents.

"I'm afraid we have the makings of dinner but it's going to be very late even if we start cooking now. Want to take care of the dogs and then meet us at Patty's? I think this is a punt kind of night and greasy food is on tap," Dad said. It was obvious whatever was going on was not at all good. He loved Gam like a second mother. This was not easy for him.

"Patty's it is, Dad," I said and proceeded to hug everyone in the room.

When I got to Papa, I whispered, "I'm sorry the part of me that could help isn't here. I wish I could, Papa."

He looked at me and winked, a knowing smile on his lips.

Helena and I left to go take care of the dogs, who were sound asleep when we arrived. I hunched that Gale at minimum was deaf, but Helena disagreed. Violet attached herself to my girl, just as she had my grandma. It had to be a girl thing; it was cute no matter what.

With dogs taken outside after lots of prodding and belly love and subsequent feeding, we helped them settle back into their luxe doggy beds. I knelt down with Gage and could not believe how supportive those things were. Helena straight up cuddled Violet to the point of puppy snoring.

A couple more minutes of petting and loving observation followed, with Helena declaring, "We're getting at least one, maybe two," as we left my grandparents' house.

We then proceeded to Patty's and found Mom and Dad, who both looked to be sleep deprived and extremely sad.

Mom stood and hugged me, wiping her nose and eyes a couple times. Helena hugged Dad.

We all sat and I tried to break the mood by talking about the dogs and school, but the mood remained. There were large sections of small talk, but the somber mood never left the table.

As we got in the car to leave, Helena turned to me and said, "Babe, I have this idea. What if every time you came back here to do the orchard or school or farm stuff, I go and stay with your grandma? I have a selfish reason for this, so let me just be out with it. I lost both of my grandmothers by the time I was eight. You have two grandmothers who I adore. I don't care if it's an hour or four or eight. Can I really be a permanent passenger on your flights back here?"

I smiled, leaned over and kissed her. "Of course you can, love," I replied.

The plan at least cursorily made in intention, we headed back to my parents' house, where the intention was then communicated.

My mother enveloped Helena in her arms and both of them wept. Dad and I had to leave the room as the scene had a tragic feel to it. Watching the whole thing was heartbreaking.

"Helena is positively unreal, Paul," Dad said and handed me a glass of water.

"I agree, Dad. I feel like an insanely lucky man to have her in my life," I replied and took a drink.

As we settled in to bed that night, Helena whispered, "I love this family so much."

"You have no idea the impact of your words, Helena. What you promised to do today was unreal," I said, pulling her close.

We both crashed hard that night after the day that was had.

The morning began a cadence that lasted five full days. Put simply, we drove to the hospital, where I dropped off Helena. I then went to the orchard and tended everything that needed attention. From there, I went to my grandparents' house and spent time with the dogs. Next, I went to Rick's school and did whatever Papa G or Dad asked me to do. Next, I went to the farm and did whatever Mom or Uncle Lou or the Rodriguez's needed.

The Rodriguez family is essentially Uncle Lou's in-laws. They were full partners in the farm with my grandparents and Mom. From the stories I've heard, Papa's life was saved at one point by an invention Aunt Julia's uncle made. The intertwining respect and love between both families ran very deep, generations long.

After I left the farm, I would go back to the hospital, visit with my grandma a bit with Helena and anyone else in the room. From there, we either took care of the dogs again or went back to my parents' house.

This pattern did not change for any of the first five days we were in Charleston.

At the start of day six, my grandmother was released and allowed to go home. She had remained unconscious for a full week. On the morning of the sixth day, she was wide awake, as though nothing was out of the ordinary.

Her unconsciousness had been caused by a rogue infection in her brain. My grandfather had disallowed quite a bit of testing to take place as he'd diagnosed the whole thing and had gotten to the root cause of it the day she had gone to the hospital. He was not equipped to deal with her care at home, so he relented and allowed the hospital to treat her within the boundaries he allowed.

Papa had worked in that hospital for decades, diagnosing both conscious and unconscious patients. He was well-respected—he had saved thousands of lives, simply by pointing doctors to problems they had no way of finding.

The long and short of Gam's issue was that her body was becoming less resistant to common bacteria literally found everywhere. The type of healing Papa did was rooted deeply in the person's willingness to be healed. Thing was, there was little to heal for her unless time traveled backward, and this drove him nuts. Her condition was therefore managed with diet and supplements. If she got woozy, she knew to get to a hospital.

Also, it was advised that her energy levels would fluctuate wildly. As such, a wheelchair was introduced for the times that she really didn't have it in her to walk.

So, on the day that Helena was to drive back to Columbia, the cadence changed. After breakfast, we drove to my grandparents' house, where I left Helena and went on with the orchard/school/farm cadence. When I was done with all of my responsibilities, I returned to my grandparents' house, where I found Helena and Gam sitting out on their deck with the dogs.

"Well, look at this," Gam began, "The Paulie has returned to us. What say you, child?"

"Hello, you two. How was the day?" I replied.

"Magical. This girlfriend of yours is a true keeper. You're not being an idiot, are you, child?" Gam asked, lowering her brow.

"I intend to keep her, Gam," I replied.

"This is a good thing, indeed. Are you going to keep coming here until school begins? My heart is already missing this girl, but I certainly understand there are preparations to be made."

"I will absolutely be here, Gam. And, we have already made plans for both of us to be here on a weekly basis. So, you'll only be missing Helena for about a week or so before we'll be back," I explained.

"Yes—she and I have talked about this and I truly love the plan. I will still miss her in the interim. We have become quite close," she explained.

"Aw Gam," Helena began, "our time together means the world to me. I have loved this week so, so much. I cannot wait to come back!"

Grabbing Helena's hand, Gam said, "Helena, you have made a difficult situation so much easier to handle. I am so thankful for your help."

As soon as she said this, Papa walked in and announced that dinner was ready. We had plans with Mom and Dad at Patty's, ironically, given the last experience we had there.

So, we exchanged our goodbyes and I promised my presence there the next day.

When we got in the truck, Helena grabbed me and kissed me. "You gave me love, you gave me a bigger family and you gave me the chance to feel like I've been able to have an honest to God grandma again to boot. By damn, Paul Glassburé— you are about as perfect a man as I could have ever imagined. I am not at all looking forward to sleeping without you for the first time in weeks."

I looked deeply into her eyes. I truly could not believe she was in my life.

"It'll only be four days, Love. I think the time will go quickly with all there is to do," I replied.

Dinner at Patty's was immensely lighter and much more fun than the last experience. Dad laughed the way I expected him to laugh. Mom smiled the way I loved to see her smile. Helena soaked in every moment in a way that touched my soul. The food wasn't too bad, either.

When it came time for Helena to head back, she drove me to the airport so that I could pick up the vehicle Dr. Szymanski had arranged for me. Essentially, it would stay in Charleston for the duration of my education—it would be my transportation from the airport each week that I flew home.

Low and behold, we found a full-sized pickup truck, not unlike mine. I went into the terminal to retrieve the keys and was handed a note with them. It read:

Greetings, Paul!

I was able to convince the higher ups to secure you a ride that allows you to maintain the functionality you have with your own vehicle whilst in Charleston. We'll have to come up with a name for her, as it's only right.

Best,

Ted

"Once again, your influence proceeds you," Helena gushed.

"This is such a nice gesture. I was worried about the farm and orchard work I do without a truck," I said, looking over the hitch and bed of the truck.

"I don't want to go, Paul," she said, wrapping her arms around me.

I squeezed her tightly. I wanted to feel her heart next to mine; I knew I was going to miss her.

"The time will fly, babe. Four days will sail by," I said, still feeling her heartbeat.

"But… Paul, I fall asleep listening to your heart. It's the most uncanny thing, but it's the single most comforting thing I have ever experienced. Right now, with you close, I feel so at peace," she replied, putting her head on my shoulder.

We stood there for a good couple minutes not talking or moving.

As the sun set behind us, I knew it was time. I didn't want Helena getting home too late, and I knew the drive was a good couple of hours, plus.

"It's time, you. I want you to get home before the pitch black of night settles in," I lamented.

"I know. I just don't wanna," she replied, unmoving.

After another couple minutes, she relented and let go.

"I hate this, Paul. I don't want the fact that you are away to feel like this," she said, her eyes looking two inches deep into my brain.

"Try something for me: close your eyes, take a deep breath and try to feel my heartbeat in your mind," I suggested. I had done a notable amount of research in the area of the human mind. It is remarkable what is possible with intent, especially when partnered with meditative states.

She looked at me quizzically, but then relented and closed her eyes. I could almost see the moment when she realized that she could feel my heartbeat from memory. You see, she had listened to my heart so much that the frequency of the rhythm was something she could hear, if she allowed herself to become quiet.

A single tear fell from her eyes. "You really are with me, my love. This is beautiful," she gushed.

"Now you see; there literally, will never be a time in your life when I won't be with you. This is as true now as it will be when we are old, stinky people. I have trusted you with my heart, Helena Upton. Please keep it safe," I said as she opened her eyes.

Indeed, we are old, stinky people, currently. Bite me, ingrate.

She kissed me. "There will never be a time in my life, Paul Glassburé, where I won't hold that heart as close as I can to mine."

With that said and a final kiss, I loaded her into the truck and watched her drive away. As the car faded into the distance, I felt our separation. I decided that this dictated a conversation with Blue. As such, I called her and asked if I might be able to stop by. She welcomed it.

So, I took my as-yet-to-be-named school truck and drove to the land of my bald brother and his angelic bride. The twins were two months old at this time.

I arrived at my brother's house and texted him that I had arrived. I didn't want to wake the babies if they were asleep.

He happily opened the door and welcomed me in. That dome of his was just magic back then— magic.

"Hey, Paul! It's great to see you! College is about a week away, right? Well, the master's work that was supposed to be bachelor's work, that is," he jested.

"Yeah. I am transferring to SCU to follow my psychology professor. I also truly enjoy my astrophysics professor, too," I replied.

As I was talking, Blue walked up and hugged me tightly.

"You have questions, Paul. Let me help," she said without prompting.

The twins were asleep in their room. Both parents carried monitors, one on Annabelle and the other on Josephine.

We went out onto their patio and Blue gave me another hug.

"Helena headed back today. I know this is hard," she said.

"Yeah, but I can't quite understand why, Blue. I mean, I care deeply for her, but I can't figure out why it hurts like this when we're apart," I explained.

Blue looked at me and said, "There are people in our lives that extend the meaning of our own. I have seen this with both my and your parents, and certainly feel this way about your brother. I have to believe that Helena simply adds something to your life that enriches it. When she is away, you feel this," she replied.

"I've known you forever, Paul. *Not once* has there been a girl in your life, but quite a few attempted to bribe your sister and me for a chance to do so. I know this was your choice. Heck—I had to be the bad guy more often than not because I knew what you wanted, but our sister wanted what *she* thought was right for you. I respected the absolute bejesus out of you for it. Because of this, I knew when the one you chose was in your life, it would change you. From the sounds of things, brother, she has," Larry pontificated. He was nice from time to time.

"I mean, maybe. I just can't reconcile this. I know how I feel, but the physical sensation of her being away is not something I was prepared for," I reasoned.

"Paul, tell me this: do you know why Helena is infatuated with your heart?" Blue asked. For context, this topic was never discussed with her. If this is the proof you need that she was an angel put here on Earth, there it is. Now quit yer complainin'. Dammit.

"I… I don't…," I stammered.

"She has known your heart for years, Paul—since she was a little girl. *Years* of her life have been spent dreaming of finding that ticker of yours. She told all in her circle that she'd know when she found you. Thing is, she'd know she found you if your heart matched the one in her dreams. The explanation of this is something my Momma told me a long time ago, and it was something I've *believed* ever since as I proved it with Larry. Trust this feeling as proof that you searched for the same thing—and found it in her," Blue preached. By the end of this, she was holding both of my hands.

"I seriously don't know what to say," I said, stunned.

"It's best you just accept what you've been told, Paul. My bride has a talent for communicating things that are rooted in truth that supersede rational thought," Larry interjected.

Blue moved from me to kiss Larry and then sat back down. She looked at the monitor of Josephine and smiled.

"Is everything going okay with the twins?" I asked, seeing Larry investigate his monitor as well.

"Yes. It's just something to watch them sleep. There are such wonderful things happening in those young minds. It's something to simply witness it all," Blue explained.

"I can't be nearly as prophetic," Larry said, still looking at his monitor. "I just like knowing they are safe and healthy."

"Thank you both for the time. I know this was out of the blue and we all have full days tomorrow. I'll get out of your hair and head home," I said, sensing the parents wanted to devote more attention to their monitoring efforts.

"Don't feel you need to rush away, Paul. We love having you here," Blue said, looking up from the monitor.

"I genuinely appreciate that, Blue. I should head home given the day that waits for me tomorrow," I explained and got up.

Blue walked over and hugged me tightly. "You are always welcome here," she said mid-embrace.

"Thank you," I said, hugging her tighter.

"I'm glad you are happy, Paul. Eighteen years is a long time to wait for a relationship. I'm just glad it's working out the way that it is. Don't be a stranger, okay?" Larry requested kindly.

"Thanks, Brother. I want to be a good uncle to those twins of yours. I promise to not be a stranger. Besides—it sure looks to me that Hatch and Dylan are going to get married sooner than later. There was talk on our flight back about getting a wedding together by the end of the year. I think the planning to do such a thing will be intense!" I said, separating from Blue.

"He told me the same thing. I think they are looking to get married between Thanksgiving and Christmas, so yeah, it's going to be interesting," Blue added.

"They make the best, most unlikely pair I can imagine," Larry offered.

Blue wrapped her arms around my brother and said, "When love is purely intended, nothing else matters."

She's a descended master of the living. Literally, that's what she is. There is no other explanation.

I quietly made my exit and headed home.

As I pulled into the driveway, Helena called to say she was home. We agreed that it was bittersweet that we were apart.

Thing is, it was silly for us to feel this way. The next four days flew for both of us. On my end, my days were literally orchard, Rick's school, farm, Gam. On Helena's end, it was pack, move, school, repeat. She continued to help her dad get his office and classroom set up and had medical school orientation in the mix, too.

When the day arrived for me to head back, a sizable tropical depression started speeding toward Charleston. So, I changed my flight plan to a much earlier time, finished my packing and did a very quick touch-up at the orchard before heading out.

It was a good thing, too. No more than five minutes after I had taken off, my air traffic controller came on the radio to tell me that they were closing the airport due to the severity of the storm. He encouraged me to fly faster and get on the ground as soon as possible.

So, I heeded the warning and sped up. I had landed and just finished my taxi into my parking spot when the wind and rain finally caught up. Out of complete kindness, the entire ground crew helped me get Bessie torn down and protected my luggage from the rain. I got soaked, but my stuff got into my truck with just a couple drops on it, compliments of the extremely kind ground crew.

After going through my paperwork with the gate agent, I headed home. This was going to be the first time I slept in the condo, provided the furniture was still going to be delivered.

As I pulled in to the parking lot, I spotted something. My gut told me something was wrong, so amid the torrential rain, I ran to investigate.

I found a tiny black kitten, shivering from both fear and cold. Instinctively, I picked the critter up and got into the condo. I immediately called Blue, who told me to make sure the kitten got warmed up and fed a very bland diet. She was going to drive up the next day to check him out.

Helena arrived a short time later, panicked.

"Why was your truck door open, Paul? I closed it, but it's soaked. What's…" she said as she rounded the corner and found me holding the swaddled kitten tightly to my chest, wrapped in a towel. I was still dripping wet.

"Who is this, now?" she asked, kneeling down. The kitten was still shaking.

"I don't know, babe. He needs our help, if only for tonight. He was getting beaten up by that storm. I didn't see any other cats in the area, but to be fair, I really didn't look too hard," I explained.

"I so, so, get it. Let me get you and the little fella a fresh towel," she said and kissed me.

The three of us sat there for about an hour. Eventually, the wind and rain stopped and I decided to try and find where the little cat may have come from.

Thing was, there was no sign of other cats anywhere. I looked under bushes, all around the pond and under cars. A couple of my neighbors saw what I was doing, and after a quick explanation, pitched in. After scouring the area, we'd found no signs of cats, kittens or nests anywhere.

So, I thanked my neighbors and returned to the condo, where I found Helena feverishly looking on her phone for something.

"What are you looking for?" I asked.

"I've sent Savannah out on a scavenger hunt to get him food. Blue recommended this really specific food, so I sent Savannah out to find it. I was looking to try and aid the search," she explained.

"You reached out to Blue?"

"Nope. She somehow knew to find me with you outside. I dunno," she said.

With that moment of consternation complete, there was a knock on the door and our furniture was delivered. As soon as the movers were done, Savannah appeared, bearing kitten fare.

"I shall sit on my couch and review my finds," she began, sitting on the couch she had picked out. "I found the food and bought all that the one store had. I also got him bowls, kitten toys, a scratching post, a litter box and a bed."

"Thanks Savannah! The food is perfect—it's exactly what Blue recommended. Let's see if he's hungry," I said. Helena was holding the still-bundled kitten. Tiny, faint purrs were audible.

Savannah washed the new dishes and put half of one of the cans in one of them with a little bit of water. Again, this was a Blue recommendation.

Helena carefully put the little guy in front of the food and it was gone in seconds. His little eyes looked up at us, hypnotically forcing us to give him the rest of that can.

Again, the food was gone in seconds. So, I called Blue and asked for some advice.

"From the pictures Helena sent, he's probably no more than three or four weeks old. Let his system digest the food and, in an hour or so, give him a little bit—maybe two or three teaspoons—of whole milk. Try to find the most natural stuff you can, okay? I'll bring some with me tomorrow to help supplement his diet over the next two weeks or so. We need to mimic mom at least a little bit with him being so young.

"Keep the solid food feedings to no more than three a day. He'll be hungry in-between, so give him milk at those times. You should likely introduce the litter box to him soon after the meal, too. Sound like a plan?" she asked kindly.

"As always, thank you Blue. You have helped so much," I replied.

Savannah took a turn holding the kitten while I got the litterbox established. Helena researched the introduction process. Once I was confident the box was ready to go, he was placed in it, dug a little bit and used it. He was smart from jump.

"He needs a name. We can't keep calling him 'kitten'," Helena professed.

"Is Storm too intense? I want to honor what he survived if that makes any sense," I suggested.

"In keeping with that theme, why don't we name him Vick after the weatherman on channel three? Vick Storm is about the most intense weather guy I've ever seen," Helena offered.

"I think that works. Savannah, what say you?"

"I like it—Vick fits him perfectly. What he survived will always be part of his story. I think now, it's about giving him the best life possible. I'm not a cat person in the least, but that tiny thing is special," she replied, picking him up after his potty trip.

"It is decided. Vick the black cat," I proclaimed. I liked it too with my significant experience as Vic on Cythis.

"Let's not age Vick prematurely, Paul. For at least a little while, he's a kitten," Savannah corrected.

"Noted," I acknowledged. Savannah has done this to me for decades. This was but the beginning of the torment.

Vick somehow knew the bed was his and curled up in it immediately. Well, to be honest he sorta fell in, clumsily gathered himself and curled up. He was anything but stable on his feet. I think he slept in that thing until the next morning, as he groggily stretched and looked at me with tired eyes when I went to check on him before making breakfast.

The fact Vick had slept as well as he had was especially impressive as Helena had kept our tradition of intricate lingerie alive, given it was our first night in the condo. It was an especially lively session given the fact that it was both a new place *and* our brand-new bed. It was broken in extremely well that night. The cliff notes: layers of intertwined lace, blindfolds. Let your savage mind roam and you'll likely get less than half of the night right. Bottom line, we were anything but silent for a good part of that night,

The groggy cat thing worked out nicely, as my sister-in-law arrived minutes after I checked on the sleepy guy and was able to examine him and give him a couple precautionary shots before he ate. She wanted to give him the medicine before food was in his belly, so this whole thing worked out well. I hadn't been looking forward to his hunger fit, which happened immediately after Blue left.

"He looks perfect, Paul. Just be aware that he is very, very young. I'm going to guess he's *just* over three weeks old right now. His claws are apt to get caught on things, so watch for that as they are really brittle right now. Use the milk I brought as both in- and between-meal nutrition. I think a full can, twice a day is about right for about another week.

"Once his teeth are mostly in, we should look to add dry food to the mix. This won't be for another couple weeks yet, so we can talk about that later. But, like any baby, he may gnaw on you from time to time. He'll grow out of it, but those gums may be super sore over the next couple weeks. Still—tiny kitten teeth and tiny kitten nails *hurt!*

"Do you have any questions?" she asked kindly. She was holding him the entire time—his purr likely woke the neighbors.

"No—thank you, Blue. Can I get you any coffee or make you breakfast before the drive back?" I asked.

"That is such a kind offer, Paul. Unfortunately, I have appointments that I have to get back for. I will plan another trip here and will be able to spend more time then. However, I will gladly accept whatever coffee you have available," she said.

She had brought a travel mug with her, so I filled it while she said her goodbyes to Vick. I swear to you he understood her. I wish I could have captured the interaction on video—Blue's connection to animals was uncanny.

I put the lid on the mug and gave Blue a hug once the Vick goodbyes were complete.

"Thank you for the short notice visit, Doc. How much do I owe you for today?" I asked.

"Given all pertinent facts, this and all future visits are free, Paul. Should you wish to pay anything, please support the shelter," she requested, referencing the shelter she co-founded with her brother Red. It was one of the only no-kill, nonprofit facilities in the country to offer the level of care it did to all of the animals. The whole thing was run on donations of money and time from other veterinarians.

"Consider it done. Thank you again for coming all this way.".

"Your house is lovely, Paul. I will look forward to our breakfast together for the next time," she said, grabbed her coffee and was off.

Vick then devoured a can of food, found his bed and fell asleep quickly.

Helena emerged from taking a shower. "Is Blue already gone?" she asked.

"Yeah. She had to get back for appointments later in the morning. She was here shortly after eight if you can believe it," I replied.

"Unreal. Vick check out okay?" she asked, wrapping her arms around me and kissing me. "Unreal stuff last night. My heart is *still* racing, Paul. *Wow.*"

"He is good; we have a plan. I would agree that our activities last night upped the game in ways I didn't think the game could be upped," I replied and kissed her.

We had orientation at USC later that morning, so we ate breakfast and headed to campus.

What is absolutely absurd is that, after orientation and with just two outliers, the next three-and-three-quarter years followed an insanely predictable pattern at a high level. Let's cover the pattern first.

At the end of class on every day and on Saturday mornings, we flew back to Charleston. Helena was dropped off at my grandparents' house to spend time with Gam. I touched up the orchard, went to Rick's school and to the farm and did whatever needed to be done for forty-five minutes in each place. I'd then head to my grandparents' house, visit with Gam and Papa—if he was there— and we'd fly back. The exception to this part of the pattern: Saturdays, we flew down at 11:00 and flew back at 4:00. I spent time wherever I was needed and Helena first helped me at the orchard and then visited with Gam. Papa drove her back with him if he left before I left for the school or farm. A minimum of one dinner per week was spent with my family. Sundays, we had dinner with the Upton clan without fail.

During the week, we'd get home and make dinner, study for no more than two hours, play with Vick until he got tired and then go to bed. He alternated time between my and Helena's lap as we did our school work, which I found to be adorable.

We went to school throughout our summers, albeit with slightly lesser class loads so there was time for relaxation here and there. This allowed Helena to accelerate her way through her ancillary coursework so that all the rest of her time in college was able to be spent focusing on internal medicine. She decided to isolate her efforts on the cardiovascular side of medicine and formed her genius self into one hell of a cardio surgeon and specialist in the process of doing so.

The summer work also allowed me to maintain my pace in all areas of my studies, making it possible for me to truly earn my doctorate in psychology in four years and for sure my masters in astrophysics, too. I felt I'd be close to a doctorate there, too, which in the end I was.

So, in this three-and-three-quarter year chunk, I earned my master's degree in psychology and was nearly done with my doctorate. I was more nearly done with my master's in astrophysics, though in truth the work I was doing with my research partner, John, and Dr. Szymanski was never at the master's level. On paper, that was what I was earning based on the college's guidelines, which did not consider the publications or research as part of my studies.

The work we did, however, lead worldwide exploration based on our findings. My logic was featured in major science journals as I'd published over one-hundred white papers with my name on the byline. We found planets, evidence of dark matter everywhere and accurately predicted the movements of objects never before measured.

The first outlier: Dylan and Hatch got married in the gap between Thanksgiving and Christmas during our first year at SCU. Charlie was born just over a year later. Both events slightly amended the cadence enough to be considered a disturbance to the pattern.

The second involved Sam and Eva coming to see us at the end of this chunk of time.

Before I dig into this, it is worth mentioning that Sam, Eva and I talked to Helena constantly about my dimensionally wandering self and all it entailed. She asked questions—good, probing questions—throughout. It makes zero sense to detail every one as there were well over two-hundred conversations on this topic, and it always went the same way. The takeaways were always Helena learning and accepting a little more and the four of us getting closer.

At the three-and-three-quarter year mark, we were dangerously close to hitting our respective goals. Helena had moved through her studies with a proficiency that proved she was right where she needed to be. She would graduate from medical school in four calendar years, thanks to the summer supplements.

I was a millimeter away from my doctorate in psychology and had done more than twice what I needed for a master's degree in astrophysics. I was bitter about this at times—really, sourly bitter.

So, when I got the call from Sam that they were coming up with news, it hit me when I was in a mood.

We met for lunch on a Wednesday. This lunch spawned a three-ish month blitz that I still can't properly comprehend. Both Helena and I had turned twenty-two by this time.

"So—you two, the assignment on Xsip is nearly done. By sometime right around graduation—in around three months—it will be time for that part of Paul to return to Earth. Because of this and the massive time gap in place, we have more than a lot to do. Both families have to be prepared. Professors need to be prepared.

Documentation needs to be prepared. The time gap is going to be ridiculously hard on Paul to resolve, so it is up to us to craft a path for him forward. It could cause all kinds of things, from fainting to heart issues to far worse.

"Helena, I need to be extremely clear here: in one fell swoop, Paul's memory will be wiped of approximately seven years. Though it will remain local in your boyfriend's brain, it won't be accessible due to the enormity of the gap. You have to realize that Paul was fifteen when he started the assignment on Xsip. He's had no way to communicate with anyone at all about anything and thinks this has been nowhere near as long as it has due to the time difference between Earth and Xsip.

"I should mention that the work completed is positively unreal. What he achieved saved around two-trillion lives. He is going to have so much to tell us.

"I digress. The other thing is that Eva and I have to derive a strategy for finals work as that is likely to happen the moment he returns. This is on us to figure out as there is no way all this work is for nothing.

"Congratulations, by the way!" Sam said with no explanation whatsoever.

"Congratulations for what, Sam?" I asked, full brat in play.

"The baby, idiot. Helena, how are you feeling?" he replied.

"What?" I asked, shooting a look at my girl.

"I'm, like, two days late. I didn't think much about it," she explained.

"Go to the doctor. She'll explain," Sam offered, every bit the satirist.

"That was awful, Sam," Eva criticized and hugged Helena. "I didn't want to say anything, but *Sam* apparently decided for the both of us. Regardless, this will be incredible for the Paul coming back. Here's the thing, sweetie: we are here to help you. You will need help. Are you willing to do this?"

"I'm not sure what to say," Helena responded. "Paul, seriously, I've been on birth control forever. This should not have happened."

Sam gently grabbed her hand and said, "No birth control was stopping this from happening. I'm profoundly sorry for saying anything."

"Wait, wait, wait. Is this the child lost on Cythis?" I asked, recalling what I had heard the baby say as he died. My brat self changed in a hurry.

"Yes, Paul—it is," Sam said smiling.

"Oh my God," I said, tears falling down my sourpuss face.

"What is happening?" Helena asked, grabbing my hand with her free one. Sam still held her other hand.

"I will never forget that feeling, Helena—ever. I was so young, but I will never forget hearing him say 'goodbye'," I explained, reliving that horrible moment.

"Let me get this straight: I am pregnant with a child some part of Paul and another part of me lost a bunch of years ago on some planet in a different dimension? Am I understanding you correctly? How in the world…" Helena stammered.

"Helena, look at me," Eva began. "I was there. I know this is a *bunch* to digest, but you have to find some way to make peace with it. This is going to be unbelievable for a bunch of reasons. Trust me when I say that this child chose his entry point specifically and refused to wait for you to be ready. He *decided* you were ready. You are, in every possible meaning of the word.

"Paul, you have things to do. Get them done," she said flatly.

I had purchased a ring from a guy at Papa's urging three months prior with the intention of proposing sometime around graduation. The guy I bought the ring from was the grandson of the guy Papa had gotten Gam's ring from. Stanley Marks was Ted Marks' grandson—Ted served with my great, great grandfather in the Army. Like everything else, I loved the familial connection, so I went with the suggestion.

Gam coached me through every aspect of it. She sat in my meetings with Stanley, choosing what she did based on what she had cleverly pulled from Helena over time. I spent a fortune on it, again at my Gam's direction. "You do this once, Paulie. One time, you get to see her eyes light up for the first time. Do not minimize the importance of that moment," she explained as I made my final decisions.

I had the ring but not one clue how to propose. Let's table that for the moment.

The lunch ended with a fairly specific plan to address the entirety of the Upton clan, then the University staff, then the Glassburé lot. Sam and Eva took point on all of it.

As we got up from that lunch, Helena immediately enveloped me in a tight embrace.

"How in the world are we going to do this, Paul? How…"

"Helena, I need you to hear me. Not just with your ears, but with your heart. If there is one thing we both have trusted from the very beginning, it's that our lives are governed from someplace bigger than we are. We found each other in an unlikely place at what turned out to be perfect timing.

"I believe to the core of what I am that this is no different. If this is really all happening, there is more to celebrate than I can ever properly say," I explained, holding her tightly.

"What Paul said," Eva added, wiping copiously falling tears from her face.

Putting It All Together

A doctor exam two days later proved that Helena was pregnant. Her doctor explained that frequent sex could result in pregnancy, despite the use of birth control. Helena scoffed at this, but ultimately conceded that we had successfully gotten pregnant on the one-millionth-of-one-percent chance of doing so and walked out of the appointment.

I decided to propose in the same place we met the next weekend. So, with Dr. Szymanski's help, I quickly got together a plan to fly both families out with him in a different plane that I financed, and I altered my flight plan on Bessie for Friday to include the trip to Hawaii. Dr. Szymanski would fly everyone two hours ahead of me, which was something of a Herculean task to put together but, with help, I pulled it off.

When we got into the plane for what should have been our normal trip to Charleston, Cassie was waiting in a seat in the back. She had packed all of Helena's additional clothes and toiletries for me and had the ground crew load all of our luggage into Bessie.

"Are you coming to Charleston with us, Cassie?" Helena asked, completely surprised by her presence.

"Something like that, yeah. Sit with me back here, Hells? I hate flying with a passion and trust your man as much as I trust myself to fly this thing," Cassie said.

"Sure," Helena replied and shot me a look.

I smiled, turned on the loudspeaker and in my best smug pilot voice said, "Ladies, thank you for joining us today. Please get your seatbelts fastened as we are about to begin our taxi from the gate. No questions will be entertained until we reach our final destination. Snacks and drinks are in the fridge in the back. Blankets and pillows are in the cabinets on the side. Enjoy your flight."

As soon as I was done talking, I nodded at my ground crew, who had been briefed on the plan, and was pushed back.

I never closed the cockpit door when Helena and I flew because she'd sit in the copilot seat we would chat on the headsets. This time, I closed the door so that my check-ins wouldn't tip Helena off to the plan. She'd know something was up, but I even changed my refuel point to throw her off.

When we landed to refuel, I peeked in the back and found both women sound asleep, both wrapped up in blanket cocoons. We got a full belly into Bessie, I got a coffee with espresso in it and got back into the sky in about thirty minutes, give or take a couple. The girls never woke up through the refueling or the noise I made getting into and out of Bessie. Apparently, those blankets were truly magical, keeping human beings unconscious at times they, in no way, should be.

Six hours later, we landed in Hawaii at the same airport I'd landed at previously. The girls slept through the landing and taxi to Bessie's parking spot, which was next to Dr. Szymanski's ride.

The ground crew helped me get all the luggage unloaded into a waiting car. I was able to do all of my final work both with Bessie and the airport before gently waking the girls and ushering them into the car.

It was almost dinner time. My plan was to quickly drop all of our stuff off in the hotel lobby and then take Helena out to the bench where we first sat. The family would sneak up behind us, and I would propose.

Well, Cassie and I got the bags into the lobby while Helena was still waking up in the car. Cassie then went off to find the families and I went back to nervously get Helena out of the car.

"Why in the world did you fly us here, Paul?" she asked mid-yawn, taking my outstretched hand.

"Just a fun little getaway for the weekend, you," I replied and led us toward the bench.

"What about my time with Gam? What about the orchard? What about…"

"Helena, I promise it's all under control. I *promise*," I said as we got close to the intended bench.

"Paul, Gam and I had plans this weekend. We have things to discuss. I need to…"

"Helena Louise, I need you to calm thyself," Gam said from somewhere behind us.

"Gam? Why?" she stammered.

"Sit, child. Listen to Paulie," she instructed.

"What is going on?" she pointedly asked as we sat down.

I had the ring in my shirt pocket. I got up, turned to face her and saw everyone start to walk towards us.

I looked deeply into her eyes and gently grabbed her hands.

"Helena, from the moment we met and sat on this bench, I knew I'd found someone special. For years now, you've proven to me that you are so much more than that. You're the woman I need to spend forever with," I said and knelt down.

I produced the ring from my pocket and asked, "Helena Louise Upton, would you marry me?"

Her sleepy, confused eyes got very big and then *very* teary. "I would have said 'yes' the first time we sat on this bench, you."

I put the ring on her finger and the collection behind the bench erupted.

Helena knelt down and kissed me, tears still falling from her eyes.

"All of this isn't because of the bean in my belly, is it?" she asked, crying.

"No, my love. I've had the ring for a couple months. This was the right time, all things considered," I explained.

"Congratulations you two! Paul, thank you for allowing us to be part of this. I cannot believe you did all that you did for us," Dr. Upton gushed.

Cassie attached herself to our kneeling selves, crying her own tears.

"I have considered you my brother since I met you, Paul. Thank you for being my big brother," she said through heavy tears.

I stood us up, squeezed Helena and Cassie tightly and said, "Dr. Upton, I wouldn't have wanted this any other way. I cannot thank you enough for enduring my insanity to be here with us. I have dinner planned; is everyone ready for a little walk on the beach?"

There was boisterous, strangely hard to understand replies.

The group included our parents, my grandparents, her grandfather, Sam, Eva, Dr. Szymanski, Cassie, Savannah, Larry, Blue and the twins, Dylan, Hatch and Charlie. I could not resolve plans with her uncle Saul, unfortunately. Dr. Upton promised to record it all and send him the footage as a consolation.

I'd planned for the meal to be at the place Dylan, Hatch and I had breakfast. The owners were incredibly happy to have the chance to be part of the celebration.

Yeah, celebrate, we did. All of us—plus about two-hundred of our closest Hawaiian friends. There were so many hugs that night I felt I might pop with one more. Despite the crowd, we had time to talk as a family, and the baby was disclosed.

As soon as Mom heard this, she started to cry. She came over to me and whispered, "It's him, isn't it?" and wrapped her arms around me. She then proceeded to wrap her arms around Helena and completely soaked her shoulder with tears. The emotion spilled over to Dylan, Cassie, Savannah and Helena, too.

As the night wound down, Dad pulled Sam and me aside and asked, "Is this child really the same boy that was lost all those years ago on that planet with those awful men that killed my son, like, five times or something?"

"It is, Jonah. When you meet him, you will recognize him," Sam replied.

"I didn't die, Dad," I interjected.

"Am I wrong to wonder how that's possible? And yes, son, you were very dead many times. I will never forget this as long as I live and likely will never forgive you for it, either." Dad continued, rubbing his forehead.

Sam put his hand on Dad's shoulder and said, "You're not wrong about the absurdity of this, Jonah. I can't in good faith explain it, though. I simply promise you this: he will make you incredibly proud, just like his father who did, in fact, die many times on Cythis."

There was a tear in Dad's eye after Sam said this. No other words were spoken.

The night ended with hugs, more tears and a sense of family in our combined realms. I still feel such a connection to that night for this reason alone.

When we retired to our room, Helena lamented, "Babe, I didn't plan for this. I... No... No lingerie."

"Well, Fiancé, what if we introduced something different on account of the night?" I asked, gathering her in my arms.

"I'm listening," she replied and sunk into me.

"Pregame, and however many rounds we have between tonight and tomorrow morning cannot be in the same place. The floor counts as one big place. This limits us to the bed, that chair thingy, the balcony, the floor and the two or three options in the bathroom depending how you look at it. Oh—and hands may not be used for clothing removal once buttons, clasps and zippers are undone. Up for the challenge?" I proposed.

"Clarification: pregame in the morning counts in this, too?" she asked, looking at me intently.

"It does," I replied and kissed her.

"I like the thinking here," she said and tripped me onto the floor. "Let's get this floor thing out of the way because it's *way* too convenient."

That night, we crossed off the floor, balcony and chair thingy. When we woke up the next morning, the bed, bathroom counter and shower were subsequently removed from the available list.

"Are we really doing this forever, Paul? I mean, like, officially and forever more, you are mine and mine alone?" she asked as water careened over us in the shower.

"Was there ever a question in your mind that we weren't, my love?" I replied and kissed her.

"I mean, no—but having a ring changes things. Not in a bad way, though. I mean, seriously—I was your only and you are my only. Can it seriously be that we will be this happy forever as each other's onlys?" she asked.

"Well—the way I see it—we made a choice somehow to exclude anyone *but* each other. As we have said countless times, we mutually had opportunity, sometimes encouraged or arranged by family, to pair us with someone else. We never took the offer. The first time I allowed myself to surrender to the possibility was with you, in this hotel. I am happy to spend the rest of my life celebrating this fact," I replied and kissed her again.

"You seriously will take me, and me alone, as your only?" she pressed.

I backed her into the wall and initiated session number two for that day in the shower.

"Did you want me to say no?" I asked seductively.

"You're dead, Paul Glassburé," she breathed and pushed me off of her and out of the shower.

She grabbed my hand and led our soaking wet selves to the bed, where she aggressively pushed me down and got on top of me. "I want to make one thing abundantly clear to you," she began sternly, slowly moving her hips. "I will hold you to every promise made, Paul. One of those promises is in regard to intimacy.

"When I'm fat and pregnant, nothing in our sex life changes. *Nothing.* When we are both doctors with all of our responsibilities, nothing in our sex life changes. Should I perceive anything changing, I reserve the right to remove the very penis that is inside me now, stuff it, and have it preserved so that at least I will still be able to have what I expect.

"Now, flip me and finish this like the man I expect you to be," she demanded, every bit the drill sergeant.

I did as I was told and session number two on the bed finished with us holding one another tightly, reflecting on the truth of us. Well, that's what I was doing, anyway. She whispered some semi-understandable somethings whilst biting my ear.

The lot of us spent the day as a family in and around the Dolby house. Our parents seemed to grow an incredibly tight bond through the day, with both fathers talking shop and football and both mothers talking babies, sunsets and wine.

We had dinner at another one of Dylan's favorite places and were again joined by quite a few islanders. Papa knew so many of them through his practice and introduced me. It was quite an education to see how he masterfully navigated each conversation.

"Every relationship is yours to curate and grow, Paul. I have every confidence," he said to a nervous me after one of the conversations. The enormity of the responsibility was something I was still trying to adjust to.

Seeing this, Dr. Upton walked over and said, "Son, you are talented. Your grandfather has done a masterful job of preparing you. If you are agreeable, Olaf, I would like to see Paul lead the next conversation. What do you think?"

"I believe this is a brilliant thought, Thomas. Paul, why don't you take the next one?" Papa asked, smiling.

"I'll certainly try," I said hesitantly.

"There is no 'try' in your being, Paul. We are here; heed all that you know," Dr. Upton encouraged.

Well, not only did I take the next conversation—I managed *all* of them for the rest of the night, over a period of maybe two hours. When it was known that I was taking over Pop's practice, all of his patients found me and talked quite a bit.

The night ended with our extended family watching the glow of the moon against the undulating waves. We all met the next morning in the hotel for breakfast and flew home a short while later.

When we got home, the preparations for my "return" began in earnest. The map was made by an army of people, including Helena, Cassie, Savannah, Eva, Mom, Dr. Upton, Mrs. Upton, Dr. Szymanski and Dylan, who demanded to be part of it.

Friends, families and targeted college staff were briefed multiple times by Sam and Eva, who did an incredible amount of educating in ever-more-intensive conversations. There were tears, shock, concern, lots of questions—and then resolute acceptance by all.

The night before I returned, Helena asked that we take time to be together and talk through everything one more time.

"Paul, should I be scared that I'm going to lose you?" she asked as I held her on the couch.

"Not at all, babe. There will be a *ton* of memory loss. After any of the other assignments, I have to allow time to sync up my memories. At worst, it's been a few hours and the topics were more about school things or sibling arguments. I've never had to deal with a gap this big. I mean—it's *years*, love. I was fifteen when this all started. Not only am I going to have to absorb some nasty memories—that part of me is going to need to acclimate to almost all of high school, undergraduate, master's and quickly gain doctorate-caliber knowledge in two major areas. This is all happening at finals time. I am not handling the stress involved particularly well," I explained.

"Sam mentioned something about the pond, babe. I think he has a plan for the education aspect, but I didn't follow. His bigger concern was for your health. I guess fainting is expected and lots of stress on your heart. I am a thousand percent ready for that part, but the rest scares me. I just can't get my head around the mechanics of this. I know in time it'll make sense but, for now, it's hard to reconcile," she began and looked up at me. "Paul, we are in this together. If there is one thing I am confident in, it's that we can make it through anything. I am here, my love, and I am going *nowhere* without you."

I kissed her. I knew I'd get through all of this with her at my side.

The day ended with me fighting sleep. I was concerned that when I woke up, so much would be lost that couldn't be recovered.

Well…

You know how the return went. It was the furthest thing from easy, but we got there.

When last I had you current, I was in the extreme upper atmosphere, preparing for a descent into a massive lake. Remember?

As I began heading toward Earth's surface, I looked at the energy all around the planet and in the immediate space between it and the Moon. I couldn't put my finger on it, but something was very amiss.

Just as I had experienced in the past, the energy bubble was gentle to a point and then I was a floppy human falling with no control. Why this happened near water, I've never clearly understood. Somehow, it is funny to someone. What or who that someone is, I do not know.

I saw the boat's lights in the distance as I crashed into the water.

"Stay there, Paul. I'll come get you," Dr. Upton yelled in the distance.

A spotlight was placed on me and I treaded water for a few seconds.

The boat slowed and the engine was shut off. I swam around to the back of the boat and climbed up on the ski deck.

Cassie jumped down next to me and gathered me into her arms. She was crying so hard I found a loss for words I couldn't reconcile. The emotion of the moment spilled over to everyone else on the boat.

"You're okay, right, Paul," Eva said through big emotions.

"I'm just a little damp, but yeah. Cassie, can you tell me what's wrong?" I replied after a couple moments.

"I thought you were dying, Paul. I thought… I thought that dream I had last night was real and you were really hurt," she lamented, her arms still wrapped extremely tightly around me.

"Cassie, sweetie… Look at me."

Her red, emotion-covered face looked up at me. She was so sad.

"I'm right here. I'm okay. I promise you—I'm okay. I need to know about this dream, though. Let's get off this deck and dry off, okay?" I asked.

She did not move.

So, I wrapped us in an energy bubble and moved up to the deck.

We were then engulfed by every set of arms on the boat.

"Y'all, I'm sorry. I think everyone knew this was going to be hard, and it proved to be a bigger challenge than anyone forecasted. I am all better now, and don't want any of your very hungry bellies to remain so. I will talk about anything you wish to discuss. Not one question is off limits in terms of what I just did.

"Captain, can you please take us back to shore? I believe you and I have a scotch or two to consume," I said. Dr. Upton and I had made a thing of having a glass or two of scotch during all of the planning sessions over the past couple years.

"You promise you're okay, son?" he asked.

"I promise I am."

"Okay, then," he said and went back into the cabin.

The group, including Cassie, Helena, Savannah, my parents, Mrs. Upton, Dylan, Hatch, Eva and Sam, remained in some way attached to me during the trip back.

Before I got off the boat, I grabbed Sam.

"They somehow seem to have followed me. We have little time," I whispered.

"Let's see what they do. There may not be a cause for concern," he replied.

When we got off the dock, Helena grabbed my hand and led me to a gathering of what looked like everyone.

"Before you change, your wet self answers questions. I inspect later. Do you understand me?" she asked, glaring into my eyes.

"I do," I answered, feeling the intensity of her emotion.

I was placed in a chair facing the entire group. I was dripping wet.

"Where did you go?" Hatch asked, emotion lacing his words.

"I found the closest energy band sourced from the Milky Way's black hole and merged my energy with it to heal. I was out maybe three quarters of the way to the Moon, though I was not close to it so I could protect it," I replied.

"Why an energy band and not the space hospital?" Eva asked.

"One of the things I learned in my last assignment was how best to use what is available to me. Space hospitals fix enough to make one functional. I wanted something different given the situation at hand," I answered.

"Are you okay?" Mrs. Upton asked, tears falling from her eyes. For that matter, Cassie, Savannah, Mom, Helena and Dylan were actively dabbing at their eyes.

"I need all of you to close your eyes. ALL of you," I said as forcefully as I could without being forceful.

I stood and raised the group about a foot off the ground. I wrapped each person in an energy bubble and then attached both Earth and a specific energy from the Moon to each one.

"Allow what you feel to help you relax. There should be no more tears here today, no more hurt. Breathe deeply and feel," I thought.

After a couple minutes, I felt the emotion release and the energy even things out. I felt comfort in each person, so I removed the bubbles and set them down.

"I have no idea where you learned to do that but, oh my God, Paul," Eva gushed.

Mrs. Upton walked over to me and hugged me. "I don't need to understand how or why. Thank you," she said.

"I think the baby felt that, Paul. My Lord!" Helena said, rubbing her stomach.

"Let's see," I said and looked at my son. He had a little smile on his face—I think he knew I was there.

"Yep, looks like it," I confirmed.

Helena wrapped her arms around my still wet self. "You're allowed to change now," she said and kissed me.

I changed and the dinner proceeded as it should have from the beginning. Conversation was what one would construe as "normal" if that makes any sense. In truth, I think the group had been through a whole lot in a short amount of time and normalcy was preferred.

As the night grew longer and people started to leave, the time grew closer for me to head back home.

Mom, Cassie, Savannah, Mrs. Upton and Helena pulled me into the kitchen.

"Paul, I feel as though something is concerning you. Are you willing to say what?" Savannah asked. The collective women focused intently on me.

"I'm getting married tomorrow, Savannah. That's really all…"

"I saw you talking to Sam on the boat. Did you see something when you were up in space?" she pressed.

"If I say yes does it change anything? Would you believe me if I said no? Look: I don't want any of you to be afraid, or nervous, or any of the things that take away from the day tomorrow.

"My dream, Paul, had a very dead you in it," Cassie said.

"Me, too, son," Mom agreed.

"Did you actually see me in this dream—my face? Or, did you know it was me but did not see my face?" I asked.

Both women thought for a second and then shook their heads no after looking at one another. I took this as a confirmation neither had seen my face in their death dreams.

"I won't say the dream wasn't real. But I don't believe it was forecasting. Even if it is, know you are safe and I'll somehow get on. I promise you," I encouraged.

This seemed to suffice, as the group disbanded and Helena collected me and pulled me outside.

"I did not inspect you for damage, boy. I find it difficult to believe you are perfectly okay after the happenings today. I'm worried about you, Paul," she said, melting into me.

"I'm okay, Love. I promise you," I replied.

"I will not believe you until I know for sure," she said and thrust her hand down my pants. "Well, at least we're okay in that department."

"Unkind, Helena Louise," I said and took a deep breath.

"What you did to me for the entirety of today was unkind. I totally knew it would be challenging, but I genuinely believed you were going to have to be hospitalized after all the fainting. Please tell me you're truly okay, Paul. I need to know this," she pressed.

"Helena, what I did today—tonight—was fix me in the way I know how. I should have insisted on doing this from the beginning. But I am whole. My memory is good. My knowledge gaps are gone. Everything is all synched up. I promise you: I am truly okay," I confirmed.

"Tomorrow, boy… Tomorrow it becomes a forever thing. We become a forever thing. Are you completely okay with this?" she asked and kissed me.

"I cannot wait to make it official, my love," I replied, and squeezed her tightly.

I said my goodbyes to the "women of hitchdom" and Dr. Upton before painfully leaving Helena to go home.

As I drove, I reveled in the happenings of the day. I literally returned from Xsip, got a couple big college degrees, reconciled seven years of memories and discovered I was getting married to one of Ania's connected lives and we were finally having our child. Unbelievable.

When I got home, I sat with Vick for a good amount of time. Poor little guy had been horrified by me earlier in the day. Eventually, he went and had a bite to eat and curled up in his bed.

I decided to take a quick peek at space under the cover of night, so I went out by the pond and launched into space via an energy bubble.

In the distance, I saw something on fire. My first inclination was that the surviving Xsint had somehow navigated from their dimension to ours. Thing was, I couldn't get a read on the object or objects and, in truth, this hypothesis was ridiculous.

Each dimensional plurality is separated by defined boundaries. The only thing that rationally can pass through those boundaries is extremely specific energy. So, the Xsint would have to match that energetic profile to do the same thing, and that was nearly impossible.

Regardless, this remained a possibility in my mind. If it wasn't the Xsint, something aflame appeared to be speeding toward the inner solar system.

I slept soundly for the most part that night, despite a couple big things. Firstly, I was getting married. Secondly, the Earth assignment was starting really quickly. Neither item should have allowed me to sleep, but I did.

The next morning, I again craftily got up into space to try and figure out the fire thing. Oddly, it was nowhere in sight. I looked for a short while, but didn't get an energetic or visual read on it. I checked Earth's atmosphere and the area around the planet and didn't see the abnormalities I had when I first looked. So, I headed back to get ready for our nuptials.

We were getting married on Dr. Upton's property. Neither family was particularly religious, so we had settled on a friend of Mrs. Upton's to marry us. When he asked about a rehearsal, Helena looked at him and said, "I'm walking up next to you. You are saying stuff, we are saying stuff, rings are put on and a kiss ends it. What do we need to practice exactly?"

So, there was no rehearsal.

I arrived at my prescribed time and was ushered by Cassie into the guest room to wait.

Maybe ten minutes later, Dad knocked on the door and paid me a visit.

"Big day, son. You feeling okay?" he asked excitedly and set two small glasses down on the end table.

"I am, Dad! I cannot believe we are getting married!" I replied.

"It's going to be a wonderful day, son. All of the people look to be here. It's my job to do two things: have a quick drink with my son and then get you to the altar," he said and produced a flask from his coat pocket.

He poured the contents of the flask into the two glasses and handed me one.

"To a wonderful new beginning, a merging of two families," he said, raising his glass.

"Here, here," I agreed, and we imbibed.

"You ready?" he asked. "It's time."

"I am, but I need to know how long you've had that flask. Do we have a problem we need to discuss?" I pressed.

"Bought it yesterday, son. I might use it a whole bunch more, though. The convenience is *lovely*," he prodded, and led me out of the room.

Helena and I had written our own vows as our story was not a traditional one. We wanted to make the promises to each other that we believed were needed, given this.

So, I shook the pastor's hand and took my place to his left.

A guitarist began to play and Dr. Upton and Helena walked from the patio toward the altar. The whole setup was on the part of their property by the lake. The backdrop was the lake—it was gorgeous.

Helena and Dr. Upton walked up to me. He kissed her cheek, hugged her and then shook my hand.

"Welcome, everyone, to the celebration of the marriage between Helena Louise Upton and Paul Christopher Glassburé. This is a blessed day for Paul and Helena," he began.

In the distance, I heard what sounded like really mild thunder. It was brilliantly sunny that day.

"Paul and Helena found one another unconventionally and have written their own vows. They have instructed me that the vows should be the ceremony, and having read them, I completely agree," he said.

There was more thunder, just a touch louder than before.

I leaned into the preacher and whispered, "We might need to speed things up."

He looked quizzically at me, and I shot a look back to him.

There was another clap of thunder, this time much louder. People became restless.

"Helena, I will love you, protect you and never ever stop, forever. I'll love our kids and your family and even Savannah if I have to. This ring proves it. Your turn," I said, putting the ring on Helena's finger, cutting the preacher out of the process.

She seemed to understand, and said, "Paul, I will love you, support you, worry about you, love your family and love our life together, however that looks. This ring is yours to notify others they can't have you," she said and put my ring on.

More thunder. Whatever was coming was close. I felt it.

"I can kiss her, right?" I asked the frightened preacher.

Helena grabbed me, kissed me, and proclaimed, "We're hitched. Everybody, stay safe now!"

As soon as her final word left her lips, my fear was confirmed.

"HUMAN PAUL… PREPARE TO DIE!" a familiar chorus bellowed.

There are two things you should remember before we proceed: Earth's atmosphere is really wet, especially in the Atlantic South—and I still don't know how these things exist.

Proceed.

"Go be safe. I have work to do. *Please*, Helena," I begged, kissed her and began to fill myself with a rage unlike anything I had ever felt. The energy from the sun filled my veins and the power of Sagittarius A coursed through my body.

I let out a deafening yell, and added, "IT'S MY WEDDING DAY. PREPARE TO SUFFER!"

I quickly covered the entire area in an energy bubble, leaving the lake exposed. I hovered over it and waited. They still weren't visible to me.

There was a bright flash. The Xsint accelerated through the lower atmosphere. As I expected, Earth's atmosphere thrashed them. Three made it through, but were notably weakened. I grabbed a bunch of water and accelerated it in an energy bubble at the Xsint. This seemed to hurt two of them.

So, I did it again and extinguished two of the fire beasts.

One Xsint was left, and seemed to be unharmed for the most part. I had nicked it with my water bombs, but it was still extremely strong. It was seemingly motivated, too.

"YOU WILL DIE, HUMAN!" it yelled and advanced toward me.

A spray of fire spears were thrown at me but I dodged them.

I figured that energy was likely the best tool to use at this point, but I had little time—the Xsint was accelerating toward me *absurdly* fast.

More spears were thrown and one hit my side. I was okay but was bleeding, and running out of time. Another spear was going to head my way any second now and the Xsint was uncomfortably close.

I grabbed energy from the lake and Earth, adding it to my own. I added it all into a powerful stream of energy that I propelled toward the Xsint as I, too, quickly advanced. I needed to use my own acceleration to strengthen the force of my attack. I felt the combination of it all would end this—energy fragmenting energy.

I was bleeding badly from my side. This had to end and I had to get repaired.

Well…

I was right and I was wrong about my approach.

The energy ripped the Xsint apart as I'd thought.

But…

It did so unevenly. Though I had completely dispatched the Xsint and returned the sanctity of calm to Earth, the tip of a freshly made energy spear tore through my chest before it faded into nothing.

My movement upward slowed and then stopped.

For a brief moment, I was suspended in the sky.

Tears filled my eyes.

"I'm so sorry, Helena," I whispered.

"Relax, Daddy. I promise: it's going to be okay. Please don't be sad," I heard a voice say. I didn't recognize it.

I began to fall.

Blood streamed from my torso as I danced with the unconscious delights of shock.

My eyes fell hopelessly shut—and I crashed into the lake.

Notes and Acknowledgements

The first draft of this book was completed in my Aunt Bonnie Ross' kitchen, ten days after her untimely passing. I feel it only right that this happened, given her tremendous support of me as a writer.

The next installment of this series is upcoming...

Thanks to:

Bambi Sommers for exemplary editing; Courtney Lindemann for continuing to make me a better writer; Jesse Burke for unbelievable artwork and true partnership in creativity; Stoney deGeyter, Ken Biltz, and George Styles for allowing me to wallow in their respective wakes as authors; Larry Smithmier and Jonathan Whittenton for being both critics and encouraging support; Kevin Syzmanski for the unknown yet fortuitous use of his last name; Darin Strachan for being the first person to ask me to sign a book. Darbs, you have no idea how much this *still* means to me.

Thanks as always to you, the holder of these words—for taking the time to read them. As an author, this is the single greatest compliment I can receive.

If you ever see me out and about with a printed copy, I will happily sign it!